ROOT
OF
ALL EVIL

ROOT
OF
ALL EVIL

A Laurel Highlands Mystery

by Liz Milliron

LEVEL
BEST BOOKS

Copyright Page

Root of all Evil
A Laurel Highlands Mystery

First Edition | August 2018

Level Best Books
www.levelbestbooks.com

Trade Paperback ISBN: 978-1-947915-05-3
Also Available in e-book

Printed in the United States of America

To my parents, Gary and Mary K. Lederman, who introduced me to Nancy and Agatha, the two best literary friends a girl can have.

ACKNOWLEDGMENTS

I am not the first author to say, "it takes a village to make a book," nor will I be the last. Here is mine.

Most importantly, thanks to my husband, Paul, and my kids, Mary and Michael, for their support of this crazy writer thing. It all started with the suggestion to "take the summer off and finish your book." If not for that, my road would have gone in a completely different direction. I love you all.

My gratitude to my critique partners—Annette Dashofy, Tamara Girardi, and Jeff Boarts—is hard to put into words. They never let me take the easy way out and although I sometimes (okay, often) want to whine "But it's hard!" every suggestion makes me a better writer. I would not be where I am without you guys.

Hank Phillippi Ryan hasn't been the only author who said to me "when your book is published," but she was the first. An amazing writer and person, she never fails to encourage and support others, no matter what stage of the writing journey they are at. Mwah!

Cynthia Kuhn rocked my world when she invited me, a then-unpublished author, to join the Mysteristas blog. It was the first time I did something as a "real author" and it was a huge confidence boost. Thank you.

Much love to all the members of Sisters in Crime and Pennwriters who have helped and encouraged me along the way. The only reason I cannot name every one of you is the acknowledgements would be longer than the book.

I cannot leave out thanks to Trooper Robyn Mungo and Corporal Brian Carpenter of the Pennsylvania State Police, and assistant public defender Charles Van Keuren for keeping me straight with regards to police and legal procedure. Any errors in these pages are entirely my own.

Thanks to Debra Evans-Rhodes in the Fayette County Commissioner's office for the wonderful tour of the county courthouse. I hope I've done that historic building justice.

Lastly, thanks to the ladies at Level Best Books—Harriette Sackler, Verena Rose, Shawn Reilly Simmons, and Angel Trapp. You made Christmas 2017 a truly magical season!

ROOT
OF
ALL EVIL

CHAPTER 1

Sally Castle studied the menu for a moment, then put it down. "I'll try the Fero lemberger and a tower of onion rings, please." She looked across the table at Colin Rafferty, her colleague from the public defender's office. The usual crowd at Lucky 7, men and women in varying levels of business and business-casual clothing, milled around their table. "Split them with me?"

"Sure. A bottle of Miller Lite for me." He slid the beer list back in the holder.

"Miller Lite?" Sally asked as the waitress jotted down their order and walked off. "How long have you worked in Fayette County again?"

Colin shrugged. "Almost two years and I know. You have some great local brews. I'm not a beer connoisseur." He fiddled with the position of the salt and pepper shakers.

Had it been that long? "Anything new this week?" she asked, leaning on the table, the dark brown wood reflecting the muted overhead lighting.

He pushed away the cut-glass shakers. "Got assigned a new case today. De'Shawn Thomas, misdemeanor possession. This will be the third time I've been in court with him for the same damn charge. What the hell is the point?" He averted his gaze, studying Uniontown's well-dressed business-class, all relaxing at the end of a hard week.

Sally remembered the young hotshot who'd arrived believing public defense was rock bottom. Their regular end-of-week outings were part of trying to change that. Sometimes she thought she was getting somewhere. Other times, like now, maybe not. "Colin, I know it's frustrating. But say you were in a high-priced private practice. Is defending someone's trust-fund kid from his third DUI in six months any different?"

"No."

The waitress reappeared with the beer and a glass of red wine. Colin took his bottle. "Red wine with onion rings?"

Sally sipped the wine, which had a unique aftertaste: a hint of oak and a slight peppery kick. The menu said it was good with grilled meats and she could taste why. "Sure." It would go great with the classic bar finger-food.

They killed five minutes with small talk about their work until the waitress returned with the appetizer. Sally leaned forward to inhale the delicious sweet smell from the tower of fried snacks, then picked one off the top. "Got any big weekend plans?" she asked before biting into it. Sweet, salty, slightly greasy, and a burst of flavor from the herb seasoning in the crust. Yes, perfect with her wine.

He tore apart an onion ring and popped half in his mouth. "There's a film noir festival tomorrow. The Killers. D.O.A. Might go to that."

"Film noir. One of my faves."

"Well, you're welcome to join me." He finished off the other half of the onion ring, wiped his fingers, and took another swallow of beer. "Then it's my mother's sixty-fifth birthday on Sunday. After the year she's had, we're doing it up big."

"How is your mom?"

"Good. Three months out, the doc is still happy with her numbers. The big thrill for her? Her hair is back."

Sally pointed at him. "Hair is important. Unlike men, women rarely look good bald. It's terribly unfair."

"I'll take your word for it. Anyway, the party should end soon enough to get home to watch the Steelers game."

She rolled her eyes and took a second onion ring. "You and your football."

"Hey, I may not care much about the beer, but I do love the sports."

The door opened, letting in a breeze that sent the pile of napkins on their table to the floor. Sally leaned over to pick them up. Above her, she heard Colin mutter and it sounded a lot like profanity. She sat up with the napkins and brushed hair from her forehead.

Colin's lighthearted expression had evaporated. He rearranged the standup cards listing available desserts and beers, trying to obscure his face.

"What's wrong?"

"Nothing."

"Bullshit."

He ducked his head, his chest almost flat to the table. "A guy I don't want to see just walked in."

Sally craned her neck as she looked toward the door, but even the height of the bar-style chair didn't allow her to see well over the crowd. She lifted herself up.

"Get down!" Colin hissed, pulling at her sleeve.

"What the hell?" She dropped back into her chair, still not seeing anyone who would upset her colleague this much. "Who is it?"

His gaze darted around the room. He took a hurried gulp of beer and stood. "Never mind. I have to go to the men's room. Be right back." He headed toward the restrooms, snaking his way through the crowd, bending frequently to make sure he was behind other people, and keeping out of sight of the door.

Once again, Sally tried to see through the crowd, but no one caught her eye. Who had walked in who would upset Colin so much?

⚜⚜⚜

Jim Duncan took his bottle of Black Magick imperial stout and thanked the bartender. Why had he agreed to meet Zelinsky here? The bar, popular with the downtown Uniontown business scene, was way too crowded. He should have insisted on a quieter place to catch up with his fellow Pennsylvania State Trooper. Someplace where he could sit, get a bite to eat, and get Zelinsky's impression of his new trainee.

As Duncan scanned the crowd for Zelinsky, his gaze lit on another person. Sally Castle, sitting all by herself. Maybe this was a good place after all. Zelinsky could wait a few minutes. Duncan took a circuitous route to Sally's table and came up beside her. "Only you would pair red wine and onion rings."

She started, but relaxed when she recognized him. "Red wine goes with anything, I've told you this before." She lifted her glass and winked.

A good sign. "You here by yourself?"

"No." She pointed at the empty chair and a Miller Lite bottle. "After work drinks with a friend."

"Your friend likes Miller Lite?" Clearly a friend without good taste.

She suppressed a laugh. "Colin isn't a beer snob, Jim. Not everyone has your discerning palate."

"Colin." Sally was here with another guy. A bad sign.

"Colin Rafferty. We work together." She grinned. "If I didn't know better, I'd say you were jealous."

A man in a dark blue suit edged behind Jim. "Sally, we've been friends how long?"

"A year or so."

"You have other friends. Some of them are men. I wasn't jealous of what's-his-name, the baseball trainer."

She brushed hair from her face. "Anyway, why are you here? This isn't your scene, all the suits."

"I'm on training duty for a new trooper. It's her second month. I want to talk to the previous FTO, get her impressions."

Sally took a bite of onion ring. "Is there a problem?"

"No. I don't like to let what happened before color my opinion, but I feel like I'm having a hard time connecting with Aislyn McAllister. That's the trainee's name. Thus far, she's not very talkative. Hasn't shared anything besides the fact she's from Natrona Heights in the two shifts we've worked so far. I hope it's not me."

"I'm quite sure it's not you. You're one of the nice guys."

He lifted his beer in thanks. "It's a point of pride. I can count on one hand the number of folks I've had to fail out of training." The Black Magick was excellent, bourbon flavor with chocolate notes. "By the way, I'm working first shift tomorrow. Supposed to be a great day if you'd like to go out on the reservoir with Rizzo and me." Rizzo, his golden retriever, loved Sally. The weather forecast was calling for a perfect fall day: blue skies, mild temperatures, fluffy clouds. The water would be filled with boaters trying to cram in as much outdoor time as possible before the winter snows froze everything solid.

"I might be meeting Colin for a film noir festival." She took in his expression and a smile spread across her face. "Ah ha! You are jealous."

Duncan had a horrible track record with women. Just ask his ex. However, after a year of friendship, maybe this was Sally's way of telling him she was sick of waiting for him to make a move. "Do you want me to be?" He studied her face.

Sally flushed and turned her attention back to her food.

Okay, maybe not. He paused. "You come here a lot?" With the friend who drinks Miller Lite?

"Every Friday. I've been mentoring Colin this last year and it's part of our ritual." She tore a piece of onion ring off the stand on the table. "Speaking of Colin, where the hell is he?"

Ah, she was mentoring. He should have known Sally wouldn't date a man who made such horrible choices in beer. Duncan looked around, even though he had zero idea what this guy looked like. Everybody was paired up, chatting, and snacking after a hard week's work.

"He said he was going to the men's room. I didn't think guys took that long."

"Not usually." Duncan set his beer on the table. He stood and stretched to his full six-foot-three so he could see over the crowd. "Caucasian, early thirties, white shirt, dark suit, gold tie?"

"That's Colin. You see him?"

"Yeah, he's by the restrooms. Looks like he's arguing with someone." Duncan dropped back down, the crowd of people blocking his view.

Sally's eyebrows puckered. "Who's he arguing with? Can you tell?"

Duncan took a pull from his beer. "A guy in a suit. He had his back to me. Hold on." He stretched up again, pushing up on the table to try for a bit more height, and looked in the direction of the restroom.

Rafferty was nowhere in sight.

CHAPTER 2

Saturday morning, Duncan and his trainee headed to the town of Confluence immediately after roll call. Duncan was armed with a travel mug of coffee, brewed at home. McAllister opted for a bottle of Mountain Dew. Duncan shuddered but didn't say anything. To each her own.

Brilliant red and orange leaves dotted the green grass of the town square. Duncan waved out the cruiser window to a few folks going into the bike shop, maybe for a quick tune up before they hit the bike trail by the river that led into Ohiopyle proper.

"Where are we going?" she asked as they turned the corner toward the seedier side of town. Confluence was a town of contradictions. Nice homes and restaurants could be across the street from run-down trailers and beat-up buildings, the Casselman River cutting through it all.

"To visit one of my informants. When we get there, let me do the talking."

She frowned and looked out the window at houses in need of a little fresh paint, or at least a power wash. "Why?"

"Two reasons. First, you're a new face and Eddie can get a little squirrelly with new people."

"And the second?"

Duncan weighed his response. He liked field training and wanted every new trooper to succeed. Four out of five times, his trainees were a pleasure to work with and the training period was a smooth success. But the universe had a way of keeping him humble. Instinct told him McAllister was going to be that one time out of five. She was a bit too fast off the mark, aggressive where she should be assertive. That was Zelinsky's assessment and his observations over two days confirmed it. "Because I said so." She started to speak and he cut her off. "You want to succeed at this job, you learn when to take orders without question. This is one of those times. My informant, my rules. This first time, you're an observer. Got it?"

She scowled, but said nothing.

They pulled into a gravel parking lot on the outskirts of the town. A soot-streaked one-story building with blacked out windows was the only structure on the lot. The town limits gave way to farmland, a few shabby houses nearby. The honk of geese carried through the air as they made their morning progression overhead. A scarred metal door, the only entry, was shut. Duncan shut off the car. "Let's go." Once he was out, he detected the homey tang of wood smoke.

Next to him, McAllister stood ramrod straight, tension coming off her in waves as she studied the building. She was keyed up. He'd told her this was an informant. A trooper should always be alert, but her posture went beyond that. She wasn't only prepared for trouble.

She was hoping for it.

All the signs of an eager beaver ready to prove she had what it took. It was a good thing as long as it didn't get out of hand.

Duncan weighed his words as she faced him. "Before we go in, let me make one thing clear. I don't expect to be challenged when I give instructions. My job is to make sure you're ready to be on your own. Yours is to learn and get ready."

McAllister's face darkened and she scuffed the gravel with the toe of her boot. "Yes, sir."

"I don't need to be called 'sir.' Did you ever visit a CI with Trooper Zelinsky?"

"No."

"I've worked with this guy before. I'm not expecting trouble, but you always stay on guard. They aren't called criminal informants for nothing. But this isn't an interrogation."

"Aren't you asking questions?"

"I am. But there's a push and pull. It's an art. You have to remind a CI you're in charge, but you don't want to push too hard or he'll shut down. That's why I want you to watch this first time. We'll review later." Without waiting for a response, Duncan went and pounded on the door.

The viewing slide opened, revealing eyes as dark as a bottomless well. Stanley, the ever-present bodyguard slash doorman. "We're closed," a gravelly voice said. "Besides, you know better than to show up dressed like that."

"Can't help it," Duncan said. "I need to talk to Eddie V."

"Official business?"

"Yes and no. Official visit. But it doesn't necessarily have anything to do with Eddie."

The eyes narrowed. "You carrying?"

Duncan held up his arms. "Really?"

The man snorted. "I got a job, too. Stay there." The cover slammed back.

"I know you said this guy is your informant, but I don't like the look of this place." McAllister took in the deserted parking lot and the windowless, cinderblock building. "Nothing good can be happening."

"It's okay. I've been here before," Duncan said. "This is where Eddie does business. Neither he nor Stanley want trouble, not here."

"If you say so." McAllister continued to visually sweep the lot, her gaze never resting on any one thing.

After a few minutes, Duncan heard the repeated scrape and thunk of locks being unfastened. The heavy metal door opened to reveal the hulking form of Stanley.

"He'll talk to you," Stanley said. "But you better have been telling the truth. That he's not who you're looking for."

Duncan beckoned to McAllister and they entered, Stanley close on their heels, towering over them. To McAllister's credit, she didn't flinch.

Eddie V was in the room he called his office, sweat glistening on his paunchy face, red hair gleaming in the light. Smoke swirled through the air, a stale smell. Eddie didn't believe in smoke-free environments. "Duncan, what a surprise," he said in his soprano voice. His eyes flickered over to McAllister. "Why, you rogue. You hang out with all the pretties, don't you? Who's the new one?"

Duncan felt rather than saw McAllister's chest swell with indignation. "Nice to see you too, Eddie," Duncan said. "This is Trooper McAllister. Let's not get off to a bad start. She doesn't know you like I do. Understand?"

"I suppose." Eddie tapped his hands on his gigantic stomach. "To what do I owe the pleasure of your company?"

"I want to know what you know about meth labs," Duncan said. "Specifically, any in Fayette County."

Stanley growled and Eddie's face turned scarlet. "I don't mess with drugs, Duncan," he said. The venom in his words didn't match the high pitch of his voice. "I don't deal them, I don't use them, and I don't tolerate them."

"I'm aware of that."

"Then why are we having this conversation?"

"Because if anybody would know if someone local is cooking, you would."

"What have you heard?" Eddie challenged him, but his face relaxed ever so slightly.

"Pittsburgh Narcotics has a credible lead," Duncan said.

Eddie smirked. "And I should help you why?"

McAllister muttered under her breath.

Duncan caught the words "show him who we are." Luckily Stanley had not because the big man didn't move. He wouldn't have let a challenge to his boss pass. Duncan kept his voice firm, reasserting control, but chose his words carefully. "Oh come on. After everything we've been through?"

The chair groaned as Eddie leaned back. The silence was heavy. "I've heard nothing about meth activity in the Laurel Highlands."

Duncan's move. "Would you know who to ask?" He stole a glance at Stanley, still attentive but staying in the shadows.

Eddie squinted. "They're notoriously secretive people, meth producers. They don't mingle socially, if you know what I mean." He sat up and pulled a cigar out of a drawer. "But I might know of a couple of people to ask. If I was feeling generous."

Duncan placed his business card on the table and slid it toward Eddie.

"I have plenty of those," Eddie said, clipping the end of the stogie. He lit it and puffed, filling the claustrophobic office with acrid smoke.

"Have another," Duncan said. Push, pull. Eddie tried to pick up the card, but Duncan held it firm, pinning it to the table with his finger. "I encourage your generosity, Eddie," he said. "Meth is bad for business. Bad for yours and bad for mine."

Eddie tugged the business card out from beneath Duncan's finger. He slipped it into his shirt pocket without looking at it. "Your point is made, Trooper First Class Duncan," he said around the stogie. "Trooper McAllister, was it? A pleasure meeting you." Eddie's gaze never wavered from Duncan's face. "Stanley, show the troopers out. Their business here is finished."

☙ ☙ ☙

Saturday morning, Colin was still missing in action. The previous night, Sally had searched the bar with no success. She accepted Jim's offer to look in the men's room, but no Colin. He'd left half a beer and a light coat behind. No word, no warning.

He'd invited her to join him at the film festival, but when she called him on his home number to follow up she'd gotten his voicemail. It was unlike him to issue an invitation and not provide details or make plans. Perhaps he assumed she'd get the information on her own and either show up or not. She checked the paper. The festival started at nine in the morning and ran all day. It was now nine-thirty. She called the ticket office, but the bored man who answered didn't remember seeing anyone matching Colin's description, confirmed there was only one ticket window, and said no one else was working ticket sales who might be able to help. Sally knew the theater; a small, historic one-screen place in Uniontown, so she knew the man was not merely brushing her off.

Maybe Colin had decided not to go to the festival. Plans change. Sally dialed his cell number. Voicemail. "Colin, it's Sally. You never called me about the film festival. Anyway, you left your coat behind. Call and let me know if you want me to bring it to you or hold it until Monday." She left her home and cell numbers.

She puttered around her apartment for the rest of the morning, the windows open to let in the fresh Indian summer breeze and the sounds of Saturday-morning residential traffic. This was weird and entirely unlike her co-worker. He didn't disappear and he didn't blow people off. Sure, there were half a dozen reasons for him to not return her calls; they were friends, not lovers. If his plans had changed, he was under no obligation to clear it with her or even tell her about it.

Except her criminal law attorney sixth-sense was tingling. She and Jim had definitely seen him arguing, but there'd been so many people in the crowded room, she hadn't seen the person's face or any identifying features. They'd asked the bartender and a couple other people if they'd seen Colin, but didn't learn anything. The bartender had been busy and other patrons had been too caught up in their own activities to notice two people talking.

She flopped down on her couch and looked at the clock on the TV. Almost noon. She'd gotten no response to her messages. She dialed Colin's cell, but once again got voicemail. Had he put his phone on do not disturb during the movie? "Please, call me back. If you're at the film thing, at least send me a text between pictures so I stop bothering you."

She didn't have his address handy, but she could get it. Normally she'd consider it extreme, but his failure to answer her calls meant a drop-in visit just might be warranted.

CHAPTER 3

Duncan's follow-up conversation with McAllister after leaving Eddie's was unsatisfactory. "I don't see why you didn't push harder," she said. "I would have."

"Oh?" They'd returned to regular patrol duty around the county. The open grasslands were turning brown-gold in the sun, but the mountains held a healthy amount of green in their rolling sides. Occasionally they passed a pasture of cattle or horses out enjoying the warmth, as though they too knew winter was on its way.

"It was clear to me he knew something and was playing games. If you'd reminded him who we were, maybe you'd have left with information."

Again, aggression instead of assertion. "Eddie didn't need a reminder. I told you, it's a conversation not an interrogation. If you have to beat cooperation out of your CI, it isn't really cooperation, is it?"

She said nothing, but her expression told him she wasn't sold on the approach.

Vindication came just before Duncan and McAllister ended their seven-to-three shift. His cell phone rang. Caller ID showed a blocked number. It hadn't taken long for the visit with Eddie to yield a result.

"Are you sure you want to answer that?" McAllister asked.

"I know who this is. And he doesn't leave messages." Duncan stepped away from the barracks to give himself a bit of privacy as troopers rolled in from their patrol duty, or arrived to get ready for the next shift. The fall breeze tugged at his campaign hat. "This is Duncan."

"Got some news," said a male soprano voice.

"Eddie," Duncan said, looking around. Nobody around but McAllister. Perfect. "What is it?"

"Aaron Trafford is back in town. My sources tell me he was at The Beer House last night looking ugly and angry. Like always."

Aaron Trafford had been arrested the previous fall for meth production. When the charges were dismissed, he disappeared. If he was back, that wasn't good news. "Where there's smoke—"

"There's probably a fire," Eddie said.

"Did this associate of yours speak to Mr. Trafford?"

"No," Eddie said. "Mr. Trafford is not someone who encourages conversation. But given his past alleged activities, I thought it was worth calling you."

"Appreciate it," Duncan said. "If you hear anything else—"

"You'll be the first to know," Eddie said. "Only because you're right. Meth is bad for business. If nothing else, it brings more police to Fayette County. Besides. I like having you owe me."

Duncan snapped his phone shut and slipped it into his shirt pocket.

"Was that a flip phone?" McAllister said, her attention diverted. She held up an iPhone in a purple case. "I hate to break it to you, but this is what a cell phone looks like these days. I didn't peg you for a technophobe."

"My phone makes calls, it texts, and it has a camera," he said. "I don't need or want to be connected all the time. When I'm fishing, I like to fish. Without distraction."

She lifted her eyebrows. "Was that your guy?"

"Yes." Duncan told her about the information from Eddie. "Trafford was arrested last fall and the case was dismissed. Caused a big uproar."

Troopers filed out of the barracks. Shift change was over. It was time to go home, but this bit of news required action.

McAllister glanced at the patrol cars as they left the parking lot. "What are we gonna do?"

Duncan spun his key ring around his finger, noting the inclusive pronoun. McAllister wasn't one to bolt at the end of a shift. Good. "How would you feel about making an unscheduled visit?"

☘☘☘

By mid-afternoon Saturday, Sally had given up finding Colin by phone. She'd left half a dozen messages, some on his home machine, some on his cell. If he went to the film festival, there had to be breaks between pictures where he could check his phone. Whatever he was doing, he wasn't of a mind to return any of her calls.

She debated her next move. She could swing by his apartment. But Colin was a grown man, not a child. He was under no obligation to her. What if he was engaged socially, maybe with a woman? As far as Sally knew he wasn't seeing anyone, but that could change. It would be pretty embarrassing for him if she showed up while he was amorously involved.

She had his jacket. Perfect excuse. October weather in the Laurel Highlands could change on a dime and he might need it come Monday morning. She could drop by to return it. She checked her contact information for him on her phone and drove over to his apartment building, a plain, brick building at the southern edge of Uniontown. Away from the downtown bustle, modest homes on small wooded lots, probably built during the boom-days of the coal industry, lined the streets.

Colin wasn't home. He didn't answer his buzzer at the front door and the parking spot that corresponded to his apartment number was empty. Of course, it was a sunny day. He might be out enjoying the good weather while it lasted, maybe gone hiking at nearby Ohiopyle State Park. He'd mentioned his mother's birthday tomorrow. Maybe some family had come into town and he took them out. Cell service could be spotty; that would explain why he wasn't answering his phone.

An elderly man wearing a plaid flannel shirt and stained twill pants pushing a gray, heavy-duty trash can rounded the corner of the building. "Can I help you?"

"Maybe." She came down to the sidewalk. "I'm looking for Colin Rafferty, apartment 3D."

"Not here." The man wheeled the trash to the curb.

That's not helpful, Sally thought. "Have you seen him? My name is Sally Castle. Mr. Rafferty and I work together. I have his jacket and I want to return it before Monday. He hasn't answered my calls and I'm a little worried about him."

The man dusted his hands on his pants. "You should be, after the visitor he had this morning."

Sally's legal antennae perked up. "What visitor? Did you get a name?"

"Nah. I'm Bernie Trout, by the way. Building superintendent." He didn't offer to shake hands, something that made Sally very grateful considering Trout's dirty fingernails.

"Was it a man or a woman? What did this visitor look like?"

"A man. Nasty."

"Where did you see them?"

"Outside Mr. Rafferty's unit. I was on my way to fix a leak in 3E." Trout pulled a paisley neckerchief from his pocket and wiped the back of his neck. "Not that tall, little taller than you. Shaved head. Ugliest tattoo I've ever seen on his neck. The leather jacket he was wearing looked tight enough across the shoulders that I was sure it'd bust a seam if he shrugged."

It didn't sound like anyone Sally knew as a client from the office. "Did Mr. Rafferty let him in?"

"No. In fact, he looked like he had the piss scared out of him when he opened the door. I'm not surprised. I only saw the stranger once and I damn sure hope I never see him again."

Hmm. "You hear their conversation?"

"A bit." Trout replaced the kerchief. "It wasn't friendly."

"What did they say?"

Trout shrugged. "Don't remember. Like I said, not a guy I wanted to notice me so I ducked into the utility room to stay out of sight."

"Think. You didn't hear anything, not even a few words?"

The man frowned. "Mr. Rafferty said something about how he'd changed his mind. The guy said, 'We had a deal, legal eagle. You might have changed your mind, but I didn't. Best keep that in mind.' Close to that. Then he left."

"What did Mr. Rafferty say?"

"Nothing. He looked pale as new milk. Less than fifteen minutes after that, I noticed his car was gone. Hope that helps." Trout nodded and disappeared around the building.

Colin had been in an argument last night. Sally had the super's report of an unfriendly stranger today. Same guy? No. The man she'd seen last night had a full head of hair and he'd been wearing a suit, not a biker jacket. She'd gotten that much. The Lucky 7 crowd was business: legal, accounting, a few others. No matter how busy, a tattooed man with a shaved head wearing a leather jacket would have been noticed.

She'd check Colin's office. Sure, it was the weekend, but the law didn't stop because it was Saturday. She could get in. She'd be careful not to get too nosy when it came to his cases. Then again, they both worked for the same office. Bryan Gerrity, the public defender and their boss, might not be happy with the snooping, but it wouldn't compromise any legal business. Privilege covered all of them.

She drove downtown and parked her tan Camry on a side street. The Fayette County courthouse was a massive gray stone edifice, built in 1892. None of this modern glass and steel. If ever a building proclaimed "law and order live here," it did. Located on East Main, on the edge of downtown proper, there was a small park with benches and a memorial at the corner, a nice place to have lunch on a warm day. Since it was Saturday, there was little foot traffic. Across the street from the courthouse, a neon sign advertised the services of a bail bondsman. The trees out front had russet leaves streaking the green, a hint that the Indian summer was fighting a rearguard action against the onset of fall.

Sally pressed her finger to the biometric lock and ducked in the backdoor. Then she headed to the basement and the public defender's office. Inside, she locked the door behind her and snapped on the lights. Of the two desks in the front, one was neatly organized, one piled high with papers. Being in the basement, the office had no windows to let in the sun. Colin's office on the interior was especially cave-like. Sally turned on the brushed nickel LED desk light.

Papers were strewn everywhere, sticky notes on the lampshade and the phone, none of them remarkable. Sally flipped through the file folders sitting on the desk. De'Shawn Thomas, the case Colin had mentioned the previous night, was on top. But it was exactly what he'd said. Simple misdemeanor possession.

She put aside the Thomas file and kept searching. Drawers of office supplies, a chain of paper clips, forms, and folders. This was a bust. She looked around at the walls. Colin had hung his diploma from law school, but nothing else. No family pictures, not even a dusty plant. When he'd arrived, Colin had disdained such things, proclaiming his stint in the office would be short. His sole concession to personal items were two mugs, black with gold trim and the iconic Pittsburgh Steelers logo. One for each of their two most recent Super Bowl wins. Colin had attended the games; they were his most treasured office possessions.

Sally flopped in the desk chair and eased herself in a half circle, stopped, and repeated the arc. What was she missing?

She returned her attention to the desk surface and the message pad caught her eye. Not because there was anything on it, but the top sheet was indented. She studied the marks. It was the standard office pad and she could tell it was Colin's handwriting. He'd pressed so hard when writing, he left an imprint on the page below. She grabbed a pencil and lightly shaded the marks. "You'd better fix this."

Bernie Trout had described a visit from a tattooed guy. Is that what Colin had been arguing about at the bar? No, couldn't be. The argument had occurred before Colin had his run-in with Mr. Ugly. Who had mentioned a deal, something Colin wanted out of. That could be the problem that needed to be fixed. Except Colin had written this note at work, also before the encounter with Mr. Ugly. But the deal could involve a third party, the recipient of the note. Or Colin simply needed help.

Had he mailed the note or delivered it to someone in the courthouse? And if it was another courthouse employee, who?

CHAPTER 4

I t was late Saturday afternoon when Duncan and McAllister pulled up in front of a modest red-brick ranch house in Dunbar, surrounded by fields of sun-browned grass. The white shutters gleamed and the yard was as neat as Duncan would have expected a retired trooper to keep it, although he was certain that the mums in the front garden, with their cheerful orange and red flowers, were not the work of his old friend.

"Who lives here?" McAllister asked.

"Former trooper and a buddy of mine."

"What are you hoping to learn?"

"Fitz was the lead investigator the last time Trafford was on our radar. I'm hoping he'll remember something that'll help us out." Duncan slid out of his Jeep.

The clunk of wood drew him to the back yard, McAllister trailing. Fitzpatrick was stacking firewood. "Well, I'll be damned. Jim Duncan," Fitz said. He shook Duncan's hand, then held his out to McAllister. "Who's the new face?"

"Fitz, this is Trooper Aislyn McAllister." Duncan flexed his hand. Fitz still had a firm handshake. "McAllister, Trooper First Class Daniel Fitzpatrick."

"Retired," Fitz said. "You've got a good grip for a little lady."

"You've got a good grip, too, for an old guy," McAllister said.

Fitz barked a laugh. "What do you want with a broken-down retiree?" He waved at the brick patio. "Let's sit. My back is killing me."

"Who said I wanted something?" Duncan asked.

"I did. Can I get you anything? You like your beer dark, if I remember." Fitz pulled a few weathered chairs onto the patio.

"We better not. Shift ended at three but we're still in uniform. You know how it is." Duncan took the proffered chair. McAllister sat beside him. "Aaron Trafford."

Fitz spat into the ground. "Damned scandal. That case pretty much ended my career."

"What happened?"

"It was a standard drug bust, right until we got into the courtroom. All of a sudden, the defense is claiming I didn't include the pseudoephedrine in the warrant. Got it all thrown out." Fitz leaned back, his leisurely posture contrasting with the fire in his eyes. "You think I'd be so stupid as to leave raw production materials off the contents?"

"You didn't make a mistake?"

"No, I didn't make a damn mistake."

McAllister broke in. "But if you didn't, then the warrant was changed. Who would do that? And when?"

"Damned if I know. Clerks, paralegals, attorneys—they all would have touched it after the search was complete." Fitz leaned his arms on his knees. "I would swear, under oath, that warrant was good. Hell, I did swear under oath. I was on the stand when that mealy-mouthed assistant public defender started in on 'mistakes of old age' and that shit. And he pulls out this piece of paper that sure looked like my warrant, but it couldn't have been."

"Which attorney?" McAllister said.

"Colin Rafferty," Fitz said. "That boy looked like he'd be at home anywhere except the public defender's office. Way too slick. But I suppose he did his job, got his client off."

Rafferty. Sally's friend. Huh. Did Sally know her co-worker had been involved in the Trafford case? She probably did, it was a small office. "What did the prosecutor say? He must have stuck up for you."

"Nope. Alex Costanzo. Another city boy. The lot of them belong in Philly, not Uniontown."

Duncan let the statement pass. Despite the presence of high-end resorts like Nemacolin and Seven Springs, Fayette County—and by extension, Uniontown—was still mostly blue-collar, where attorneys in nice suits would be looked on as distrusted outsiders. "He didn't challenge Rafferty's claim?" That was puzzling. In Duncan's experience, the prosecution was usually more vigorous in standing up for the police—as long as the police gave them something to stand up for.

"He went through the motions. But in the end, he rolled over and apologized for taking the court's time. Trafford walked," Fitz said. "After the judge dismissed the case, Costanzo talked long and loud in front of the press about how he had nothing but respect for the PSP, but there would be a thorough investigation to ensure that such lapses wouldn't occur again."

"I can't believe everyone ignored your experience," McAllister said.

Fitz snorted. "That was part of the trouble," he said. "People started saying how after thirty years, I'd burned out. The stress had finally gotten to me. After the trial, I insisted there had to be another explanation. Costanzo gave me some bullshit about how he could understand I wouldn't be sharp. After that, seemed like they kept me away from anything big. So I retired."

Duncan glanced at McAllister. Her forehead was wrinkled, looking as distressed as he felt. "That's more than a little disturbing, Fitz. If the warrant got changed between the day you served it and the day of the trial, you know what that means."

Fitz spat again. "Yeah. It means you've got a rat somewhere in the Fayette County Courthouse."

⚜ ⚜ ⚜

Sally paced her apartment. Sunday afternoon and still no phone call. Frustration was edging out worry. She called Jim.

"I'm heading out for some fishing if you want to join me," he said, the rattle of metal boxes coming over the line. "Conditions on the water should be perfect."

"I'm not calling for social plans. Has the PSP heard anything about Colin Rafferty being missing?"

"Your co-worker?" A beat of silence. "No. I'd have called you. Why?"

"What's up with the pause? You know something?"

Another beat. "Not really. Nothing definite. What's the problem?"

"I haven't seen him since Friday night. I've called him at least a dozen times and he hasn't answered. It's both irksome and worrying."

A dog barked in the background. Jim's golden retriever, Rizzo. "Well, he is an adult. But if you're really worried, you can file a missing persons report with the Uniontown police."

Missing persons report. "That might be extreme right now. Thanks, Jim. Enjoy your fishing." She hung up.

Before escalating the matter to the police, she'd make one more trip to Colin's apartment.

⸙⸙⸙

This time, Colin's blue Mazda was in its spot. So why no return call?

She was almost to the front door when Colin came flying out, focused on his phone. "Colin. Didn't you get my messages? I've been calling."

He pulled up and blinked. "Sally. What the hell are you doing here?" He grabbed her arm, looked around, and pulled her around the side of the building.

She shook her arm free. "Relax. I've been trying to get in touch with you since Friday night. What on earth are you looking at that's got you so distracted?"

Colin's gaze darted up and down the street and his face was flushed. "I was checking for…never mind. Look, I really appreciate your concern, but don't worry about it. There's something I need to handle."

"Can I help? I thought you had your mother's birthday party today. I wouldn't want you to miss that."

"It is, but…I have to take care of this first." He continued to scan the street. Except for a man a few houses down mowing his yard, the area was quiet. "Thanks for the offer, but I have to do this alone."

"Colin, you're freaking me out." She snapped her fingers in front of his face to get his attention. "What is going on?"

He stopped obsessively checking the street to face her. "It's nothing, Sally. Well, it's something, but something I have to handle myself. I blame you, making me all responsible and everything." He gave a faint huff that might have been an attempt at a laugh.

"Is it related to the stranger who was here yesterday?"

Colin's reaction was unexpected. He seized her shoulders. "Did you see him? More important, did he see you? Tell me he didn't see you."

She felt his fingers tighten on her shoulders. "Colin, you need to calm down." He was not doing anything to reassure her. This wild behavior was out of character. Way out of character. Whatever he said, he was in trouble. "Your super told me. Let go, take a deep breath, and tell me what the heck is eating you."

He released her, sighed, and ran a hand through a shock of sandy brown hair. "I can't. Not right now. I have to go." He took a step away then stopped. "I'll tell you in the morning. Promise." He got into his car and pulled away without another look.

Sally stood frozen, staring after the retreating taillights until they rounded the corner. She'd hoped finding Colin would answer her questions and put her at ease. He'd been with friends. He'd have some explanation for the tattooed stranger that made perfect sense. Instead, she was standing on a residential Uniontown street wondering what the hell could turn her easy-going, unflappable colleague into a high-energy bundle of nerves. Colin might want to keep her out of it, but...too late. With the questions piling up in her brain, Sally was firmly sucked into Colin's whirlpool. She cherished her weekends, but this time Monday couldn't come soon enough.

CHAPTER 5

D uncan's cell phone rang right before first-shift roll call on Monday morning. He waved McAllister into the room of gathering troopers while he answered it.

"12679 Jumonville Road."

There was no mistaking Eddie's voice. "What's there?" Duncan said.

"Let's just say you will find a visit enlightening," said Eddie.

After the meeting broke, Duncan and McAllister headed out to the address on Jumonville. Might as well make the tip their first stop of the day. Cottony white clouds drifted through the rich blue sky as they drove past fields full of rippling golden grass and cornstalks. "Should we get a search warrant first? In case we want it?"

"Even with a reputable CI, visual verification is good to have. Jumonville isn't that far and we can always start the warrant application in the car."

"Lights and siren?" McAllister asked, reaching for the controls.

Tempting, but they didn't want to scare off anyone who was on site. "No. Let's go in as quietly as possible. See if we can catch anyone. In the meantime, affidavit forms are in the glove compartment. Get writing."

They pushed the speed limit on the way. As soon as they exited the car, Duncan noted the signature stench of meth production. It put a damper on another perfect fall day, overwhelming the dusty scent of the dry leaves fallen from the oak trees in the yard.

He gazed at the rambling Victorian farmhouse and could see traces of elegance through the faded blue paint and sagging white shutters. Gabled slate roof, big windows, wrap-around porch, and a bay window perfectly positioned to catch the afternoon sunlight. Beautiful place. Ruined now.

"Is this how multi-cat houses stink?" McAllister asked, holding her hand over her nose.

"Wouldn't know. I'm a dog guy," Duncan said. "I think we found our lab, though. See the windows? All papered over. I can't be sure from here, but that looks like an industrial quality lock on the front door."

"There's trash over here." McAllister walked over to some overstuffed, heavy-duty trash bags stacked by the road.

"Don't touch anything without gloves," Duncan said. "Better yet, don't touch."

"If you insist." McAllister bent over the bag, inhaled and gagged. "Same smell, maybe even a little stronger."

"All right. Now's the time to get that warrant signed and call in some search assistance."

"What kind of assistance?"

"Someone with a hazmat suit. I've gone into some dirty places. I'm not going into that." He jerked his thumb toward the house, walked to the car, and picked up the mic.

"You're the boss, Boss," McAllister said.

"Don't call me boss. Let's make a few calls, get the emergency response guys to back us up, find a judge, and we'll get this party started."

McAllister grinned. "I love a party."

⚜⚜⚜

Sally arrived at the courthouse Monday with no more idea of what Colin could be involved in than when she'd seen him speed away Sunday afternoon. That visitor. The very idea he could have seen Sally sent Colin to a tailspin. What was up with that? When she'd called Jim, he'd definitely paused like Colin's name meant something. Jim had glossed over it—or tried to—so that something had to involve the police. She parked in the rear; the sun beating down on the pavement lent the faint odor of melted asphalt to the air. She passed through the employee entrance and waved to the deputy on duty, heels clicking on the worn flooring.

Colin had promised her an answer in the morning. Well, it was morning.

The bitter, acrid scent of burnt coffee hit her nose the moment she got into the office, overlaying the ever-present musty basement smell. The desk belonging to Doris—one of the office secretaries—was empty and spotless, computer monitor black. She hadn't started the coffeemaker. Maybe Bryan? What was he doing in the office at seven on a Monday morning?

One thing was sure. It wasn't Colin. In the time he'd worked there, he had yet to arrive before eight-thirty.

Sally dropped her purse and briefcase on Doris's desk. "Hello? Anyone here?" No answer. The door had been locked. Sheriff's deputies manned the front and rear building doors, so the chances of an intruder were low. Nonetheless, Sally fished a can of pepper spray out of her bag. Maybe someone had come in Sunday night, turned on the coffee pot and forgotten to shut it off. It was unusual for anyone to be in on a weekend. If they had to meet a client, they did that at the jail behind the courthouse. Sally sometimes took advantage of the empty office to get some dedicated prep time if she had a case. But she brought her own coffee. The cheap machine didn't make single cups. That implied either a long night or multiple people.

She checked the pot on the little table in the reception area. Sure enough, the dark liquid was sludge. She quickly touched a finger to it and tasted. No amount of sugar and creamer was going to save it and the carafe was probably wrecked, too.

Bryan's office was dark. In fact, all of the rooms were dark, except one. Light streamed out of Colin's office. Had he forgotten to turn off the light last Friday? Had to be. Except she distinctly remembered turning it on, then back off, when she came in on Saturday. There was no noise, not even the rustle of paper.

She crept into the room, expecting to see an empty desk or maybe Colin catching an early morning nap.

Colin's head was face down on the surface in a grotesque parody of someone who'd fallen asleep over his work. Blood pooled around him and on the floor, dull and sticky-looking. The air tasted like pennies. In his temple was what looked to her like a very large gunshot wound.

She clapped a hand over her mouth and grabbed the doorway for support. Whatever Colin's trouble, she never guessed it was this bad. She took a couple of steps and stopped. Colin was seated at the far side of the desk, back to the wall. There was no way she could do anything to help him and the police would not thank her for mucking up the crime scene. In fact, she shouldn't have touched the door frame.

She backed out of the room and hurried to her office to dial 911.

CHAPTER 6

D uncan eased into an open spot in front of a stately red-brick house on East Main in Uniontown, a block away from the castle-like courthouse. Here on the edge of downtown, some of the buildings showed off older architecture, a throwback to more prosperous times. "We're going to Judge Monaghan's on the second floor. Got the affidavit?"

McAllister waved it at him.

They got out of the car and walked to the courthouse. The scene in front of the building stopped Duncan in his tracks. The presence of a Uniontown black-and-white, lights still revolving, and the county coroner's wagon in the No Parking zone, significantly undermined the building's message of law, order, and strength.

What the hell? He quickened his pace, McAllister trotting to keep up. He stopped short and turned. "Here." He took his out his wallet and handed McAllister a twenty. "There's a coffee shop not far from here. Down the street, across from the old State Theatre. Go buy yourself something. Me, too."

"You can't be serious. You're sending me on a snack run?" McAllister waved her hand at the official vehicles. "With all this?"

"Stop and think a moment," Duncan said. "Something is definitely going on. I'd like to know what it is before we see the judge, even if it's unrelated to our investigation."

She stared at him, uncomprehending. "So we ask the Uniontown guys."

"They may not want to share information," Duncan said. "Territorial politics at its finest. I'm going to go in and check it out."

"You mean snoop."

"I prefer 'get the lay of the land.' Make sure we aren't walking into a minefield. If I know any of the guys on scene, they'll be more willing to talk to me than a newbie. In the meantime, you go get some food—and keep your eyes open. If anyone's hanging around, say in that little green area at the corner, talk to them. See what you can smoke out."

"What if it's nothing to do with us?"

"We go see Judge Monaghan, get our warrant and get out of here."

McAllister grinned and took the money. "You are very devious, Trooper Duncan."

"It's called experience, McAllister," Duncan said. "Meet me at the judge's chambers when you're finished unless I text you."

"That piece of history you carry sends texts?"

"Don't be a smart ass. Get going."

McAllister headed down the street while Duncan walked inside. After passing through security, he paused to speak with the sheriff's deputy manning the checkpoint. It was business as usual on the first floor. "I saw the action outside. What's going on?"

The deputy jerked a thumb at the stairs. "They got a real mess downstairs in the Public Defender's office. Uniontown PD is here, but they aren't saying much."

Sally. Was she okay? Duncan hurried down the stairs to the basement, his footsteps echoing in the stairwell. A ring of chairs surrounded the waiting area, overhead fluorescent lighting harsh over the tiled floor. During court week they'd be full. Now they were empty, but there was a definite commotion focused near the public defender's office. A vise clamped around his chest.

A young uniformed officer from the Uniontown police department stood outside the office's partially open door. "We didn't call for help. Thanks," he said.

He looked young enough to be in high school, and a little wild-eyed at confronting a state trooper, but the kid stood his ground. Duncan gave him credit for that. "I'm not here to help," he said, "Officer…"

"Edmonds," the kid said. "Tim Edmonds. Sir."

"Officer Edmonds." Duncan pulled out his badge. "Don't have to call me sir. I'm here on other business. Since I am, do you need any assistance?"

"No, we got it under control. Thanks."

Duncan tried to sneak a look inside the office, but Edmonds's stance blocked his view. "What's up?"

"Call this morning about a dead body."

Dead. Duncan's heart skipped a beat. Not Sally. "Can you tell me who?" he asked, trying to keep his voice calm.

"Maybe you should talk to the detective in charge."

"Officer, I have a friend who works in this office. I'd like to know she's okay."

Edmonds paused and glanced at the door. "The deceased is Colin Rafferty. He's a member of the staff."

Rafferty? The guy who defended Aaron Trafford? And Sally's friend from the bar last Friday. The coincidences kept coming. That Trafford returned and a new lab cropped up wasn't hard to believe. His attorney turning up dead, that was a more disturbing thing. More importantly, where the hell was Sally and was she okay? "I think I would like to speak to the detective." When Edmonds didn't move, Duncan continued. "As I said, I have a friend who works here. Also, Mr. Rafferty's name has come up in a matter I'm investigating. Might be nothing, but I wouldn't be doing my job if I didn't find out."

Edmonds waited a moment, then leaned into the office. "Detective Killian. Got a state trooper here. Says he's needs to talk to you."

A middle-aged man wearing an off-the-rack suit appeared. "Detective Larry Killian, Uniontown PD." He stuck out his hand and Duncan shook it.

"Trooper First Class Jim Duncan." He showed Killian his badge. "Your officer tells me the deceased is Colin Rafferty. Is there somewhere quiet we can talk?"

"Follow me." Killian led the way from the office, scuffed shoes thudding on the floor. He opened an unmarked door that led to what was almost certainly a utility room that had been repurposed. A plain table and four chairs dominated the space. One of the chairs was occupied.

Duncan stepped inside and pulled up. "Sally?"

"Fancy meeting you here," Sally said.

She looked like hell. Her face was pale and she clutched a sweater around her shoulders even though the air in the room was stuffy, not chilly.

But no wounds, at least no physical ones. Had she encountered the shooter? "Are you—" He swallowed his intended words as unprofessional. "Ms. Castle. How are you?"

A smile, albeit a wan one. "As well as can be expected when you find a friend and colleague shot."

She'd come on the scene after the fact. At least she hadn't run into anyone leaving. Finding a dead body was bad enough.

"Ms. Castle," Killian said. "I need to talk to the trooper. Then I'll be in to get your statement."

Sally's head snapped toward Killian. "Wait, what?" She gripped the sweater. "Why? Trooper Duncan is a good guy. I'm sure whatever you need to talk to him about can wait."

"Ms. Castle," Killian said. "It's likely my conversation with him won't take long. I don't want to hold up a state police officer for his entire morning."

"I understand, but I have been sitting here for quite some time already. At least it feels like it's been a while. He wasn't here. I was. I found my co-worker shot in the head. I would think talking to me would be the most important thing on your to-do list right now." Sally's voice rose steadily, cracking a bit at the end.

"Ms. Castle," Killian said, an edge coming into his voice. "I appreciate your situation, but you—"

"Detective, if I may." What Duncan really wanted to do was wrap his arms around Sally, escort her home, and pour her a glass of wine. Maybe a glass of something stronger, given her morning. Tuck her quilt around her and assure her that everything would be okay. That wasn't going to happen, at least not right now, not in front of another police officer. He had to be solicitous, but professional. She'd understand, he hoped.

She looked up at him, and Duncan saw the exhaustion written on her face. The mute appeal. "Ms. Castle," he said, lowering his voice. He looked her in the eye, willing her to read the intent behind the official-sounding words. "I know you want to go home. Something's come up that may be related to this morning. I need to move on that quickly, which means I have to ask you to wait just a few more minutes. I promise, the detective and I won't be long. How about we get you a cup of coffee, huh?"

"It's burnt. No good." Sally mumbled and ran her hand through hair that had already been yanked out of its twist.

"I'm sure someone in this place has coffee." Duncan patted her hand and turned to Killian. "Give me a minute."

Duncan obtained a cup of steaming black coffee from another office on the floor, ignoring the undisguised curiosity of the occupants. He brought it to the tiny room and set it in front of Sally. "Drink that."

"Didn't happen to bring any creamer, did you?" she asked, giving him a weak smile.

"Take it black this time," Duncan said. "Something tells me you need it."

CHAPTER 7

"This'll do." Killian opened a door and flicked on the light. Another small room half-filled with boxes, presumably of cleaning supplies. Someone had stuffed a shabby wooden table and a couple of chairs inside. "Sit down." He settled into a chair and unbuttoned his sports coat. "You know her? Ms. Castle?"

Duncan finished a text to McAllister instructing her to get the warrant signed. He took off his hat and dropped it on the table. The room smelled stale. Dusty. "We met on a case a year ago. We've crossed paths a few times since on various investigations," he said.

"I hope she's not going to be difficult." Killian pulled out a notebook and uncapped a pen. "Public defense is a pain in the ass if you ask me."

There was just enough room for Duncan to pull out a chair; the sound of the legs scraping the floor loud in the enclosed space. Killian's attitude was not uncommon among cops. "Detective, may I offer you some advice? One investigator to another."

"Go on."

"Tone it down. Right now, Ms. Castle isn't an attorney. She's a person who found a friend and co-worker shot. Be gentle."

Killian fiddled with his jacket. "You said you needed to talk to me."

Sally would no doubt pull herself together. That was who she was. Duncan leaned forward. "Tell me about the scene."

"Why?" The Uniontown detective's chin jutted.

Oh for the love of... "You've heard about this suspected meth activity. I'm here this morning to get a search warrant signed for a likely location. In addition, I have information that Aaron Trafford is back in the area. I assume you're familiar with Trafford."

"What a screw-up that case was. The PSP botched that one for sure. But what's that got to do with Rafferty?"

Duncan held back a retort. Not the appropriate time or place for an argument. "Rafferty was Trafford's attorney."

Killian narrowed his eyes and said nothing.

"New lab, Trafford back, now Rafferty dead. Any cop worth his badge would wonder if there's a connection."

Killian grunted.

"Tell me about the scene."

Silence and Duncan thought the detective might refuse. But then Killian thumbed through his notes. "Call came in a little after seven. Unit dispatched to the public defender's office found a white male, one GSW to the head. Right temple." His expression told Duncan that the detective would rather not have said anything.

"Powder burns? Shell casings?"

"No burns. We're still looking for casings."

"You haven't found a day planner or calendar with appointments in it? Maybe on his computer?"

No response. The overhead light flickered.

"Coroner say anything? Time of death?"

Killian capped the pen. "Usual mumbo-jumbo, doesn't want to commit until the autopsy. I've got my doubts about this kid. Weird, even for a coroner."

That description fit only one deputy coroner Duncan knew. Tom Burns, whose humor could make even seasoned investigators flinch. Duncan stood. "If you find anything during the course of your investigation that leads back to Trafford, I'd appreciate a call." He handed Killian a card.

The detective took it without looking. "This is my murder, Trooper."

"I'm not interested in taking your investigation. I'm only concerned about how it may affect my drug case." Duncan picked up his hat and left Killian glowering at the table.

Duncan paused outside the PD's office. No point hanging around. If Burns was the deputy coroner, he'd be willing to talk. And who knew what McAllister had dug up.

Duncan headed upstairs. Once outside, he put on his hat and looked around. The bright October sunshine, and the accompanying light and warmth, were as welcome as if he'd emerged from a coal mine. Sally would also be more than happy to share with him when he called her later, maybe after his shift. Why did their conversations always deal with murder and mayhem?

※ ※ ※

Sally sat in the room, picking at the rolled edge of the paper coffee cup. It was a semi-used storage space, but cleaned out in preparation for something. Maybe to be used as an office. It was eerily quiet, as though she was the only person in the courthouse. Which couldn't be true. There'd been people all around when she'd been ushered out of her workspace, shock glazing her senses.

The room was hot, but she was icy cold. Thank God for Jim. She'd recognized the concern under his calm, professional tone, seen it in his eyes. Most importantly, he'd brought her fresh coffee and if he could have put a shot of whiskey in it, he would have. She took another sip. The coffee had been so hot initially she hadn't been able to drink it safely. All right, girl, time to pull yourself together.

Poor Colin. As the shock of seeing him wore off, her natural investigative logic kicked into gear. Argument, disappearance, panic, murder. It created a straight line of reasoning, the end of which was obvious, murder. But what caused the argument?

Where the hell was Killian? She'd forgotten her watch this morning, her phone was in her purse back at Doris's desk, and the clock in the room was broken, so she had no idea how long she'd been sitting there. She knew it was past the seven-fifteen shown on the cheap, battered wall clock. She'd found Colin a little after seven. What made him come in to the office so early? He rarely walked in before eight-thirty, usually closer to nine. She'd have been shocked to find him alive in that office at seven, never mind dead.

Random killing? She dismissed the idea. Wrong place and too early. Someone would need to know Colin was in the office. The door had been locked. That meant Colin had known his killer and let him in. She felt a crawling sensation across her neck.

Then the evidence of the coffee. The machine wasn't the best, but it took hours for the brew to become truly undrinkable. That meant Colin had come in unusually early, or the pot had been left on the burner since last night. She doubted Colin had come in at three in the morning. But yesterday was Sunday. He'd specifically mentioned the birthday party and the Steelers game...and he'd missed both. He might grudgingly skip the football, but he would if the issue was big enough. But what could be important enough to make him miss his mother's birthday, her first after being declared cancer free?

She closed her eyes, forcing herself to picture his body. He wore the same clothes as when she saw him the day before. That meant he'd come to the courthouse after that. To do what? Something related to the Friday argument or the tattooed visitor?

Sally started as the door opened and Killian came in. "Sorry. Things took a little longer than expected." He pulled out a chair opposite her and sat, flipping to a clean sheet in his notebook.

"Why was the trooper here?"

Killian raised an eyebrow. "May I have your full legal name?"

Damn. Well, she'd tried. "Sarah Marie Castle."

"How long have you been with the public defender's office?"

"Three years."

"How long have you known the deceased?"

"Colin joined the office a year after I did."

"Take me through your morning."

Sally ran down the basics. She'd arrived early, discovered the burnt coffee, seen the lights, and found Colin.

"Was it normal for Mr. Rafferty to be in the office at that time?" Killian asked, not looking at her.

"No. It was extremely abnormal," Sally said.

"When was the last time you saw the victim?"

"Yesterday."

"How did he appear? Calm? Normal? Agitated?"

Sally thought. "Agitated. But that wasn't the first time." She related what she'd seen in Lucky 7 on Friday.

Killian paused in his note taking and looked up. "Who did he argue with?"

She played with her cup. "I told you. I didn't see the man's face."

"And Mr. Rafferty left immediately after this incident?"

"Yes…well, I assume so. He didn't come back to the table to get his jacket or tell me he was leaving."

Killian jotted a note. "What was Mr. Rafferty like as a co-worker? Did you get along with him?"

"Usually." Sally focused on the cup. "When Colin started, this job was not where he saw himself. He wanted to be doing high-priced private defense. I'd been working with him and bringing him around. You know, helping him to see that public defense isn't a dead end."

"Was it working?"

"I think so. I mean, he appeared relatively happy."

"Did he have problems with anyone that you know of, maybe your boss?"

"I don't know. But the man in the bar Friday night was not Bryan Gerrity." She rubbed her forehead. "Colin was okay Friday morning. We had a normal day and we went to Lucky 7 for happy hour, like we always did." Coffee gone, she threw the paper cup in the trash.

"Then he argued with someone you didn't see, disappeared, and when you found him yesterday he promised talk to you today."

"That's correct."

Killian studied his notes. "Let's return to this morning. Did you see Mr. Rafferty's car when you arrived?"

Sally paused, staring at the wall. "I don't…no."

"You don't know or no, you didn't see it?"

Sally's neck warmed. "No, I didn't see his car. Maybe he got a ride to work."

"There's only the three of you in the office?" Killian asked. The pen scratched as he wrote.

"No. Seven attorneys and two secretaries."

"Who has access to the office?"

Sally didn't like where this was going. "All of us have keys."

"Did Mr. Rafferty have enemies as a result of his work?" Killian asked. "Disgruntled clients? Or a relative of someone who was convicted, someone prone to violence?"

Sally thought over what she knew of Colin's cases. "Not that I know of. And I doubt a civilian could get in here after hours."

Killian looked up. "Do you know someone with the initials DT?"

DT? De'Shawn Thomas? Was that why Colin was at work? But why would he meet about such a minor case on a Sunday? Easy, he wouldn't. "Not personally and I'm not in a position to discuss our clients without a little more information from you so I don't violate attorney-client privilege. Why do you want to know?"

"Anything else you want to tell me?"

She squelched the urge to hit Killian with the broken clock and folded her hands on the table. "No." She maintained eye contact. "Do you have a time of death?"

Killian shook his head and smirked. "Sorry, Ms. Castle. We're not prepared to divulge that information."

What a jerk. She should have hit him with the clock.

CHAPTER 8

While Duncan waited for McAllister to return to the patrol car, he saw a bagged body on a gurney emerge from the courthouse. Tom Burns maneuvered it down the stairs by the main entrance. Duncan rushed forward. "Let me help you with that."

"Thanks." Burns looked up, saw Duncan and gave a wry smile. "I should have known."

Duncan followed him out to the coroner's van, pausing as a woman talking on her cell phone, completely oblivious, barreled on down the sidewalk. "Coincidence, I swear."

"Right. Face it, Duncan. Trouble follows you like your devoted dog."

Duncan pulled open the back door of the van. "As long as I'm here, what can you tell me?"

Burns shoved the gurney, laden with what Duncan assumed was Colin Rafferty's body, inside and slammed the door. Then he looked around. Seeing Detective Killian hovering at the top of the stairs, he muttered, "Call me later." Raising his voice, he said, "Thanks for your help, Trooper." With a wave, Burns got into the van and pulled away.

Duncan watched the receding taillights. He glanced back at Killian, who turned and headed inside without acknowledging his counterpart.

A few minutes later, McAllister returned, cutting through the garden seating area at the corner. She held a paper bag and a carrier with two cups in one hand and a folded paper in the other. "I hope you like scones," she said.

"That's fine. You get the warrant?"

"Right here." She waved the folded paper. "And I have a fresh pot of gossip."

"Good. Get in the car." He took the paper bag and walked back to where he'd parked. The scones were still warm and smelled like pumpkin spice. "What's the gossip?" He took a bite.

"A few secretaries were standing around, taking a smoke break," McAllister said. "They heard Colin Rafferty from the Public Defender's office was killed."

"They heard right." He ran down what little Killian had said in their interview. "The lead detective wouldn't give me much else. No obvious connection to our case."

"Only if you believe in coincidence." McAllister took a bite of scone. "We get a tip Aaron Trafford's back, find a probable lab, and then Trafford's attorney is killed? Yeah. Absolutely no connection."

Duncan took another bite. McAllister had good taste, although now there were crumbs on his uniform.

McAllister took a sip of her latte, the scent of cinnamon and cream filling the car. "Anyway, one of the secretaries overheard the Uniontown detective asking about CCTV footage and weekend maintenance staff."

"Detective Larry Killian. We talked."

"He give you anything at all?"

"Only that Rafferty was shot," Duncan said. "Other than that, he was pretty tight-lipped." Duncan took another bite.

"Why would they be interested in weekend staff?" McAllister asked.

"Not sure, but it tells me they're looking at who might have been in the building on a Sunday evening, which gives me a hint as to time of death." Duncan brushed the crumbs off his shirt, put the used napkin in the bag, placed his coffee in the cup holder, and fastened his seat belt.

McAllister followed suit. "Would anyone have been working on a weekend?"

"No clue," Duncan said. "We can also hit this from another angle. I know the woman who found the body. First, however, we have a search warrant to execute."

⁂

Back out in the still-deserted sitting area, Sally tried to peer into the office. The people who'd been observing the goings on from other offices had returned to their daily grind. Sally couldn't tell if Burns was still inside or if he'd left with his grisly baggage.

"Ma'am, your purse." The officer held out her maroon Coach bag, mercifully free of fingerprint powder.

"Is the coroner still here?"

"Not my place to say, ma'am," he said. "Hope you have a better afternoon." He went back to his post.

"Sally, there you are." Bryan Gerrity came up beside her. "You okay?"

Sally nodded, eyes still on the office. "I guess so. I'm having a hard time processing the fact that Colin's dead. I feel like I should be grieving, but I'm kind of numb." Side by side, they walked up the stairs to the first floor. The two sheriff's deputies were checking a couple of visitors through the metal detector. Few others were around. They'd most likely gone back to work.

She could barely see out the glass windows of the front door, but enough to tell the coroner's van was gone. She could see reporters and camera crews from all of the Pittsburgh and local media clustered on the sidewalk with their cameras and sound equipment in the bright sunshine. Another harried Uniontown officer prevented them from entering.

"Don't feel bad." Bryan shook his head. "It'll set in later, when it's quieter." He stared at the stairs leading to the basement. "God, I can't believe this."

"Did Killian interview you yet?"

"I had to talk to the press first. I made a brief statement expressing our general sorrow at the loss of a colleague, said further details would be forthcoming. They threw out a lot of questions, but I wasn't hearing them."

"Right." Sally shivered and it wasn't from a chill. The air conditioning in the courthouse had been shut off a week ago, when the overnight temps plunged to the forties. The truth was starting to hit her. Colin was dead. She'd never razz him about his careful appearance or sloppy handwriting again. "Did the police mention the initials DT to you?"

Bryan's forehead puckered "DT? No, why?"

"Something Killian threw out during my interview. It sounds like Colin was meeting someone last night with those initials. The only person I could think of was that new case. The guy Colin's defended before."

"Did you mention him to Killian?"

"No. He didn't give me reason to potentially violate privilege so I kept my mouth shut."

"Good." There was a pause and Bryan shrugged. "I can't think of anything important enough that Colin would skip Sunday night football. Certainly not that case."

Exactly what Sally had thought. But if her friendship with Jim had taught her anything, it was that cops didn't ask pointless questions.

They stood in silence. Sally's mind churned over the facts as she knew them. DT, huh? Could there be another person with those initials and had that been the person who visited Colin's apartment, the one he was afraid of? Had that been who he was meeting last night, the person who needed to fix…something? She needed to look at Colin's office again. "When can we get back in?"

"Not any time soon. I've already called around, postponed any meetings we have with prosecutors or court appearances," Bryan said.

Damn. That meant the police would confiscate any information that might lead to the identity of DT. She sighed.

"Sally, you look frazzled." Bryan patted her shoulder. "Go home, have a glass of wine, put your feet up. Hopefully we'll be able to get in tomorrow. I'll call you tonight to confirm."

"Okay, thanks." Sally shouldered her purse and headed to her car, grateful for the warmth of the sun. Go home? Yes. Glass of wine? Definitely. Put her feet up? Not a chance.

CHAPTER 9

The Special Emergency Response Team had arrived by the time they returned to Jumonville Road. A highly-trained unit, SERT members were better equipped to handle high-risk searches, such as the suspected meth lab.

"Here's Trooper Duncan. He can answer all your questions," said Trooper Alan Porter, who'd been securing the site, as Duncan walked up. "Troopers David Gryzbowski and Anthony Dawkins."

"Gentlemen." Duncan didn't consider himself a small guy, but the SERT troopers looked like they could have folded him in half and put him in a back pocket. Both were built like NFL linebackers and wore hazmat suits.

"Afternoon," Dawkins said. His baritone voice matched his cocoa-colored skin and eyes. The sun gleamed off a bald head. "You the one calling the shots on this?"

"I am. This is Trooper Aislyn McAllister." Duncan scanned the property. "So, Dawkins and Gryz—" He struggled with the Polish name.

"G," Gryzbowski said. He grinned, blue eyes looking out of a face that had seen a little too much sun. His hair was closely cropped, leaving him almost as bald as Dawkins.

"Thank you," Duncan said. "You two ready to get started?"

"Waiting on you," Dawkins said. "Must say, never had the dubious pleasure of searching a suspected meth lab. They stink as much as the feds say they do."

Duncan eyed the equipment on the ground. "Ramming?"

"Safer," Gryzbowski said. "If it's really what we think it is, the next stop for this house is demolition. You said no one is here?"

"That's the assumption. You see anyone?" He looked at Porter, who shook his head.

"Then we have the luxury of taking the time to beat down the door. I'll wait with you in the vehicle." Gryzbowski pointed at the heavy-duty truck parked in the driveway.

"McAllister, come with me," Duncan said. "Nothing for you to do out here. Porter, you can take off. Thanks."

Porter nodded, headed back to his patrol car, and drove away.

Gryzbowski led Duncan and McAllister to the SERT truck as a couple of other team members joined Dawkins.

McAllister handed the warrant to Duncan. "You want to read it?"

"You wrote it, you do it." The warrant covered everything including the proverbial kitchen sink when it came to drugs, and not just the meth. If they got to court and it said otherwise, there'd be hell to pay.

McAllister keyed the mic and read the contents of the warrant over the loudspeaker. As expected, no one came out.

"How long do you want to wait?" Gryzbowski asked.

Duncan glanced at McAllister, who gave a thumbs up. "I think that's enough time," he said.

Gryzbowski keyed another mic and said, "Dawkins, we're a go."

They watched the video monitor as the team breached the door and entered. Methodical and brisk, they cleared the house. Images of dilapidated rooms, bare except for boxes and what looked like oversize chemistry sets, streamed over the video cameras. One room contained a table laden with what appeared to be plastic baggies containing pale chips of stone. As anticipated, no other people were present.

After a few minutes, Dawkins' voice crackled over the radio. "Congratulations, Duncan. You found yourself a meth lab."

"We can see it. What exactly is there?" Duncan said, looking at McAllister.

"We got raw materials, equipment, and finished product. Some packaged, some waiting. And a god-awful smell."

"Copy that." Duncan faced his companions. "Step one accomplished," he said. "Now on to step two, the hard part."

"We need to get this place condemned and scheduled for demolition after we remove the evidence," Gryzbowski said, jerking his thumb in the direction of the house, battered door hanging like a broken tooth. "Damn shame. Bet it was beautiful before it was a meth lab. Who owns it?"

McAllister consulted the warrant. "Someone named Genevieve Marnier."

Gryzbowski frowned. "The guy who met us, Porter, said you were looking for a suspect named Trafford."

"We are," Duncan said.

"How's he connected to this Marnier woman?"

Duncan gazed at the house, which looked despondent in the shaded sunlight. "No freaking clue."

⁂

The first thing Sally did when she got home later Monday morning was pour herself a generous glass of merlot and call her sister. Her modest apartment building, tucked into a shady street away from Uniontown's downtown area, was a soothing balm to her soul after the morning she'd had. Her front corner, third-floor unit offered a nice view of the single-family homes and tree-lined street. No balconies and the building wasn't pet-friendly, but one couldn't have everything. She wasn't home enough to take care of an animal anyway.

Colin's shooting was all over the news and Noreen was frantic. After assuring her sister that everything was fine and Sally wasn't in danger, she kicked off her shoes and found her favorite cardigan, the one that was a bit ratty, but too cozy to part with. Wine in one hand, pencil and paper in the other, she settled into her couch.

Distance from the scene was working its magic. Plus Sally's sister always described her as a cat: too curious and determined for her own good. "And we all know what happened to the cat," Reen would inevitably say.

Sally had been in the criminal law game long enough to be able to read between the lines of Detective Killian's questions. He had a suspect. The mysterious DT. Why? Because he must have found something that indicated Colin had an appointment, either a note in his day planner or something on his computer. She was certain the cops had found the case file identifying De'Shawn Thomas, so there was already a name to go with those initials.

Detective Killian had been snide, which helped burn away Sally's shock. Sure, cops and defense attorneys rarely were best buddies. Her friendship with Jim was an anomaly. But Jim would never have been that callous with a witness.

She took a sip of merlot and set the glass on a coaster on the end table. She was missing something. A little detail that didn't mean much in the immediate aftermath, but was important.

She didn't want to, but Sally closed her eyes and tried to picture the scene. Colin dead, sitting in a chair, blood everywhere. His Steelers mug, half filled with coffee, nearby. The other Steelers mug, filled to the top.

She opened her eyes and reached for her pad. Those commemorative mugs were Colin's most precious office belongings. He'd gone to both of the Super Bowls. There was no way he'd use that mug for a client meeting. Clients rated a polystyrene cup. Someone important—a friend, a colleague—would be the only person allowed to use the other mug.

What else? She closed her eyes again, picturing the desk. It had been bare except for the mugs. No files, no loose papers, no notepad, not even a pen. But if it had been a client meeting, Colin would need the case file for reference, and pen and paper for taking notes. Unless the client had taken the file or pad. Sally scribbled another note and took a healthy gulp of wine. She'd have to call Killian with all this, of course. As soon as she was finished.

She figured the meeting had to have occurred late afternoon or early evening on Sunday; after the birthday party, but before the primetime football game. Next question, why hold such a meeting at the courthouse? Because it was Sunday night. There'd be no one around so there would be more privacy. But there were CCTV cameras all over the place and anyone with Colin would easily be identified. That meant whoever the other person was, it was also someone who wouldn't look out of place if he or she was seen on that footage.

An important person who wouldn't look out of place at the courthouse. That led her to one conclusion. DT was a county employee.

CHAPTER 10

The search of the house on Jumonville occupied most of the morning. By the time Duncan and McAllister left the scene, it was almost noon. They grabbed a fast-food lunch and headed back to the barracks to do some more in-depth investigating.

"I want you to hunt down Genevieve Marnier. Current address, phone number, whatever." Duncan threw his crumpled bag into the trash. "And see if she has any priors." He slurped the rest of his Coke and tossed the empty cup after the bag.

"Right. What about the property?" McAllister shook the remaining fries out of their paper holder and stuffed them in her mouth.

"I've got the house. When you're done, we'll pool information."

"Okay. I have a question though."

"Shoot."

She paused. "We're patrol cops. Shouldn't we be out driving our area? I mean, the PSP has an investigative division, right?"

Duncan studied his trainee. Deciding she was curious instead of confrontational, he answered. "Criminal Investigation, yes. I do things differently," he said. "I don't like handing over my cases until I absolutely have to. Over the years, Nicols and I have come to an…understanding, if you will. As long as the routine stuff gets done, I can work my cases. Since you're with me for the month, that means you do what I do."

"Works for me." McAllister gathered up her own lunch remains, tossed them in the garbage, and walked off with her oversized cup of Mountain Dew.

He glanced at his watch. He still needed to check on Sally. By now she was probably back at her apartment. If he didn't get a chance to at least call before the shift ended at three, he'd stop and see her. Work first.

He logged into one of the shared computers and pulled up the records on the house. Genevieve Marnier had owned the property for thirty years, previously with a Peter Marnier. Duncan assumed that was her husband. The mortgage was long paid off. Property taxes up to date. The search had only turned up drug paraphernalia. No clothes, no furniture, no appliances. The grass had been flattened where a car—a smaller one, judging by the spot—had been parked. There'd been nothing in the battered garage except cobwebs and dust. No tools, no car maintenance materials, nothing. Not really surprising. Only a moron lived in a house where someone was cooking meth.

McAllister returned holding a sheaf of paper. "I found the homeowner."

"Excellent. Where?"

"Genevieve Marnier's current address is an assisted living facility, Running Waters. Been there for a couple years, according to what I found. I'm guessing she's either too old or too sick to keep up with the property. No other phone number besides the facility. No criminal record."

A big, grand Victorian would overwhelm an old lady. Ripe pickings for someone looking to establish a meth facility. "All right. Let's see what we else can find on Mrs. Marnier." Duncan inched his chair over and pulled up another one, scraping it across the floor. "You type."

"Why me? I mean…you're already there. Is this some kind of training task?" McAllister unscrewed a bottle of Mountain Dew.

"Damnit, McAllister. What did I tell you about doing as I say?"

Her face hardened. "I'm asking if there is a specific reason I need to be the typist."

"This isn't a hazing thing because you're new and it's not because you're a woman, if that's what you're thinking. I am the slowest damn typist in this entire barracks. Ask anyone." He pinched the bridge of his nose. "You want to finish this before dinner, you type. You want to spend all night? Then sit down, and I'll start hunting and pecking."

She sat, settled the chair, and pulled the keyboard closer. "You're a dinosaur, you know that?"

"No, I failed computer keyboarding in high school. Happy? I can use the damn thing. I'm not fast. We need to move fast."

"Why didn't you say that in the first place? We're starting with Genevieve?"

"You got it."

McAllister's fingers flew. "What if the person running this lab isn't Marnier? Are we looking for family connections?"

"Yes."

"What if we don't find anything?"

"Then we'll try something else. We have to start somewhere."

McAllister had no response.

"According to my property search, the house was purchased in 1968 by Peter and Genevieve Marnier. He died in 2007," Duncan said. "Let's start by seeing if we can find a marriage license."

The computer hummed for a minute, and results popped up on the screen. "Marriage license for Peter Marnier and Genevieve Taylor from 1957," McAllister said. "I think this might be the right couple. Here's Peter's death certificate, 2007."

"Any kids?"

More tapping. "Two, a son and a daughter." Before Duncan asked, McAllister continued. "Son never married and here's his death certificate. Coal mine accident in 2002."

A couple of troopers passed, grinning at the sight of Duncan hovering over the shoulder of his trainee. He ignored them. "What about the daughter?"

"Working on it." A minute later, she read from the screen. "Daughter married...son of a bitch."

"What?" He leaned in.

"Married in 1982 to Alexander Trafford." She searched again. "Birth certificate for their son, Aaron, dated 1986." She pointed at the screen.

"Genevieve Marnier is Aaron Trafford's maternal grandmother."

"There are death certificates for both parents. Car wreck in 1994. Damn. Maybe Aaron went to live with her?"

Duncan jotted a note. "I would say possible, even probable, his grandmother was his guardian."

McAllister leaned back. "Very convenient for Mr. Trafford that his grandmother's house is empty."

"A little too convenient." He stood. "Print that stuff."

She headed for the printer as it whirred. "Who's paying the property taxes on the house?"

"Computer doesn't say. But they're up to date, so someone's paying them."

McAllister collected her printouts and followed Duncan back to the desk area. "Think it's Trafford taking care of granny because she can't manage the house?"

"Possible. Or he doesn't want his grandmother living in his drug production facility because she'd get in the way. Or because it's not safe."

"Is he the type to care?"

"Who doesn't love his grandmother? We'll find out where the account's money is coming from. We can go to the facility tomorrow, see if Aaron has visited his grandmother lately. If we're lucky, we'll find out who's paying her bills."

"What if he hasn't? And what are the chances it's not him behind this new place?"

"Trafford's already been arrested for meth production once. If that warrant hadn't been tossed, he'd be in prison. That, coupled with the fact he's been seen locally, moves him to the top of my suspect list. All he would need to know is that his grandmother's house was empty. He moves in, sets up shop, and doesn't even have to explain ownership of the property."

"Think he was living there?"

"No. Too risky. That doesn't mean he isn't renting somewhere else and cooking on Jumonville Road. He'll want to stay relatively close."

McAllister emptied the bottle and used a perfect jump shot to send it to the trash. "Too bad Eddie can't give us a location."

"He can't give us one yet." Duncan glanced at the clock. "It's time to knock off. I'll see you tomorrow." He grabbed the keys to his Jeep. Eddie would come through. He always did.

⸙⸙⸙

The adrenaline crash hit Sally late that morning and she fell asleep. Persistent knocking on her door woke her around five. She blinked at the clock, rubbing sleep from her eyes. She'd get rid of her visitor and call Jim. He should be off duty by now if he'd been in uniform this morning.

She threw aside her quilt and headed for the door as the knocking continued. "I'm coming. Keep your pants on." She mumbled under her breath, words her mother definitely would call "unladylike," and pulled on her slippers as she rushed down the short hallway. "Yes, yes, what do you—" She pulled open the door.

Jim stood in the dark blue-carpeted hallway, hand raised to knock again. "Don't worry. I planned to keep my pants on."

She felt the heat rise in her face, but couldn't keep her gaze from flickering to the faded jeans that showed off his lower body. Damn. "What are you doing here?" Great, just great. Nice opening.

He raised one eyebrow. "Thanks. Good to see you, too."

"I didn't...what I meant..." Get a grip. "I didn't expect you. I was just thinking of calling."

"Well, here I am. I wanted to make sure you were okay after this morning. Professional courtesy."

She stared at him for a second. Coming to her senses, she stepped back. "Sorry, I'm not...come in. There's no reason for us to stand in the doorway." God only knew what he was thinking. Asking him in should have been her first line.

Sure enough, he stepped inside, hesitating slightly. "How are you doing?"

"This morning was rough, but I'm better now." She closed the door. "Take off your pants, stay awhile." The heat crept down her neck. "Coat. Take off your coat and stay awhile." Oh for...she was going from bad to worse.

He turned a laugh into a cough, then slipped out of his leather jacket, and handed it to her. "How many glasses of wine have you had?"

She took his jacket, warm from his body, and hung it on the rack of ornate iron pegs in the hallway. "I had one when I came home. But I just woke up from a nap, so I'm a little...can I start over? Jim, nice to see you. Come in. Let me take your jacket." She adjusted her hair, which had come out of the messy bun while she slept.

"I liked your first opening. It's rare to see you off your game."

This was worse than when she'd seen him at the bar Friday. Both times she acted like a sixteen-year-old twit instead of a thirty-three-year-old professional. She headed for the kitchen. "Want something to drink? Dark beer, right? Will this do?" She held out a bottle of Edmund Fitzgerald porter from the case next to the fridge, along with a bottle opener.

"Perfect." He popped off the cap and threw it in the garbage. "Right temperature, too."

That was a complete accident, but Sally played it like it was intentional. She'd already made an idiot of herself with the doorway scene. At least he'd relaxed. "You need a glass?"

"Bottle is fine." He followed her into the living room, where he sat in the overstuffed arm chair. "Any leftover jitters?"

She picked up the quilt from the floor and returned to the couch. "Once I started the interview with Killian, I was good."

"Told him you would be." His gaze drifted to her shoulder.

Her sweatshirt had slipped down. She tugged it back into place. Was that disappointment in his eyes? Should she have left it? Too late. "I'm pretty sure he didn't think so."

"I got the feeling Detective Killian has some very firm ideas when it comes to defense attorneys." He lifted the bottle. "We can't all be enlightened, you know."

She should have left the sweatshirt alone. "What exactly happened? I didn't spend time examining Colin's body. Too...you know."

"Understandable." He set down the beer on the polished wood coffee table. After a second, he put a magazine under it. "I don't know much more than you. Single GSW to the right temple."

"Killian didn't tell you anything?"

"He's being a bit territorial."

She picked at the edge of the quilt. "Why? Wouldn't the state police be involved?"

"Because he can be. Uniontown is a full-service force. They do their own thing and call if they need help."

"But you were there."

"Getting a search warrant signed on an unrelated matter." He studied her, his face unreadable. "I did find out that he's looking to see if there is CCTV tape and asking about Sunday night staff."

Sally waited, but Jim didn't elaborate. For a moment, she allowed herself to be distracted by his sweater, maroon and soft, cotton-blend not cashmere knowing him. It was snug enough to show off his torso and shoulders, but not skin tight. She forced herself to focus. "I was thinking after I came home." She told him the conclusions she'd reached. "If Colin met someone on Sunday night, that would play into Killian's question about Sunday. But he normally didn't work weekends. And I certainly can't think of anyone important enough to rate a commemorative Super Bowl coffee mug."

"Importance is relative."

He had a point. The person only had to be important to Colin. "Anyway, what was the search warrant for? If you don't mind my asking."

He paused. "I'm sure you've heard about the suspected drug activity in the region. McAllister, she's the trainee I told you about Friday, and I found a house where there's evidence of meth production. The warrant was for that."

Sally got the impression he was debating whether to tell her more.

He must have decided against it, because he didn't continue. When he spoke again, it wasn't about the warrant. "You should call Killian. Tell him what you told me."

"I don't think he'll care."

"You're a witness in his homicide. If he's any kind of investigator, and I'm sure he is, he'll at least listen." Jim paused, his gaze lingering on her shoulder, then stood. "Thanks for the beer. I'll be going, let you get back to sleep or whatever." He headed toward the kitchen with the empty bottle.

Sally jumped up and the quilt fell to the floor, jumbled color on the brown carpet. "Can I get you another?" She'd finally gotten him over to visit and once again the whole conversation had been about work.

"No, thanks. Won't do for me to get busted for DUI on my way home." He rinsed the bottle, put it in the recycling can, then stood in the entrance to the kitchen, spinning his key ring on his finger.

"I don't want that." Damn it. It was dinnertime. She could ask him to stay.

"Besides, I have to get home and take care of Rizzo. Marge had some event to go to for her kids."

Damn it again. Marge, his neighbor, often lent a hand with the dog. Why did she have to be busy tonight? "Okay, well...thanks for stopping. Tell Rizzo I said hi."

"Will do." He paused. "Take care." Then he turned and left.

Sally groaned and sagged against the granite countertop. If only she hadn't acted like a complete fool when he arrived. She'd probably scared him off. But he had come to see her. That had to mean something, right?

She returned to the living room, folded up the quilt, and hung it on the back of the couch. Jim had mentioned a new meth facility. Colin had represented a guy on meth charges who'd vanished after the case ended in a mistrial. Aaron Trafford. Everyone thought it was a lock for conviction and the decision had stunned the entire courthouse staff. Was he back? Was that what needed fixing? How? But the initials didn't fit. She looked at her clock. Six-thirty. A little late to call Detective Killian. That unpleasant chore could wait until tomorrow.

CHAPTER 11

Duncan and McAllister headed to the Running Waters Assisted Living facility immediately after roll call Tuesday morning. As Duncan pointed out, they could combine the drive out with their patrol duty. From what they'd been able to piece together, Genevieve Marnier had sole custody of her grandson for almost four years after his parents died when he was eight. At age twelve, he'd been transferred to the foster system, staying with various families until he was eighteen. Something had happened with Genevieve that made Child Protective Services think young Aaron would be safer with strangers than his grandmother.

Running Waters looked like any other assisted living facility: a low building, lots of windows and landscaped with a big garden of colorful mums around a man-made pond. The inside was decorated with soft pastels and innocuous flower prints that were so common that they lacked identity. The dining room was set with formal place settings while elderly residents lounged in an oversized sitting room full of hotel-decor furniture, waiting for their next catered meal.

After showing his badge and identifying himself and McAllister, Duncan said, "We're here to see Genevieve Marnier."

The receptionist pointed to an elderly lady sitting by a window, sunlight glinting off her white hair, head nodding. A colorful afghan covered her lap. "Over there," she said. "Hopefully it's one of her good days." The receptionist turned away to answer the phone before Duncan could ask what she meant.

They walked over. Duncan touched the lady's shoulder to wake her. "Genevieve Marnier?" he asked, when the faded blue eyes opened. "Trooper First Class Jim Duncan from the state police. This is my partner, Trooper Aislyn McAllister. We'd like to talk to you."

Genevieve blinked and patted him. The skin on her hand looked like tissue paper, blue veins prominent. "What a nice looking young man you are," she said. "But I'm afraid you're too late. My Pete got here first. He should be home soon. It'd be lovely if you could stay to meet him."

Oh boy. This was going to complicate things. "Mrs. Marnier, I'm looking for your grandson. Aaron."

Genevieve peered at him, eyes unfocused and filmy. "A grandson? Young man, I just got married. What kind of girl do you think I am, having a grandchild at my age?"

The troopers stepped out of Genevieve's hearing. At least Duncan hoped so.

"I don't think she's going to be helpful," McAllister said. "Sounds like she's got dementia."

"I noticed."

"Now what?"

Now what indeed. He approached and tried again. "Mrs. Marnier, I'm from the state police. Do you understand me?"

"She probably doesn't get a word you're saying," a woman's voice said from behind him.

Duncan turned to see a kind-faced black woman in a nurse's uniform. "I was afraid of that. Do you work here?"

"I'm one of the nurses. Tricia Milkins. Mrs. Marnier has late-stage Alzheimer's. They brought her here two years ago, when she needed more personalized care. As I understand, she's been in a couple different facilities ever since she almost burnt her house down. Her husband, Peter, has been dead for a while but she thinks he'll be home any moment. Poor dear never gets any visitors. It's rather sad. Is there something I can help you with?"

Duncan glanced down at Genevieve, who was now staring out the window, humming. "I'm looking for Mrs. Marnier's grandson. A man named Aaron Trafford. Have you seen him? Medium height, shaved head, extensive tattoos." At least that's what he'd looked like at trial last year.

"No. Like I said, she hasn't had a visitor since she was brought here. At least not that I've seen," Milkins said, shaking her head. "She talks about a grandson sometimes, but it's hard to tell when she's lucid and when she's having one of her spells."

"Pete'll be home soon. You can talk to him then," Genevieve said. There was spit at the corner of her mouth. She had started to tremble, but Duncan didn't know if it was nervousness or a symptom of her dementia.

"I know, dear. You sit here in the sunshine and wait for him." The nurse bent over, wiped the old lady's mouth, and adjusted the afghan. She turned back to Duncan. "Sorry I can't be more help to you."

Duncan looked at Genevieve, who had resumed her humming. "Who would I speak to so I can find out who pays her bills?"

"Stop in the office. They might be able to tell you." Milkins pointed.

The troopers thanked her and headed for a door off the lobby marked Office. The stark white contrasted with the gentle pastel decor of the rest of the building. A woman inside sat at a computer. "Excuse me," Duncan said. "I need to know who pays for one of your residents. Genevieve Marnier."

The woman squinted at him. "I need a warrant to show you confidential information about a resident."

"Someone is using her house for illegal activity. Whoever is paying for her to be here might be able to help us."

"I can't release anything, sorry."

McAllister started to argue, but Duncan cut her off. "Can you at least tell me how the bill is paid?"

The woman pursed her lips, but pulled up a file on the computer. "Mrs. Marnier's bill is paid monthly on an automatic electronic funds transfer from a bank account."

"Not Medicaid?" McAllister asked, using her phone to tap out a note.

"No, only state-run facilities take Medicaid. Private ones, like Running Water, take payment in cash."

Electronic funds transfer from a bank. He'd need a warrant for information about the account, such as whose name it was in. Duncan thought. "She must have a contact for emergencies. Surely you can tell me that."

Again, the woman fussed, but eventually said, "Her attorney, Mr. Lester, is her emergency contact. He has an office in Uniontown." The woman wrote down the address and handed it over. They thanked her and left.

Outside, McAllister slipped on a pair of Ray-bans. "Well, that was useless."

"Not entirely. We know Genevieve is probably clueless as to what's happening at her house, no one has been to see her, and we got a name of someone we can ask more questions. Didn't you handle any investigations in your first month?"

"Nothing like this."

Every new trooper came out of the academy a hard charger, thinking everything fell into place, despite what they'd learned in the classroom. "Quite often, this is a long game. We have more facts. Might not know what to do with them yet, but we will. Patience is one of the most important skills you need as an investigator."

She bit her lip, clearly processing his words. "Then on to Mr. Lester?"

"On to Mr. Lester."

As she got into the car, McAllister looked around the grounds, neatly decorated and green, but clinical at the same time. "I hate these places," she said, wrinkling her nose. "My pap ended up in one. They smell like death."

Duncan had to agree. Running Waters was pretty, but it wasn't where Duncan wanted to spend his retirement. Shuffling along the stone paths, looking forward to rice pudding for dessert. "I know what you mean." He slid into the car.

"Oh shit." McAllister got in beside him. "I didn't...do you have someone close to you, like a parent, in one of these homes?" She looked genuinely distressed.

"My folks retired to Arizona a few years ago." He started the car. "Hell, my dad skis in Flagstaff every winter. I meant I hope I go fast, even if it means being shot in the line of duty."

McAllister sighed with obvious relief. "I'd say I'd help you, but I don't think it would make a good impression if I shot my FTO."

⚉⚉⚉

Despite Bryan's concerns, Sally returned to work on Tuesday. Now that they were one man down, there'd be more to do. Plus, she had better resources at the office, which meant more opportunities to match DT to someone at the courthouse.

She was skimming the building directory when there was a knock on her door. She looked up. "Detective Killian."

"Ms. Castle. Do you have a few minutes?"

Even if she didn't, she'd take them if it meant getting more information about who killed Colin. She suspected Killian knew that. "Of course. Sit down." She gestured at a metal chair with a vinyl seat. "How can I help you?"

Killian lowered his bulky frame onto the chair. "Do you know if Mr. Rafferty was in debt?"

She stared him. Debt? Wasn't everyone in debt to some degree? Colin had not lived extravagantly. His suits were nice, but not designer. She'd been to his apartment building, clean but modest. His car was a few years old. "We didn't discuss personal finances," she said. "Not in detail. But I wouldn't find it surprising. It's expensive to go to law school and the salary of a county employee, even an attorney, is not exorbitant."

"You never talked about money?"

"No. I mean, not beyond very general topics. What prompts this question?" Now that Killian brought it up, it was odd. She and Colin had talked about a lot of personal things: his mother's illness, their love lives or lack thereof, but never money.

"He never asked you for a loan?"

"No, why?"

"What about your boss, Mr. Gerrity. Did the victim ever ask him for a loan?"

"I find it highly unlikely Colin would have asked anyone in this office for money. Again, why do you ask?"

"Perhaps I should talk to Mr. Gerrity." Killian moved to stand up.

"Let me save you the trouble." Why was Killian so set on keeping information from her? "I am ninety-nine point nine percent sure Colin never spoke to anyone in this office about a loan. Not me, not Bryan Gerrity, no one. I can't say it any clearer."

Killian stood, the chair scraping the floor. He had a satisfied smirk on his face, as though she'd reacted exactly the way he hoped she would. "Thank you for your time, Ms. Castle. If you don't have any information—"

"Wait. While you're here." Sally told him about the lack of files, the coffee mugs, and her conclusions. But as she spoke, she could tell from Killian's expression he didn't think she was on to anything. "I thought I should tell you."

"I'll keep those observations in mind." Killian shook her hand, a brusque, impersonal gesture. "I'll be sure to call if I have any other questions. Don't get up, I can show myself out." He left.

It was clear Killian didn't attach much importance to what she'd said, either because it didn't fit his ideas or because he knew something she didn't. She'd be charitable and assume it was the latter.

Bryan came into her office. "Did I just see Detective Killian leave?"

"Yes. He came to ask if Colin had ever asked me for a loan."

"A loan? Why?"

"Killian didn't say, but it's possible Colin had money troubles." Sally drummed her fingers on her desk. "Did he ever ask you for money?"

"Change for the vending machine, but I think you're talking about something a little bigger. No, he didn't." Bryan squinted. "You're thinking about something. What?"

She told him the same thing she'd told Killian about the files and mugs. "Does that make sense to you?"

"It does. But I'm just as in the dark as you are." He set another pile of folders on her desk. "More cases to review. All of these need to be dealt with until we hire another lawyer."

Sally waved a hand and Bryan left the office. Colin had been in debt and it sounded to her as though it was significant if Killian was asking about loans. Maybe DT wasn't a county employee after all. He, or she, could be someone who gave loans or who brokered them. If the loan fell through, that would explain the note. "You'd better fix this" could refer to financial arrangements he was counting on. Except all this brought her back to that Sunday meeting. Would Colin see such a person on a Sunday night at the courthouse?

CHAPTER 12

After leaving Running Waters, Duncan and McAllister proceeded to Trafford's last known address. Duncan took the opportunity to tell McAllister more about the state of Fayette County and the rural landscape dotted with farms. But the young couple living at Trafford's former residence denied ever talking to Trafford or even knowing him.

"Now what?" McAllister asked when they returned to their car.

"McAllister, I know this is new to you and you're trying to learn. But the constant asking of now what is really getting on my nerves. It sounds vaguely accusatory. Like you think I should have this wrapped up by now."

"Sorry. I meant what do you think our next step should be?"

"Let me ask you. What do you think?"

She leaned on the car. It was obvious she hadn't been prepared for the question, but she needed to be involved, not merely be a tagalong observer. "We've checked relatives and last known address. Both were a bust."

"Yes."

"We should talk to last known associates. But we don't know any, do we? Except for his attorney, Rafferty, and he's dead. What about your informant, Eddie?"

She was thinking. Good. "I called him earlier, but he didn't answer. Eddie will contact me if he has information. In the meantime, you're right. Let's check known associates."

They returned to the barracks, delayed slightly by the need to pull over a driver for a speeding violation. They were soon forced to admit they'd hit another dead end. Most of Trafford's few friends were either in jail or had left the area for parts unknown. "This is infuriating." McAllister hung up the phone in disgust after her third fruitless call. "And the public thinks the police can find people at the drop of a hat."

Duncan crumpled the paper from which he'd been working and tossed it in the trash. "Yeah, funny how they skip this part in the TV shows."

"Could Eddie have been wrong? I checked recent drug arrests. No mention of Trafford."

"It's always possible, but Eddie isn't usually wrong."

She tilted her head. "You've got something in mind."

"I'm wondering if we should talk to the ADA who prosecuted the last case, Alex Costanzo. He might remember something that will point us in the right direction. Plus prosecutors have their own information grapevine. He might have heard something."

"You got it, Boss." She emptied her bottle of Mountain Dew.

"I told you before, I'm not your boss. An FTO is not a boss."

McAllister grinned. "I know. But 'you got it, FTO' doesn't have the same ring to it."

"You're impossible." Duncan tossed her the keys. "You drive. I'll call the district attorney's office."

⇟⇟⇟

The receptionist at the DA's office told Duncan she could squeeze them in if they arrived before ten, so he instructed McAllister to push the speed limit. This time, they parked on a side street strewn with gold and brown leaves, and went in. "Once we're inside, I'll lead, you follow," Duncan said as they stood outside the DA's office.

"But—"

"It'll be on you to be sharp in case I miss something. What isn't said is often more important."

"Are you expecting Mr. Costanzo to be less than forthcoming? Because it kinda sounds like you are."

Was he? There was no reason for Costanzo to hide anything. "It's likely the prosecution on the Trafford case thought they were let down by the police. That wouldn't make them feel great. At the same time, the police, specifically Fitz, thought the ADA could have fought harder. That means there aren't a lot of good feelings around this one."

"Okay, but do you believe he's going to be uncooperative?"

"I'm not sure. It never hurts to be alert. Ready?"

She nodded and they entered the office.

The district attorney's office had fancier digs than the public defender. Nicer furnishings, better paint job on the walls. "Trooper First Class Jim Duncan," he said, showing his badge to the receptionist. "I'm here to see Alex Costanzo. This is Trooper McAllister."

The young woman glanced at McAllister, then focused on Duncan. "Just a minute." She picked up the phone and dialed an extension. "Trooper Duncan here to see you." She paused. "You told me you could get him in. Yes, I'll tell him." She hung up. "He'll be out in a minute," the woman said. "He has to finish something. Can I get either of you a cup of coffee?"

"Not me, thank you."

McAllister shook her head.

Costanzo emerged from a back office a few minutes later. He looked impeccable in a tailored suit, but Duncan thought he detected a trace of annoyance on his aristocratic face. "Trooper Duncan. What can I do for you?" Costanzo asked. "I can't help you much in the Rafferty shooting."

Why would he think they were there about Rafferty? He should know the PSP wasn't handling that. "We're not here to talk about Mr. Rafferty."

"Why else would you want to see me?" Costanzo arched an eyebrow, trying for a tone of disdain, but Duncan could read the hint of surprise in his voice and eyes.

"It's about Aaron Trafford. This could take a few minutes."

"I don't have a lot of time right now. That case was a fiasco."

"I promise we'll be quick, just a couple questions," Duncan said. "Can we talk in your office? Where we can be comfortable."

Costanzo huffed and eyed McAllister. "Who's she?"

"This is Trooper Aislyn McAllister. She's in training." Duncan waved at McAllister, who nodded in response.

"You didn't mention there were two of you." Costanzo smoothed his tie, subtle gray-on-gray striped silk.

"Sorry if you got the impression I was alone. Is that a problem?" Duncan watched Costanzo's face as he studied the younger trooper.

"I wasn't expecting a group discussion." Costanzo turned back to Duncan. "Fine. Follow me."

Costanzo led the way to an office that was cluttered, but tastefully decorated. A couple of framed diplomas hung on the wall. He took a seat in an oversized leather armchair behind the massive mahogany desk. A far cry from the utilitarian furniture in the public defender's office.

Duncan sat in a leather wing chair and indicated that McAllister should do the same. Her face held a careful, neutral expression. Because she was angry over what could be perceived as a slight or because she was busy cataloging Costanzo's reactions? "As I said, we're here about Aaron Trafford."

Costanzo sat and leaned back, crossing his legs. "Complete disaster. The press was outraged, but what can you do? It's unfortunate the trooper screwed up. Why the interest in a trial that's almost a year old?"

Duncan resisted the desire to defend his friend. "Yesterday, the PSP raided a meth lab."

"And?"

"The property in question belonged to Trafford's grandmother and we've received information that Trafford is back in Fayette County," Duncan said. He glanced at McAllister, who was studying Costanzo, and continued. "Naturally, we'd like to verify that fact and find Trafford if he has returned."

"Why aren't you questioning the grandmother?" Costanzo asked.

"Mrs. Marnier has Alzheimer's," McAllister said. "The staff at the facility told us she hasn't had any visitors."

"We've checked Trafford's known associates without much luck. We wondered if you had any information from the old trial or if you'd heard something since then that could help us," Duncan said.

Costanzo narrowed his eyes and licked his lips. After a moment, he straightened. "I'm not in the habit of maintaining a correspondence with accused criminals."

"Of course not and we don't mean to imply that you do. We—"

"I haven't heard anything from Mr. Trafford since last year. Now, if you two don't need anything else, I'm very busy." The message was clear: Get out.

Duncan stood and McAllister followed suit. "Thank you for your time," Duncan said. "Here's my card. If you would call if you do hear anything, I'd appreciate it." Costanzo reluctantly took the card and the troopers left.

Once they were back in the slightly overheated car, Duncan turned to McAllister. "Thoughts?"

"I don't like him. He reminds me of my uncle. Used to getting his way and not above doing anything to get it."

"Whether you like him isn't relevant." The information about the uncle was the first personal note McAllister had shared. Duncan tucked it away for later reference.

"He wasn't happy about there being two of us present and I don't know why he'd care. I also don't think he's being honest about Trafford. He got fidgety and started blinking when you started asking about him. His eyes kept moving off to the left, which would indicate he was thinking about a story."

"Anything else?"

"He said he hadn't heard from Trafford, not about him. I doubt they've been in constant communication, but I think he's seen Trafford a lot more recently than he claims."

"Good job," Duncan said as he pulled away from the curb.

"I seriously don't like him, though. He's used to getting his own way. A bully."

"You're going to run into a lot of people you don't like in this job. And a lot of bullies. Some of them supposedly on your side. You can't let that get to you, at least not on the outside. Blow off the steam later over a beer with the crew from the barracks."

"Is that what you do?"

Duncan started the car. "More often than I'd care to admit to a civilian."

She sat up a little straighter. "Now wh...I mean, I guess that leaves us with Genevieve's attorney. Lester."

"Yes. Here's hoping he knows something."

There was a moment of relative silence, then McAllister cleared her throat. "If you don't mind my asking, aren't we being narrow-minded?"

"What do you mean?"

"Well, there might be other people with a motive for killing Rafferty. Shouldn't we look for them?"

"You're right, but finding Rafferty's killer is Detective Killian's job. Ours is to find out who was running that meth lab. Is Trafford back in business, or was someone squatting on his grandmother's vacant property? I'll talk to Lieutenant Nicols about maybe setting up some surveillance, see if anyone comes back. Although with the bust on the news, it's unlikely."

"To know, we need to find Trafford. How are we going to do that when all we've racked up are dead ends?"

Duncan turned on to Route 40, heading west, sun blazing into his eyes. "If I knew, McAllister, I'd have him already."

⚜ ⚜ ⚜

Sally locked her computer and grabbed her purse. "Bryan, I'm going out." No answer. She looked down the hall. Her boss's door was shut. There was no reason to bother him, not for this. She went to the front of the office where Doris was busy filing. "Hey, Doris. I have to run out. If Bryan asks, I'll be back in half an hour. An hour tops."

Doris pushed the drawer shut and brushed a lock of graying hair from her forehead. She always seemed like an elderly neighbor to Sally—friendly, concerned, and determined to know everything about everyone. She'd been at the office longer than Bryan or Sally, something she reminded them of frequently. "Where are you going?"

"I have to take care of something."

"What kind of something?"

No point trying to get by Doris with a vague answer. The woman thrived by hunting down information. "Something related to Colin based on Detective Killian's last visit. Look, I'll be back soon. You and Bryan both have my cell number if you need me. I've handled all my cases for the morning and I'm not needed anywhere until after lunch." Sally placed a hand on the doorknob.

"Is this related to the murder?"

"Could be. Oh, if any mail comes for Colin, put it on my desk."

Doris pulled her cardigan tight, a faint frown on her face. "I'm supposed to give Mr. Rafferty's mail to that detective."

"And you will. After I look at it. Please, Doris. I wouldn't ask if it wasn't important."

The older woman sniffed. "Don't be silly, of course I will. But I want to know what you find. Deal?"

"Deal. I promise. Thanks." Sally left the office. Doris might seem like a nosy old lady and, heaven knows, Colin had been frustrated with her persistent questions more than once. But Sally knew Doris considered all the others in the office her kids. She'd do anything she was asked to help find out who shot Colin.

⚜⚜⚜

A short time later, Sally parked outside Colin's apartment. His car was gone and the small side lot was virtually empty. The building super, Bernie Trout, was hauling out several heavy, black trash bags. She locked her car and hurried over. "Excuse me, Mr. Trout was it? I don't know if you remember me."

He tossed the bags into a dumpster next to the building then faced her. "You were here looking for Mr. Rafferty the other day."

"Yes, Sally Castle. Have you cleared out Mr. Rafferty's apartment?" Probably not. It had only been a day.

"Not yet." Trout headed back to the building. "Cops finally took down their tape and said I could start emptying it this morning. Good thing. I gotta get it ready for a new tenant."

"Then no one's come by or called to take Mr. Rafferty's remaining things?" She crossed her fingers.

"Nope." Trout opened the front door and Sally followed. "I called his emergency contact, his mother. Guess she's been sick so she's gonna call a service to come clean out the place. Said she'd get back to me with a time to expect them."

"Would you mind if I took a look inside? Or would you prefer if I call Mrs. Rafferty for permission?"

Trout's eyes narrowed. "Why do you wanna get in there? Cops already took a bunch of stuff."

"I want to have a look around for myself. Mr. Rafferty was a friend. Since his mother lives in Pittsburgh, maybe I can help her by boxing up things, winnowing through what's left, and tossing the obvious garbage."

Trout paused, then removed a large bunch of keys from his belt loop. "Guess it's all right, you working with Mr. Rafferty and all. You got his mom's phone number? You know, to tell her if you took anything?"

"Not on me, no."

He unlocked the door and pushed it open. "Okay. You tell me what you take and I'll write it down for her. Lock up when you leave."

Sally thanked him and went inside. She put her purse on a small discount-store hall table. When Colin lived there, the apartment had been sparsely furnished, a typical bachelor pad. Now there were unmistakable signs that the police had taken belongings. Drawers were open, file folders empty. There was a bare spot next to a flat-screen monitor where a laptop computer had undoubtedly been. A fleece throw was on the floor, the cushions of the couch lopsided. The police had searched, but not left a neat scene behind them.

She straightened the cushions, then headed to the bedroom in the back. It had also been searched. Clothing was all over the bed, which had its covers piled on top in a jumbled mess. She opened the dresser drawers to see a tangle of socks, T-shirts, and underwear. What had the police been looking for? Better question, what had they found? She opened the closet. The dress shirts and pants were still on their hangers, but pushed to the back. Shoes were haphazardly stuffed in cubbies, not even matched up. Sally removed them and looked, but the cubbies held only footgear. She stood on tiptoe to run her hands over the top shelf and knelt to look in the back corners of the closet. Nothing.

She returned to the living room where Colin's desk was, the only piece of quality furniture in the apartment. She checked all the drawers. Many of the hanging files were empty, only past utility bills and other miscellany remaining. There was no evidence of a calendar or day planner. In a small top drawer, she found a stack of credit cards held together by a rubber band. At least a dozen of them, Visa, MasterCard, all from different banks. None of them were signed, but all of them were in Colin's name. Why hadn't the police taken the cards? Unless Colin still received paper statements. The police might have decided they didn't need the actual cards if they had paper, which would provide a record of account activity.

She found a document-sized box in the bottom of the last drawer. She opened it. Inside was a thick stack of papers with the University of Pittsburgh Medical Center logo at the top. Bills from the Hillman Cancer Center, along with statements with charges for individual physicians. A few were for procedures. These were his mother's medical bills. Sally glanced at the totals and nearly choked. Even with insurance, the amounts were staggering, thousands and thousands of dollars. Had Colin been paying his mother's bills? How? No way he made this kind of money working for Fayette County. She picked up the stack of credit cards and it clicked. Detective Killian had talked about Colin asking for a loan. He must have been putting the bills on credit. Either he needed money to pay off the bills themselves, or he'd been using the credit cards to pay the hospital and needed cash to pay the cards off.

Sally replaced the stack of UPMC papers. Knowing about the debt was interesting, but it didn't help her. Well, it provided possible motive, that was true. Finding proof that Colin had tried to obtain illegal loans, or was unable to pay off money to someone, that would be even more helpful. Maybe he'd hidden something else. She leaned back and the chair squeaked. Where? The office? That had been thoroughly searched by the cops. Any confidential information, such as case files, had been taken by Bryan. The active cases had been redistributed, the closed ones filed away. There was nothing in Colin's office. Where else would he hide something?

Sally ran her fingers over the antique desk. When Colin had purchased it, he'd been giddy over the fact it was so old. Old desks in fiction often had secret compartments. Did this one? She sat up, and inspected the cubby holes and drawers. If she were to build a desk with a secret hidey-hole, how would it compartment open? A notch or a lever. She opened the top drawer. There, at the back of the drawer, under the desk top.

A side panel of the desk popped open, revealing the compartment. She reached forward to catch it as it fell. "Yes," she breathed. Inside the space was a three-subject notebook, the kind students used. She set aside the panel, took out the notebook, and flipped it open. At first glance, it was gibberish. Not names, not addresses. It looked like the word scramble puzzle from the paper, but not quite. Lines of numbers, followed by letters, more numbers and either a star or an X. Sometimes, the numbers ran sequentially: 150304, 150305. Sometimes there were gaps. Some of the stars were colored in, some weren't.

She replaced the desk panel, but kept the notebook. She'd have to turn it in to the police and explain where she got it. But not before she took a crack at figuring out what it meant.

CHAPTER 13

Duncan waited until Tuesday afternoon before he visited the coroner about the Rafferty autopsy. He started McAllister on a search for any property that Trafford might own and told her to give priority to any hits in a one-hour driving radius from the Jumonville Road house. "And get me a standard background check on Colin Rafferty."

McAllister didn't move. "I'm confused."

"Why?"

"You said before it wasn't the state police's job to find the Rafferty shooter. Our responsibility is the drug case. So far, I can't see where there's any evidence linking the two cases. I'm wondering why you're changing your mind."

Saying "because I said so" wouldn't satisfy McAllister any more than it would a child questioning a parent. "I'm not. Not really."

"Why can't we get the CCTV footage from the courthouse? Then we see who's on it, and bam. Killer caught."

"Maybe. I'm sure Killian already has that film. But CCTV isn't always as helpful as you think it would be."

She narrowed her eyes. "You said Killian isn't likely to share. Got it. I still don't see the connection."

"You're right, it's not obvious. I can't shake the feeling there's a link here. I can't see it yet, but it exists."

"So you're basing your decision on a hunch. I thought we worked in facts?"

"We do. It's true you can't make an arrest or conduct a search on a hunch." It never ceased to be a challenge: helping a new officer learn to balance hard facts and instinct. "The longer you do this job, you'll come to realize you shouldn't ignore your gut. Don't ask me how you'll know. I can't explain it. After thirteen years I just feel it. There is something there and it's important."

There was a long beat of silence while she mulled his words. "What are you going to do?"

"I'm going to Uniontown. The autopsy on Rafferty should be done by now. Maybe the results will give me the connection I'm looking for."

Another pause. "Whatever you say, Boss." She walked away before Duncan could remind her, yet again, not to call him "boss."

He left the barracks and drove to the coroner's office, a squat, yellow brick building on Peter Street, a couple blocks away from the county jail. Duncan was always amused there was a post office in the same building. Most of the morgue occupants were not likely to need a mailman. He parked on the street.

Burns was hosing down a metal table. "Duncan. Didn't expect to see you." Shadows illuminated by the bright fluorescent lights rimmed red, watery eyes. Burns had not slept in a while.

The cold, clinical nature of the room always made Duncan feel like he was the subject of a science experiment. "You look like hell."

"An unnamed drug dealer buys it in Uniontown, nobody gives a shit about the autopsy," Burns said. "A county lawyer gets shot—"

"You can't get the results fast enough."

"Yup." Burns headed for the office. Back at his desk, he turned up the radio and took a hit of coffee, before grimacing and heading to a small sink. He poured the offending liquid down the drain. "I hate coffee anyway. What can I do for you?"

"I don't want to pile on."

"But…"

"I need the basics about the Rafferty autopsy."

Red eyes or not, Burns' gaze was shrewd. "Why do you care? It's not your case."

Duncan knew the deputy coroner would share, but Duncan also knew he had to give his friend a plausible reason in case someone questioned it. "The deceased might be connected to the prime suspect in another investigation," he said.

"Sure he might." Burns returned to his desk and picked up a report from on top of the pile on his desk. "We did the physical exam yesterday. You know the speed of toxicology. Colin Rafferty, height and weight, blah, blah, blah."

"Skip to cause of death."

"Single gunshot to the head. Judging by the angle, the shooter was over him, firing down and standing close enough to leave traces of powder burns." Burns pantomimed the shot. "Mostly likely standing to the side, slightly behind the victim."

"Exit wound? Defensive marks?"

"No on both counts. We recovered a single bullet from inside the cranium. In my very limited experience, I'd say it's a 9mm. But that's a guess."

The caliber alone was not useful. "What else?"

"Not much." Burns tossed aside the report, flopping into a battered rolling chair, which creaked as he leaned back. "Full toxicology isn't back, but I'm not expecting anything. Want to know what he had for dinner?"

"No. What about time of death?"

"Body was cold and stiff. Death occurred at least eight but not more than thirty-six hours before it was discovered. Imprecise, but the point is he'd been dead a while." Burns rubbed his face, then ran his hands through his hair, which looked like he'd done that a few dozen times already. "I'd say he died anywhere from Friday morning, which is impossible because I think someone would have noticed a corpse in the middle of the day, to Sunday night. He must have been involved with something important to be in on a Sunday. Does your girlfriend work weekends?"

"She's not my girlfriend."

"That's a pretty fast denial there, buddy." Burns grinned.

Duncan refused to rise to the bait.

"Nobody moved him either," Burns said. "Based on evaluation of lividity, his head hit that desk and he never twitched again."

Duncan considered that information. "Manner of death?"

"What else? Homicide by person, or persons, unknown."

"Thanks, Burns. I owe you one."

"Hell, at this point, you owe me way more than one. You're lucky I'm not much of a drinker." A ghost of the deputy coroner's usual humor broke through the fatigue. "I'll let you know if something pops on the toxicology report. As it turns out, Detective Killian hurt my feelings."

"You, the victim of hurt feelings?"

"The guy's attitude at the scene implied I did not take my job seriously." Burns snorted. "I consider that a professional insult."

⇟⇟⇟

Back at the barracks, Duncan tossed his hat on a desk as McAllister walked up. "Coroner say anything helpful?" she asked.

"You first. What did you find?"

"Aaron Trafford is not listed as the owner of any property in Allegheny, Fayette, Westmoreland, Greene, Washington, or Somerset counties. My conclusion is that he either rents or owns under a false name, if he lives around here at all."

Or he was living with someone, a friend or a girlfriend. "If I was a meth dealer, I wouldn't want my name on a property deed."

"I also called police departments in those counties," McAllister said. "Asked if there'd been any meth activity recently. Aside from Pittsburgh, nothing."

"Nice work."

"Thanks. Are you going to let me know what you found out?"

"Not much." He recapped what he'd learned from Burns. "No defensive wounds and the shooter got close enough to leave powder burns."

"Rafferty knew his attacker."

Add that to the speculation Sally had shared with him Monday night, it didn't seem like there was much of a connection with his case after all. An attorney didn't invite a known drug dealer into his office at a county building and sit still while said drug dealer put a slug in his brain. "What about the background check on Rafferty?"

"I wasn't sure how deep you wanted me to go," McAllister said. "No prior arrest record. He lived in Uniontown in a very modest neighborhood, drove a pretty basic car according to vehicle registration. He was, however, in a crapload of debt."

"Loans?"

"Credit cards." She paused. "When I say crapload, I mean metric crapload. He's got at least six accounts and his balances are sky high."

"Do you think he's rate shopping? You know, getting an introductory rate, transferring the balance, rinse, repeat?"

"No. All the cards have high balances. So high, my bet is they are maxed out. Or almost. If he's only making the minimum payment, it's the equivalent of a fifteen-year home loan." She paused and shrugged. "I studied accounting. Figured I needed something to fall back on if the police thing tanked."

"Is he? Only making the minimum payment?"

"I can't tell from what I ran. I'd have to get a full financial picture. Should I?"

It was tempting, but... "No. That would require a subpoena and we don't have cause. Sometimes the hunches don't pan out."

"You got it, Boss." She fed the papers into the shredder.

They couldn't get the records, but boy did Duncan want to. His sixth-sense was quivering. Something was there, dancing just outside the scope of his knowledge. Something important. "Well, Rafferty is a bust. We'll have to find Trafford another way."

"He must be living somewhere."

"Yes. With a girlfriend, a friend, a relative we don't know about." Duncan rubbed his eyes. "We need to get back on patrol."

"Should we go to the meth house?"

"Not unless we have to. The place was stripped clean in the bust. If there was something to be found, we'd have found it and it's still pretty volatile. No, someone has to know where this guy is." Fayette County was a big place, with a lot of empty space. Trafford wasn't a ghost. His facility was here, which most likely meant he was around. Just like with the lab, all the police needed was one break and they'd have him.

CHAPTER 14

With nothing pressing on her calendar, Sally took Wednesday morning off to drive to Pittsburgh. Colin's mother, Deborah Rafferty, lived in Mount Lebanon, in a small Cape Cod. Surrounded by trees, the house was on a little cul-de-sac where the neighboring houses were of the same style. Smaller homes, red brick, built in the mid-twentieth century above single-car garages, small yards, older trees. A far cry from the spacious million-dollar homes built later, but perfect for a single, older woman.

She threaded her way between some aged wicker porch furniture and knocked on the door. After a few minutes, it opened. "Mrs. Rafferty, hi. Sally Castle, we spoke on the phone last night."

"Yes, yes. Colin's friend. Come in." Deborah pushed open the front door and Sally stepped inside. The interior was a tad dated, with plaid, tweed furniture in the living room, but it was immaculate. A window air-conditioner hung out the side window and Sally glimpsed a small kitchen off the back. Like the front room, the decor showed its age, but the laminate counters and linoleum floor gleamed.

"Please, sit down." Deborah indicated a wingback chair and took a seat on the couch. "Would you like something to drink?"

"No, thank you." Sally studied her hostess. Deborah was a small woman with the emaciated look of the recently ill, but even in complete health she would be bird-like in stature. She wore a University of

Pennsylvania sweatshirt and dark blue sweatpants. A bold patterned scarf covered her head and her brown eyes glowed with determination and spunk. Instinctively, Sally liked this woman. "First off, I'm sorry about Colin. He was your only child?"

"Yes. He was a good boy. Mostly. He had a streak of his father, always looking for a big payout, but he had a good heart." Deborah folded her hands. "The police said he was found by a co-worker. Was that you?"

"Yes." Sally paused, not sure how to continue. The woman was just out of cancer treatment.

"Do you think he went quick?"

"I, uh…"

Deborah fixed Sally with a piercing stare. "Miss Castle, you don't have to step around me. I buried my husband when Colin was ten. I raised him, worked, and now I'm going to bury him. I know I don't look like much, especially after the chemo, but that's just looks."

"Colin probably died pretty quickly. The shot was directly to his temple and I understand the shooter was very close. People talk about instantaneous death and I don't know if that's possible, but this was as close as you get."

Deborah closed her eyes and crossed herself. "That's a blessing anyway. I'd hate to think of my boy bleeding out and suffering."

"I'm surprised you aren't more…upset. I can't imagine losing a child."

Deborah opened her eyes. "I cried plenty when the police called me. Now I'm mostly angry." She tilted her head. "But you didn't come all the way from Uniontown to give me your condolences."

"No. I, uh, also wanted to wish you a belated happy birthday. And congratulations on your remission. Colin talked a lot about it."

"Thank you. But you didn't drive an hour plus to say that, either."

Mrs. Rafferty was sharp and tenacious. Sally withdrew the box of bills and the notebook from her briefcase. "I found these in Colin's apartment. I went over there last night to see…to see if I could find anything that might help explain his murder. This box is full of your medical bills." She handed it to Deborah.

She ran her hand over the lid, blue veins prominent through the pale skin. "Colin was insistent. He would pay these. 'I'll take care of you, Mom. Don't you worry.' Like I said, a good heart."

"Do you know how he paid them?"

"No clue." Deborah set aside the box without opening it. "I'd ask and he'd assure me that he had it covered."

"I found a stack of credit cards in his desk. Could he have used those?"

"It's possible, I guess. They'll give a credit card to anybody stupid enough to fill out the application these days, or so it seems. I tear up an offer a day." She pointed at the notebook in Sally's hands. "What's that?"

"I found this, too. It doesn't make any sense to me. I was hoping you could shed some light on it." Sally handed the notebook over.

Deborah flipped through the pages, lips moving as she silently read. "I'm sorry, no. It's all Greek to me, as they say."

"I never saw him work on them, but did Colin like word puzzles, like the Jumble?"

"Those scrambled words?" Deborah chuckled. "He hated those. Way too easy. Same with the crossword. Even the ones in the big papers, the ones that are supposed to be incredibly difficult, he'd have them solved in no time." She handed back the notebook. "Sorry I can't help you."

Sally took it. "Do you mind if I keep this?" Deborah shook her head and Sally slipped it back into her briefcase. "What about Colin's attitude the last few months? Aside from being worried over your health, did you notice anything unusual?"

Deborah twisted her wedding band and stared out the window. Pale cream curtains were pulled back to let in the autumn sun. A bird perched on the A/C unit. "He was worried about me, of course. I don't know what it was that tipped me off, but he was into something big. Something that made him nervous, I think. I asked of course, but he brushed me off. I thought it was the hospital bills. Then this last month he changed."

"Changed how?"

"It's hard to put into words." Deborah continued to stare out the window. The bird chirped and took off. "He was still nervous. Scared, almost. But very determined at the same time. 'Whatever happens, Mom. You're going to be okay. I'll make sure of that.' I remember him saying that one day. He'd come up and we'd gone walking around Schenley Park after one of my appointments."

It sounded like Colin had been anticipating something. "Any idea what he meant?"

"Probably the life insurance. A woman from the insurance company called this morning. Colin took out a big policy and I'm the sole beneficiary."

"How much?"

"The lady said seven hundred and fifty thousand dollars. I was stunned."

Deborah wasn't the only one. Three-quarters of a million? "When did he do this?"

"Three months ago, I think she said."

It was the kind of policy someone took when they were expecting to die and wanted to provide for loved ones. But Colin had been a healthy guy in his early thirties. Not someone who believed he'd be dead ninety days later…unless he'd been in trouble. Trouble that made him fear for his life. That much money would satisfy his debts and leave some cash for his mother. "Can you think of anything else?"

Deborah turned her attention from the bird that had returned to its perch to Sally. "He admired you. I could tell the way he talked about you. Oh, not in the romantic way." She laughed gently. "Professionally. In fact, it was just a few weeks ago when you came up again."

"I did?"

"Yes. He said, 'I've done something, Mom. Something I'm not proud of. But I'm going to fix it. You'll be disappointed when you find out, and so will Sally. Hopefully I'll make you both happy with the fix.' He stopped being so nervous after that. More…determined. Wistful, but determined."

The two women sat for a moment, then Sally noticed Deborah's eyelids were drooping. Sally had imposed long enough. "Thank you so much, Mrs. Rafferty. For your time and for letting me keep that notebook."

The blue-veined hand shook a little as Deborah clutched Sally's arm with surprising strength. "Find out what Colin was into, Miss Castle." Her brown eyes were over-bright and her voice wavered for the first time. "Whatever my boy was doing, find out and bring him some peace."

🌱🌱🌱

Late Wednesday morning, Duncan and McAllister drove south on Route 119. The October sun shone on fields shading into gold, the sky the intense blue of Indian summer. The maples and oaks were showing more than a spotting of color. Prime leaf viewing season was right around the corner, something Duncan knew would bring hoards of tourists to the area. More reason to find Aaron Trafford quickly.

"Face it, Boss. The Pirates are a lost cause," McAllister said.

"They are not a lost cause. Just missing a few pieces."

"They said that last year and the year before that. Your love of baseball is coloring your view."

A battered black Dodge ahead of them swerved slightly, then pulled back into their lane.

Duncan scoffed. "I could say the same thing about you and football. The Steelers need a new quarterback before the current one cashes it in."

"That'll happen before the Pirates find this mystical missing piece."

The Dodge swerved again. The car slowed slightly, making McAllister tap the brakes. Then the Dodge sped up again.

"The guy ahead of us," she said, scowling. "You think he's drunk? Midday on a Wednesday?"

"Could be. We can—"

The light ahead of them turned red, but the Dodge never slowed, shooting through the intersection and setting off a cacophony of horns as drivers slammed their brakes.

McAllister flipped the switches to turn on the patrol car's siren and lights. "Guess we're about to find out."

It seemed as though the Dodge was going to try and make a break for it. It sped up, but when the marked Ford easily closed the distance, the Dodge's driver must have changed his mind. The black car slowed and angled to the shoulder of the road, eventually rolling to a stop.

McAllister parked behind it, killing the siren, but left the lights revolving. "Should I?" She waved at the Dodge.

"I'll be right behind you. You talk to the driver, I'll check the car. Remember, a traffic stop—"

"Is one of the most dangerous situations. Got it." She adjusted her hat and got out of the car, hand on her Sig.

Duncan followed. The Dodge could have been a dictionary illustration for the phrase "beater car." The black paint was dull, blasted by who knows how many Pennsylvania winters, a few patches of gray on the trunk and panels. The bumper was held in place with twine. Sunlight glared off dirty windows, making them effectively opaque. Unsure whether there was a passenger, Duncan angled his approach and laid his finger against the holster release of his gun.

"Hey there," McAllister said. Friendly, but firm. "You know why I pulled you over?"

"I dunno," a reedy voice said. The words were slightly slurred. "I'm just out for a drive."

Duncan kept half his attention on the exchange between McAllister and the driver, but he searched the backseat as best he could through the grime-covered windows. Crumpled fast food bags. Tattered magazines with half-naked women on the covers. No bumper stickers or other decorations. The wheel covers were missing, revealing the lug nuts. The rubber of the tires was a tired black, with tiny cracks in the sidewall. The tread was worn in several places. He glanced at the windshield. The inspection stickers were current. He'd be willing to bet money had changed hands there.

McAllister continued. "You drove right through that red light back there."

"I...I did? You sure?" The reedy voice was lethargic. "I didn't see no light."

"Whether or not you saw it, you ran it. I'm gonna have to see your license and proof of insurance."

"Oh, um, okay. I, uh, got the license here. Just a sec." There was a pause.

Pennsylvania had dispensed with registration stickers; they'd check that when they ran the plate. Duncan took a good look at the driver, whose attention was focused on McAllister. A scrawny white male. Maybe late twenties, early thirties. He was wearing a faded red T-shirt that looked like it needed a wash, and jeans more gray than black. Duncan was willing to bet they'd hang off the guy's hips if he stood up.

He fumbled in a battered leather wallet for his license, then reached over to open the glove compartment. Duncan tensed. "I keep the envelope with the registration stuff and insurance here," he said. He took out an envelope and thumbed through the contents. "I, uh...looks like I don't have the registration confirmation page no more. But I got the insurance card." His fingers trembled as he held out the crumpled paper.

McAllister looked at the license. "Benjamin Gearhy? This picture doesn't look like you. Your insurance is expired."

"I, uh, was sick. Lost a lot of weight since that picture was taken. I sure thought that was the right card. Must have accidentally thrown out the new one." The driver tried for a laugh, but it came out a nervous titter.

"If you'll just wait here." McAllister returned to the patrol car.

Duncan continued to visually search the car. The front seat had more garbage. A six-pack of Iron City. One can missing. There it was, in the cup holder, top popped open. "Sir, you know it's illegal to drive with an open container," he said.

The driver jumped. "Oh, uh, didn't know there was two of you." He swallowed, larynx bobbing. His eyes were watery and bloodshot. "It's empty. I should have taken that out of the car. Forgot." Another tittering laugh.

McAllister returned. "The car is registered to a Dominick Branson. This license was reported stolen." She held up the license before pocketing it.

"Oh, uh, no, see...I, uh, thought it was stolen, but, uh, found it." The driver looked from McAllister to Duncan, blinking like an owl. He twisted his shirt and wiped his upper lip with his forearm. He bumped the open can and it fell to the floor, spilling golden liquid that barely fizzed.

"I thought you said it was empty." Duncan gestured to the open beer can.

"Oh, uh, I thought it was."

"Sir, step out of the car please. Slowly." McAllister took a step back, hand still on her sidearm.

"Why?"

"Nothing major, just a standard roadside sobriety test while my partner checks your vehicle."

Gearhy or Branson, or whatever his name was, got out. "Look. This is all a big misunderstanding. I can explain."

Duncan leaned into the car, while McAllister started the sobriety test. Locating the lever, he popped the trunk. Opening it, he saw boxes filled with plastic baggies. Some were filled with the familiar rock-chips of meth, others with dried leaves Duncan was quite sure was marijuana. He picked up a bag of each and returned to the front of the car. "Don't suppose your explanations cover this?" He held up the baggies.

Gearhy twisted like a landed fish. McAllister held him firm. "I...funny about that," he said, now truly sweating.

"We'd love to hear." Duncan and McAllister had focused their search on Trafford's old known associates. Perhaps they should have looked for new ones.

McAllister's gaze hardened. "You don't happen to know a man named Aaron Trafford, do you?"

Gearhy shook his head, eyes wild. "Never heard of him."

"You expect us to believe that?" She tightened her grip on her Sig. "Let me ask again. Do you know Aaron Trafford?"

Shaking like a leaf in a strong breeze, Gearhy looked from Duncan to McAllister. "I, uh...I think I want a lawyer."

McAllister glanced at Duncan. "Boss..."

Duncan read the mute appeal in her eyes, but there was nothing he could do. "The man asked for a lawyer. Cuff him, take him to the patrol car, and I'll call for a tow."

McAllister's lips thinned to a line as she followed instructions and hustled the suspect to their car.

He understood her frustration, but there was no point pushing Gearhy here and now. He wouldn't change his story. The chances these drugs weren't somehow connected to Trafford? As Duncan's grandfather would say, "Slim to none, and Slim just left town."

CHAPTER 15

After lunch on Wednesday, Sally sat behind a tottering pile of case files. Some of them were hers, but most were Colin's, awaiting her review and subsequent action. The courts were not going to wait for their office to hire Colin's replacement.

Her mind was only half on the task. She was positive Colin had used the stack of credit cards to pay his mom's medical bills. That easily explained his being in debt. He was either making regular payments on the cards or he wasn't. She put aside the files and opened the calculator app on her phone. Assuming maxed out cards, and average interest and minimum payment rate from her own credit cards, she ran the calculation. "Holy shit," she whispered, staring at the screen. The number that stared back at her was unreal, almost her entire salary.

A knock at her door interrupted her thoughts. She looked up to see Killian. "Detective. What can do I for you this time?"

"Ms. Castle. Do you have a minute?"

She rubbed her temple. "As you can see, I'm a little busy." When Killian didn't move, she understood the question for what it was: polite formality. "What do you need?" If nothing else, she'd get a break from reading.

"You didn't tell me you knew De'Shawn Thomas," Killian said.

"You asked if I knew anyone with those initials. I said not personally, which is the truth. I've never met Mr. Thomas."

"He was Mr. Rafferty's client."

"Yes, but I said I'd need more information before I discussed any of our clients. You failed to provide context."

Killian leaned on the metal doorframe. "Have you seen Mr. Thomas lately?"

She twirled a pen. "No."

"Are you his attorney now that Mr. Rafferty is deceased?"

"In all likelihood, Mr. Thomas's defense will be transferred to someone else in the office. That could be me."

"Isn't it odd you haven't met him, then?"

Killian wasn't asking questions that violated attorney-client privilege, but he was trying to trap her into saying something about a man whose only connection to Colin's murder was his initials. Almost a textbook definition of a leading question. "Is Mr. Thomas a suspect? Is that what this visit is about?"

"I'm not at liberty to say." Killian smirked.

"Then I'm not at liberty to discuss Mr. Thomas further." She stood. "Anything else?"

Killian straightened, put his hands in his pockets, and narrowed his eyes. "You're refusing to talk to me?"

"Until you give me some details, yes. Either Mr. Thomas is a suspect, in which case there are procedures this office has to follow, or you're simply digging. Either way, I don't have time for this." She pressed her fingertips to the desk. "Your call, Detective."

Killian smoothed his tie. "I'll be back. Thanks for your time, Ms. Castle." He walked off and moments later, the sound of the door slamming echoed through the office.

She let out her breath. She sorted through the stack of folders and found the case file. Thomas had been arrested a third time for misdemeanor marijuana possession. Small time charge and an automatic plea bargain. She hurried down the hallway to Bryan's office and knocked on the open door.

He looked up from his computer screen. "Hey. You finished getting up to speed on the new cases?"

"Almost. I have a question about De'Shawn Thomas." Sally held up the folder. "Misdemeanor drug possession. On the day I found Colin's body, Detective Killian asked if I knew anyone with the initials DT. Thomas is the only person who fit, but I didn't say anything since he's a client. Killian just left. He came by to ask about Thomas. He wouldn't say whether Thomas was a suspect, but why else would a homicide detective be interested in a two-bit drug offender? And why would said drug offender be a suspect anyway?"

"Close the door." Bryan indicated a chair. "The police found a note for Sunday in Colin's day planner. It said DT - 8:00. They may not have looked in the files, but they probably saw the folder with the name on it. They must assume DT is De'Shawn Thomas. If Colin was meeting Thomas, it means Thomas is a suspect or he's the last person to see Colin alive. Either way, they want to find him."

"How do you know this?"

"I stayed Monday until they left. Has Thomas been in?"

Sally tapped the file against her palm. "No. If this is the case you assigned Colin the Friday before he died, I wouldn't expect he'd even done anything with it."

"It is."

She continued bouncing the file against her hand. A meeting with a misdemeanor client at eight o'clock on a night the Steelers played primetime? "What time does a Sunday night football game start?"

"About eight-thirty, why?"

"Then it doesn't make sense." She told him what she knew of Colin's plans for that Sunday. "How do we know Thomas even showed up?"

"We don't. By the way, do you know Colin's mother?"

Sally blinked. "Deborah? Yeah, I saw her this morning. Nice woman."

"Did you know her maiden name was Torberg?"

Deborah Torberg. It took a full ten seconds for the implication to sink in. "Be real. Colin met his mother on a Sunday night at the Fayette County courthouse? She lives in Mt. Lebanon. She's a cancer patient. He'd just seen her at her birthday party earlier that day. Why would she be in Uniontown that night? If he wanted to meet with her, he'd have done it earlier."

Bryan lifted an eyebrow. "If he went."

Sally had assumed Colin wouldn't miss the party. She could confirm that with a quick call. "Besides, why would he refer to his mother by her maiden name initial? It's...ludicrous." Sally huffed. "I want to see the CCTV footage for Sunday night. Let's find out for sure who was here."

"We're not going to see it and you know it. But you can be sure the police have." Bryan turned back to his computer. "Besides, there is no way in hell we're going to be allowed near this case. You found the body. Colin was a co-worker. Clear conflict."

"Fine." Bryan might be right. That didn't mean Sally had to simply accept it. She stood.

He narrowed his eyes. "Where are you going to do?"

"What else?" She opened the office door. "I'm going to find De'Shawn Thomas."

"You have other cases."

"Don't worry. I'll get to those, too."

☙☙☙

Duncan left the interview room at the Uniontown booking station, closed the door, and took a deep breath. Gearhy, although that was almost definitely not his real name, proved to be more stubborn than the everyday driving under the influence and drug bust. He stuck by his request to talk to a lawyer, the only words that had passed his lips since arriving at the facility. Duncan was pretty sure Gearhy was just a mule, responsible for transporting the drugs, but it would be nice to get a confirmation.

He checked his watch. One o'clock. Someone from the public defender's office should be here soon. He wasn't sure whether he wanted it to be Sally or not.

McAllister came up to him, Lt. Dan Nicols right behind her. Nicols was the commander of the Uniontown barracks, but it was unusual to see him at the booking center. "Lieutenant. Didn't figure on seeing you," Duncan said.

"I was here on other business and heard about your suspect." Nicols nodded to McAllister. "What's the story?"

"We picked him up on 119. He'd blown a red light. Definite DUI. Boxes of meth and marijuana in his trunk," Duncan said. "He gave us a stolen ID. McAllister, you find anything?"

"Yes." She glanced at the paper in her hand. "The suspect's real name is Alexander Monahan. His prints were in AFIS. He was arrested two months ago for possession, no intent. Has around half-dozen arrests on similar charges." She handed the sheet to Duncan.

He scanned it. "What kind of drugs?"

"Marijuana and OxyContin. No meth." She glanced at Nicols.

The lieutenant took the print-out from Duncan. "Has he said anything?"

"I want a lawyer," Duncan said. "He's smarter than most."

"You think he's been coached?"

"Possibly. We're waiting on someone from the PD's office now."

Nicols handed back the sheet. "Keep me posted."

McAllister spoke up. "Sir, based on the presence of the meth, isn't it logical to assume Monahan is transporting for Trafford? Shouldn't we hit Monahan with that?"

"The man asked for a lawyer, Trooper," Nicols said. "It's hands off until he gets one."

"But if we know it's Trafford—"

"I applaud your initiative, but we don't know it's Trafford." Nicols shook his head. "We can't continue to question a suspect once he's lawyered up."

"Yes, sir. I understand that. I just think we've got an opportunity here and I'd hate to see us waste it."

Duncan gave his commander a swift look. "Trooper McAllister, it won't hurt us to wait. The PD should be here shortly. Lieutenant, I'll let you know what happens."

Nicols nodded and left without another word.

Duncan faced his trainee. "Ever the hard charger."

"I don't know what you mean."

"Yes, you do. You're new, you want to make a good impression. Hell, so did I. You'll learn there's a time for going all out, and there's a time to take a breath and wait. This is a time to wait."

McAllister's expression was stony. "We know it's Trafford. How many meth dealers can there be in this county?"

"You're right, not many. But this isn't a good time to push. Listen to me." Duncan held up a finger. "If Monahan hadn't asked for a lawyer, you'd be absolutely right and we'd already be in that room."

No response.

"Trafford has already skated once. I don't want to lose him again. It sucks, but it means we're careful and wait."

"Yes, sir." McAllister crossed her arms and stalked to the end of the hall.

By quarter after one, Bryan Gerrity had arrived. "Trooper Duncan? Is the trooper at the end of the hall with you?"

Duncan held out his hand. "Yes, Trooper McAllister. Your client has been rather...obstinate. Got to tell you, that's not good from our perspective."

"I know how it goes," Gerrity said, voice dry. "Let me talk to him and see what we can do." He entered the room and closed the door. Ten minutes later, he emerged.

"Well?" Duncan asked. McAllister had gotten over her fit of temper and come back to stand next to him.

"It's pretty clear to me he's terrified." Gerrity looked from Duncan to McAllister. "I take it he's not scared of you."

McAllister started to respond and Duncan waved her off. "We pulled him over for a traffic violation and a suspected DUI. When we ran his license, it came back flagged. We've since learned he's not the owner of the license. A vehicle search uncovered the drugs. I understand if he's nervous, but I assure you we've done everything by the book. Including calling you the second he lawyered up."

Gerrity made a calming motion with his hands. "Relax. I'm not saying you were out of line. But my client is quite adamant he has nothing more to say." He glanced at McAllister and focused on Duncan. "You know Sally Castle, correct?"

Duncan nodded.

"She speaks very highly of you. Because of that, I'll tell you this in confidence and I'll trust you not to abuse my good faith." Gerrity stepped closer and lowered his voice. "It is my professional opinion that Mr. Monahan is convinced talking to you will be worse for his health than going to jail for possession." He took off his glasses, polished them, and put them back on. He fixed Duncan with a stare. "Do with that information what you will."

⚜ ⚜ ⚜

After Bryan left for the booking center, Sally called the number listed for De'Shawn Thomas. Disconnected. His address was a run-down apartment building a few blocks south of Uniontown's downtown area. Sally found the phone number of the building superintendent, who confirmed Thomas hadn't been home since Sunday afternoon. It wasn't looking good for Mr. Thomas. The police would want to know why he disappeared if he was innocent and it was a valid question.

Sally looked at the case file. Thomas had been arrested on a street corner in the city that was a known hangout for small-time drug dealers. Early in the afternoon, it was unlikely anyone was there. She'd stop later with Thomas's mug shot. Maybe someone had seen him.

As she continued her search for information that would help her find Thomas, she noticed the docket number on the case. The construct tugged at her memory. Of course the format looked familiar; every docket number in Pennsylvania was set up the same way. She'd seen it somewhere else.

She pulled out the notebook she'd found at Colin's. Without knowing more about its contents, she'd been unwilling to turn it over to Killian. She ran her finger down the first column of numbers. They could be a snippet of a docket number, or a code based on the court identifier. She continued her search until she found what she thought could be Thomas's case number.

She plugged the numbers in Colin's notebook into what would be the rest of the number. Her heart skipped. It matched the court record. She looked at the rest of the information in that row. The middle column contained the number two-point-five. The third column had a star, unfilled.

Her pulse quickened. She picked up another of Colin's cases. Sure enough, that docket was in the notebook as well. This time, the second column was blank and the third column contained an X.

For the next half hour, Sally worked through the files. In each case, there was a corresponding entry in the notebook, many with filled-in stars in their third column. It was a tracking system. Colin had been keeping a record of each of his cases and categorizing them. By what? Sally could only think of one meaning behind the second column of numbers. Money. Mrs. Rafferty's words came back to her, about what Colin had said. "I've done something I'm not proud of."

On a hunch, Sally pulled up the record of Trafford's dismissed case on her computer. Sure enough, there was the notation in Colin's records that corresponded to the Trafford docket with a ten and a colored star in the other columns.

She stared at the computer screen. "Oh Colin, what have you done?"

CHAPTER 16

Sally left work early, arriving at the state police barracks around two-thirty. "I'd like to speak with Trooper Jim Duncan. Is he here?"

"I think he is," the trooper behind the desk said. "Let me call. Have a seat."

Sally couldn't sit. She paced, clutching her briefcase to her chest. Maybe Jim would tell her it was crazy and she was imagining things.

Maybe the Pirates would win the World Series.

"He'll be out in a minute. Sign the visitors' log, please." The trooper pushed forward a clipboard. A few seconds later, Jim emerged and the trooper at the desk pointed.

Jim crossed the floor with two quick strides. "What's wrong? Are you okay?" With his usual insight, he must have read her expression.

"I'm fine, but I need to talk to you," she said. "Got someplace a little more private?"

"Conference room three is open," the trooper said.

Jim nodded and guided Sally down a hall.

The room was cold and utilitarian, with chairs that weren't designed for comfort. Of course. It was a room at a police barracks, not a corporate office building. She took a seat and laid the briefcase on the table.

"I'd offer you some coffee, but this late in the day it'll be more undrinkable than usual," Jim said. "Water? Coke?"

"I don't want anything, thanks."

"Are you sure? Unless you're going to tell me about an imminent homicide, I think it would be a good idea. Calm the nerves."

"It's not anything like that." Sally pushed a strand of hair that had fallen out of her French twist from her face. "All right. Coke is fine," she said. "Sprite is better."

"Just a sec."

The lighting in the room was stark. Nothing on the walls, just a plain, slightly scarred table and inexpensive aluminum chairs with vinyl seating. Suspects were questioned in this room. She wasn't a suspect, for God's sake. But the decor, or lack thereof, worked on the subconscious to make her feel like one. She shifted in her seat.

She jerked at the sound of the door, but it was only Jim returning. He placed a cold can of Sprite and a plastic glass on the table in front of her.

"Sorry about the plastic. Best I could do," he said.

Sally shook her head. He was being solicitous, which meant he knew she was uncomfortable. "It's fine," she said. "I didn't expect the cup."

He pulled out the chair on the opposite side of the table and sat. "Okay, you're not hurt and nobody's about to shoot someone."

"Interesting order of priorities."

"But whatever you want to talk to me about must be important if you came down in person," he said, leaning back and folding his arms across his chest.

"It is," she said. "Well, I think it is. Maybe. Hell, I don't know. It bothered me. But now that I'm here, I'm starting to think I'm wasting your time." She played with the condensation on the can, trying to calm the butterflies in her stomach.

"Talking to you is never a waste of time."

She looked up and took a deep breath. What was that saying about crossing the Rubicon? "After Colin died, I went to his apartment to check on some things."

The corner of his mouth twitched. "You mean you went to nose around."

"Okay, yes. I don't know what I was looking for. Something, anything that might explain why someone would shoot an assistant public defender. The cops had cleaned the place pretty thoroughly. Then I remembered Colin had been all jazzed about this antique desk he bought because he thought it might have a secret compartment." She opened her briefcase and removed the notebook. "When I poked around, I figured out how to open it. I found this inside."

Jim thumbed through the pages. "Lots of numbers. Symbols. Do you know what it is?"

"No, but I have my suspicions. Detective Killian came by asking about De'Shawn Thomas."

Jim didn't look up, but continued flipping through the notebook. "Who's he?"

"One of Colin's clients. The day of the murder, Killian asked if I knew a DT." She paused.

Jim stopped reading and his gaze snapped to her face. "Where'd the initials come from?"

"Killian wouldn't say anything, but Bryan tells me there was a note in Colin's day planner that indicates he was meeting a DT Sunday night at eight."

"You think it was Thomas?"

"I'm not positive, but it makes sense. I'm also sure the police believe he's a suspect, especially since Killian came by looking for him."

Jim set the notebook down. "What's the motive?"

Sally tapped the notebook. "That's what brings me to this. I went back to Thomas's file, looking for anything that might even resemble motive. That's when I noticed that the first column of letters in this notebook look a lot like docket numbers. Sure enough, they are. And Thomas's is in here."

Jim's forehead creased and he motioned her to continue.

"I went ahead and started looking at the other numbers. They all correspond to dockets. Colin was logging his cases for some private reason."

"Why would he do that?"

"There are three columns in this notebook. Now, for Thomas's entry, the second column says two point five and there is an unfilled star in the third. Did you notice how some lines have an X in that third column?" At Jim's nod, she continued. "Those don't have any note in the second column. I think it's shorthand." She took a sip of Sprite.

"Shorthand for what?"

If she gave voice to her suspicions, they'd be real. Yet she couldn't stay quiet. "I can think of only one meaning for that second column of numbers. It's an amount of money."

Jim's voice sharpened. "Money?"

"A bribe. Or a payoff." She swallowed hard, then told him about what she knew about Colin's debt and his mother's medical bills. "He needed cash. He told his mother he'd done something he wasn't proud of. Jim, what if he was taking bribes from his clients?"

"That would be…well, bad is an understatement. But it's a big leap."

"Yeah, except I looked up the Trafford case. Remember, the one that was dismissed? Everybody was so sure it was a slam dunk for the DA and Trafford walked away."

Jim's expression darkened.

"Trafford's in there." She nodded at the notebook. "With the number ten and a colored star. Jim, what if…what if Trafford paid to have that case thrown out?"

Jim pushed away from the table, stood and paced. "Colin Rafferty was an assistant public defender. How would he pull something like this off by himself?"

"I don't know." Truth was, he probably couldn't. The options were too enormous to think of, but now she'd put the possibility out there she had to.

"Leave that for a moment." Jim leaned against the wall. "Although we got a tip, we don't know for certain Trafford is in the area."

"I think he is." Sally told him about Colin's tattooed visitor, the one Colin had been terrified had seen Sally. "Kinda sounds like Trafford, doesn't it? I mean, from what I read about the case and his mug shot from last fall?"

"It does." Jim's mouth thinned. "Trafford comes back, Rafferty tries to hit him up again, Trafford shoots him?"

"Maybe, except that ignores what he told his mother about trying to put things right."

"Rafferty was going to come clean and Trafford shot him to keep it all hushed up."

"Or Colin's partner shot him. Because he had to have a partner. You're right, he couldn't do this on his own."

Jim resumed pacing, footsteps deafening in the quiet room. "That book has to go to Killian. And you have to take your suspicions to Gerrity. Holy hell."

"I know. The entire office is going to come under scrutiny. Maybe the DA, even the police depending on what an ethics board finds."

Jim stared at her. "You really stepped in the shit this time."

"I know. Oh, one other thing." She told him about Deborah Rafferty, formerly Torberg, and the insurance settlement. "It's so crazy I can't even put it into words."

"Why?" He sat again. "You've been in criminal law long enough to know that devoted family members kill each other all the time."

Sally cheeks warmed, but this time it didn't have anything to do with Jim's nearness. "If you had ever seen Deborah Rafferty, you'd know why. The woman is a stick. She's not strong enough to do something like this."

"You don't need to be especially robust to fire a nine millimeter into someone's head."

"I don't even think Deborah could pick up the freaking gun."

Jim held up his hands. "Okay, okay. I'm only saying it's a valid line of inquiry given the initials and the money involved. But I agree with you. A woman recently out of cancer treatment doesn't drive over an hour on a Sunday night to meet her son at his place of employment."

"Especially when he saw her earlier."

"You're sure of that?"

"Yes. I called Deborah on the way here. She confirmed Colin was at her birthday party. He was distracted, but he was there." The heat left her face. "I'll call Killian tonight and give him the notebook. After I make photocopies of the pages, of course."

"Of course." His smile was faint and disappeared quickly.

Too quickly. "What?"

"You said Rafferty had to have an accomplice. There's only one place I can think of where an accomplice would work."

Sally's midsection suddenly felt hollow. The best place for said accomplice would be the district attorney's office.

⚜ ⚜ ⚜

Duncan escorted Sally back to the barracks entrance. "Promise me two things."

"Maybe."

"Get that notebook to Killian and talk to your boss."

She chuckled. "I hate talking to Killian and this is going to become a complete shit storm, but of course I will. What's the second thing?"

"Stay out of this."

Any trace of levity in her face faded. "I can't do that. Killian's got his mind made up. I know it and that's not fair. Besides, how would you feel if one of your friends here was gunned down like Colin was?"

"Sally, I'm not joking." He resisted the impulse to brush aside the hair stuck to her cheek. He was at work, after all. Proprieties had to be observed. "If Aaron Trafford is involved, things are serious. He's not a guy you invite over for Sunday brunch to meet the folks. You get in his way and he'll kill you without any hesitation."

"I promise I'll be careful," she said, voice neutral.

It wasn't what he'd asked for, but it was all he was going to get. At least for now. "How about we meet for dinner tomorrow? I'm off. We can go to Dex's." Their favorite place in Uniontown, Dex's had good atmosphere and a great Reuben.

"And you can try and get me to back off. I know your methods, Jim Duncan." She poked him, then sobered. "I didn't waste your time?"

"I told you. Not gonna happen." He almost continued, but the trooper behind the desk coughed, a noise that sounded suspiciously like a laugh. "Call me if you need anything or to let me know about tomorrow."

"I will. Thanks." She shouldered her purse and left.

"Smooth, Duncan. You almost asked her out," the trooper said.

"Thanks, Pinsky. You're a real pal."

McAllister walked up, her keys in hand. "I'm going to leave if you don't need anything."

"Nah, there's nothing to do tonight. You might as well—" He was interrupted by the buzzing of his cell phone. Blocked number. "Duncan."

"7562 Wharton Furnace Road." Eddie's high-pitched voice sounded serious. "You definitely want to check the place out." He ended the call before Duncan could say anything.

"Who called?" McAllister asked.

"How would you like a bit of overtime?"

McAllister pocketed her keys. "Was that who I think it was?"

"You got it," Duncan said. "Go get your hat. We have a visit to make before the sun goes down."

CHAPTER 17

The sun hung low in the sky, but there was still plenty of light when Duncan and McAllister reached their destination. Duncan pulled over and killed the engine. Through the windshield he could see two figures huddled under a big maple, leaves above them a fierce red. Across the road was a solitary house. A plain box in a scraggly yard. Nothing like the stately Victorian that housed the meth lab. The nearest neighbors were at least a half a football field away in either direction, grasses golden green in the fields.

The two under the tree hadn't noticed the state Ford yet. With luck, he and McAllister would be able to creep up unobserved.

"Who are those guys?" McAllister asked.

"Random bystanders? Lookouts for Trafford? Either way, let's not scare them off. Be alert, but non-threatening."

Getting out, Duncan immediately detected the pungent smell of burning marijuana. He approached the pair, angling his direction to keep both guys in view. McAllister circled the tree so she could approach from the other side. Totally immersed in their smoking, it was unlikely the two men would notice the troopers until it was too late. Duncan stopped, giving himself plenty of space if the two got squirrelly. "Afternoon, guys. Got a moment?" He hoped they were too stoned to think of running.

At the sight of the police, they took a couple steps backward.

"Stay there," said McAllister who had stopped, hand on her Sig, also at a safe distance.

The taller of the two threw down the stub of his joint and smashed it underfoot. "Hey, man." He waved, a vague motion, his eyes slightly bloodshot and voice blurry.

The second guy, shorter and stockier, shifted and stuffed his hands in the pockets of his jeans, which were hanging halfway down his ass. He didn't say anything, but his gaze, also through bloodshot eyes, moved from Duncan, to McAllister, to his companion.

If they ran, Duncan was going after that one. "Nice day," he said. "Won't get too many more of these before winter."

"'Spose not," the first guy said.

"Mind telling me your names and what you're doing here?" Duncan's voice was casual, but his nerves weren't. Strung out on pot, there was no telling what the suspects would do. He stared at his trainee, willing her to hear his thoughts. Take your hand off the gun, McAllister.

She didn't budge.

The tall guy shrugged. "I'm Nathaniel, this here is Doug," he said, indicating his stocky companion. "We wasn't doing nothing. Hanging."

Judging from the eyes and slurred speech, the joints mashed into the grass hadn't been their first hit of the day. "Looks like you've been here awhile. What can you tell me about that house?" He jerked his thumb at the run-down house across the road. It wasn't as decrepit as the meth lab on Jumonville, but it wasn't in pristine condition either, faded green paint and a sagging porch.

Doug spoke up, voice sluggish yet belligerent. "We ain't gotta tell you nothing. We got rights. You can't do nothing to us."

"It was just a question," Duncan said. He looked at Doug.

McAllister moved her hand to finger the cuffs on her belt and they clinked. "Maybe they'd rather talk at our place."

She was moving too fast. Duncan hooked his thumbs on his duty belt. "Let's not rush into anything. What do you say, guys?"

"You can't arrest us," Doug said. "I watch Law & Order. You don't have no warrant."

"You bet your ass we can," McAllister said, voice hard.

Duncan gritted his teeth. McAllister hadn't reached for her gun again, but threatening these two with arrest would be just as counterproductive. "Let's give everybody a chance to be helpful." He gave a slight shake of his head and she dropped her hand from the cuffs.

"Look, man," Nathaniel said, stepping back and putting up his hands. "I can't get arrested. I'll blow my parole. I got busted last week in Uniontown and judge said if I get caught again, I go to jail."

Duncan could see the panic in Nathaniel's eyes, hear it in his voice creeping through the drug haze. He was on the edge of running. He also seemed more willing to cooperate than Doug, who continued his tough-guy act. Duncan focused on Nathaniel. "I didn't drive out here to arrest two guys for smoking pot," he said. "I'm interested in that house. So if you know anything, now would be a good time to start talking."

"We don't know nothing," Doug said, elbowing his buddy.

"Man, shut up. You want to go to jail?" Nathaniel shoved back. "I tell you about the house, you let us alone?"

"How's this. Tell me what you know and we'll go from there."

The set of McAllister's jaw told Duncan she wasn't happy with how the situation was developing, but she stayed silent.

"Doug and me, we used to smoke behind that shed there." Nathaniel pointed to a small rust-streaked tool shed. "We figured it was a good place for a hit."

"Until the scary dude showed up," Doug said, mumbling. He must have decided to drop his act because he kicked at the ground, bravado gone.

"What scary dude?" Duncan asked.

"Couple weeks ago," Nathaniel said. "Doug and me were out by the shed and this guy comes out the back door, waving a gun, and telling us to get out."

"What kind of gun?" Duncan said.

"Man, I don't know, a gun. The kind that shoots people."

Duncan pressed. "A handgun, a rifle, a shotgun?"

Nathaniel stared. "Handgun," he said after a moment. "We didn't bother to stay and find out what kind. One'll kill you just as good as the other."

Too bad Nathaniel couldn't identify a 9mm on sight. "What did the scary guy look like?"

"Scary," Doug said, still looking at the ground.

"Man, shut up. You are so stupid." Nathaniel pushed Doug, who staggered through ankle-high grass, but stayed upright. "Shorter than you, officer. But heavier, like he works out. His hair was shaved real short, and he had tattoos all over his arms and shoulders."

"Sleeve tattoos?" Duncan asked. "The ones that go all the way from the shoulder to the wrist?"

"Nah, upper arms and shoulders," Nathaniel said.

"And the back of his neck," Doug said, pointing to his own. "Some weird, twisty thing, all black. Did I say scary?"

"You mentioned that, thanks." The description, particularly of the tattoos, matched Trafford. His hair had been longer last fall, but hair was easy to cut off. Duncan scanned the house, but saw no one.

"You gonna arrest us?" Nathaniel said, shuffling his feet. "Honest, that's all I know. We ain't been near the house since then. Not any closer than this tree. I can't go to jail. My ma will kill me."

Duncan pulled his attention back to the two in front of him. "Here's a tip, guys. You want to stay out of jail? Lay off the marijuana. Next trooper who catches you might not be as nice as I am. Now get out of here."

Doug and Nathaniel nodded so hard, Duncan thought their heads might come off. "Yessir. We'll remember that," Nathaniel said. Doug mumbled something, and the two bolted off through the field.

Duncan stared at the house and inhaled, alert for any of the scents associated with a meth lab. But all he smelled was dry grass, leaves, and the lingering traces of marijuana.

"You think they'll listen?" McAllister said.

"Not in the slightest." He moved toward the house, careful to stay back from anything that might be considered the property line.

"How'd I do?"

"Okay."

She huffed.

Duncan took a step toward the road, watching for cars, but the area was deserted. "When you question someone, a witness, or a suspect, or even just someone who might know something helpful, it's about building rapport. Tough to build rapport with threats."

"I didn't threaten them."

"Not in so many words. But you implied we were going to arrest them." He glanced at her out of the corner of his eye. "Didn't your mother ever tell you that you catch more flies with honey?"

"I prefer to swat flies. If they're too big to be swatted, they should get stuffed into a bug zapper. Get them before they get you." She stalked a few paces off, gravel crunching underfoot.

Duncan watched her from behind, taking in the stiffness in her back and the set of her shoulders. He couldn't see her face, but there had been a vein pulsing at her temple. Who was her fly? She was too emphatic for it not to be personal. Someone in her past had put her in her place, hard. From what he'd come to know of McAllister, she wouldn't have liked that. She was a fighter. The nature of her reactions thus far suggested she'd had to knuckle under. Had she given up or lost the battle? Now she was in a position of authority and it was her turn. Not for the first time, he thought "aggression not assertion." She'd reached right for the former. Why?

After a moment, McAllister returned.

"Why'd you become a trooper?" The spur of the moment question might elicit an answer.

"Why did you?" she asked, lifting her chin.

Building rapport. It didn't just apply to suspects. "It's all I ever wanted to do," he said. "Someone has to do the protecting in society. Might as well be me." He watched emotions chase each other across McAllister's face. Frustration, despair, a little anger. There was a split second where he thought she might open up, then it passed.

"Are we going in?" she asked. There was a slight brittleness in her look, but the edge had disappeared from her voice.

So close. "In? No. But we are going to knock."

Duncan climbed the uneven porch steps hemmed in by overgrown weeds and rapped on the peeling front door. No answer. He looked for a doorbell button. Finding none, he pounded again. "State police," he said, not quite shouting. "Anyone home?" Nothing.

"Doesn't look like it," McAllister said.

The faded curtains on the front window were parted, but he resisted peaking in. "Wonder who owns this place?"

McAllister wandered over to a bag of trash lying by the roadside. Carelessly thrown, it had been pulled open by scavengers. She poked through the debris.

"Anything useful?"

"Whoever lives here likes Lucky Charms. Don't suppose we could claim exigent circumstances?" The glum expression on McAllister's face said she knew the answer to that.

"Don't worry. We're off tomorrow, but we'll ask someone to come out again. If they come up empty, we'll check the property records, see if we can come up with enough for a search warrant." He headed back to the patrol car.

"This county confuses me."

"How so?"

"On the one hand, you've got the glossiness of Ohiopyle, Nemacolin, and Seven Springs. On the other hand, this." She waved at the run-down house.

"Fayette County. Playground to the rich, home to the working poor." Duncan opened the car door and got in. After a few seconds, McAllister followed suit.

He'd find out who owned the house and would go from there. If the house was a new meth lab, they'd know sooner or later. Either someone would smell it or the place would explode. Duncan hoped it was the former. Pulling evidence from an explosion would be a lot more difficult.

⊰⊰⊰

On Wednesday, as Sally had promised Jim, she talked to Bryan, alerting him to what she'd found. Unsurprisingly, he was reluctant to make a call. "Are you certain you're right? We could be opening a can of worms for nothing. Maybe it's a personal note."

"A note about what?" Sally shook out her hair. "I'm not positive, but I can't think of many other meanings."

Bryan's face and voice took on a glum cast. "It would be nice to know for sure."

In Sally's opinion, the best source of information would be Alex Costanzo, the prosecutor for all of the marked cases. She called his office, leaving both voicemail and a verbal message with the office receptionist. In between her appointments, Sally checked her messages, but heard nothing.

Maybe he was Colin's accomplice. She discarded the idea almost as soon as it crossed her mind. It was common gossip that Alex saw a future for himself as a district attorney. He wouldn't risk the position by getting caught up in an extortion scheme.

Sally decided to find him after work. Alex was a single man and a creature of habit. He almost always ate out and at the same restaurant, one of Uniontown's upscale establishments. Sure enough, Sally recognized Alex's black Mercedes with the custom plates among the dozen cars when she pulled into the parking lot. She sat in her Camry, tapping the steering wheel. Now what? She could bust in and confront him. No, too public. He wouldn't be happy to see her and would probably have her escorted off the premises. Just what Bryan needed. Not.

She could wait, see if Alex called back. But he'd had a day. If he was going to call, he would have.

The parking lot was relatively quiet. She'd wait, catch him on the way out. He might not be alone, but it wouldn't be as public of a confrontation. At the same time, he'd have to answer her.

It was almost eight before Alex emerged, an attractive brunette on his arm. Sally jumped out of her car. "Alex. Alex, wait."

He turned toward her voice, raised eyebrows lowering as he recognized her. "What the hell? Are you stalking me, Castle?"

"I wouldn't have to catch you off hours if you'd answer your messages." She glanced at the brunette. The woman's dark hair was tied back at the nape of her slender neck and smoky eye shadow showed off her almond-shaped brown eyes. The maroon velvet dress complimented milk chocolate skin; the plunging neckline exposed a touch too much cleavage. The hem of the dress ended slightly above what Sally's mother would have considered proper. The dress was more appropriate for street-walking than Uniontown's best restaurant. The woman's eyes sparkled with a touch of hardness, and Sally thought she detected the shadow of an old bruise on her jaw.

Alex tried to brush past her. "I'm busy. You'll have to wait until next week."

Sally stood firm. "I can't wait until next week." She looked at the woman. "I'm sorry I interrupted your date, but this is important. Sally Castle with the public defender's office." She extended her hand. "What's your name?"

"It's not a date." The woman glanced at Alex. "Tyra Young."

"Go wait in the car." Alex gave her a little push.

Tyra staggered on her four-inch stilettos. She shot him a look of pure loathing, but went to the Mercedes and waited while he unlocked the door.

"That was uncalled for," Sally said as Tyra disappeared into the Mercedes and slammed the door.

Alex tugged his suit coat. "So is you showing up here."

"I told you—"

"Right. Important. You've got thirty seconds." He made a show of checking the Rolex on his wrist.

"Is that a friend of yours?"

"Twenty seconds."

Asshole. "I found something that might relate to Colin Rafferty's murder. It could also influence some actions by my office, and yours." She refocused on Alex.

"What is it?" he said, voice icy.

Alex was no doubt angry, but Sally didn't miss the note of tension that crept into his voice at the mention of Colin's death. She held out the photocopied pages from Colin's notebook. "These are from a book I found in Colin's possession. Do you know what they mean?"

He glanced down. "No."

"These numbers in the first column are docket numbers of cases you prosecuted."

Alex licked his lips and adjusted his cuffs. "So what?" he asked. "Probably a personal notation."

"What kind of notation?"

"How the hell should I know?" His voice was edgy. "I don't spend my time fussing about how assistant PD's handle their record keeping."

"But you were the prosecutor. I was hoping—"

"Well, you hoped wrong. And you are way over your thirty seconds. See you in court." This time, Alex was successful in brushing past her to his car. He slid inside, the big German engine growled, and he peeled out of the parking lot with a squeal of tires.

Sally stood a moment, a bit of anger punching through her shock at Alex's behavior. He wasn't the most amiable guy and yes, she had kind of ambushed him leaving the restaurant. But why such an extreme reaction?

CHAPTER 18

T hursday was Duncan's day off, but he spent all morning thinking about the house on Wharton Furnace where his two potheads had allegedly seen Trafford. He didn't own the house. That would have come up in McAllister's search. But the owner was almost assuredly one of Trafford's associates and Duncan really wanted to know who it was. A mournful train whistle in the distance increased his sense of restlessness.

The weather was good, so he clipped Rizzo to his backyard lead, making sure the dog had water and access to his bed on the sheltered back porch. Then Duncan drove to the barracks. It was prime fishing weather, but he knew the unanswered question would dig at him all day. Once there, he ran his property search and sat back. As he waited for the results, Nicols walked up.

"What the hell are you doing here? Shouldn't you be doing something outdoorsy?"

"Probably, but you know me." Duncan told Nicols about the house on Wharton Furnace. "I decided to come in and check the ownership." Just then, the results of the search popped up. "And the winner is…Devin Carrington."

Nicols perched on the edge of the desk. "Who's he?"

"Looks like a small time criminal." Duncan clicked over to Carrington's record and scrolled. "He's been brought in on a couple of drug busts. Well, look at this. Two of them involved Trafford."

Nicols came around the desk. "Any convictions?"

Duncan read. "Looks like Carrington got a couple short sentences on misdemeanors. Trafford got a minor stint for possession on one, and skated on the second because they couldn't prove he was more than a bystander. He was with Carrington at the time of the arrest, but denied involvement and didn't have drugs in his possession."

"You didn't find anything for a search warrant when you were out there?"

Duncan looked up at his commander. "No. There's not enough here, either."

"Plenty for a return visit, though. But do it tomorrow, when you're on the clock." Nicols stood. "You've got that expression on your face. What are you thinking?"

"Colin Rafferty, the murdered assistant public defender. He was Trafford's attorney last fall." Without betraying too much, Duncan outlined Sally's suspicions.

"You think Trafford took care of a perceived threat?" Nicols asked.

"He's capable of it."

"Maybe, but that case is over and done. Would Rafferty be Trafford's attorney if he got busted again?"

"I don't know." Sally would. Duncan made a note to ask her. "If they review the old case because of impropriety on the part of the attorney, I don't know if Trafford would be retried or not."

Nicols fixed him with a dark-eyed stare. "I will remind you that it's not your job to find out." He held up his hand. "I know you, Jim. You were on the scene. The woman who found the deceased. She's a friend of yours, right? This has all the earmarks of something you'd love to get your hands on. Stay away, got it?"

"Yes, sir." Duncan cleared the search and powered down the computer. "Unless it ties into my current investigation, of course."

Nicols narrowed his eyes, but said nothing.

"I'll take McAllister by that house again tomorrow. See what we can find."

"You do that." Nicols relaxed. "Speaking of McAllister, how's she doing?"

"Okay, I guess." Out of habit, Duncan headed for the coffeepot.

"What's wrong?"

"Nothing, really." Of course the pot was empty. It was lousy coffee anyway. Duncan fed some change into the vending machine for a Coke.

"I've seen her classroom record. She's smart. Observant. She knows how to do the job and she can be good at it."

Nicols trailed him. "But?"

"I can't put my finger on it." Duncan outlined what he'd seen. "One minute she's fine. The next she's…"

"Overreacting?"

"Kind of." Duncan told his commanding officer his idea about McAllister's past relationship with authority. "There's something there. She's got the power now and she's determined to use it."

"That could be a bad sign."

"I know. Before I throw in the towel, I'd like a crack at finding out what the issue is and helping her work through it. She's got the makings of one hell of a trooper."

"I have complete confidence in you." Nicols grinned. "Now go home and, I don't know, play with your dog. Or something."

⚜⚜⚜

In between taking care of her other cases, Sally spent Thursday trying to find De'Shawn Thomas. She needed to confirm her suspicions. Of course, she could have done that by finding Colin's partner. But the thought of someone in the courthouse, the DA's office or a judge's chamber, assisting with an extortion scheme made her sicker than the time she'd ridden the Tilt-a-Whirl five times in a row.

Colin's notes seemed to indicate Thomas had not been to the office since shortly after his arraignment, almost two weeks before Colin's death. Thomas's cell phone was disconnected. A quick trip to his address of record after work turned up nothing. Neighbors said Thomas had not been home for days.

Sally had to admit: it was not looking good for De'Shawn.

Her last-ditch attempt was to troll the street corner where Thomas had been arrested for possession. She was smart enough to do it before the sun was completely down and she took a small can of pepper spray with her. The corner was in Uniontown, next to a convenience store, but there was no sense tempting fate. In the early evening there'd be less foot traffic and while Uniontown wasn't Compton, better safe than sorry.

A dozen or so young people dressed in wannabe gangster-rap attire, tight dresses, baggy shirts, sagging jeans, and sideways ball caps, were already on the street corner. They passed around a pack of cigarettes, butts and other trash in the gutter. The presence of a well-dressed white woman caused obvious amusement with a splash of wariness. "Yo, yo. You lost lady?" one of the men swaggered toward her.

Sally held up a mug shot. "I'm looking for De'Shawn Thomas."

The man took a slow step backward. "Why you looking for him? You a cop?"

"No. I'm an attorney from the public defender's office. Who're you?"

"Reggie." He rubbed his chin. "De'Shawn got a lawyer and it ain't a lady."

"De'Shawn's attorney is dead. That's why I'm here." Sally scanned the crowd. "Let's not be coy. The police are looking for Mr. Thomas. You know this. Trust me when I say it'll be a lot better for him if I find him first. If any of you can pass a message, I'll give you my number." She fished a business card out of her pocket.

There was a rumble of activity at the back of the crowd. A man stepped forward, brushing aside a few friends who muttered. "I'm De'Shawn. What you want?" Thomas was dressed much like his cohorts, sideways ball cap, oversized shirt and jeans riding low enough the waistband could be seen below the shirt. He was thin, almost emaciated, his face slightly pockmarked, ears a bit oversized for his head.

Sally glanced at the jeans. No obvious bulge of a weapon. Still, she gripped the can of pepper spray. Even if Thomas wasn't armed, somebody else in the group might be. "I need to talk to you about your attorney, Colin Rafferty."

Thomas's eyes were dark, barely reflecting the light. "He dead."

"I know. I found his body. I also know the police are looking at you as a suspect."

"How you know that?"

Sally suppressed a sigh. "I've heard Mr. Rafferty had a note in his day planner. He was meeting a person with the initials DT on Sunday night. Since those are your initials, and you were his client, it's not a huge leap in logic."

Thomas shuffled his feet and a fresh wave of muttering broke out.

"Were you supposed to meet Mr. Rafferty that night?"

After a moment's silence, Thomas responded. "I got a call from a guy saying to come to the office to see him, Rafferty. He wanted to talk to me."

"About what? Your drug charge was scheduled to go to plea bargain, correct?"

"Yeah. I don't know about what. I got there a little after eight. Lights were on, door was open. I went in, but we didn't talk."

"Why?" Sally suspected she knew.

"Dude was dead, that's why. I hightailed it outta there. Threw away my phone and haven't been home. I don't need that kind of trouble."

"Mr. Rafferty was dead when you arrived?"

"Yeah." Thomas picked a spot on his cheek. "All bloody and shit around the head. Didn't stick around to look real close."

"It didn't occur to you to call the police?"

He stared, mouth slightly open. "Lady, you crazy? I know what happens when a black man gets caught next to a dead white guy."

Sally tapped her foot. He had a point. She pulled the folded photocopies from her pocket and showed Thomas the line corresponding to his case. "This is part of your docket number from court. Do you know what the rest of it means?" She pointed. "Does it have something to do with your plea agreement?"

"No clue," Thomas said. He stared, chin stuck out.

"Mr. Thomas, I want to help," she said. "But I can't—"

"If your help is anything like the dead dude's, I don't need it. I ain't got that kind of scratch."

She refolded the sheets and put them back. "What do you mean?"

"I gotta spell it out for you? He wanted cash I ain't got."

There was only one reason Colin would be asking a client for money and it wasn't a good one. She held out another mug shot, this one of Aaron Trafford. "Have you ever seen this man?"

"Yeah. I scored some weed off one of his guys last week."

"How do you know it was one of Trafford's dealers?"

Thomas shrugged. "He showed up to collect the dough. But I don't know I'd talk to him direct and all."

"Why not?"

"Too serious. He got the smell of someone who would land a brother in a whole lotta trouble, you know?"

At least Thomas's street smarts worked. "Did you ever see Mr. Trafford with Mr. Rafferty?"

Thomas's eyes narrowed. "I don't think I wanna talk to you no more. You might be okay, you might not. I can take care of myself." He stepped back into the crowd.

"Mr. Thomas, wait." She tried to follow, but the group closed ranks and the previously benign mutters took on a more adversarial note. The sun had gone way down, casting dark shadows over the sidewalk. She was painfully aware that hers was the only pale face in the group. Even Jim might not wade into the gang by himself. She held up her hands. "I don't want any trouble. But please, I really do want to help. If one of you can convince Mr. Thomas to come see me at my office it can only be to his benefit."

She backed up. Once she was away from the crowd, she turned and went back to her car, sure that her every step was being carefully watched.

CHAPTER 19

Sally arrived at work on Friday intending to take another crack at convincing De'Shawn to come in. But Bryan derailed her plans when he summoned her to his office.

"What's up?" she asked. "Hey, before you tell me, I saw De'Shawn Thomas. He says—"

"He's been arrested for Colin's murder." Bryan leaned back in his chair. "Detective Killian informed me last night. I've already filed the motion to get his representation transferred to private counsel."

"What the hell happened?"

"He tried to rob a convenience store. Except the guy at the register had a concealed-carry and a Sig Sauer under the counter. Cops brought Thomas in for the robbery, and Killian charged him with criminal homicide an hour later."

Sally shuffled her thoughts. The arrest would definitely complicate things. "You filed that motion pretty fast."

"What did you expect?" Bryan's chair creaked as he sat up.

"I don't know. I do know Thomas is innocent of murder, though."

"You know that how?"

"I just do." Sally faced down her boss. He was more understanding than the people she'd worked with in the Allegheny County DA's office, but that only meant she was more at ease standing her ground. "It's one of those things where you don't have facts, but your gut says this guy is not

Colin's killer." It was a completely insufficient answer and she knew it, but Bryan would have to present something pretty convincing to get her to back off.

He took off his glasses and polished them. "I'm sure the police have pretty definite evidence to the contrary. Judges don't issue arrest warrants on a whim."

"They aren't always right, though. Are they?" Sally tossed her briefcase on a chair. "De'Shawn Thomas's defense is going to get handed to some private-practice attorney who couldn't care less about a street guy with two drug convictions. The real killer will walk while laughing at his cleverness at setting up some poor sap from the street."

"Damn it, you know the rules. You found the freaking body, Sally. Colin was a co-worker. We cannot keep this case."

"Then I'm just going to have to find the killer, aren't I?"

Bryan came out of his chair, rounded the desk, and strode to his door. He closed it with a bang and wheeled around. "I'm going to pretend I didn't hear that."

"Why?"

"You know damn well why." He took a step forward and raised a finger. "You are a talented attorney, Sally. A smart woman. Which means you are going to leave this case to the police and leave Thomas's defense to whomever the court appoints."

"But Bry, I can do this."

"But nothing." He resettled his glasses. "Of course you have the ability do this. Don't be absurd. I know you want justice for Colin."

"So do you. I also don't particularly care to see an innocent man railroaded."

"He's hardly innocent, Sally. He has two convictions on his record."

"He's innocent of murder." She fixed Bryan with her best courtroom-challenge stare. "Come on. You've never fought me like this. Why now when it's so personal?"

He caved. "Because it is personal. Of course I want Colin's killer found and tried. I love your passion, Sally, I really do. I've always been one hundred per cent behind you. However, the ethics here are crystal clear. This is out of our hands."

Sally paused. "Who'd the court get for the defense?"

"I'm not positive, but I heard it would probably be Ben Stilling."

Well, that wasn't the worst choice in the world. Sally knew Stilling by reputation. He'd fight for his client. But Stilling wouldn't be invested in doing any more than he had to. And he wouldn't go looking for the real killer. "Okay." She took a breath. "Let's say I come across information that might relate to Colin's death, or identify an alternative suspect. What then?"

"You're a witness. You'll hand over anything you know or learn to the police."

"Fair enough." She picked up her briefcase and went to her own office. Tell the police. Right. Except Bryan hadn't specified which police department she should tell.

☙ ☙ ☙

Friday afternoon, second shift roll call ended, and Duncan and McAllister loitered at the barracks. Other troopers departed and soon they were the only ones left. Duncan felt like he was looping. Looking for Trafford in all the same places and each time coming up empty.

McAllister got a bottle of Mountain Dew from the vending machine. "So what—" She took one look at Duncan and paused. "Do you have any plans for this shift besides our usual patrol?"

"Not a one." He spun the key ring for a car on his finger. "Your turn. What you do think we should do next?"

"Well." She stared at the wall, forehead creased slightly. "What's the Beer House? Sounds like a local bar."

"It is. What about it?"

"Your CI's first tip said Trafford had been spotted there. Maybe we ought to go ask a few questions."

"Good idea." Duncan tossed her the keys. "You drive."

"I don't know where I'm going."

"I do. Go start the car."

The Beer House was located just outside the Confluence town line. The dirt parking lot was full of battered pickups and winter beater cars. A couple motorcycles. The neon window signs were all half-lit and the sign with the bar's name was streaked with dirt.

McAllister went to the front of the car. "What are we likely to find in here?"

"As you might have guessed, it's not a high-class establishment. The clientele is…"

"Sketchy?"

"That's as good a word as any." The benefit would be he'd know a lot of the folks inside. The downside was they'd know him. Or maybe that wasn't a negative. He had a pretty solid reputation, and folks knew he didn't harass them for the heck of it. "I don't think we're likely to encounter more than a usual amount of resistance. Just remember. Our main focus is locating Trafford. Don't get distracted by anything else you see. We are trying to get people to talk to us."

"Be nice?"

"Be...polite. Firm, but polite."

"Will I see anything else?"

"Maybe. Let's go."

The interior of The Beer House was thick with the rancid smell of cigarette smoke. The lights were low, and the entrance of two uniformed troopers caused some shuffling at the back tables. Duncan nodded to McAllister, a sign that she should keep watch on the crowd. Meanwhile he angled toward the bar. "Hey, Tank."

The bartender had come by his nickname honestly, with a square build, heavily muscled arms, and a flattop haircut. "Trooper Duncan. Has there been a complaint?"

"No, nothing like that. We've come to ask about Aaron Trafford."

Tank pushed a foaming mug of beer toward a patron and faced Duncan, a wary light in his eyes. "What about him?"

"Word is he was here not that long ago. That true?"

"Whose word?" Tank made a show of wiping down the bar.

Duncan glanced around. McAllister, a table away, engaged in conversation with a couple of guys. She periodically looked up to check the other occupants of the bar. No sign of a problem from them or her. He assumed she was following her own initiative. Satisfied, he turned back to Tank. "I can't say."

"Not good enough, Duncan."

"A good cop is like a good reporter. He never gives up his source."

Tank tilted his head. "Do I know your source?"

"Yes." Of course Tank and Eddie knew each other. In a small town everybody knew everybody else and their business.

"Is he a patron of mine?"

"No, he's got his own place. But I doubt you'll see him at a Chamber of Commerce meeting." Hopefully that was enough of a hint.

Tank folded the towel he'd been using and flipped it over his shoulder. He stared off at the table area, face unreadable.

Duncan couldn't tell if the man was making up his mind to say something or not. "Tank. I'm not looking to get anyone in trouble. I want to find Trafford. You read the news. You know we shut down a meth facility a couple days ago on Jumonville Road."

"I saw." Tank still wouldn't meet Duncan's eye. "Anywhere near that kids' camp?"

"No, thank God. But it could have been."

More silence. Finally, the barman appeared to make up his mind and turned. "I don't like Trafford. I don't like his business. I got kids. I don't need them growing up with that shit in their backyards. Yeah, he was in here."

At last. Confirmation. "Alone?"

"He came in by himself. Met a couple guys in the back. They talked for maybe fifteen, twenty minutes then Trafford left."

"You know the guys?"

"Devin Carrington and Alex Monahan. Troublemakers, and I know they both got records for minor shit, but they aren't in Trafford's league." Tank leaned on the bar.

The owner of the Wharton Furnace House and the guy they'd picked up with the drugs. "Why were they talking to Trafford?"

"My guess? He wanted something. Probably front men. I warned both of 'em off, but I don't think they listened seeing as I saw in the police blotter Monahan was picked up for possession. Dumbass."

"Thanks, Tank. Listen." Duncan slid a card across the bar. "You see Trafford again, call me. On my cell if necessary."

Tank nodded, pocketed the card, and turned to attend to a customer.

Duncan jerked his thumb toward the door. "McAllister, let's go."

"Just a sec, Boss." She pulled business cards from her pocket, handed them over, then headed to Duncan. "Now we can leave."

"What was that all about?"

"Tell you outside."

When they were standing next to the cruiser, Duncan put a hand on the driver side door. "Okay, spill."

"I was building rapport."

"Stop being a smart-ass."

She grinned. "I was watching the crowd like you asked and I got to talking with those two. Asked if they'd seen Trafford. They said yes. He was in not that long ago, and met Carrington and Monahan."

"That's what Tank, the bartender, said."

"Well, my two guys? They were sitting kinda near Trafford and his buddies. They didn't hear much, but one, they thought it was Monahan, must have gotten antsy. Trafford said something like 'Don't I got a tame lawyer down in the courthouse? Just do what you're told and shut up.' Might not be the exact words, but that was the gist of it."

"They hear anything else?"

"No." She glanced at the building. "Trafford noticed them shortly after that and they took off for a different table. Guess Mr. Trafford has the reputation of being someone you don't want to mess with. I left my card, just in case."

Duncan stepped away from the door. "Good work. Your first personal sources."

"Carrington. He's the one with the house, right?" She slid into the car.

Duncan went over to the passenger side and got in. "Yes, he is."

"Let's pay him another visit. I bet I can find the place all by myself this time." She grinned.

CHAPTER 20

S ally did not go out to lunch Friday. She gave Doris strict instructions to disturb her only in the case of fire, then retreated to her office and closed the door. Over carrot sticks and blue cheese dip, she sifted through the cases in Colin's notebook, looking for a common thread.

On the surface, they were fairly mundane. Most ended in plea agreements, which wasn't uncommon in their line of work. Some of the sentencing recommendations were unusual, but not extraordinary. The crimes were all over the place: possession, larceny, criminal trespass, the majority in the misdemeanor to third-class felony range. But they did share one notable characteristic.

Without exception, they'd been prosecuted by Alex Costanzo.

That fact made Alex's parking lot statement, that he didn't know anything, suspect. Okay, maybe he wouldn't remember every single trial but none of them? Why would he lie to her? Especially since Colin was right. The same people came through the system all the time, on the same charges. If nothing else, Alex should remember the names because he'd seen them multiple times.

He had been in a hurry to leave the restaurant. She was willing to bet he hadn't even been listening as he counted down the allotted time. If she caught him when he had more time, when she'd be able to explain her concerns in depth, she'd get a better response.

Maybe pigs would fly.

Sally had never been one to back down from a challenge; ask anyone she worked with in Allegheny County. She grabbed the notebook, her purse, and headed for the front door. "I'll be back," she said to Doris.

"I thought you didn't want to be disturbed?"

"Yeah, but I never said I'd be staying here."

Sally hustled up the stairs to the first floor. If the universe liked her, Alex would not be in court. If it loved her, she'd be able to get him to give her the details she craved, ones that might identify Colin's killer.

After she was buzzed in, she stopped at the front desk. "I'm looking for Alex Costanzo."

"I think he's out. Excuse me a moment." The receptionist walked away. Sally could hear voices coming from other parts of the office and waited for a long minute. Sally knew where Alex's office was; she could continue to wait or find out for herself if he was there.

She opted to go look and hurried down the hallway. The door was closed and almost definitely locked. Damn. Out of curiosity, she gripped the knob, pushed, and the door popped open. She hesitated only a second, then slipped inside and closed the door. She'd only stay a moment, she reasoned. She wouldn't look at anything that resembled trial paperwork. If Alex walked in and found her, she'd make an excuse.

Sally paced around the room. All Alex's diplomas and certifications were framed and hung on the wall, and not inexpensive frames either. Dark wood bookshelves held thick, legal tomes. There were stacks of folders and paper on the club chair by the window. The leather wingback chairs by the desk, however, were empty. There was an engraved nameplate, part of a high-end desk set that included a leather blotter. How typical of him. More paper obscured the desk. The computer monitor was dark. The temptation to check Alex's Outlook calendar tugged at her, but she resisted. He was smart enough to set a password on his screensaver. Besides, if he had helped to arrange a murder, he wouldn't put it in his Outlook calendar.

Out of the corner of her eye, she saw a Moleskine diary. It was mostly covered with paper, but she could tell it was open. That was intriguing. She'd done enough work with Alex to know he kept all his appointments in his phone calendar, synched with his computer. What was the diary for? She shouldn't look, it was probably private. Then again, if it was so private why was the book at work and why was it open? What if it could help her find Colin's killer?

She couldn't resist. The diary was a weekly calendar layout. She flipped to the week of Colin's death and glanced at the entry for Sunday.

There were no names, but there was a line of stars by the space for eight p.m. An appointment? Something special about that time? The same time as Colin's meeting with DT, who everybody assumed was De'Shawn Thomas. In the Notes section was the word "shirt." It had been heavily circled. What did that mean? Was it merely a note to himself or something more?

She glanced at the door, then flipped through the pages for previous weeks. No mentions of Trafford, or DT, or Colin, but lots of entries for Tyra. Three, sometimes four, days a week. Sally rolled the name around in her head. It was familiar. Hadn't that been the woman who was with Alex at the restaurant? Tyra Young, that was it. Why did her name appear so often in Alex's calendar? What had he said about that night? "Not a date." The statement had been corroborated by the look in Tyra's eyes. Angry, defiant, yet…a little afraid. Sally made a note to do some research and find out more about Tyra Young.

Suddenly, the door opened and Sally whipped her hands behind her back, still holding the diary. "Oh, hi."

It was a secretary, who looked at Sally first with a puzzled expression and then with narrowed eyes. "Can I help you with something? Mr. Costanzo isn't here. You shouldn't be in his office."

Sally was cornered. Shit. If only she'd had a few more seconds before being interrupted, she could have put down the book. She couldn't put the Moleskine back now, not with the secretary watching. She'd be sure to report it to Alex. Sally was wearing a cardigan. Could she slip it under her sweater? Alex would go ballistic if he knew Sally had taken it, but she knew him well enough to know he'd make damn sure he hadn't left it somewhere before reporting it missing. Especially if it contained a record of things he'd rather keep quiet about. That would give Sally time to find a way to return it. "Yeah, sorry. The receptionist didn't know if he was here, and I had to ask him a quick question."

"How'd you get in?"

"The door popped open. He must not have closed it properly." She'd managed to slip the diary under her sweater and work it around to the front. If she clasped Colin's notebook to her chest, she could keep Alex's calendar from falling on the floor.

"He's been complaining about the lock." The secretary pointed at the notebook and a faint note of accusation entered her voice. "What's that? Did you take it off his desk?"

"No, I brought it with me. It's what I had to ask him about. Is he coming back?"

"No, he just called to say he'd be gone for the day."

"Oh, well, I'll see him on Monday then. Have a nice weekend." Sally skirted the secretary and beat a hasty exit. Behind her, she could hear the noise of things being moved around and was sure the young woman was taking stock of Alex's desk. With any luck, she wouldn't know about the Moleskine and, therefore, wouldn't know it was missing. Sally's conscience grumbled, but if she could learn something from the calendar it was worth the risk. All she had to do was get it back on Monday before Alex noticed it was gone.

⇟⇟⇟

Out on patrol, Duncan and McAllister had looped past the house on Wharton Furnace where they suspected Trafford was living. But the house stayed stubbornly silent. The fresh tire marks on the front-yard grass told Duncan someone had been there recently. Maybe that morning. McAllister hadn't been happy, but Duncan sent her home with the promise they'd try again the next day.

It was shortly after midnight when Duncan arrived home. He parked his Jeep on the gravel drive, killed the engine, and headed for the back door. He missed the sound of Rizzo's welcoming bark, but with the dog knocked out for his annual teeth cleaning, it had been better to leave him overnight at the vet's. If something happened post-anesthesia, especially since Duncan worked second-shift, there would be experienced people around to deal with it.

Rizzo's lead was curled in the grass and he could hear the faint lap of water from the Casselman running along the edge of his backyard. He reached out to unlock the back door and froze. The window to the right of the door was broken, jagged pieces glittering on the concrete entry step. It had not been broken when he'd left that afternoon. Duncan pulled his Sig and backed away, the back of his neck prickling, his body instantly on high alert.

Back at the Jeep he knelt down, using the vehicle for shelter. There were no lights in the house and no sign of movement. The front door was shut, as were the living room windows. He wanted to crash inside. But only an idiot went into a dark house against an unknown number of intruders, with an unknown number of weapons, without backup.

He pulled out his cell phone and dialed 911. "This is Trooper First Class Jim Duncan. I'm at the scene of a possible home invasion." He gave his address and waited. He disliked giving the information in plain English over an open line. When the Emergency Operations Center put the call out, anybody in Confluence with a police scanner would know there had been a break-in at his house. In this town, that was a lot of people. Helpful neighbors could come out of the woodwork, rushing to his aid. He wanted them to stay home, out of harm's way. At least until the situation was under control.

"Officer en route. Please stay on the line until the car arrives." The operator's voice crackled over the cell phone.

Kneeling on the gravel was hell, but Duncan didn't dare stand. He set the phone on the tire so he could keep his hands free. It wasn't long before a car pulled up behind him, hazard lights on but siren silent and headlights out. He didn't turn his head at the sound of footsteps and a figure sank down beside him. "That was fast," he said.

"No problem." It was McAllister, her gun already drawn. "I was close."

"Why the hell are you here?"

"Thanks for the welcome, Boss."

"I...sorry. I'm glad you came, but you should be at home."

"Leave my FTO in the lurch? No way," McAllister said, voice low. "We know if anyone is inside?"

Duncan shook his head. "I haven't seen any activity, but there could be one or more actors still on scene."

"All righty then," McAllister said. "We know whose house this is?"

"Mine." Duncan ground his teeth and stared at the front door.

McAllister whistled. "How many kinds of stupid do you have to be to break into a cop's house?"

"I don't know, but we're about to find out. Shall we?"

Wordlessly, the two troopers crept to the porch and up the stairs. The front door was locked. Duncan pulled his keys out of his pocket and opened it. Then swore.

The living room was a war zone. Lamps on the floor, bulbs shattered. The couch was stripped of its cushions, upholstery shredded. The pile of newspapers beside the fireplace was scattered, pages of magazines ripped out, basket of kindling tipped and spilled on the carpet. He edged to the kitchen door. Cabinet doors hung at crazy angles, their contents smashed on the floor. The drawers were emptied and on the floor, silverware scattered, and knives from the wooden block stuck in the table. The filet knife pinned a photo of Duncan and his fishing buddies to the middle of the table, knife point in the middle of Duncan's face. He returned to the living room.

McAllister was surveying the wreckage. "Holy shit," she said. She nudged pieces of a broken lamp out of the way with her foot. "Uh, didn't you say you had a dog? Where is he?"

"At the vet's." McAllister following, Duncan proceeded to check the rest of the house for intruders. Every room, including the bathroom, was an unholy mess, but they were the only two people there.

"Holy shit," McAllister said again, staring at the bathroom mirror. Smeared across it in gel deodorant were the words "Coming 4 u." A mangled stick of Old Spice lay in the sink, ripped towels on the floor.

Without responding, Duncan returned to the living room. He almost bent to pick up debris from the floor, but stopped. This was a crime scene. As much as he wanted to clean everything up, he needed to let forensics do their thing. He should feel something, but emotion seemed to have taken a vacation.

Outside, a car pulled up. "I'll go talk to them. You, uh, might want to take a few deep breaths or whatever. Your expression right now is scary." McAllister went out to meet the new arrivals, and Duncan heard her and another person talking. After a few minutes, she came back inside.

"It's Porter and Callahan. They're calling for a forensic team to come out. I told them we already cleared the house," she said.

Porter entered. "Damn, man." He took in the wreckage and pulled out a notebook. "When did you leave this afternoon?"

For the first time in his life, Duncan was on the receiving end of the questions he'd asked any number of victims. He couldn't stop to think about that now. If he did he'd find out his emotions weren't absent, but merely buried under a blanket of shock. The heat of anger was already threatening to break loose. If he let it, he wouldn't be any use to anyone, especially himself. "Sometime between one-thirty and two. Closer to one-thirty."

"Did you notice anyone hanging around when you left?"

He thought back to early afternoon, which seemed like five years ago. "No one I don't usually see"

"Are you sure? No bystanders?"

Duncan gave his fellow trooper a flat stare.

"Right. Small town." Porter jotted the information down. "What about when you got home?"

Duncan recapped his arrival, how he'd found the broken glass next to the back door and called for backup. "The window was not broken earlier. Someone must have smashed it to reach around and open the back door. Can't do that with the front."

"I assume you're pretty careful about security, small town notwithstanding?" Porter asked.

Duncan nodded. "Marge, she lives next door, is home most of the day. She might have seen something after I left."

"Kinda late. If she's up, I'll talk to her though," Porter said. "Do you have any idea who would want to do this?"

"Aaron Trafford."

"But how would he know that you, well we, were looking for him?" McAllister asked. "We haven't seen him and the entire barracks has been on the lookout."

"We've left our cards and our names all over the county," Duncan said.

"I hope my place doesn't look like this."

"You haven't been home yet?"

"I'm going to go out and meet the forensic team," Porter said. "You two know better than to touch anything." He went outside.

Duncan turned to McAllister. "You should have gone home. Other people would have handled it."

She looked away. "I know."

"I appreciate you coming, though."

"You're welcome." She nudged a broken lamp with the toe of her boot. "You're probably right, you know. About Trafford. My other guess would be a jilted lover, but this is overkill. Not like you've got one of those. At least not from what I hear."

Duncan had to laugh. "No, I do not."

She looked around. "You must be mad as hell. Although you look pretty damn calm for a guy who came home to disaster."

Duncan surveyed the remains of his possessions, bits of stuffing from the couch floating on the air. "I'm cooling off. But those assholes have no idea how bad they could have had it," he said, surprising himself with how calm he sounded.

"What do you mean?"

"This is just stuff." He turned to leave. "If Rizzo had been home and they'd hurt my dog, it'd be an entirely different ballgame."

CHAPTER 21

S ally parked behind Jim's Jeep and got out of her Camry. Saturday morning's brilliant sunlight glinted off the trash bags in the front yard, black contrasting with the red and orange leaves that scattered the grass. Water birds winged overhead, heading for the river behind the house. She could see Rizzo straining on the lead in the backyard, barking at the sight of her. She would greet the dog later; right now, it was the owner she was concerned with. She skirted the bags and mounted the porch steps, again thinking how the cozy Victorian house on its neat lot was more suited to a family than a single guy. The front door was open, letting the mild autumn air in through the screen.

Jim appeared, a gun in his hand.

"Uh, hi. That's a non-traditional way to greet a visitor." She pointed at the gun.

"After the night I had, I'm being cautious." He opened the door to let her in, slipping the gun into a holster at his back. He turned away, but not before she saw the dark smudges under his eyes.

Disaster-area didn't begin to describe the state of the room. She doubted there was an unbroken item in it. What she thought was dust on the surfaces of the room was, on closer inspection, fingerprint powder. Torn curtains hung at a crazy angle from bent rods, letting in cheerful sunlight that was at odds with the wreckage.

He pushed hair off his face, which was streaked with dirt and sweat. "It's a nice day. Don't you have plans?"

"Bryan heard the EOC call over his scanner. He called me when he recognized your name. I was going to meet up with my sister, but I figured you could use a hand. Helping you trumps gossip and a mani-pedi."

Jim picked up a broken lamp and dropped it into the trash bag. "What was Gerrity doing, trolling for prospective clients?"

She took a deep breath. Jim must be exhausted; he'd never have made that comment otherwise. "That was uncalled for. Bryan was concerned."

Jim halted in his work and his shoulders sagged a bit. "You're right, Sorry. I'm a little punchy. It was a long night."

"I'm surprised no one from the barracks is here to help." She looked for a clean spot to set down her purse.

Jim shook out a fresh bag and resumed his clean up. "They're working or with family. McAllister offered, but I told her to go enjoy herself."

"They didn't trash her place?"

"No. She lives in an apartment complex. More people, harder to get in unnoticed."

"She must like you if she offered to help clean."

He snorted and dropped a tattered lampshade into the bag.

"Jim Duncan, inspiring crushes in young women across the Laurel Highlands," Sally said, trying to make him smile.

"Oh please. It was a nice offer from a good person, that's all." He tied up the trash bag. "I don't suppose I can convince you to go join your sister, huh?"

"Not a chance. Hand over a bag."

They worked in silence for a time, methodically emptying the normally-spotless living room of its contents. "What happened?" Sally asked.

Jim told her, from getting home near midnight to when the last technician left at four that morning.

"Is Rizzo okay?"

"He was at the vet's. Otherwise, I have no doubt I'd have found his body." His words were casual; his voice wasn't.

She picked up the tattered magazines. "I'm surprised you didn't leave him there with all the mess."

"I couldn't. An overnight is one thing, but the vet doesn't run a kennel. Outside away from the broken glass is the best I can do." Jim examined the ripped floral couch cushions. Apparently giving them up as a lost cause, he tossed them out to join the trash bags on the lawn.

Sally helped him manhandle the broken couch frame through the front door. "You know, you never struck me as a chintz guy. Leather or suede, sure. Flowers, not so much."

"Tish, my ex, bought the furniture. I didn't get much of a say."

"Why didn't she take it all with her when she left?"

"Said she didn't want anything that reminded her of me."

Ouch. "Then why didn't you give it away and get new stuff?"

"Inertia, I guess. End of a long shift, you don't really care where you park your ass."

Living room mostly clear, they moved on to the kitchen. There was a stack of colorful plastic plates on the counter. Good thing, because the cupboards were bare and not of food. Sally made a mental note to pick up one of those giant stoneware dish sets at Target.

They didn't stop for lunch. Just as she thought it couldn't get worse, she saw the bedroom. "Where did you sleep last night?" Sally asked, piling ruined sheets, blankets, and pillows into the corner. She grabbed one corner of the mattress, springs and stuffing poking through the gashes, and heaved.

"I pushed enough of the trash in the living room aside to throw down a camp roll," Jim said, gripping the other corner of the mattress. "On the count of three. One, two…" They hoisted the mattress onto the windowsill, and he gave it a push to send it down to the ground. Outside, Rizzo yelped.

"You slept on the floor?" Sally stared at him. That, added to what she was sure was a late night, explained the shadows under his eyes and the exhaustion lines around his mouth.

"It wasn't too bad. I considered sleeping in the Jeep, but that's hell on my back."

"Got a place tonight?" Sally said, following him into the kitchen. "You can crash on my couch if you want."

"Thanks, but not necessary. A couple of the guys at the barracks offered to let me stay with them, but Marge is loaning me an air mattress. Without furniture, I'll have plenty of space for it," he said, opening the fridge. "Other neighbors have chipped in with plates and stuff. How about we take a break and order a pizza? Want a beer?" He turned, a bottle of dark beer in one hand, a lager in the other.

"Got any red wine?"

"Fresh out of wine," he said. "I can give you water or Coke."

Sally reached for the lager. "This'll be fine. Load up the meat on that pizza, though."

Jim kicked the fridge door shut. "I knew there was something I liked about you."

⁂

Thirty minutes later, they were sitting on the back porch, fresh pizza between them. Duncan declined Sally's offer to split the cost. "Payment for cleaning services," he told her. Despite saying she wasn't a big beer drinker, she had accepted the offer of a second. Rizzo sat a few feet away, quiet but on the lookout for dropped food. The sun was out, it wasn't ridiculously warm, and a soft breeze tousled some of Sally's hair that had escaped her ponytail. Why couldn't they get together like this under so-called normal circumstances? "Thanks for the help."

"Did you really think you could chase me away?" Sally shook her head and grabbed a third slice. Apparently unable to resist Rizzo's patented guilt-inducing stare, she held out a piece of pepperoni. Rizzo padded over and took it from her fingers with a delicacy he didn't normally show.

"He just pegged you for a sucker, you know."

"Oh well. Was anything stolen?"

"I'm pretty sure the purpose here was intimidation, not theft."

"Trafford?"

He wiped his hands on his jeans. "If not Trafford, someone associated with him, acting on his orders. Still haven't seen or spoken to him, but someone must have mentioned me. I haven't bothered to be subtle."

Sally finished her slice as she mulled over his words. She handed her pizza crust to Rizzo, lost in thought. "Alex Costanzo," she said.

"What about him?"

"You went to talk to him to try and find Trafford." Duncan nodded and Sally continued. "He could be the snitch. I think you're right about the warrant in the Trafford case from last fall. It would fit with everything else I've found or suspected." She filled him in on her foray into Costanzo's office, including the notes in his day planner.

Duncan closed his eyes and did a quick count to ten. "I can't believe you did that."

"I didn't mean to. He wasn't there and the calendar was open on his desk. It wasn't like it was breaking and entering."

"It's not proof of wrongdoing."

"It's really close. All those stars? Something important was going on, at least something important to Alex. He and Trafford want you off the trail. Obviously, they think this will do it."

"Then they don't know me very well." Duncan paused. "Something important could be his mother's birthday."

Her stare said volumes. "You don't believe that any more than I do. The same night and time Colin was killed? Way too much of a coincidence."

No, he didn't believe it. "What if someone saw you? You might have a target on your back if he finds out you were in his office alone."

"Like you don't."

"I wear Kevlar as part of my job."

"I spoke to the receptionist very briefly, and although one of the secretaries saw me, I managed to put her off. At least I'm pretty sure I did. It's not unheard of for someone in my office to go see an ADA. Besides, I very much doubt Alex would get one of his expensive suits dirty trying to intimidate me. It's not his style."

"You just said he was in business with Trafford. Look around. If Aaron Trafford would do this to me, an armed officer of the law, he'd have no problem paying you a visit." He leaned against one of the porch posts. "By the way, who is this Tyra you mentioned?"

"Not his girlfriend, she made that very clear. I saw her with Alex the other night. She's all over that calendar I picked up from his desk." She clapped her hand over her mouth.

"The what you picked up where? I thought you just looked at it."

Her cheeks turned a deep pink. "It was, um, kind of unintended." She told him about getting caught and how she'd taken the Moleskine planner. "As long as I get it back early on Monday, he'll never know I had it."

"You'd damn well better. It could cost you your career. And if Costanzo finds out you were rifling his desk..."

"I know, I know." She refused to look at him, a sure sign she knew she was on thin ice. After a moment, she faced him again and said, "So anyway, Tyra. Based on nothing except my observations, I'm guessing she was hired company. I've seen the same outfits and attitudes on prostitution defendants in court. Based on the calendar entries I'd say Alex was a repeat customer."

Duncan frowned. McAllister could make jokes about jilted lovers and Duncan was the first to admit his dating life had been on the quiet side since Tish left, but what Sally was saying made no sense. "I haven't had a lot to do with Costanzo, but isn't he good looking? Relatively young, straight, solid job, money in the bank. Shouldn't he be able to get a date?"

"You forgot complete asshole." She smirked. "But yes. I would expect that a man of his standing should not have to pay for sex. I'll look into it Monday. Right after I talk to Bryan about the whole Colin-Alex scheme and my suspicions about Trafford." She sobered and stared at Rizzo, who was nosing around the lawn looking for more pizza scraps. "I can't wrap my mind around it, the whole bribery thing. Why? At least Colin was trying to get money because of his mother. Alex…he's just a greedy son-of-a-bitch."

"What's the saying, absolute power corrupts absolutely?"

"More like the love of money is the root of all evil. Anyway. Sucky doesn't even come close to describing the situation, but at least we can start to clean it up."

Duncan rolled the bottle between his hands. "Watch your back."

Sally threw him a quizzical look over her drink.

"If you're right and Trafford is Costanzo's hired help, the next person they'll be gunning for is you."

"I'll be fine. I don't think that secretary is going to say anything. If she does, I'll come up with a story."

"She doesn't have to. The minute you start an ethics investigation, you become a threat. How much do you know? If Costanzo is as cutthroat as you think, he'll be looking to shut you up. Add in whatever is going on with this alleged hooker, who has also seen you, and you are definitely Alex Costanzo's worst nightmare." Maybe he should reconsider that offer to sleep at Sally's apartment. Not for his comfort, but her safety.

"You've made your point. I'll be okay. Well, at least I'll be careful." She picked up the empty pizza box and headed inside.

He followed and tossed the bottles into the recycling. "You've opened Pandora's box with this one, Sally."

She faced him. "Are you suggesting I should have left it alone?"

"No. Just making you aware of the reality. I'm not sure you're used to this. My job is supposed to be dangerous. Yours? Not so much." He held her gaze. Her green eyes were dark, devoid of their usual spark of mischief.

"Then help me out. You take care of Trafford. I'll deal with Alex Costanzo and his mess. Deal?"

She wasn't going to back down. He knew she was determined, but this felt excessive. She was, however, asking for his help. He sensed it would be better if he gave it to her. "Deal."

CHAPTER 22

That morning, Duncan had been sure it would take him all weekend to put his house back in order. With Sally's help, the cleanup was mostly complete by dinner. They were both covered in black fingerprint powder and exhausted, but the house was safe for Rizzo, who obviously found the lack of furniture acceptable considering all the jumping and racing he did once Duncan let the dog inside.

"I'm so tempted to throw his ball for him," Sally said, grinning as Rizzo ran circles around her then raced off.

"Yeah, don't. Fewer bad habits to break. Look, I owe you. How about we go out and get dinner? Not just pizza. My treat."

"I would love to." Sally picked up her purse. "But I'm pretty sure any restaurant worth anything would throw me out in a heartbeat. You can take a shower and change. I can't. But I will definitely take a rain check for a night at River's Edge."

"Count on it."

She kissed his cheek, then headed for the door. "I'll let you know how things go with the Alex and Colin situation."

Duncan caught her on the front porch. "Sally, I was serious. Be careful."

"I'm not the one chasing a drug dealer and potential hired gun." She squeezed his forearm. "I promise." The arrival of another car caught her attention. "Looks like you have company. I'll see you." She got into her Camry and pulled out, waving to McAllister, the new arrival, as she went.

McAllister strolled up to the porch. "Did I interrupt something?"

Duncan jammed his hands in the back pockets of his jeans. "She came to help me clean the place. What are you up to?"

"Who says I'm up to anything? What if I just wanted to check on my FTO?"

He raised an eyebrow.

McAllister toyed with her sunglasses. "I know you told me to take the day off. I played a hunch and went back to The Beer House."

"You did what?" She'd gone alone? Was she crazy? He stepped off the porch.

"Now, Boss." She held up her hands. "It's the middle of the day. What could happen?"

Nothing but trouble, that's what could happen. First Sally, now McAllister. What made otherwise rational women take risks like that?

"Anyway, Tank remembered me so I think he was looking out for me. Turns out my timing was perfect. Guess who I saw?"

By her triumphant grin, Duncan didn't have to guess. "Trafford."

"In the flesh. He's here. He's definitely in Confluence."

"Did you talk to him?"

"Nuh-uh. Saw him in the back of the bar and decided to come get you. I don't think he saw me, either." She elbowed him. "Wanna take a field trip?"

"You are way too perky about this. Let me get my keys and my .45. I'll drive."

Duncan wasn't thrilled that his trainee had gone off on her own, but he had to admit the excitement of finally locating Trafford edged out his disapproval.

🌾🌾🌾

As usual, the parking lot of The Beer House was crowded with older, well-worn vehicles. He parked his Jeep at the edge of the lot and checked to make sure his .45 was ready if needed. "You brought your own firearm?"

McAllister gave him a blank look.

"Oh, for the love of…you and I are going to have a talk about the whole be prepared notion. It's not just for Scouts, you know." He tucked the .45 back in its holster. "For the time being, stay close. If anything happens, I want you to get the hell out."

"But Boss—"

"But nothing." She was too new to understand the gravity of what could happen. Now wasn't the time to explain. He didn't want Trafford to come out and find them arguing. "If you don't think every person in there can wield a broken bottle with the same skill you have with a Sig, think again. You found him. Good job. Now let me take over. Only because I'm armed and you aren't."

She glared a moment, then sighed. "Guess I need to get an off-duty weapon, huh?"

"Yes. And another thing."

"Keep my mouth shut?"

"Don't antagonize him. You aren't in uniform and you aren't armed. This is not a man who will respond well to verbal threats."

"I've never directly threatened anyone."

"He won't respond well to implied threats, either." She was so new. But at least she'd been smart enough come to him before she confronted Trafford. Duncan headed inside. He paused at the bar, allowing his eyes to adjust to the dim light after the outside brightness. He glanced at Tank. The barman gave a tiny nod and looked toward the back corner. Someone had sprung Monahan, the drug mule. He and another skinny white guy were in the back with a third man. Duncan recognized the skinny guy from his mug shot: the Wharton Furnace homeowner, Devin Carrington. He could also see the tattoos on the bulky third member of the trio from across the room.

Aaron Trafford.

For a brief moment, Duncan considered going outside, phoning for an on-duty trooper, and letting them handle the situation. Then he thought being in civvies might be an advantage. He'd certainly stand out less; his target wouldn't run from him immediately. McAllister not so much. There were few women in The Beer House and none of them as squeaky-clean as the new trooper. Maybe Duncan could pass her off as a sister or girlfriend if necessary. For at least a little while. He snaked his way through the tables. Patrons barely glanced at him, all eyes on McAllister. It was like a bunch of sharks smelling a wounded seal.

"Greetings," Duncan said, coming up to the corner table. The weight of the .45 was a comforting presence at the small of his back.

"What do you want?" Carrington said, chin jutting.

Recognition dawned in Monahan's eyes and he kicked his buddy. "Dude, those are the cops who pulled me over," he said in a not-quite undertone.

Carrington's eyes widened, but Duncan focused mainly on Trafford. The drug dealer didn't twitch, simply sat back, a sardonic smile on his face. "Greetings," he said. He did a better job controlling his voice, a combination of gravel and iron, than his compatriot. "Is there something we can do for you?"

"We've been looking for you, Mr. Trafford," Duncan said, his gaze locked with Trafford's insolent stare. "We have a few questions."

"Who's we?"

"The state police."

"Oh? About what?"

"We shut down a meth lab not that long ago. I'm sure you know that."

"You don't say. Damn. I leave for a while and the county goes to the dogs."

McAllister spoke up, her voice even, hands at her side. "It was in your grandmother's house."

Trafford's gaze flickered to her then back to Duncan. "Grandma M isn't all that well. I've been thinking of selling that place for her. Should have done it, I guess. You know who trashed her home?"

"We have a pretty good idea," McAllister said.

The words pulled Trafford's attention to her. "Guess you all better get on that, then."

Duncan's attention never left Trafford's face. The intake of breath told him McAllister was about to respond, and he cut her off. "Oh, we're giving the matter our full attention. Tell me, Mr. Trafford. Where have you been for the last twelve months?"

"Here and there."

"And what have you been up to?"

Trafford smirked. "This and that."

Duncan inwardly cursed. The man wasn't going to give them anything. And he knew the cops had nothing concrete to hang on him. Not yet.

"Shame you don't want to talk to us," McAllister said. "Guess we'll just have to talk to your grandma again."

Trafford's chair legs banged on the floor as he sat forward. "You leave her out of it," he said, voice a snarl.

"We'd like to," Duncan said. "But if you can't help us, we may not have any other choice. You sure you don't want to tell us anything? We've already busted your buddy Monahan there for possession."

Trafford was silent. His nostrils flared a bit as he exhaled, but he was otherwise motionless.

"That's too bad. Are you staying with Mr. Carrington? We might have more questions for you as the investigation progresses," Duncan said.

No response.

"Guess we'll talk to you later, then. As I said, don't worry about your grandmother's house. The state police have made it their top priority. Come on, Trooper McAllister." Duncan jerked his head toward the door.

"Mr. Duncan," Trafford called. "Stay safe. Man with a nice house and a sweet dog should be careful." He turned to his companions and they all laughed.

McAllister headed out and Duncan followed, hand ready to snatch the .45 out of its holster, careful to position himself so he could watch the corner table until they were almost out of the bar. In the parking lot, he let out an explosive breath.

McAllister faced him. "Did he just admit to vandalizing your house?"

"Never get it to stick in court. But as far as I'm concerned, yeah, he did." Duncan fingered his keys. "There's only one reason for him to target me."

"We're right about the drugs."

"Yes." Duncan slid into the Jeep.

"So…I did good, right? Finding Trafford? Keeping my cool in there?" Her blue eyes begged for his approval.

"Yes, you did. Now do me a favor."

"What's that?"

"Don't ever freaking do it that way again."

CHAPTER 23

Sunday morning, Sally woke up with the same question on her mind as she'd had when she went to bed: what was up between Alex and Colin, and how did Trafford come into the picture?

After church, Sally sat down with Colin's list again. The Trafford trial. Everything fell apart because the search warrant was bad—except Jim said the trooper who'd served it would never have made that kind of mistake. Warrants were held by the district attorney and only given to the defense at the time of trial, during the discovery process. Alex was an arrogant ass, but he wasn't a moron. That trial had been the kind of high profile case he would want to shine at. He would have made sure all his legal ducks were in a row.

A case of pseudoephedrine seized, but not listed on the warrant or associated affidavit. A paralegal fresh out of college would have seen that omission. Why had Alex, an experienced prosecutor with dozens of trials under his belt, proceeded with such a problematic piece of documentation?

That was easy: he wouldn't, which meant he knew the warrant didn't cover everything that had been seized and went ahead anyway, Sally could come up with only one logical explanation: he didn't care. Why didn't he care? Because he'd shared in the payoff listed in Colin's notebook. And if Alex had shared one, he'd most likely shared them all.

Then again, maybe she was moving too fast. There were other people in the DA's office who could have switched it out. Somebody who wanted Alex to look incompetent, maybe even wind up in front of a review board. It could be someone he wronged or someone who coveted his position. She could sit and ponder it, or she could confront him and ask. Worst case, he'd continue to lie and she'd be no wiser than she was.

No. Worst case is that he'd be spooked and sic his attack dog, Trafford, on her the same way he'd taken care of Colin.

Or she could try and find some more evidence. Something she'd see for herself. De'Shawn Thomas said he'd bought marijuana from one of Trafford's dealers and that Trafford had shown up on the street corner collecting money. Chances were good he'd come back and where Trafford was, so was an opportunity to learn something that definitely tied him to Alex.

What would be perfect is if someone had seen them. Someone from the DA's office who'd been around at the time of the first trial. Sally tried to think of everybody currently in the office. Most were either new or people who wouldn't have worked the kind of high-profile trial a meth dealer would be. It would have to be someone Alex trusted not to screw it up, someone who would give the impression the DA had tried his best.

There'd been a paralegal, one Alex often worked with. Sally's fuzzy mental image sharpened. Short red hair, cheerful blue eyes, and a penchant for skirts just barely acceptable for the dignity of the district attorney. Kelly Martin. Also one of Sally's favorite paralegals, Kelly had moved last winter, somewhere south. A huge loss for the office, as far as Sally was concerned. Kelly knew more about the Pennsylvania criminal code than most attorneys.

Sally pulled up the online white pages and searched. Kelly's mother was still in Uniontown. Sally dialed, but got an answering machine. She left a message identifying herself and saying only that it was urgent she talk to Kelly. If Mrs. Martin would call with contact information, Sally would appreciate it.

What else? She couldn't just wait for Kelly to call, if she ever did. She could spy on that street corner, but the idea of going alone gave her the creeps. Going with Jim would be much better, if she could convince him it was a good idea. Sunday was his day off. It was sunny and warm, the kind of day where he'd normally be out at the gorge, fishing. But maybe he was still cleaning up after the break-in. She didn't want to call. He'd try and talk her out of her plan. Face-to-face, she'd have more luck convincing him to go along with her.

She drove out to Confluence under sunny, bright blue skies dotted with puffy white clouds. The area was hitting peak leaf season. People would be flocking to the area to sight-see. Jim would be home. He had to be.

He was. She pulled in behind the Jeep and Rizzo ran out from behind the house. "Hey there," she said, kneeling to run her hands through the dog's luxurious fur and let him slobber over her face. "Where's the big guy, huh?"

Jim came around the corner. "Right here. I wondered what the doofus was running after. Two days in a row? I'm touched, but there really isn't much to do. I'm breaking up stuff for the trash."

"I'm not here to help this time." She stood and wiped her face on her sleeve. "I need you to help me."

"Sure thing. What is it?"

"Come on a stakeout with me."

Jim stared at her for what felt like forever. "Sorry, what was that?" he finally asked. "I can't have heard you right. It sounded like you were asking me to accompany you on a stakeout."

"I did. Now, hear me out before you get all…whatever." She took a deep breath. "Colin and Alex were running some kind of racket and Colin was trying to come clean. You agree with me on that?"

"I do."

"Okay. Here's what I'm thinking. Colin was a liability. Isn't that the word you used? That gives Alex a much bigger motive for murder than De'Shawn Thomas. Alex has already extorted money from Trafford. What if Alex either paid or blackmailed Trafford into taking care of Colin?"

Jim didn't move. "Go on."

"I need to put the two of them together. Alex and Trafford. At least, I have to get enough probable cause that Detective Killian will consider another suspect. Because right now, he's pretty content to leave things as they are. If De'Shawn Thomas shot Colin, I'll eat Rizzo's dog food."

"Sometimes I feed Rizzo sirloin."

She crossed her arms and gave him her best defense-attorney "I don't buy that" look.

"If I'm following, you think you can find…something on a stakeout. Question: who's to say Costanzo didn't pull the trigger? Why does he need Trafford?"

"Because it's out of character. Alex doesn't get his hands dirty, but he's not above getting someone else to do it. You can't deny Trafford makes a better hit man than Thomas."

Jim scratched his cheek. "When and where were you planning on doing this?"

"Tonight at a known drug corner in Uniontown." She told him about Trafford's previous presence there.

"What do you think you're going to see?"

"I don't know. Maybe nothing. But it's the best idea I have."

"It's a lousy idea. I can think of a dozen things that could go wrong and that's before I give it serious thought." He clapped his hands to call Rizzo, but the dog flopped at Sally's feet and didn't budge. "You're going to turn everything over to the ethics folks. What more do you want?"

"Something that links Trafford and or Alex to Colin's death. I know, the ethics investigation will end the racketeering and Alex's legal career, but it won't necessarily prove he killed, or more likely conspired to kill, Colin."

"What if Costanzo or Trafford see you? Remember that target I talked about? If it isn't on you already, this will do it. And if it is there, it'll get bigger."

She bit her lip. "Jim, I appreciate your concern, but let me be perfectly clear. I'm going out tonight with or without you. I'd much rather the former."

"It's that important?"

"I promised Deborah Rafferty I'd get justice for her son. It would be a lot easier if you'd help me."

"What makes you so sure you're right?"

There was no way to explain. Nobody had ever questioned Jim's abilities on the job, Sally was sure of it. He'd never had to stand in front of men and women with more experience and justify himself, knowing he was right but unable to overcome their attitudes—attitudes born of years in the courtroom. He hadn't had to fight for the legitimacy of his position. "I just do."

The pause felt like it went on forever. Jim finally spoke. "Fine. Someone needs to keep your ass out of trouble." He looked again at Rizzo.

Sally glanced down. The dog was perfectly happy, tongue lolling out and leaning against her legs.

"Good thing Rizzo and I like you. Come pick me up at ten. We'll use your car, less noticeable. Come on, doofus." Jim walked back to the house, mumbling under his breath. Rizzo licked Sally's hand, then jumped up and raced after his owner.

Sally checked her watch. It was about four. Time enough to go home, eat, put on some comfortable clothes, and drive back. It had the makings of a long night.

☙☙☙

Duncan prepped for the evening by brewing a pot of coffee and filling two stainless steel travel mugs to the brim. They could be there a while and the night's forecast was calling for cooler temps. He grabbed a pair of binoculars and considered bringing a camera, but Sally could handle that. She'd have her phone. The less stuff to cart around the better.

How had he gotten into this? Easy. Sally was obstinate. Impetuous. She'd flat-out said if he didn't go with her, she would stake out some random Uniontown corner by herself. A corner where she hoped to see a man who might be a killer and had proven he wasn't above violence.

Eventually, the investigation into Costanzo and Rafferty's extortion activities would connect to Rafferty's homicide. If the connection existed. That wasn't fast enough for Sally. As usual, she wanted answers five minutes ago. Although this time was different. She pushed harder, clung to her position tighter. Similar to Aislyn McAllister, the reason had to lie in Sally's past experience, but for the life of him he couldn't think what. And as with McAllister, or with a suspect, the harder he pushed, the more Sally would dig in her heels and refuse to explain. He needed to draw her out and that would take time.

Damn it.

The last thing he did was slip his .45 into a holster covered by his jacket. Better safe than sorry. With luck he wouldn't need it.

She pulled into the driveway slightly before ten. "I went past the corner on my way here. No one's there yet. Well, no one who looked like Trafford."

"I'm not surprised. People like Trafford don't come out until they're pretty sure no one's around to catch them. You said there's a convenience store on this corner?"

"Uh-huh." She pulled out and crossed the bridge over the Casselman.

"Someone still might do a snack run for something. Grab milk for tomorrow's breakfast. Trafford'll want to cut the chances he'll be interrupted."

She glanced at the travel mugs. "What's that? I mean, I can smell the coffee, but why?"

"I debated, but my need for caffeine outweighed the inconvenience of having to answer a call of nature. Of course, we could take care of it the same way we would on a real stakeout."

"If you think I'm peeing into a bottle, you're crazy."

Once they reached Uniontown, he directed Sally to ease to the curb a block away from the corner.

"Still no Trafford," she said, chewing her lip.

"Still early. Relax." He laid the binoculars on his lap and settled in to wait.

The biggest risk was someone would notice them. But as Duncan expected, hardly any passers-by even glanced at the Camry. And those were few and far between. Most businesses were locked up and he'd have to travel a couple blocks in any direction to reach a residential area.

The first figures showed up to loiter on the corner shortly after midnight. Duncan poked Sally in the arm. "Show time." He looked through the binoculars. One by one, men appeared on the corner. Black, white, Hispanic, but no Trafford.

Sally leaned forward and gripped the steering wheel. "There." She pointed at another man who had just stepped into the pool of light. "Is that him?"

"Fits the general description," Duncan said, adjusting the binoculars. "I can't see his tattoos, but I'm damn sure not going to go up and ask."

"Who's he talking to? I wish I had binoculars."

Duncan handed her his set. "Probably his drug buddies."

Sally twiddled the focus dial. "I wonder what they're talking about."

Duncan shrugged and cracked the window. "Whatever drug dealers talk about at night under streetlights," he said. "The next deal, where they're going to cook now that the house is out of service. Whatever it is, it doesn't look like any transactions are taking place."

They sat in silence for a while, watching the huddled group of figures. Suddenly, Sally sat up straight. "Holy shit, he's here."

Duncan looked down the street. Another person had joined the group, wearing a trench coat with the collar turned up to obscure his face.

"That's Alex Costanzo, I'm sure of it," Sally said. "I didn't expect him to show. He and Mr. Trafford look pretty friendly, don't you think?"

Duncan watched Trafford and the man Sally identified as Costanzo exchange words. "If you define 'friendly' as 'not shooting each other,' then yeah, they're friendly."

"I wish we could shake them down or something."

"We're here to observe, remember?"

The sound of shouting reached them, but the words were unclear. The coat collar fell down, revealing Costanzo's face. He pushed Trafford roughly a couple times and jabbed a finger at him. Trafford tried to shove back, but Costanzo stepped aside and Trafford stumbled past him.

Costanzo smoothed his hair, pointed again, and smiled. The rest of the crowd had stepped back. "See that you do," Costanzo said, the words audible now that silence had come over the street.

Costanzo straightened his coat and walked away from the group, down the street toward the parked Camry.

"Shit," Duncan said. "He's going to see us sitting here. If we pull away now, it'll be suspicious."

Sally twisted toward him. "Kiss me."

Not what he expected to hear. "Wha—"

Before the word could leave his mouth, Sally grabbed a fistful of his shirt and pulled him close, planting her mouth on his. Her lips were warm and soft. She smelled of cinnamon, coffee, and fresh baked goods.

As suddenly as she'd started, she broke away. "He's gone." She sat back in her seat and brushed her hair out of her face.

Duncan was speechless for a moment. "That was all you could think of?" he asked as he came back to the present.

Sally flipped the visor down to peer into the mirror. She pulled a lipstick from her purse. "You said it yourself: if we pulled away, we'd have been noticed. But no one pays attention to a couple making out in a car. Looking at that kind of display makes people uncomfortable." She shot him a sideways glance. "Why Trooper Duncan, I do believe you're blushing. Did I startle you?"

"Shit. I'm not blushing. Just…give me some warning next time."

Sally laughed. "Where's the fun in that?" she asked. "Seeing him really was a surprise, though. I hoped to get some information I could work with, but we hit the mother lode."

"You didn't expect to see who? Costanzo? Isn't that why we're here?"

"Yes, but it's still kind of jarring. It's a street corner at night. What is a county prosecutor doing hanging out with drug dealers on a Uniontown corner?" Sally dropped the lipstick back in her purse.

"When I talked to Costanzo, he said he hadn't seen Trafford since the trial." He forced his brain to think of what they'd learned, and not be distracted by Sally's lips or her vanilla-cinnamon scent. "This means you're right and Costanzo could have hired Trafford to kill your buddy before he ruined everything."

She chewed a fingernail. "They argued about something. 'See that you do,' he said. What should Trafford do?"

"Keep his mouth shut? Pay more money? I can think of several possibilities."

"Indeed." She put the Camry in drive and pulled away.

"So this is the end of it," Duncan said. "Talk to Gerrity in the morning, let Killian know you saw Costanzo and Trafford—"

Sally shot him a look. "At an illegal stakeout?"

"Despite my misgivings about this whole affair, it's a public corner and you have the right to sit there and observe. No expectation of privacy. It should be enough to get Killian to at least entertain other ideas."

Her shoulders twitched in what might be a shrug. In that instant, Duncan knew Sally wouldn't let go of her investigation until she had proof positive of Trafford's guilt.

Headstrong. Impetuous. Damn it.

CHAPTER 24

The three names continuously ran through Sally's head as she arrived at work Monday morning. Alex and Colin, the conspirators. Trafford, the hired muscle when Colin wanted out of the game. It made perfect sense.

"You did what?" Bryan asked when she presented herself in his office and recapped her Sunday night activities.

"I had a friend with me."

"Oh, dear God, Sally." He dropped his glasses on his desk. "Do I know this friend?"

"Um." Would the nighttime surveillance get Jim in trouble? He'd agreed to go, but Sally was uncertain he'd be thrilled about her telling Bryan. "Yes."

Bryan eyed her, but said nothing.

"Don't worry, my friend was armed in case it all went sideways." She moved a pile of paper and sat down. "Don't you see? Colin wasn't killed by some low-level druggie. It was Alex, protecting his ass. He must have hired or otherwise gotten Trafford to do the dirty work." She drummed her fingers on his desk. "What about the CCTV footage? Are you sure we can't see it?"

"Absolutely." He picked up his glasses. "Close the door."

She did, and returned to her chair.

"I wish you'd drop this." Bryan leaned forward, voice low. "If you're right, and Alex had Colin killed to protect himself, what'll he do to you?"

"Tell me something." She crossed her arms. "If the situation were different, would you be telling Colin this?"

"Yes. Because it's not about you being a woman, it's about you being a lawyer. You're not a death investigator. Call Killian and let the system work."

"How long will that take? We need to move on this now. Alex could easily leave and Trafford might disappear again."

Bryan put on his glasses. "The last thing I want is to be down two assistant public defenders. For the last time. Call the police. Tell them what you saw. After that, I'm sure you have work on your desk. Work associated with your job. Go do it. End of discussion."

Sally knew a dismissal when she heard it. When she reached her office, she dutifully called the Uniontown police, but Killian was unavailable. She left a message. "It's very important he get that as soon as possible."

"I'll see to it, ma'am."

She hung up and thought. Mrs. Martin hadn't called and neither had her daughter. Sally tried the number again. No answer. If the greeting hadn't said it was the Martin residence, Sally would have thought the number wasn't good any longer. She left another message.

Maybe she didn't need the CCTV or to talk to Kelly. She knew the name of the cleaning company the county contracted. How hard could it be to get a list of their employees, or even the name of the person who'd been working Sunday night? That might give her the information she needed. She looked up the company's phone number and dialed. After she identified herself, she said, "I need to speak with HR." There was a pause while the receptionist made the connection. Sally repeated her introduction. "I need the names and phone numbers of your weekend employees. It's for a case I'm working." Not her case, but it was a case.

"I'm sorry, I can't provide that information without proper authorization," the woman said.

"It's very important. It might mean a man's life."

"That's terrible, but as a lawyer you should know the rules. I cannot provide that information without a warrant."

Sally hung up. Damn it all. There had to be a way to get the names without breaking the law or ethics. She went to the front of the office. "Doris, question for you."

"What is it?" the older woman asked, not stopping her filing.

"Do you know anyone from the cleaning company who works nights? Specifically who might work a weekend?"

"Like Sunday?" Doris turned around. "As in the Sunday Colin was killed?" The gaze over her bifocals was like Superman's X-ray vision.

"Well, um, yeah. Sunday is the weekend."

"I overheard you and Bryan a little bit ago. I heard him tell you to leave this alone and I can't say I disagree with him."

"Oh come on, Doris." Sally took a step closer. "Tell me you don't want to find out who's responsible for murder in this office. What I really want is the CCTV footage from that night. I can't get that. But I know there was a guy here. If you have a name, I'd appreciate you giving it to me. Colin wasn't your favorite person on the planet, but think of it as doing him a favor. Better yet, a favor for me."

Doris closed her eyes and her lips moved. Prayer? Cussing? She opened her eyes, crossed to her desk, and wrote down some names. "I have no idea who was here. But I see one of these three people most of the time on Friday nights when I leave. Maybe one of them can help."

"Doris, you're gold. Thank you." Sally took the paper and returned to her office. She had a few cases to deal with first. After that, if she could get a little help from the internet, she'd have contact information for the three names in no time.

※ ※ ※

The discovery of Costanzo and Trafford's familiarity changed everything as far as Duncan was concerned. It brought a new angle to the drug investigation. If there was some kind of relationship, even one that wasn't entirely cordial, between the dealer and the ADA, there was little wonder Trafford had returned to Fayette County.

It also opened up new possibilities in Rafferty's murder. Duncan was less positive that the Costanzo-Trafford duo was responsible. Sally was so convinced of her solution she'd fit any fact to her ideas, instead of the other way around. But the idea was an avenue that needed to be explored. If Killian wouldn't listen to Sally, maybe he'd listen to Duncan.

It was essential he interview Costanzo again. This time, evasive answers wouldn't fly. Good thing they worked second shift and could corner him the minute he left work. Get his undivided attention.

"About Aaron Trafford," McAllister said as they grabbed their patrol car for the shift. "You think he's living with Carrington at the Wharton Furnace house?"

"I'd bet my pension on it. We've got time before we can interview Costanzo. Let's go see if we can get ourselves an invite inside that house. Keep your eyes open for anything that'll let us get a search warrant."

They were halfway to Wharton Furnace Road when a call came over the radio. "Possible fatality at the Twin Oaks Motel. Any troopers in the area, please respond."

Duncan wanted to pass the call off to someone else, but dead bodies took precedence. The Twin Oaks, located approximately ten miles northwest of Uniontown, was best known for its rooms-by-the-hour business and was relatively close. It was even sort of on the way to their destination. It was almost certainly a drug overdose. He keyed the radio mic, giving his information and McAllister's. Then he flipped on his lights and siren, and sped toward the motel.

The day was Indian-summer warm, but heavy clouds put the parking lot into shade. The Twin Oaks looked exactly like what it was: a shabby place that catered to guests looking for anonymity. It wasn't on the way to any of the area's tourist spots, such as Ft. Necessity or Fallingwater. You didn't just happen upon the Twin Oaks, which made it perfect for its purpose. Two wings of rooms, white exterior streaked with grime, windows covered by polyester curtains, and faded blue doors with tarnished bronze numbers.

The door to Unit 115 was open and the housekeeping cart was outside. Parked in front was a tan sedan, one of those cars no one ever noticed because of the common make and bland color. Like Sally's Camry. A middle-aged man and a woman in a housekeeping uniform stood in the parking lot, the woman's face pale but not as paper-white as the man's.

"What are we likely to see here?" McAllister asked. She looked a little green.

"Depends on what's inside. Heart attack, pretty clean. Violent death, could be messy," Duncan said. "If you start feeling nauseous or light-headed, go outside. Don't hurl on the scene. First dead body can be rough." He waved at the two employees. "Tell you what, you start with them. I'll check what's in the room."

What was in the room was a lot of early 80s style furnishings on a blue industrial carpet that had to have been picked for ease of cleaning. Duncan's gaze took in the deceased's naked body lying on its back on the bed, eyes wide and unseeing. Alex Costanzo. Shit. What was he doing at the Twin Oaks? Okay, Duncan knew what he'd been doing, but why?

Blood oozed from multiple holes in Costanzo's chest. It soaked the sheets on the bed, the air heavy with the coppery scent of blood overlaid with a sweet smell of perfume, the beginning of decay, and the musk of sex. His clothes were piled on a chair. A box of condoms was on the cheap pressboard nightstand, a couple of empty wrappers beside it. A used rubber was on the floor. A second one hadn't been removed from the victim's genitalia. No cell phone in sight. No wallet.

Duncan didn't need to get close to know Costanzo was dead. "Son of a bitch," he said. The last person in the Rafferty-Costanzo-Trafford triangle. At least, the last person who might talk to the authorities. Sally's idea was looking better and better. And now, unless Carrington or Monahan cracked or Duncan could get inside that house on Wharton Furnace, the investigation into Trafford would stall.

First things first. He pulled a pair of nitrile gloves from his belt.

The light was on in the bathroom. The plastic shower curtain was streaked with water and the thin blue towels were damp. Several long, dark hairs curled around the drain. No personal items brought from the outside, but the motel-supplied bottles of shampoo and conditioner were half empty and the soap was unwrapped, wet, and in the shower niche.

He'd seen enough for the moment. One actor, possibly more. Considering the victim, and what Duncan and Sally now suspected Costanzo had been involved in, likely more.

Once outside, he stripped off the gloves and keyed his radio. "This is Duncan. I need the coroner, an ambulance, and a forensic team at the Twin Oaks." He joined McAllister and the two civilians. "Who called the police?"

The woman held up her hand. Her skin was the color of curdled milk. "He's dead, isn't he? He has to be, it looks like a bad slasher movie." Her voice was calm, but a thin calm that could crack at any moment.

"This is Janelle Murray, she's one of the motel's employees," McAllister said, pointing at the woman. "Carl Hopfelder. He's the Twin Oaks' manager."

"What's your job here?" He looked at Murray. Beside him, McAllister continued to take notes.

"Housekeeping," Murray said. "Carl told me room 115 was ready for clean up."

"It was an hourly rental," Hopfelder said. "I usually give it thirty minutes before sending the cleaning crew in."

"Sir, why don't you go with Trooper McAllister and give your statement." He looked at McAllister. "Take him over by the car."

She beckoned to the manager, who followed her.

Duncan took enough time to watch McAllister begin her interview with Hopfelder. He took out his own notebook. "Ms. Murray. Do you need to sit down? Can you tell me what happened when you went in to clean up the room?"

She gave a shaky nod. "I'm okay. When I opened the door, the room kind of stunk. Not that unusual because it always stinks after…"

"Sex." Duncan finished the sentence.

Murray swallowed. "This was different, all funky-like. I flipped on the light, and damned if the guy wasn't still there. Naked as anything and all bloody."

"Where was he?"

"On the bed. The covers and sheets were all messed up, and I saw the box of Trojans, so they must have done it. The sex. I realized the funk smell was blood, but not only that."

"What else?" Duncan paused in his note-taking to look at her.

"Really heavy, spicy perfume. The cheap stuff that tries to pretend it's expensive."

"Go on."

"I couldn't move. Then I screamed. Carl said the thirty minutes were up and people should be gone."

"That all? That's a pretty disturbing scene to come across when all you're expecting are dirty bed sheets." He jerked a thumb toward the room.

"You got that right." She shivered in the warm sunlight.

"Are you sure you're okay? I have a blanket in the car. Ambulance is on its way."

"Don't need an ambulance."

"You're shivering. That's the onset of shock." Duncan glanced over at McAllister, who appeared to be doing fine. "I appreciate your help, but if you need to take a break—"

"No." Murray's voice firmed up. "I wanna get this over with. I called to the guy, but he didn't move. I was going to check for a pulse, but," she swallowed again, "didn't seem like the thing to do, you know? I called 911 and told Carl that 115 was messed up."

"Did Mr. Hopfelder see the room or the victim?"

"No. He mighta seen the guy when he checked in, but not like he is now." Murray nodded toward the room, arms clasped around her body.

"Did you touch anything?"

"The door. The light switch. Might have leaned on the doorframe. I didn't look close, you know?"

"I understand." Duncan slipped his notebook into his pocket. "Let's get you that blanket until the EMTs get here. We'll eventually need your fingerprints for elimination purposes. Here's my card if you need to call me later."

Murray took the card and Duncan fetched the blanket from the trunk of the patrol car. She refused to sit in the backseat, preferring to sit at picnic table underneath a shedding maple in front of the motel. McAllister took Murray's place, and Hopfelder joined his employee.

"What did he tell you?" Duncan asked.

"Room 115 was rented for three hours by a Mr. Ralph Commons. Commons paid cash. Unfortunate, but I suppose if you're meeting someone for a quickie you wouldn't want a credit card record."

"I expected no less. Did he see this Mr. Commons?"

"He says no. He's lying. There aren't any other employees in the main office. Hopfelder's scared of something or someone. Plus this Mr. Commons said he was meeting a woman. How would Hopfelder know if he didn't speak to the victim?" She snorted. "How stupid do people think we are?"

If a high-powered county official paid for secrecy, no wonder Hopfelder was acting squirrelly. "Get used to that. People lying. But good thinking. What else?"

McAllister consulted her notes. "That's his car there, the tan one. The woman didn't stop at the office. Mr. Hopfelder figures she knew the room."

"Hopfelder didn't see her arrive or leave?"

"He saw another car pull up about thirty minutes after Commons registered. A woman got out. Hopfelder thinks she was tall, but she was wearing a scarf over her head, giant sunglasses, and an overcoat, so he didn't get a good look at her. He didn't see her leave."

"What kind of car?"

She flipped through the pages. "Dark, two door. Some sort of compact. Hopfelder thinks it could be a Honda or a Hyundai. No clue as to model or year, and he didn't see a plate."

"There are only a few hundred of those around." One day, someone would pull up in a fire-engine red Lamborghini, just to be helpful. He straightened his hat. "I called for the coroner and a team. We keep everyone out until they get here."

"He's dead?" McAllister put her own notebook away.

"Oh, yeah."

"Who is it?"

"Take a look. Remember—"

"Don't puke on the scene." McAllister finished the sentence with a tight smile.

They entered the hotel room. Flies were already gathering on the body.

Next to him, McAllister gagged slightly. "Shit. Is that who I think it is?"

"Yep," he said. "Alex Costanzo."

CHAPTER 25

As the late-afternoon sun washed the gold and red of the trees gracing the edge of the property at the Twin Oaks, people swarmed over the scene. A photographer took pictures from every possible angle while techs dusted fingerprint powder in the room and the rental car. A run of the plates told Duncan it was registered to a small local outfit, where you could still get away with paying cash. The agreement in the glove compartment was in the name of Ralph Commons. The woman at the agency claimed not to have seen her customer. Duncan would see about that.

Members of the forensic team stuck little markers where evidence had been found. Burns worked over the body, whistling.

"Would you please stop?" Duncan closed his eyes and pinched the bridge of his nose. He'd been hoping Costanzo would break open the Trafford investigation. Damn it.

"You know the song. Whistle while you work," Burns said, carefully examining the corpse.

"Don't think this is the work they meant," Duncan said.

Burns didn't turn away from his task, but he did stop whistling. "Why wouldn't a guy like Costanzo, who has to be known throughout the county, go farther away for this kind of assignation? What's that saying about shitting where you eat?"

"If his lady-friend, or whatever you want to call her, was local and unable to get away, he might stay. Maybe he'd rely on his notoriety to keep people quiet." It fit perfectly with Costanzo's personality, arrogance. "What can you tell me?"

"Four gunshots to the chest and one to the groin. Shooter was probably standing in front of him. Within a few feet, but not close enough for powder burns."

"Time of death?"

"I'd say less than three hours. Of course, that's preliminary until—"

"Right, autopsy. Before or after sex?"

"After. There's semen in the condom."

"Was he on the bed when he was shot?"

Burns surveyed the bed, the thin, tacky floral bedspread jumbled under the victim. "Hard to say. He's flat on his back, so he could have been standing at the end of the bed and fallen. But he wasn't shot in the bathroom then dumped on the bed."

"He and the paramour finish having sex. She gets up, he's lying there, she shoots him." Duncan looked around. Cheap paneling, gaudy mirrors, worn carpet, gold-flecked plastic tile in the bathroom. None of it spattered with blood. "Or they're standing at the end of the bed, she shoots him, and he falls over. Either way, she showers to clean herself up, then leaves." He made a mental note to ask about blood in the shower drain.

"Or someone else comes in and shoots him while she's in the bathroom." Burns placed paper bags over Costanzo's hands.

"Skin or blood under the fingernails?" Duncan said, although he suspected what the answer would be.

"Not that I can see. No defensive wounds. That tells me he was caught off guard by a stranger, or he knew the shooter and wasn't expecting trouble." Burns examined Costanzo's head. "No bruising, no contusions on the skull. Just wham, bam, thank you ma'am. All nice and neat."

Duncan pointed to the bloody genitals. "That's not neat."

McAllister came into the room while Duncan and Burns talked. "Do you always joke around at a crime scene?" she asked the deputy coroner.

Burns looked at Duncan. "She's new, isn't she?" He faced McAllister. "Come talk to me in a year. We have to keep our sanity somehow in this business."

"Trooper McAllister, this is deputy coroner Tom Burns. Don't mind him, he's harmless." He turned to her. "Find anything in the car?"

McAllister pointedly turned away from Burns. "Miscellaneous junk. Short brown hairs and cashmere fibers that will probably match the deceased." She jerked her thumb toward an overcoat that was thrown on a chair. "We found his cell phone. Couple of calls this morning. One text after he checked in that only says 115."

"Sending the room number to his lady friend. Is there a name on the text?"

"Just a number."

Duncan tapped his thumbs on his duty belt. "We'll get Costanzo's phone records, trace the number. Anything else?"

"Nothing of note. It'll be up to the lab. You finished in here?"

He glanced at Burns, who nodded. "Almost. Anybody in the surrounding rooms see anything?"

"They're all empty. Manager said most business rolls in after the sun goes down," McAllister said. "Neither of the two outside heard a gunshot. At least not that they can remember or will admit."

Duncan shook his head. No one ever heard or saw anything.

McAllister waved at the deceased. "He get shot before or after?"

"Oh, after," Burns said. "You see—"

"I don't need the play by play." McAllister cut him off. "I'll be outside, see if I can dig up anything else."

Burns turned the body to look for exit wounds. "Speaking of digging, I'll probably be able to dig some bullets out for you for ballistic evidence. I've heard stories about Mr. Costanzo. It'll probably be the last, if not the only, nice thing he did for anyone."

McAllister snorted and walked out.

"Burns?" Duncan turned to his friend.

"What?"

"Not everybody here knows and loves your unique brand of humor. Do me a favor. Shut the hell up."

Burns didn't look offended. "If you insist." He glanced at the door, McAllister visible in the parking lot. "Is she single?"

"Are you eyeing up my trainee at a murder scene?"

"What can I say? I don't get out much and where else am I going to find someone who doesn't think my job is morbid?"

Duncan turned to walk away.

A member of the forensic team approached, holding a small plastic evidence bag. "Trooper, look at this. Shell casings, 9mm. There aren't any holes in the walls, so probably from the bullets in your victim."

"Nine mil, eh?" Duncan took the bag. "Do me a favor. Run ballistics and see if there's a match from this victim to the bullet that was recovered from the Rafferty homicide in Uniontown last week." He handed back the bag.

He headed outside and over toward McAllister, who was surveying the lot. "Sorry about Burns."

"What a jackass," she said. "I don't think he's very serious about his job."

"His mouth often gets the better of him, but he's good. No one I'd rather work a scene with. He's right though. To work a job like ours for any length of time, you have to develop a mental defense."

"You don't joke like that."

"Everybody is different."

"If you say so." McAllister's voice was doubtful. "Shot through the groin, huh?"

"Yeah." His insides tingled just thinking about it. "They've found nine mil shell casings."

"Same caliber as the gun that killed Rafferty. But..."

"But what?"

"I don't know. This one feels different. Does that make sense?"

A good sign. "Yes, it does. Be interesting to see if ballistics can make a match." He paused. "Follow up with the forensic team, make sure they've taken as many pictures as possible."

She waved toward the room. "I guess that's what you call ending with a bang."

He stared at her. "And you think Burns' humor is bad?"

⚜⚜⚜

Monday afternoon around five, Sally crested the stairs on her way out of the courthouse. She jerked to a stop when she saw Jim enter the building. A younger, blonde trooper trailed him by a step. That had to be his trainee. What were they doing there at this time of day?

"Jim," Sally called.

He halted mid-stride and changed direction, while the other trooper kept going toward the DA's office.

"Kind of surprised to see you here," Sally said. "Who's that?"

"Trooper Aislyn McAllister."

"I hate to tell you, but if you're looking for someone, you'll probably be disappointed. Most people have left for the day."

He looked over at Trooper McAllister, who was standing outside the office door—not all that patiently, judging from the tapping of her fingers on her belt. "Go on in," he said. "Uniontown PD should have sent someone over to secure the victim's office. Nobody leaves until we finish our interviews."

Someone must have buzzed her in, because she opened the door. She stepped inside and held the door. "I can wait for you, it's not a problem."

"Go. I'll be right behind you."

Sally saw the young woman shoot her a look, then shrug, and let the door close. "Jim, what is going on?"

He held up a finger and waited until the door clicked shut. Then he looked at Sally, his expression betraying an internal conflict. "Alex Costanzo is dead."

"Dead? How?"

"Keep your voice down." He looked around the lobby. "He was shot this afternoon at the Twin Oaks Motel."

"What was he doing at the Twin Oaks?"

"Really?"

"I know why people go to the Twin Oaks, but...Alex?" Being at a seedy motel was more out of character for the fastidious ADA than extortion. "Was it Trafford?"

"It's too early to say."

"It has to be. First Colin, now Alex. The only thing that connects them is this scam and Trafford. Somebody must have seen something. I bet if you canvas the surrounding rooms you'll find reports of an ugly guy with a shaved head and lots of tattoos."

Again, Jim's gaze darted around the lobby. "We don't know the two deaths are connected."

"Oh puh-leeze. Don't give me that official bullshit."

He ignored the comment. "I need you to do me a favor."

"Anything, you know that."

"When you were at my place over the weekend, you mentioned a woman. Tyra Young. Did you find any more information on her?"

His cloak-and-dagger attitude was rubbing off. The skin on the back of Sally's neck tingled, like she was being watched. "No, I've been too busy. I can stay for a bit and do that now, if it'll help."

He paused. "Yes, anything to give us a leg up. Also, I want you to think about your recent interactions with Costanzo. Did he mention anything to you that might indicate he had been threatened, or anyone who had a gripe with him? You know, more than usual."

"Nothing leaps to mind, but I'll think while I search." She turned back to her office.

He reached out and grabbed her arm. "Sally, this is going to hit the news and be a huge story. I'd appreciate it if you'd keep quiet until the official announcement."

She studied his face, taking in the set of his jaw. In other words, he really shouldn't have said anything to her, but he was grasping at straws and hoping she could help.

"My lips are sealed."

He nodded, released her, and went to the DA's office. She watched as he entered, then headed back to the basement. Fortunately, Bryan and Doris were gone for the day, especially Doris, so there were no prying eyes around. If Jim wanted information on Tyra, he could have it. But the two attorneys connected to Trafford shot? That was too much for Sally to ignore.

⚜⚜⚜

As he went inside the DA's office, Duncan's conscience battled his common sense. He really should have waited and let Sally find out from the news and the state police PR flaks. He should look for Tyra Young on his own, not farm the work out and certainly not to a civilian. But he trusted Sally to be discreet. And, quite frankly, there'd be a ton of pressure to find the killer of an ADA quickly, even if he was found in a compromising situation. Duncan needed all the help he could get.

The DA's receptionist accosted him the minute he stepped inside. "Trooper, what is going on? An officer from the Uniontown police department is keeping everyone out of Mr. Costanzo's office. The female trooper who came in ahead of you said almost nothing, only that we had to wait. Our employees want to go home."

"I'm sorry, Ms...."

"Stewart."

"Ms. Stewart. There's been an incident involving Mr. Costanzo."

"What kind of incident?"

"He's been shot."

"Shot?" Stewart blinked rapidly, mouth open. Recovering, she asked, "Is he okay?"

"He's dead."

"Oh my God. Who shot him?"

"I don't have any other information for you right now. I understand it's inconvenient, but we need everybody to stay here until we've conducted interviews. And someone needs to stay until we've finished the search of Mr. Costanzo's office in case we have questions."

She nodded. When she spoke, there was a decided tremble in her voice. "I'll...I'll pass the word to everyone to hang tight. Can I tell them about the shooting?"

"I'd rather you didn't. We'll handle that." He took a step, then stopped. "Before you do that, do you have access to Mr. Costanzo's calendar?"

Stewart nodded and returned to her desk. "Let me pull it up for you."

"I'm specifically interested in whether he had any personal appointments this afternoon."

She tapped on the keyboard. "He was in court this morning, but they adjourned at noon. His afternoon looks free."

"Has he had any visitors recently, especially people you might not know? Say in the last week?"

"His only visitors have been on court business and I know all of them," Stewart said. She straightened and her hands shook. "Someone has it in for county lawyers. First Colin Rafferty, now Mr. Costanzo. Were they killed by the same person?"

"Have you ever seen this man in the office?" Duncan held out Trafford's mug shot.

She looked at it. "No. I'd remember someone like that."

"Thank you." Duncan pocketed the photo. "Go tell everyone here that we're going to need to talk to them before they leave. I'll also need a list of visitors from the last two weeks."

"Naturally we want to cooperate, but I'm going to have to clear that with DA Harding."

Of course she would. "Is Trooper McAllister in Mr. Costanzo's office?" The secretary nodded and Duncan strode off.

Inside, McAllister was going through desk drawers, hands gloved. She looked up. "Was that your public defender friend? The one who was at your house Saturday?"

"Yes. I asked her to help me find someone who might be connected to the deceased."

"You sure that's a good idea?"

Duncan tugged on his own gloves. "It's a little...unorthodox, but I trust her. What have you found?"

"So far, not a whole lot. His computer is locked, so I can't get into his email."

"The tech guys can do that, but we probably won't find anything. Costanzo was likely smart enough not to conduct illegal operations using county email."

McAllister nodded. "There's some snail mail, court papers, an envelope from the bar association. None of it interesting or related to Trafford."

"Don't limit yourself. Not yet."

"Understood. But unless people now send secret messages in professional-development mail, I don't see anything."

"What about a day planner?"

There was a pause while McAllister sifted through the contents on the desk. "No day planner. Should he have one?"

Sally hadn't returned it yet. "According to my source at the public defender's office, Costanzo had a day planner. One that detailed a lot of appointments with a Tyra."

"Who's Tyra?"

"I think she's a local prostitute." At least Sally thought so.

McAllister snorted. "Repeated appointments with a hooker. Today his body turns up, riddled with bullet holes, at a fleabag motel. He couldn't find a better place?"

"I'm guessing he needed somewhere outside Uniontown proper. He wouldn't want to be seen taking a lady of the night into his apartment. Traveling up to Pittsburgh might also be problematic."

"Too far away for a quickie."

"The Twin Oaks might have been as good as it got. As much anonymity as you can pay for." He looked around. "Let's speed this up. You go interview everyone here. Get contact information for any employee who's absent so we can follow up."

"Check."

"Take Trafford's picture. Ask if anyone saw him or this Tyra. Or if Costanzo had any other visitors he may have argued with. That Uniontown officer still here?"

"Yeah, why?"

"Let's enlist his help getting all this stuff boxed up and labeled. Computer, desk contents, the works. I'll be back in five."

CHAPTER 26

Colin shot. Alex shot. Right after suspicion of the legal scandal came to light. Sally's intuition screamed that they were wasting time with Tyra Young. But if Jim insisted on more information, Sally would provide it. What she found in the county arrest records for Tyra prompted another search.

She was still studying the results when Jim entered her office. "I hope you have something. I'm putting my neck out talking to you."

Sally turned her monitor so he could see it. "See for yourself."

"Tyra Monique Young. Arrested three times this year for prostitution. Currently on probation." He straightened. "That's confirmation of your suspicion, but not news. Incidentally, you didn't return that Moleskine."

"I haven't had the chance."

"Well, hand it over." He held out his hand.

She pulled it out of the desk drawer where she'd stashed it and laid in on his palm. "What are you going to do with it?"

"Figure out a way to slip it in with the rest of the stuff we take from the office. That way it gets entered into evidence and you're off the hook." The ghost of a grin flitted across his face. "You're welcome."

"Thanks."

He flipped through the planner. "Looks like you're right, though. Costanzo may be her biggest customer based on this. Why? Aside from wondering why a county prosecutor is frequenting a prostitute in the first place. It only seems to be Tyra and there has to be a reason."

Sally clicked to another tab on her browser. "I'm going to guess it has something to do with her brother, Elijah."

"What about him?" Duncan looked back at the screen. He frowned. "You're kidding me."

"Nope. Arrested four times this year for drug possession. All four times, charges were dropped." Sally shook her head. "One time, yes. Four? That's ridiculous."

"Please don't tell me Colin Rafferty represented Elijah Young. His name isn't in Rafferty's notebook."

"No, Elijah Young was not one of Colin's clients. But." She leaned back. "All four times, the DA dropped the charges for insufficient evidence. Someone in the Uniontown police department must have been furious. Guess who represented the Commonwealth?"

"Alex Costanzo."

"You got it." Sally leaned forward. "Who, according to you, was killed earlier this afternoon."

He stared at the computer screen. "I think Miss Young and I need to chat."

"Here's her current address and phone number. I looked it up once I saw the history on her brother." She stood and handed the address to Jim.

He gave the information a quick read. "They don't match."

"What doesn't match?"

"We found Costanzo's cell phone at the scene. He sent a text with the room number, but Tyra's numbers don't match."

"Could be a burner phone." In fact, it probably was. Alex wouldn't want a number in his cell phone traced to a prostitute. "Do you think she's connected to Trafford?"

He slipped the address in his shirt pocket. "If she is, I'm going to need a stiff drink or three."

He left and Sally shut off her computer monitor. Jim was right. Elijah Young had not been listed in Colin's notes. But if the DA had decided not to prosecute, there wouldn't have been a docket number. Either there was another list out there somewhere or Alex had been working a side venture by himself.

When Duncan returned to the DA's office he checked with McAllister on the status of her interviews. "A couple to go, but so far no one has seen, heard, or smelled Aaron Trafford since last fall," she said. "I thought he might have come after hours, except everyone I talked to said Costanzo wasn't one for working late if he could avoid it. Nobody knows who Tyra is."

"I do. Tyra has a brother who can't seem to stop getting arrested, but who is very skilled at avoiding trial."

"You get that from your public defender source?"

"Yes." He took in the dubious look on McAllister's face. "I admit, it's an unusual relationship. But Ms. Castle and I have a history."

"A history."

Her tone spoke volumes. McAllister had made assumptions about his friendship with Sally. "Not like that. Jeez."

McAllister made a tsking sound, shaking her head. "She's good looking."

Time to cut this conversation short before he got into trouble. "You said you're almost finished?"

McAllister smothered a grin, but returned to business. "Yes. I've got contact information on a couple people who aren't here at the moment." She tapped her notebook on her palm. "You know, I'm surprised. Is being a lawyer so distasteful they have to troll the streets for a date?"

"We're going to find out as soon as we're done here." Duncan looked over the boxed items from Costanzo's office. The box wasn't sealed yet, awaiting his signature on the chain of custody form. He opened the lid just wide enough to slip in the day planner, then sealed it, signed the form, and taped it to the box.

"What was that?" McAllister asked.

"What was what?" He should have sent her away. Damn.

"You slipped something into the box. What was it?" She cocked her head. "A day planner? You get that from Ms. Castle?"

"Never mind. Go finish up." Note to self: he needed to practice his sleight of hand, especially in front of eagle-eyed trainees.

⚜⚜⚜

It was well after six when they headed back to the car. "Hey, do we need to talk to Killian?" McAllister asked, sliding in and buckling up.

Duncan fastened his seatbelt and started the car. "No. Costanzo may have worked in Uniontown, but he was killed outside Killian's jurisdiction."

"But the 9mm shell casings—"

"Until ballistics can match them to the Rafferty shooting, it's not worth pursuing." Duncan pulled out. "I'm not inclined to bother Detective Killian until I have to."

"But why not?"

How to explain and be diplomatic? "Some local law enforcement officers are…prickly when it comes to sharing with us. They see it as an unwanted intrusion into their territory."

"You're telling me Killian is a bit on the provincial side."

"That's one way of putting it."

Tyra Young's address was in a brick and siding row-house in a neighborhood typical of housing for workers when the coal industry peaked, but had fallen on hard times, like a lot of the county. The windows were covered with cheap mini blinds that had been discolored by the sun. Dented metal trash cans sat next to the door. No car, but it was still early; Tyra might not have hit the streets yet. "You lead," he said and gestured to the door.

"A woman-to-woman talk?"

"Something like that."

McAllister rapped on the faded, dirt-streaked tan door. "Ms. Young, Trooper McAllister with the state police. We'd like to speak with you." No answer. McAllister knocked again. "Ms. Young, state police."

The lock snapped back, and a statuesque black woman opened the door but left the chain on. She was dressed for work in a tight, purple micro-mini dress, four-inch heels, and heavy makeup. "What do you want?"

"Are you Tyra Young?"

"Who's asking?"

"State police. We need to ask you a few questions," McAllister said. "Do you know Alex Costanzo?"

Tyra spat and McAllister stepped back to avoid it.

"That's a yes. You don't like Mr. Costanzo very much." McAllister's voice was mild.

"I'm busy. If you came by to get my opinion of that shit-eating scumbag, you've got it." Tyra moved to close the door.

McAllister blocked it with her foot. "Where were you earlier this afternoon between noon and four-thirty?"

"Why?"

McAllister glanced at Duncan, who nodded. "Alex Costanzo was shot this afternoon. He's dead."

Tyra's face didn't move. "Good."

"Ms. Young, where were you this afternoon?"

"Why do you care?"

McAllister checked her notes. "Your name appears multiple times in Mr. Costanzo's day planner. Four times last week, three the week before. The week before that—"

"All right, all right. I got it," Tyra snapped. "I was home, sleeping."

Again, McAllister stopped Tyra from closing the door. "Can anybody confirm that?"

"Honey, are you deaf or stupid? I said I was sleeping. If you know where to find me, you know I live alone. Nobody saw me sleep." Tyra put her hand on her hip, striking a pose, but the door remained barely open.

"Ms. Young, where is your brother Elijah?" Duncan asked.

Tyra flinched. "He's gone, moved to Pittsburgh. Homewood."

"Do you have his phone number or an address?" Duncan studied her face. The makeup on her right cheek didn't quite hide a yellowing bruise.

Tyra shook her head. "No, he's, uh...between addresses. No phone. Couldn't pay his cell bill, so it got cut off."

"You don't have any way to contact him?"

"Nope." Tyra shifted from foot to foot. "When he needs to talk to me, he borrows a friend's phone. He called me couple nights ago."

"Just to catch up or did he have something specific to talk about?" Duncan asked.

"Shootin' the shit, but it wasn't a long conversation. He ain't a talker. Don't know why he calls at all."

McAllister peered through the opening, but Tyra moved to block her view. "Ms. Young, do you own a gun?"

"No. What do I need a gun for?"

"As I mentioned, your name appears quite frequently in Mr. Costanzo's calendar. What's the nature of your relationship?" McAllister asked.

Tyra's lip curled. "He would tell you it was business. But honey, trust me. It was plenty personal." They waited, but Tyra didn't offer any further information. Finally, she said, "Is that all? 'Cause I got to get ready for work, unless you all gonna arrest me."

Duncan and McAllister exchanged a long glance. "That's all for now," McAllister said, handing over her card. "If you happen to hear from your brother, tell him we'd like to talk to him. You can give him my number."

Tyra took it with her fingertips, like it was a dead snake. "Sure. You have a good night." Her voice dripped sarcasm. She waited for McAllister to move her foot, and then shut the door and slammed home the dead bolt.

When they reached the car, McAllister looked back. The window blinds twitched. "She's lying. Just like the people at the motel. A freaking county attorney is shot and the whole world clams up." McAllister got into the car.

"I told you. Everybody lies, and nobody sees or hears anything." Duncan followed.

"I don't understand why honest people do that."

"Lots of reasons. They're scared, maybe they think they'll get in trouble, maybe they're involved and are trying to fool us, or maybe they hate cops. Pick one."

"Tyra wouldn't let us in or open the door to see into the house." McAllister buckled up. "And how does she have a business yet personal relationship with Costanzo?"

"Do I have to answer that?"

"I guess not."

"No smart person lets a cop into her house without a warrant. Maybe her brother is inside. She mentioned Homewood. Let's call the Pittsburgh Bureau of Police. By the way, did you notice her cheek?"

McAllister nodded. "The makeup didn't cover up the bruise. Did she get it as a result of her work or through an accident?"

"Could be either." He shot her a sideways glance. "That was another good interview. You're getting the hang of it." He'd also noticed a pattern. When she was working with a victim, she was softer. More approachable. Put her in front of an aggressive interviewee, and she dug in her heels beyond the normal police determination to control the situation. Interesting.

"Thanks. But...why Tyra?" McAllister buckled her seatbelt. "I mean, so Costanzo liked hookers for some reason. But why did he spend so much time with her?"

Why Tyra indeed? There were a lot of unanswered questions, but Duncan was sure of one thing based on their interview. Tyra Young absolutely hated Alex Costanzo's guts.

CHAPTER 27

The meeting with Jim delayed Sally's departure from work and she didn't get home until almost six-thirty. The news of Alex's death had knocked the wind out of her, but it had also made her more determined. Sally knew because Jim was a cop, he could not ignore the fact that Alex had been found at the Twin Oaks, with its reputation as a location for paid-sex encounters, or the fact that a known prostitute's name featured so prevalently in Alex's calendar. It wasn't a mystery to Sally. High-powered men used hookers all the time. Tyra was either a distraction or she was tied to Trafford in some way. A third possibility made the puzzle more complicated; in Sally's experience, a simple answer was almost always the right one.

At her apartment, Sally heated some leftovers for dinner. The last thing she'd done that day was get addresses for the members of the cleaning staff Doris had identified. It wasn't too late to visit each man.

The first visit was a bust. The man had been out of town all that weekend with his family, away at Cedar Point. She'd have to get confirmation from his employer that he'd been off, but Sally didn't get the feeling he'd lied. Plus, the kids in his living room were wearing amusement park shirts. No, he wasn't the guy she was looking for.

She parked in front of her second destination. Name number two, Roy Pasquale, lived in a quiet residential area. The houses were plain, but the owners tried to make them attractive. The tiny yards were mowed and there were flowers in pots or small gardens. Flags for the Steelers, the Pirates, and the Penguins flapped outside metal storm doors that were pitted, but washed clean. A pot of orange mums was in the front window of the Pasquale residence, a bright pink kiddie bike with silver streamers propped against the front. A working-class neighborhood, but one that had some civic pride.

Sally rapped on the metal door. The man who answered wore a faded Steelers T-shirt and cargo pants. A wine-colored birthmark covered a portion of his neck, at least up to where a shirt collar would be and maybe higher. "Yes? Can I help you? We ain't interested in buying anything or taking any surveys, if that's why you're here." He spoke through the storm door, voice muffled.

"It's not." Sally held out her court identification. "Are you employed by CleanRite, the company that has the contract for the county courthouse?"

"Yes. Why?"

"Did you work the night shift, a week ago last Sunday?"

His eyes were wary. "Uh, yeah. I did. Is there a problem?"

"I'm not sure." Why didn't he open the door? "Do you mind stepping outside? Talking through the Plexiglas is awkward. Or I can come in."

Pasquale mulled over her words, then stepped out, pulling the door shut behind him. His feet were bare and he didn't let go of the door handle. "Is this better? Kind of late to be reporting an issue with my work from a week ago, isn't it?"

"This isn't about that, well not directly." How did she want to proceed? Best be honest. "You know, of course, that Sunday was the night Colin Rafferty from the public defender's office was murdered."

He twitched. "Oh, yeah. Right. The cops called about that. Not sure I can tell you anything I haven't already told them."

"What did you tell them exactly?"

"I worked the night shift. It was pretty quiet. Mr. Rafferty said hi when he came in, but he went right to his office. I'd already cleaned in there, but he said he wouldn't make a mess." Pasquale gave a nervous laugh. "Not quite a true statement, but I guess he didn't do it, did he?"

"Did you see anyone else that night?"

He shifted his weight back and forth. "No."

"No one? Not even this man?" She handed him Trafford's mug shot.

His hand gripped the photo, crinkling the edge. "Sorry. Didn't see anyone that night." He handed back the picture. His gaze was open, no blinking, but there was a nervous tic at the corner of his right eye and his voice shook ever so slightly. "Is that all? It's almost dinner time. My wife and kids are waiting."

"One last thing." Sally hitched up her purse. "Did you hear anything? Voices or anything that sounded like a gunshot? Running?"

"No. Wait, yes. I was coming off the elevator and heard footsteps. Kind of fast, I guess they could have been from running. And I heard the front door shut, but I only saw the guy's back. Black guy, skinny. I guess I did see someone, huh?"

His statement didn't help. It bolstered the police case that De'Shawn Thomas was the killer. She handed him a business card. "If you remember something at a later date, would you please call me?"

He glanced at the card. "Sure thing Ms. Castle. Hey, you didn't work with the guy, did you? The one who was murdered?"

"I did. He was a friend and I want to know what happened to him."

"Well, uh, if I think of anything I'll be sure to call you. 'Night." He hurried inside and shut the door with a thud.

Sally was certain Pasquale wasn't going to call her, just as she was certain he was holding something back. Why? He'd flinched when she gave him Trafford's photo and he'd tried too hard to look her in the eye. Conclusion: Pasquale had met Trafford before…and that meeting had scared him shitless.

※※※

Sally's cell phone buzzed as soon as she parked at home. "Jim, what's up?"

"I was hoping you could meet me for a drink. Dex's?"

It was almost seven. "Sure, but I haven't changed out of my work clothes. You want to meet now?"

"Be there around eight. I'll be waiting." He clicked off.

Sally had enough time to shower and change into something more comfortable, jeans, a light v-neck cashmere sweater, and her new ankle boots. Dex's wasn't fancy and this wasn't a date, but Jim had called to ask her out. The least she could do was make herself presentable.

He was there when she arrived, in the back corner booth he preferred. She took a minute to study him. He was seated, but she was sure the dark jeans would fit perfectly, as did the forest green Henley-style shirt. He was drinking some kind of dark beer, a glass of deep red wine was across from him.

She slipped through the tables and slid into the booth. Then she lifted the glass. "You shouldn't have."

"Merlot. From Australia, I think."

"It's perfect." She waited for him to say something. When he didn't, she continued. "What did you want to talk about?"

"You want anything?"

"I can eat."

Jim signaled to a passing waiter and they placed their order.

"You're stalling." It wasn't like him.

"McAllister and I interviewed Tyra Young." He told her about his meeting. "There's something there."

"I agree, but I don't see how Trafford fits in with that."

"Sally, I know Trafford's on your radar. But he doesn't have to be involved in everything."

"He's involved in this somehow." She told him about her meeting with Pasquale and his reaction to Trafford's photo. "Ten to one Roy Pasquale has seen Aaron Trafford and the meeting wasn't a friendly chat."

Jim sat back. "In one of our interviews, McAllister found a witness who told us he heard Trafford say he had a tame lawyer at the courthouse. What if we're looking at this wrong?"

She swirled her wineglass. "What do you mean?"

"What if Rafferty and Costanzo didn't extort money from Trafford? What if he paid them of his own volition?"

"You're saying he bribed them. He was arrested, looking to get out of the charge, and offered them money." She finished her drink. "What about the others?"

"The others could be extortion. We have Thomas's statement to you on that."

"So, Colin kept track of the payment in the same way he did the others because it was one more instance of corruption, just not extortion." She rubbed her forehead. "Is it too late to get a whiskey, neat?" The food had come while they were talking and she picked at her burger. The conversation had stolen her appetite.

Jim eyed her over the rim of his glass. "Probably not. I didn't know you drank whiskey."

"Only in times of great stress or depression." The waiter walked by and Sally ordered her drink. "Okay, we've got the extortion. On top of that, Trafford paid for legal 'protection,' for lack of a better word."

"Maybe. I'm just spitballing."

"When Colin threatens to expose everything, Trafford shoots him. Where do the Youngs come into this?"

"They might not. That might be a separate set of motivations."

"Come on. How many legal rackets can one guy run?" The whiskey arrived and Sally took a healthy gulp. It burned going down, but it was better suited to her mood than red wine.

"I don't know. You could be right and I'm overcomplicating things."

"You think?"

"But Costanzo had some kind of hold over Tyra Young. I'm willing to bet it has to do with her brother."

"Maybe they paid Trafford to get rid of Alex." She took another slug of whiskey.

"You're making Trafford out to be a gun for hire."

"Tell me it's impossible." She finished her drink and set down the glass.

"It's not probable." Jim reached over and moved the tumbler away from her. "Trafford has an extensive record and violence is certainly part of it, but hired assassin isn't there."

On second thought, the whiskey might have been a mistake. Their meeting, which had been pleasant despite the topic of discussion, had assumed a somber feel.

"Let's go." He called over the server and asked for the check. They didn't talk while they waited for it, and when it arrived, Jim pulled a credit card out of his wallet and handed it over.

She fumbled for her purse. "What do I owe you?"

He waved her off. "My treat. Do I need to drive you home?"

"No, I'm okay." If he came over now, she might do something rash and that would be bad. Or maybe not. She wasn't sure.

The check paid, Jim helped her up, grabbed his jacket and they left Dex's. Standing in the parking lot, he spun his keys on his finger. "Sally, look. I know the situation isn't...pleasant for you."

She snorted. That was an understatement. Colin had been a friend and the closest thing she'd ever had to a protégé. She'd sat in front of his mother and promised to find his killer. Almost a week later, Sally had made zero progress, but she had shown Colin to be as dirty as some of his clients.

"We'll figure it out." He eyed her. "I'll ask again. Do I need to conduct a field sobriety test before you get in that car?"

He wouldn't. Who was she kidding? He absolutely would. "No, I'm fine." She fished her car keys out of her purse and promptly dropped them.

Before she could move, Jim picked them up. "On second thought, you don't get a choice in the matter. Get in the Jeep."

"What about my car?"

"Get it tomorrow. You don't live that far away. You might be a bit late for work. Better than wrapping that Camry around a light post."

She yanked open the Jeep's passenger door. "Fine. Fair warning. If you drive me home, you'll end up walking me to my door, and I won't be responsible for what happens next." There. She'd said something. His move.

He stared, face inscrutable in the shadows of the parking lot light. He was going to say yes. Oh God. What if he said no? Damn whiskey.

But he simply pointed at his Jeep. "I'll take my chances. Now get in."

They completed the short trip in silence and once at her building, Jim walked her up. He unlocked the door, pushed it open, and handed over her keys. "Now I'll be able to sleep."

"You sure you don't want to spend the night on my couch? Make sure I don't have a seizure or something?" She could hear her heart thumping at her tipsy, brazen words and she was sure he could hear it too.

He took a step closer, expression unreadable, just a slight twitch in the strong line of his jaw. He was going to come in. "I don't think you're drunk enough for that. I should go." He brushed a soft kiss on her cheek. "Sleep well, Counselor." He stepped back, turned, and jogged down the stairs.

Sally sagged against her doorframe, her heartbeat at least twice as fast as normal. Damn. Next time, she should skip the whiskey. Or make sure he had one with her.

CHAPTER 28

Tuesday morning, Duncan arrived for first shift with two different sets of thoughts in his head. The more pleasant ones involved Sally. He should have stayed, if only to see what did happen next. Then again, the timing wasn't quite right for that. She hadn't been drunk, but she'd definitely been tipsy. That comment about not being responsible for what happened? Not something she'd normally say. Sam Duncan had raised his son to be a gentleman. A gentleman did not take advantage of a woman who wasn't in complete control. That didn't preclude some interesting dreams when Duncan finally crashed into bed.

The second set involved Costanzo. Sally was sure his death was connected to Rafferty. Duncan wasn't ready to break in either direction. But two things could help him make up his mind. The autopsy results and ballistics.

Immediately after roll call, Duncan called the coroner's office while McAllister went to follow up on ballistics.

"Once again, I'll skip the boring parts," Burns said. "COD was a gunshot that severed the aorta. He might have bled out from the others eventually, but the aorta was the killer."

"The one in the groin. Was that post-mortem?" Duncan asked.

"Are you seriously asking me that? Don't answer. I've no clue. I can give you some psychological speculation, but that's it."

McAllister told him the shootings felt different. She was right, but Duncan didn't have extra time to spend on that thought at the moment. "Skip the speculation. Time of death?"

"Based on body temp, lividity, and rigor, he'd been dead for less than three hours before he was found." Burns' voice was tired, the black humor missing. It wasn't hard to explain. An assistant public defender and an ADA within a week.

But the time of death window was less than that, since Costanzo had checked in slightly before two and had been found less than two hours later. "Anything else?"

"Not really. Preliminary blood alcohol within limits. I already told you about the semen." He paused and Duncan imagined him rubbing his eyes. "I'll call you when we've got toxicology."

Duncan hung up as McAllister walked up with a paper.

"I've got good news, bad news, and I-don't-know-what-it-is news," she said. Like Burns, any trace of levity was gone, her face sober.

"What's the good news?"

"We have a ballistics report. Bullets are definitely from a 9mm."

Common enough. "What's the bad news?"

"They don't match the Rafferty shooting." She grimaced and handed over the report. "Does that mean we have two shooters?"

"It means we have two guns. The simplest explanation is two actors. But it's not necessarily right." Duncan scanned the report. "What's the rest?"

"Ballistics did show the weapon in the Costazno shooting matches one in Pittsburgh last summer," she said.

Pittsburgh? "You get the details?"

She handed over another sheet of paper. "Shots fired in Homewood, no victims. At the scene, Pittsburgh Bureau of Police picked up a Marshawn Watkins. I ran his name. Couple of weapons charges, assault, possession, misdemeanor theft."

"They recover the weapon?"

"No. Watkins didn't have it on him; PBP got him for possession with intent. He gave them a story about an argument between two guys, one fired at the other, both took off. He couldn't identify either man. There were no other witnesses."

"If there was no victim, how'd we get a ballistics match?"

"Bullets were recovered from a car and a utility pole at the scene. Since Watkins didn't have a gun on him, they ran ballistics hoping to find a match that way, but no dice. Could be Watkins was in the wrong place at the wrong time."

"Could be he's full of shit and got rid of it before he was arrested." Add another name to the mix. "What about the phone number from the text?"

"It belongs to a prepaid phone that was recovered from the motel room. It was wiped down. No prints. We're still trying to find out where it was purchased, but it was probably paid for in cash."

Duncan handed back the papers. "Call Pittsburgh. See if you can find any information on known associates for Watkins, something that might tie him to Uniontown or Fayette County. I'm going to call Killian."

She frowned. "The ballistics don't match. You weren't going to call unless we found a connection."

"Changed my mind. I think we need to talk to him."

After a couple rings, the Uniontown detective's voice came over the line. "Killian."

"Detective Killian, this is Trooper First Class Duncan from the PSP. You may have heard that Alex Costanzo was shot at the Twin Oaks Motel yesterday. I responded to the call."

"And?"

"Have you heard about the extortion scandal involving Rafferty and Costanzo?"

"Nothing definite, but the rumor mill has been going full speed on the subject. Get to the point."

"I think we have to face the possibility that the two homicides are connected."

"I have my suspect. De'Shawn Thomas." Now Killian sounded annoyed.

"With this latest homicide, you should reconsider. Given the collaboration between the victims, it would be shortsighted to do otherwise. At least I think so."

Silence.

"You haven't found a murder weapon, have you?"

More silence.

"Has the name Tyra Young come up in your investigation?"

"No, but I haven't put your guy Trafford on the scene either. Only Thomas."

"I think we should re-interview him. Together. Maybe he can help both of us."

"I'm not releasing him."

"I'm not asking you to." Duncan waited. "Detective, I'm not trying to steal your investigation. I have enough on my plate. I want to make sure the right guy is taken into custody. I know you feel the same."

Yet more silence.

"How about this? We meet this afternoon, one o'clock. I'll let you handle the details. If the results of that conversation show it really is two separate homicides, I'll leave you alone." McAllister had used the word provincial. That was Killian all right. Investigating the murder of an ADA was touchy enough without local police politics muddying things.

Killian grumbled, but agreed. Duncan hung up just as McAllister returned, sheaf of paper in hand. "What'd you find out?" He reached for the papers.

"More details on Watkins's priors. I called Pittsburgh. They weren't able to give me a lot, but one name did come up that was interesting."

"Don't drag it out."

"When Mr. Watkins was picked up last summer, he had a friend with him." She pointed to a section of the report.

Elijah Young. Tyra's brother.

⚜⚜⚜

What Sally wanted to work on Tuesday morning was proving her theory about Trafford. Her actual duties turned out to be more mundane: continuing existing negotiations on the cases she'd inherited from Colin. In addition to returning phone calls and emails regarding proposed pleas from her existing caseload. As a result of her conflict between heart and duty, she moved through the morning on autopilot.

Okay, Jim might be right. If Sally was a cop, she'd be foolish to zero in on one suspect like this. But she had one luxury at her disposal he didn't. She didn't have to keep an open mind. She was doing this as a personal favor to Deborah Rafferty and could conduct her investigation any way she damn well pleased.

Jim. She'd thought about last night when she walked the few blocks to Dex's to get her car earlier. It had been a good thing he'd insisted on driving her home, she could admit that. Whiskey on top of red wine? What had she been thinking? Then the alcohol had lowered her usual level of decorum, not that she regretted a single thing she'd said. It was no surprise he'd opted to go home. Look up "good guy" in the Urban Dictionary and there'd be a picture of Jim Duncan.

Damn it.

Doris came in around eleven with some packages. "These are for you, they're are addressed to Colin. I'd give them to Bryan, but he's out today." She turned to leave.

"Doris, wait a minute." The older woman paused and faced Sally. "I'd like to get your opinion, if you don't mind."

"Opinion on what? You look terrific and that state cop you've been hanging out with is quite the catch."

Sally's neck warmed. "Not that kind of opinion. It's about Colin. You know what's going on."

"With him and Mr. Costanzo? I'd never have guessed it."

"You and me both. The police have arrested De'Shawn Thomas."

Doris pursed her lips. "Young, skinny black guy. Misdemeanor possession."

"That's him."

Doris thought for a moment, then shook her head. "He doesn't look the type. Then again, how many times do people say that and the suspect in question is a serial killer?"

"I can't get it out of my head that there are better candidates. Aaron Trafford, for one."

"I remember him. He definitely looked like a murderer, straight out of a TV show. But why?"

Sally sat back. "I found a record Colin had been keeping of the cases he and Alex collaborated on. Trafford's trial last fall was on it. Colin made comments to me and to his mother about a mistake he'd made and how he was going to put it right."

"You think Colin was killed because he was going to turn himself in?"

The older woman was sharp. "Yes."

"If that's the case…wouldn't Mr. Costanzo have more to lose in that scenario?" Doris took one look at Sally and continued. "Think about it. Mr. Costanzo fancied himself as someone who was going places. If he were to face charges, wouldn't that have ended his career? Trafford could disappear, he's done it before. But Mr. Costanzo…"

"What?"

"Well, you know him better than I do, of course. But he always struck me as proud. Arrogant. Even if he was cleared, wouldn't the whiff of scandal be enough to ruin him? Would he risk that?"

Sally tapped her fingernail against her teeth. It was a good point. "Knowing what you do of Alex, do you think he'd shoot someone?"

"Put in a corner, one he couldn't escape, or didn't think he could escape, who knows? Does he own a gun?"

"No, he doesn't. It was part of a trial once. I was observing, not participating. Anyway, he was questioning a firearms expert and specifically said he wasn't a gun owner and didn't know anything about them."

"It wouldn't be hard to get a gun, would it?"

"Not especially. I doubt his background raises a red flag." The idea clashed with what Sally knew of Alex's personality. "Alex...he strikes me as a white-collar crime guy. Conspiracy, yes. Not murder."

Doris shrugged. "If you say so. But there's something else to consider."

"What's that?"

"From what I understand, there are a lot of names in that notebook. Any of those people could be responsible, I would think. Revenge. Looking to make sure it doesn't happen again." Doris went to the door and stopped, hand on the knob. "If I were the person running this show, I'd be looking at them, too."

⚜⚜⚜

Duncan was about to leave when Nicols walked up. "Trooper Duncan. What's the latest on that meth investigation?"

The meth lab, right. The Costanzo shooting had driven it out of Duncan's mind.

Nicols' gaze was shrewd. "Maybe you need to hand over the homicide. Focus on one thing at a time."

"No sir, I can handle it." Nicols knew how Duncan felt about passing off a case. It was cheating. "I'll get back to the drug investigation. Promise. I need to run down one lead on Costanzo."

"Good thing you have an extra set of hands, then. But don't let your overdeveloped sense of responsibility get in the way of closing something." Nicols strode away.

In other words, finishing one investigation was better than letting two of them linger. Especially ones that were high profile.

McAllister came up, swishing the contents of yet another bottle of Mountain Dew. "Let me guess. The lieutenant wants some results."

"Yes. And he's reminded me that we have another investigation." He pointed at the bottle. "Don't let that explode all over you."

"Relax, it's been opened." She held it up, unscrewed the cap, and took a gulp. "Back to business. You're talking about the meth lab."

He'd have to find a way to give each item equal attention. Maybe he'd luck out; Sally was right and everything was related. "Yes. When we last saw Trafford, he was arguing with Costanzo on a street corner in Uniontown."

McAllister had the bottle halfway to her mouth, but stopped. "We did?"

Damn it. He hadn't told her about his nighttime foray with Sally. "Well, the last time I saw him he was."

"When did you do that?"

"It doesn't matter right now."

"It doesn't?"

"Not as far as the drugs are concerned. It might…look, just put it aside."

She grinned. "Whatever you say, Boss. But the last time you and I saw him, he was in the bar. With Monahan and Carrington."

"Monahan, who was arrested with drugs in his car."

"And Carrington owns the house on Wharton Furnace Road."

"Then let's go visit Mr. Carrington." Duncan grabbed some keys and headed out, McAllister right behind him.

CHAPTER 29

By mid-morning, Sally wanted to scream in frustration. She'd methodically searched for every name in Colin's list and had come up empty. People were in jail, in other parts of the state, in other states; most importantly, none of them had been seen in the Fayette County courthouse the night Colin was killed. If only she could get her hands on the damn security footage. She'd know exactly who'd walked in the door.

Only two people fit the criterion in her opinion: Thomas and Trafford. Assuming Colin's and Alex's deaths were connected, and how could they not be, only one name remained in play. De'Shawn Thomas was in jail. That left Trafford as the last man standing. It raised another question, one she hadn't thought of. There were metal detectors at the doors. How had he gotten the gun into the courthouse? Then again, she'd seen stories all over the place of people beating security measures. Trafford was a career criminal. Surely he'd know how to smuggle a gun into a secure building.

Maybe Sally was going about this wrong. Instead of trying to put Trafford on the scene when Colin was shot, maybe she needed to focus on linking Trafford to the new meth facility. If she did that, it might give the police the opening they needed to then prove Trafford was the shooter in both homicides.

Jim had told her a little about the current investigation. The house in question belonged to Trafford's grandmother, who'd raised him. The grandmother had Alzheimer's. She'd be no help, but maybe her house would.

Sally looked at the clock. Eleven. She could take an early lunch. She had a meeting that afternoon, but she could run down to the house, snoop around, be back in plenty of time. She grabbed her purse. "Doris, I'm going out for a bit. Quick question. That meth lab, the one they found last week. That was on Jumonville Road, right?"

Doris stopped her filing, folder half in the drawer. "Yes, why?"

"Just wondering." She hoped Doris wouldn't press it.

No such luck. "There is no reason for you to be asking about that unless…you're planning on going out there. What on earth for?"

"I told you, it's nothing." She wilted under Doris's stern gaze. "Okay, fine. Those other names are a bust. The police are pretty sure Trafford is behind this latest lab. It's his grandmother's house, after all."

Doris's eyebrow twitched.

"My thought is that if I can help the police make that connection, they will have a reason to arrest Trafford, dig more into his activities and prove he killed Colin. And Alex." Alex was a dick, but that wasn't against the law, and definitely not a justifiable reason for homicide.

"I'm no expert, but isn't that rather dangerous? Your friend in the state police would not approve."

"That's why I'm not going to tell him." Sally stepped over to Doris and rested her hands on the older woman's shoulders. "I'm quite sure the police cleared anything dangerous out of the house. I'll be extra careful and I'm only examining the outside. I won't go in. But promise me you won't say anything to Jim if he calls."

"I won't lie to him for you."

"I wouldn't expect you to. I'll settle for you not picking up the phone the second I'm out the door. He's hip-deep in work and this will only unnecessarily add to his stress. I won't be long." Sally left. No, Jim would not approve. But she fully planned to make this a quick trip.

The sky had turned a vivid blue, with a generous helping of thick clouds that looked like whipped foam. The forecast said storms were on the way. When she parked in the weed-choked driveway of the Victorian farmhouse on Jumonville Road, the sun dappled the nearby trees, which were heavy with gold and red leaves. The yard was overgrown with wildflowers and saw grass.

Only now that she was there, she recognized the futility of her task. Any evidence of Trafford's presence would be inside the house, not outside, and that had been cleared out by highly-trained members of the state police. If there was anything to be found, they'd taken it.

She should leave, but she stood mesmerized by the sight of the house. The architecture captured her imagination. She saw it with fresh paint, the porch pristine, comfortable wicker furniture, and a swing inviting a person to sit and relax. Not this sad, decrepit pile waiting to be torn down.

Out of the corner of her eye, she saw movement and turned her head. A woman was power-walking down the road, dressed in a lime-green track suit, arms pumping in time with her brisk steps. Even from a distance, Sally could see the silver hair was cut into a stylish bob.

As the woman got closer, she called a greeting. "Good afternoon! I wouldn't go near that house if I were you. We were all told to stay away."

"I wasn't planning on it." Sally hoped the woman would pause in her exercise. If she lived nearby, she might have information.

She stopped, her breath a bit quick from the pace, but that was all. Up close, her face was lined; she was in her mid-sixties or close to seventy. But the deep brown eyes were keen and she sized up Sally with a shrewd gaze. "Nice young lady like yourself didn't stop for no reason. You aren't one of those people who buy cheap houses and fix them up to be sold, are you?"

"No." Sally smiled and held out her courthouse ID. "Tell me. Do you live around here?"

"Dorothy Warren. My husband, Stuart, and I live down the road. I guess that qualifies as being a neighbor in these parts."

"Did you know the owner of this house? Genevieve Marnier?"

"Yes." Dorothy's smile was wistful. "Genevieve, Pete, Stu, and I played cards regularly. Gen was a mean pinochle player. Of course, that was before Pete died and she got sick."

"Did you ever see her grandson, Aaron?"

"Oh yes." While Dorothy spoke, she gazed at the house. Heavy clouds rolled in, obscuring the sun. "He was such a delightful child, so friendly and helpful. Gen adored him. He was good for her, especially after Pete was gone. She was getting more and more confused, but she was heartbroken when they took Aaron away from her."

"Who took him away?" Jim hadn't mentioned anything about this.

"Social services." Dorothy continued to speak, but her expression said she was remembering better days for the house. "As I said, Gen's confusion grew worse. At times she didn't know where she was. One night, the kitchen caught fire. She didn't do anything, just watched it. Young Aaron tried to put it out, but the fire department came. Gen didn't remember what had happened. After that, they decided she wasn't capable of caring for a child, and Aaron was sent to foster care."

"How old was he?"

"Twelve? Thirteen? Not very old." She shook her head. "Gen really went downhill after that. Alzheimer's is a cruel disease."

Sally let the silence linger for a minute before she spoke again. "Do you know what happened to Aaron?"

"I heard he bounced around the foster system for a while."

Sally was willing to bet the move hadn't been good for anyone involved. Adolescence would be a tough age for something like that, and Aaron might have been angry at being forced to leave his grandmother. "Have you seen him recently? Aaron?"

"Oh heavens, no. I haven't seen him in over ten years."

"Are you sure? Shaved head, lots of tattoos, built like he works out a lot?"

"I did see a man like that once as I was walking by. But I'm sure it wasn't Aaron. He had the most beautiful head of thick, wavy brown hair."

"Was this man with anyone? What was he doing?"

"I didn't see anyone else. He was taking boxes out of the house. I assumed he was someone who'd been hired to clean things out so it could be sold. I would have stopped to chat, but I was in a hurry that day."

Sally thought it was better Dorothy hadn't stopped. If that had been Trafford, the contents of the boxes might have been more than knick-knacks and he almost certainly wouldn't have appreciated the interruption of a nosy neighbor.

A stiff wind started and the sky had darkened while they talked. Now a slow roll of thunder rumbled through the air. "Good gracious," Dorothy said. "I better get going unless I want to get wet. You take care, now." She resumed her brisk walk.

Sally thought she might as well go, too. Dorothy could talk about Aaron's lovely hair as a child, but the adult could easily have shaved it off. She'd mention this to Jim, see what he made of it.

The rain came, light at first but rapidly picked up. Still Sally stared at the house. The story made her feel sorry for Trafford. How would his life have been different if he'd grown up with Genevieve?

A crack of lightning jolted Sally out of her reverie. She was soaked. She definitely had to go so she could dry out and look presentable at her afternoon meeting. She turned to open the car door.

It happened without warning. A whoosh that might have been her imagination, then an explosion. She crouched next to her car, arms covering her head as burning debris fell around her. She felt the heat of fire, heard the crackle of the flames and the hiss of water as it hit the fire, smelled the acrid tang of smoke in the air. When she dared look up, the sight took her breath away.

The stately old Victorian farmhouse was an inferno.

※※※

When Duncan and McAllister pulled into the driveway at Carrington's house on Wharton Furnace Road around eleven on Tuesday, there was a dirty white Honda Civic near the garage. "Trafford owns an early-model Buick, right?" McAllister asked.

"Yep."

"Then who does the Honda belong to?"

"Run the plate."

McAllister tapped on the onboard computer. "Devin Carrington. No outstanding tickets, registration and insurance is up to date." She squinted through the patrol car's windshield. "He's the homeowner of record?"

"Yes." Duncan opened the car door. "And it looks like he's finally at home."

The two troopers climbed the steps onto the tiny porch. McAllister stood to the side, hand on her Sig, while Duncan knocked. "State police." No answer.

A second, more forceful knock and accompanying ID, said a little louder, got a response. One of the men from The Beer House opened the door. Carrington. He was dressed in a plain white undershirt and jeans, and held a cigarette in his left hand. "Can I help you?" he asked, holding the door open just enough to see him, but not the inside of the house.

"We're looking for Aaron Trafford," Duncan said, showing his badge. "Is he here?"

Carrington took a drag off the cigarette. "You can't come in." Smoke wafted out of his mouth as he spoke.

"I didn't ask to come in. I asked if Mr. Trafford was here."

The crunch of footsteps on gravel made Duncan look toward the driveway. He gestured to McAllister, indicating she should stay focused on Carrington.

It was Trafford, in a tight tank shirt and a pair of cargo pants. "Did I hear my name?"

Duncan stepped to the porch railing. "You did. I have a few more questions for you. Can we go inside? Kind of crowded on this porch."

"I already said no," Carrington said, his voice a little petulant.

Trafford smirked. "Now Dev, don't be rude. No reason the troopers can't come in."

Carrington hesitated, then opened the door wider. McAllister kept a tight grip on her sidearm and Duncan laid his finger beside the release on his, then both troopers entered. McAllister continued to watch Carrington, while Duncan faced Trafford, who followed them and shut the door.

"Your grandmother's house. I'm sure you know by now it's been condemned," Duncan said.

Trafford's expression was bland. "I do. Damn shame Gran won't get any money out of a sale."

"When we spoke, you said you didn't know who might have been cooking in the house."

"That's right."

"Any names come to mind since then?"

"Not a one." Trafford's voice held a mocking note.

Duncan considered his next question. "Why are you back in Fayette County, Mr. Trafford? Last time you were here things didn't end amiably. Considering your record, I'd have thought you'd stay away."

"I missed my grandmother."

He's playing with us, Duncan thought. "Since your return, you haven't taken up with any of your old pals? Someone told us you were seen on a street corner known for drug activity."

Trafford paused, the light in his eyes malicious. "Nope."

McAllister did not take her eyes off Carrington as she spoke. "Then you won't mind if we take a look around and verify that for ourselves. Considering we have a witness statement that contradicts you."

Carrington, who'd been quietly smoking, stubbed out his cigarette with a violent motion. "Hell yeah, I mind. This is my house. I'm the one you need to ask."

Trafford chuckled. "Dev, don't get excited. The troopers are just doing their job." The mocking expression and tone returned to Trafford's voice. "If they want to waste their time with us instead of finding the person who's taking advantage of poor old Gran, we should let them. Maybe then they can find the asshole who ruined her home."

Duncan held Trafford's gaze. They needed Carrington's okay to search, since he was the homeowner. But it was clear who was in charge: Trafford. Duncan made a silent bet with himself that Carrington would follow Trafford's suggestion, no matter what.

After a weighty pause, Carrington answered his friend, voice surly. "Fine. Go right ahead."

"And troopers," Trafford added. "Take your time. Don't want it said later that we rushed you and you missed something. We'll wait here."

The two troopers exchanged a quick glance. Trafford was certainly acting like a man who had nothing to hide. "Let's take advantage of the permission," Duncan said under his breath as he and McAllister left the front room. "Don't trash the place, but be as thorough as you can."

Two hours later, a fierce thunderstorm had come and gone, and Duncan was forced to admit Trafford had outmaneuvered them. There was no evidence of any drug production equipment or packaging, never mind the actual drugs. The kitchen garbage contained a blackened banana peel and some coffee grounds. All the other trash cans were empty. He walked into the living room where Trafford waited, a self-satisfied grin on his face.

"There's a garage out back," Duncan said, once again meeting Trafford's amused gaze. "Mind if we take a look out there?"

"Oh, I think you've spent enough time and effort, Trooper," Trafford said, leaning against the wall and hooking his thumbs in his belt loops. "You want to look at any more of the property, you'll need a warrant. I'm afraid Dev's courtesy only goes so far."

McAllister entered the room, holding a thick stack of cash. "Mr. Trafford, do you usually keep several thousand dollars in your possession?" She handed it to Duncan.

He fanned them. All twenties, the bills were not new. A quick glance told him that the serial numbers were not sequential. They were bundled into stacks of one thousand dollars, ten of them. "This is an awful lot of money to have lying around," he said.

Trafford shrugged. "I sold my car. Guy paid cash. Said he didn't have a checking account."

"That would be your Buick?" Trafford nodded, and Duncan continued. "When did you sell it and for how much?"

"Yesterday," Trafford said. "He paid ten grand for it."

"Ten grand for a fifteen-year-old Buick?" McAllister asked.

Trafford shrugged. "I asked for five or best offer. The guy offered ten. Who was I to turn him down?"

"You have a receipt?" Duncan asked.

"Nope. It was a cash transaction and I didn't see the need. It's not illegal to sell a car on your own in this state."

No, it wasn't. But the lack of proof was inconvenient for both sides. Without a receipt, Trafford couldn't prove his claim. Of course, Duncan couldn't disprove it, either. "Did you know the buyer?"

"Nope. He answered the ad. Can I have my money back?" Trafford held out his hand.

"I'm sure you remember his name. What was it?"

Trafford's shoulders twitched. "Tom something? Tim? It was real common. I sold the car, Trooper. That's not a crime. I don't have a receipt and I don't remember the buyer's name. Also not a crime. Give me back the cash."

Duncan bit back a curse as he handed it over. "When was the last time you saw your grandmother?"

Trafford tensed. "I can't remember. I don't like those places. They're as depressing as shit."

McAllister's voice was taut. "You said earlier you missed her."

"I do. That doesn't mean I like nursing homes. I see her other places."

Another true statement, but McAllister was right. Inconsistent. Duncan made a mental note to follow up and check whether Genevieve Marnier had taken any day trips from Running Waters. "You haven't been in her home lately, either."

"Nope."

"That reminds me. We haven't had time to notify her that the house has been condemned. Trooper McAllister, let's make sure we do that today." Duncan watched Trafford's eyes, which had become narrow and hostile.

"You leave her alone, you hear me?" The muscles in Trafford's arms tightened. "She's sick and she doesn't need your shit. I'll tell her. I take care of her."

Duncan exchanged a look with McAllister. "You do? I'm confused here. First you claim you came back because you missed your grandmother. Then you said you don't visit. Now you tell us you take care of her. Which is it?"

"Screw you. I said I take care of her. You leave her alone." Trafford's hands clenched into fists.

"Tell me, Mr. Trafford," McAllister asked, "where were you Monday between noon and four?"

"Here."

"Can anyone confirm that?" Her tone almost matched Trafford's in aggression.

"Sorry, you'll have to take my word for it. Dev was out and no one else was around."

Duncan hoped McAllister wouldn't get into a pissing match, but he didn't want to undermine her authority by telling her to back down. He studied Trafford's posture, which had relaxed again. "You know Colin Rafferty was killed recently."

"So you told me at the bar," Trafford said, voice deadpan.

"By a strange coincidence, the ADA in your trial, Alex Costanzo, was also murdered. Yesterday, as a matter of fact. Someone said they saw Costanzo with you this past Sunday night." Duncan watched for any sign of reaction to his words.

Trafford was silent.

"Can you tell me where you were that night?"

"I was home. I went out. I went to town. I might have gone to Uniontown. Hell, if I'd known my movements were going to be so interesting, I'd have kept a diary. Looks like I'm shit out of luck there." Trafford sneered. "It's a damn shame those lawyers are dead. Police need to do a better job with that whole law and order thing. Now. Unless you have any other legal reason for being here, I'm going to ask you to leave. Well, Dev will ask you since it's his house."

Carrington had stayed quiet during the entire exchange, but he piped up on cue. "Yeah. Get out."

Duncan exchanged a look with McAllister. The set of her jaw said she was still on edge. Time to go. "We'll be in touch about your grandmother's house."

They headed for the door, but McAllister stopped and turned. "You said you placed an ad for the car. What paper and when did it appear?"

Trafford's eyes narrowed. "Why do you care?"

"Because I want to know."

"The Herald Standard. Sunday."

"Last Sunday or a week ago Sunday?" Duncan asked, catching on to the purpose behind the question.

"A week ago." Trafford answered slowly, gaze flicking between the two troopers. "Didn't you say you were leaving?"

"We did," Duncan said. "Have a nice day." He beckoned to McAllister, who gave Trafford a stiff nod, and left.

Outside, McAllister cursed and scuffed her foot through a pile of dead leaves. "What a waste."

"Not entirely," Duncan said. "That was a lot of cash. No one in his right mind pays ten thousand dollars for a Buick LeSabre that old." He studied her. "You okay? You seemed a little wound up in there."

"I don't like people like him," she said, her voice a growl.

"What, criminals? Hardly surprising considering your chosen profession. I'd be more surprised if you did." But her reaction was more than a cop's natural distrust and dislike of a lawbreaker.

"Bullies." She climbed into the car and clicked her seatbelt, the expression on her face dark.

Interesting response. But Duncan let it lie for the moment. Instead he slid into the driver's seat and said, "Nice question about the ad for the car. Good instinct."

"Be interesting to see the classifieds for that day." McAllister sat back, still glowering, but her voice lost its pugnacious edge. "He's awfully touchy about Grandma. And very scattered in his answers. He takes care of her, he missed her, but he doesn't visit? What the hell?"

Duncan gave the house one last look and backed out. "Genevieve's bills are paid by funds from a bank account. How does the money get in the bank?"

"And where does it come from?"

"I think we know that."

"You think Trafford uses his drug money to pay the nursing home and property taxes?"

"The property taxes, definitely. It gave him a production facility. The nursing home, probably. Everybody has a soft spot. When we get back to the barracks, I'll put in some requests to look at Genevieve's bank records. You see if you can scare up a copy of the classifieds for last week Sunday."

"Yes, Boss." McAllister sighed. "You know, if I'd known about the paperwork and research involved in this job, I might have chosen a different line of work."

CHAPTER 30

Sally had a long afternoon.

After the farmhouse explosion, she called and waited for the authorities, then had an interview with a very nice, but very stern, member of the state police. She notified Bryan and told him what happened. He was rather curt when he told her to go home and not come back to the office. He'd cover her afternoon. Sally had never heard that side of him and she supposed he'd let her have it when she went to work tomorrow. She had, after all, pushed it a little far and she considered apologizing on the spot. But she was wet, smelled like smoke, and figured a weak phone apology was insufficient, so she accepted her dismissal. She'd make it up to Bryan somehow.

Back at her apartment, she showered, changed into her most comfortable sweats, brewed a cup of tea, and heated some leftover pasta carbonara for dinner. Maybe she'd go to bed early.

The pounding on her door jolted her out of a half-doze. What the hell? Had she parked in the wrong spot? "Hold on, I'm coming." She unchained the door, telling herself she should have checked the peephole first, but she was too tired.

Dressed in jeans and a sweater, Jim's face was like a thundercloud. A vein pulsed on his forehead. Instinctively, she took half a step back.

"May I come in?" His voice was low with a hint of steely anger under the layer of good manners.

"Uh, sure." She stepped back to let him in, then closed the door. "I guess you heard about this afternoon."

"Oh, I heard all right." He crossed his arms in front of him. "I was surprised enough when my buddy, Alan Porter, informed me that the Jumonville Road house had exploded, but we had a witness. Witnesses are usually good things in a situation like this. I thought it was a neighbor, maybe someone driving by. Imagine my shock when Porter told me our witness was one Sarah Marie Castle. News delivered with a smirk, by the way."

Sally swallowed hard. Jim hadn't raised the volume of his speech one decibel and his tone was icily polite. But at that moment, she'd rather have faced Aaron Trafford. "Jim, please. I can explain."

"Explain." He raised his fist to his mouth, then pointed at her. "Sally, what the...hell were you doing there? Do you understand how dangerous meth houses can be?"

"I thought the PSP cleaned it up."

"We took the materials, the product, the production apparatus. But a lab is never really clean. That's why the houses get condemned."

As he spoke, she heard another tone under the anger. Worry. Learning she'd been at the scene had upset him and she melted a little inside at the thought. "Okay, but with all the stuff gone I didn't see much to fuss about. I didn't think anything was left to explode."

He sighed. "One of the by-products of the process is metal residue. My guess is that there was a leak somewhere and when the storm hit, the water reacted with the metal and caused the explosion." He came over and placed his hands on her shoulders, warm and firm. "Are you okay?"

She could feel the tremor in his muscles through the touch. "I'm all right. I wasn't close enough to get hurt. A little bit of debris hit my car, but all small stuff. Seriously, I'm just...tired." Without much thought, she leaned on him, prompting a strong, comforting embrace. She sagged, relishing the sense of safety.

Jim held her for a long minute. "Tell me," he said when they broke apart. "What were you doing on Jumonville Road?"

"Let me get you a beer first." She fetched the drink from the kitchen and they went to the living room to sit. Once there, she curled up in her quilt, wrapped her hands around her still-warm mug of tea and told him about her conversation with Dorothy Warren. "How much do you want to bet those boxes were filled with drugs?"

"I wouldn't take that bet." He stared at the floor and Sally could practically see the wheels turning in his head.

"That should get you a search warrant, shouldn't it? Of the house where he's staying, or where you think he's staying?"

"We've already been there." He told her of his visit to Carrington's. "Trafford may have been moving drugs from one place to the other, but since we came up empty on a search it's going to be hard to get a warrant for another one."

"You didn't find anything?" She set aside her empty mug. There had to have been something.

"Just a very large amount of cash and a story we don't really buy. We'll be looking into that." He brought his gaze back to her face.

"You've got to go back. There has to be something to incriminate him in two murders. A gun, something. Maybe you need to get Devin Carrington on his own and question him."

"Sally." Jim set the bottle on the floor and leaned forward, arms on his knees. "I get that this case is important to you. Colin was a friend, you made a promise...you told me. But honestly? You're worrying me and more than a little."

"I told you, I'm fine."

"Staking out that corner was bad enough. You took evidence from Costanzo's office, you went to a dangerous scene and don't tell me you didn't think it was dangerous, and now it sounds like you're telling me to find an excuse to question a witness."

Sally stared at her hands.

"You're a defense attorney, for God's sake. You should be telling me all the reasons I can't pull Carrington in for questioning. I always thought you were pretty level-headed. What gives? Please don't tell me 'nothing,' either. I'm not stupid."

She closed her eyes, fighting tears brought on by frustration and exhaustion. She used the quilt to dab her eyes. "I know sneaking into Alex's office and taking that book was wrong. I...panicked and didn't think. Alex and Colin were involved in an extortion racket, subverting the system. How would you feel if you learned something similar about two of your colleagues in the PSP?"

"Pretty damn angry."

"Exactly. As for why I went to that house...you and I aren't so different, Jim." She took a deep breath. "Killian has arrested a man for

Colin's murder. It's the wrong guy. Would you want to see an innocent man go to jail?"

"That doesn't explain why you're stuck on Trafford."

"Because it's the least complicated explanation. What do they call that? Occam's Razor? Use the hypotheses with the fewest assumptions?"

"Something like that."

"Trafford is the fewest assumptions. I need to figure out how he did it. How did he get into the courthouse, past the security and video, and into the office? I'm sure he had means, and he definitely had motive if we're right about his 'tame lawyer' comment. He was threatened by the idea Colin might bolt. I need to show opportunity. I get justice for Colin, and De'Shawn Thomas doesn't go down for a crime he didn't commit." Sally picked at the edge of her quilt.

Jim's grin was faint, but there. "What about Alex Costanzo?"

"Yeah, him too. I guess."

They sat in a silence broken only by the sound of the occasional passing car from the street below. Then Jim said, "Okay, I get all that. There's something else, though. What is it? I've known you for a year and you've been awfully stubborn at times. Not like this."

She'd been crazy to think she could hide anything from him. "Before I came to Fayette County, I was with the Allegheny County DA."

"Yeah, you mentioned that once."

"I was young, new. I spent a lot of time there knowing I was right, but not sure enough of myself to hold my ground against older, more experienced attorneys. Not just men." She'd put it all behind her, or she thought she had. "Women, too. I didn't know how to stand up for my opinion."

"And now you do."

"Yes. It's probably not something you ever had to deal with, this need to earn your credibility." She got up to take the mug and bottle to the kitchen. She heard Jim follow her. Once there, she put the containers on the counter and turned.

He leaned in the doorway. "What makes you say that? You think I showed up to roll call my first day and hey presto, everybody listened to me?"

"But you're so…" She waved her hand at him. "You."

He arched an eyebrow in response.

Was she being unfair? "I've never seen you in a situation where you weren't in charge. Respected."

He chuckled. "Because you met me when I had twelve years on the job. Believe me, there were plenty of older troopers who made me work for it when I was new. Folks who made me justify how I tied my bootlaces. A few made it pretty clear they wouldn't be interested in what I had to say until I'd spent a few years in the trenches. Not Fitz, my FTO, but others. It's something I swore I wouldn't do when I became an FTO myself."

"I can't see you being that way."

"Thanks for that. Look. Everybody can have a good idea, Sally. Or a bad one. You don't have to justify yourself to me." He paused. "But I know you. You have to be careful. If you're wrong and it results in an innocent man going down, it'll crush you."

His words made sense and his concern was touching, but still. She had to stick to her position. "I'm right about this, Jim. I know I am. I feel it. You understand that, right? Instinct?"

"I do."

"I know you and I have to do things differently. You have to explore all options because that's how you do your job. Eventually you'll get to where I am because I know you're a smart guy and Trooper McAllister seems pretty on top of things, too. Just don't ask me to stop doing what I'm doing. I can't." She bit her lip, waiting for his response.

He waited a bit, mulling over her words. Then he pushed away from the doorway and took a step forward, holding out his hand. "I know better than to argue with you. Just remember. I've got your back. No questions asked."

She grasped his hand, strong and firm, yet gentle. "Thanks."

CHAPTER 31

On Wednesday morning, Bryan barely spoke to her at the coffee pot. He stirred his creamer with too much vigor, sloshing liquid on the floor. After wiping it up, he stormed off.

Sally followed him to his office. "Bryan, yesterday. I'm sorry. It won't happen again."

"It better not." He sat down and focused on his computer, refusing to meet her eyes. "I cut you a lot of slack, Sally, because you're a good lawyer. I suggest you get back to being a lawyer and let this rest. There are other people to carry this one to completion. Understand?"

"Bry…" He looked up. When Sally couldn't detect anger in his eyes, she continued. "Are we at least agreed that Colin's partner in this was most likely Alex Costanzo? The amount of power needed to pull this off, the timing of Alex's death. It's too coincidental, don't you think?"

Bryan's gaze softened. "All the more reason you should stay clear unless someone asks you a question. Then you answer truthfully and promptly. You don't want to get any more mixed up in this than you are. For your own good and the good of this office." He looked back at his work.

Sally recognized a dismissal when she heard one. Back in her own office, she slumped at her desk. What did she have? Colin's notebook. There had to be more than that. The list of dockets and numbers and symbols might indicate something was amiss, but a prosecutor would need more. Lots more.

Had Colin kept additional information as insurance? It made sense. Wouldn't he want more than a simple list? She went to Colin's empty office, stripped of anything the police considered evidence, all cases reassigned. It looked even sadder with the bare desk and walls. Colin's few personal possessions were in a box, ready to be sent…somewhere. His mother, probably.

Sally searched the desk looking for false bottoms or sides, checked for loose carpet, and looked behind the filing cabinets. Nothing. There weren't any hidden safes, but she checked behind the framed diplomas just in case. No luck. The parchment was exactly what it looked like.

She bit her lip, staring at the barren space. Of course she didn't find anything. The police would have found it when Colin was murdered. And if they hadn't, the ethics folks would have.

The box of personal effects drew her eye. Colin's mother. He trusted her. If there was more evidence, something that pointed to a link to Trafford, he might leave it with her for safekeeping. Deborah Rafferty might not even recognize it for what it was. Sally would drive up to Pittsburgh tonight after work.

She picked up the box and walked toward her office. What Trafford had said, "a tame lawyer." Jim had posited it could mean Trafford had bribed someone to keep him out of jail. That wouldn't be Colin. Or not just Colin. A simple assistant public defender wouldn't have the power.

It brought her back to Alex, who'd been an ADA. If Trafford had a highly-placed attorney on his payroll, that would definitely be protection from jail. Colin had to be killed because he threatened to expose past crimes. But there must have been a falling out between Alex and Trafford for the drug-dealer to have shot his protector. Or maybe with the threat of the ethics investigation, and the likelihood that Alex was going to jail, he'd become expendable.

But Alex wouldn't put himself in that position. He was smart. An asshole, but smart. He'd have something in his possession to keep Trafford in his place. But where?

His office. If she had been Alex, would she have kept anything incriminating there? On the one hand, it was a public space. He might have preferred to keep any proof of wrongdoing elsewhere. On the other hand, what was more secure, and less likely to be a suspected hiding spot, than the office of a county prosecutor?

Doris came in with the mail. She dropped it on Sally's desk, but didn't leave. Instead she looked over the top of her glasses, a small frown on her face.

"What is it, Doris?"

"You. You're thinking of something. I can tell by your expression." Doris's voice held a disapproving note. "Didn't I overhear Bryan tell you to get back to work? You're still thinking of Colin and that dirty drug-dealer, aren't you?"

Was Sally so transparent? She'd have to work on that. "He told me not to do anything, Doris. I can't help thinking, can I?"

"I suppose not." Doris still didn't move. "What are you thinking about?"

Sally eyed the plump older woman. The office mother. Would Doris run to Bryan? Probably not. She might snitch to Jim if she thought Sally was in danger, but not Bryan. He was just another chick to be mothered. Older, maybe, but still a chick. "Well, this extortion thing is pretty settled as truth, right?"

"I thought so."

"But my friend, the cop, had another idea." She told Doris about the tame lawyer comment. "If that's the case, wouldn't Alex keep some record? Something he could use as leverage to protect himself if Trafford ever crossed a line?"

Doris folded her hands. "I suppose. Mr. Costanzo was very thorough in everything else. I don't see why this would be different. What's your point?"

"Where would he keep it?" Doris blinked and Sally pressed on. "Don't you think he'd keep it close to him? Safe? Say in his office?"

Comprehension dawned on Doris's face. "Oh no you don't. Look here. I'm only a secretary. But I've worked here long enough to pick up on some things." She wagged a finger. "You're thinking of searching Mr. Costanzo's office. You have no ethical, legal reason to be there. The police already searched. If something was there, don't you think they'd have found it?"

"But if they didn't know what they were looking for, maybe they missed something. It's possible."

"It's irresponsible." The secretary turned to go, but stopped at the door. "Bryan has enough to worry about without you going rogue and breaking into what I am quite sure is still considered a crime scene. No one has any reason to go there except the police. My advice? Stay out of it and do your job." She left, closing the door firmly behind her.

Doris was right. No one had any business in Alex's office except the police. Sally picked up her phone and dialed.

⸙⸙⸙

Duncan and McAllister were on the road late Wednesday morning when Duncan's phone rang. "Hey."

"Did you find any of the original materials from the blackmail scheme? In Alex's office?" Sally asked, voice low.

Wherever she was, she didn't want to be heard. He thought over what they'd taken from the office. "Not that I remember, no."

"You need to go back and look. As soon as possible." She clicked off.

He slipped his phone back into his pocket and glanced at McAllister in the driver's seat. "When we were at the DA's office, right after Costanzo's body was found, we didn't find any details about Trafford or the extortion scheme, did we?"

"Nope."

He tapped the door. "Another item on the to-do list. We need to search that office again."

She glanced at him. "Why?"

"Got a tip. This time we need to specifically look for materials that might relate to the racket with Rafferty or anything that draws a line from Costanzo to Trafford."

"Tip from whom? Ms. Castle?" she asked, eyes narrowed.

"From a reliable source."

"We'll need another warrant."

"I know." They'd be at the courthouse. It would be easy to get a signature.

She glanced at the dashboard clock and made a turn that would take them into downtown Uniontown. "We're back on Trafford? You must trust this Castle woman a lot, Boss."

"We were never off Trafford. He's one suspect among many for Costanzo's murder. A man can be guilty of more than one crime at a time, you know." He watched the grassland give way to the outskirts of the city. "And yes. I trust Ms. Castle." She was sometimes infuriating, but he trusted her. He reached for some of the extra affidavit forms he kept in the car and started writing.

"Speaking of Trafford, I pulled the classifieds for that day he said he placed the ad. I couldn't find it."

Duncan wasn't surprised. The whole story had been weak. A defense attorney would argue that Trafford had misremembered the date or the paper, but the more realistic explanation is that the whole thing had been a lie.

They reached the courthouse and McAllister parked. "I thought we wanted to see Tyra Young again today."

"It's only noon. This search probably won't take long." He finished the form and opened the door. "You do realize that talking to Tyra might happen tonight? Remember, this isn't a nine to five job."

McAllister shrugged. "I don't have any plans."

They headed inside to find a judge. Duncan had worded the warrant to give them the widest possible scope.

"I thought you searched the office immediately after finding Mr. Costanzo," the judge said, pen poised over the form.

"New information. I'm sure you've heard about the trial-rigging scandal that is currently under investigation by the state ethics board?"

The judge's nose wrinkled in distaste.

"I have information the scandal may link to Mr. Costanzo's death. We need to go back and look more closely."

The judge sniffed, but he signed the form. "Be careful, Trooper," he said, holding it out. "You could be unearthing a lot of worms with this one."

"Yes, your honor. Believe me, I'm not any happier about it than you are." Duncan took the form, and he and McAllister left. From there, they proceeded to the district attorney's office, where a disgruntled receptionist unlocked the door to Costanzo's office.

"No one's been in here?" Duncan asked. It was the same woman who'd been there the day Costanzo was shot.

She shook her head. "DA Harding was pretty clear we were to stay out until he gave the go-ahead." She walked back to her desk.

"I'm a little lost," McAllister said, closing the door of Costanzo's empty office. "Why are we here?"

Harding must have laid down the law. Even Costanzo's office supplies, usually the first things to be pilfered when someone left, were on the heavy desk. "Two reasons. First, we know, or strongly suspect,

Costanzo was complicit in altering trial materials as part of that extortion scheme."

"Like your buddy's search warrant."

"Right. I'm willing to bet the originals still exist somewhere."

McAllister set her hat on the desk and pulled gloves from her belt. "Except they've already looked in Rafferty's office, both victims' houses, and I'm sure they searched here. If it was there to be found, wouldn't it have come to light by now?"

"Possibly." Duncan took out his own gloves and put his hat next to McAllister's. "That's why we need to get creative with our search and why I wrote the warrant like I did. We search everything. Even under the carpet."

"Maybe they destroyed it."

"If you were a blackmailer, would you destroy the information that allowed you to make good on your threat?"

"What's the second thing? You used 'first' so there's more."

"Trafford." Duncan pulled out a desk drawer to looking for false bottoms and hidden niches. "Let's say he did have Costanzo on his payroll."

McAllister was pulling books from the shelves, shaking them out and tapping on the back of the unit. "His tame lawyer."

"Trafford is a nasty bit of goods." He pulled out another drawer. "If you were dealing with him, wouldn't you want insurance?"

"Abso-damn-lutely." McAllister tossed more books on the floor. "The original search warrant?"

"Yup."

"It would clear Fitzpatrick, too. Wouldn't hurt your feelings, would it?"

Fitz deserved that much. He'd retired with a full pension, but restoring his reputation would mean a lot to Duncan's old FTO.

McAllister finished with the one set of shelves and moved on to another. "Costanzo has this insurance. Something happens that makes him threaten to use it, and Trafford kills him. That the idea?"

"One of them." There was nothing in the desk. Duncan turned his attention to the chairs.

"And Tyra?" McAllister paused, a book in her hand.

"We'll get to her, McAllister. One thing at a time."

CHAPTER 32

Early Wednesday afternoon, Sally stared at her computer screen. Jim hadn't called, but there'd been a state police cruiser parked in front of the courthouse when she came back from lunch. Ten to one he was upstairs with his trainee pulling apart Costanzo's office.

If only someone there had seen Trafford. Of course, that was exactly the type of question Jim would have asked, especially after they'd seen the argument on that street corner Sunday night. Had he talked to everyone? Would it be an ethics violation for her to ask? Just to confirm, of course.

Her desk phone rang, jolting her from her reverie. The number on the caller ID was unfamiliar. "Fayette County Public Defender's office, Sally Castle speaking."

"Sally! It's Kelly Martin. My mother said you called looking for me."

"Kelly, yes. How are you?" Sally looked again at the number on her phone. It was local. "Are you in Uniontown?"

"I am. Mom said you were pretty insistent. Must be about something important."

"It is. Kelly, do you remember Aaron Trafford?"

When Kelly spoke again, her voice was dead serious. "How could I possibly forget?"

"He's back in town. I know it was a year ago, but I need to know if you ever saw him with Alex Costanzo or in the DA's office."

"I saw on the news that Costanzo is dead. You think it was Trafford?"

"He's a good candidate in my book, but I need to put the two of them together. If you've seen the news, you also know about this extortion scandal that's brewing and the fact that an attorney from my office was killed."

"I do."

"I think Trafford's involved in that, too."

Kelly paused. "Sally, I'm only home for a few days. I don't want to get involved in this. I'm engaged. Trafford is trouble. Walk away."

Walk away? Not possible. "I can't."

"You should, you really should." The fear and concern in Kelly's voice was almost tangible.

"You've seen them, Alex and Trafford." Silence. "Kelly, please. Help me with this. When were you ever one to back off just because it was hard? Two men are dead, two offices under the taint of corruption…if you know something and you stay quiet, you'll never be able to forgive yourself even if you go back to wherever you're living these days."

"South Carolina." Kelly's sigh echoed over the line. "You're right. But this isn't a conversation for the phone. Can we meet for a late lunch?"

Sally had already eaten, but she might be able to squeak out and call it a meeting if the reason were compelling. "What about dinner? I can leave early."

"Okay then, dinner at four. Where?"

"Dex's." Sally rattled off the address. After she hung up, she called the restaurant and made a reservation. No way was she going to risk not getting a table.

☙☙☙

Duncan surveyed the office. "Shit."

Books were piled on the floor. They'd cleared the desk of its contents, which now sat in stacks on the floor. They'd tapped on every surface, checked under every drawer, looked behind every frame. Nothing.

McAllister blew hair from her face. "Maybe he really did destroy everything, Boss. We didn't find anything at his house, we're not finding it here. How many more places can we look?"

Duncan wouldn't have believed it. Still didn't. But facts seemed determined to prove him wrong. Criminals had done stranger things than defy a cop's expectations. He glanced at his watch. Two-thirty.

The door opened and the receptionist stuck her head inside the room. "Is there anything I can do for you?"

"Ms. Stewart, right? Tell me." Duncan stepped over a load of books. "Is there anywhere else, besides his home, Mr. Costanzo would have stored important items? Papers, books, boxes…anything?"

Stewart shook her head. "He was pretty uptight about his stuff. Work never went home. He liked to keep it all close by and arranged to his liking. He'd have an aneurysm if he saw the mess in here."

He probably would and not for the reason she was thinking. "Thanks. We'll try and put it back as best we can. Should be out of your hair by quitting time," Duncan said.

McAllister mumbled something that was almost certainly profanity as she started to re-shelve the books.

"Thank you. By the way, do you know when this office is going to be released? You know, when it'll no longer be a crime scene?" Stewart gave an apologetic smile. "Naturally, we want to get a new occupant in here. And, well, the vultures are circling."

"Vultures?" Duncan asked.

"People after supplies." Her cheeks pinked a little, maybe with embarrassment. "You know, the staplers and pens. Plus Mr. Costanzo had a few nice pieces of furniture that some of the ADAs are eyeing up for their offices. Those wing chairs, for example. And that club chair." She pointed at a dark brown chair covered in micro suede that sat near one of the windows. "I don't know how we're going to move that one, though."

"Really?" Duncan walked over to the chair. It wasn't big. "One guy should be able to carry it. Or put it on a dolly. Heck, if I finish early enough I'll carry it for you."

Stewart laughed. "I'm not doubting your strength, Trooper, but I don't think you could. The chair is a beast. The cleaning staff hates it because they can't move it around. I don't think the stupid thing has budged an inch since Mr. Costanzo brought it in." She left and shut the door.

McAllister stopped her task. "She's kidding. I could move that chair. My mom had one like it and I used to shift it all the time to vacuum."

Duncan walked around the chair. It didn't look particularly heavy. Just a standard club chair from any one of a dozen furniture lines. No brass ornamentation, no heavy wood.

"Although now that I think about it, does that chair look odd to you?" McAllister joined him.

He looked up. "Looks comfortable, if that's what you mean. Those wing backs were awful, remember? Hard as a slab, despite the fancy leather."

"That's not it. It doesn't match."

Duncan compared it to the rest of the office furnishings. She was right. With a much more casual look, it didn't match at all.

"That receptionist, Stewart. She said Costanzo was picky," McAllister said.

"Uh huh."

"Well, this is a club chair upholstered in micro suede. Low-end of the luxury scale." She waved at all of the other furniture. "Everything else is leather and wood. Very deluxe. If Alex Costanzo was so fussy about his office furnishings, why does he have a chair in here I could get from a discount store?"

"Good question. Let's move it away from the window."

McAllister grabbed an arm and tugged. "Ugh. Is this thing weighted with granite?"

"It can't be that heavy."

"Maybe not, but it is."

He frowned. The chair was not big, and McAllister, while on the petite side, wasn't weak. He tugged on the chair. It should have toppled easily, but it didn't. Definitely weighted down. He tried to pull off the seat cushion, but it was firmly attached. "Stand back." He shoved the chair over. It landed with a thunk. Two thunks. One from the chair hitting the floor, another from something inside the base.

"You hear that?" McAllister asked.

Duncan knelt to examine the screws holding the base of the chair in place. "These are scratched. Someone has taken it off and put it back." He removed the utility knife from his belt, selected the screwdriver, and went to work. He had the base of the chair off in short order.

McAllister let out a low whistle. "Well I'll be damned. That's a lot of paper. And a metal strong box. No wonder it was heavy."

Duncan pulled out folders, and sheaves of paper held together with binder clips. The box was locked, a key not a combination. "Do you remember if Costanzo's keys had one that would match this?"

"Not offhand."

"No matter, we'll find out." He handed her a stack of paper. "Start reading."

It was trial paperwork. Notes, warrants...all things that should be part of the official record. Everything they needed to prove extortion, and most likely the collusion between Rafferty and Costanzo. Duncan was glad Sally couldn't see this. Even if she knew it before, seeing the hard proof would break her heart.

McAllister's voice interrupted his thoughts. "Boss, look at this." She held out a paper that looked like a warrant.

He took it. "Son of a bitch." It was the original for the Trafford search last fall. He scanned the contents. There it was, evidence of drug production. It would have covered the pseudoephedrine. He'd been right. Fitz hadn't screwed up. But clearing his friend's name was no recompense for the corruption staring Duncan in the face. "You find anything that supports our theory?"

"That Trafford bribed Costanzo? No." She picked up the lockbox and shook it. The contents shifted and thunked. "Maybe in here?"

"Could be. What about anything related to Tyra or Elijah Young?"

"Not that I saw, but I haven't read everything."

Duncan stood. A connection to the Youngs, Trafford, or both was probably somewhere in the mess. "Let's get a box and gather this up. Be extra careful with the chain of custody form. I'll call Nicols and find out if we should take it with us or call the ethics board. I'm betting on the former."

"Homicide trumps ethics investigation?" She looked at the pile of paper. "Quite a motive for murder, wouldn't you say?"

"That's putting it mildly." He pulled out his phone to call the lieutenant. Sorry, Ms. Stewart, he thought. We aren't putting everything back in place after all.

CHAPTER 33

Sally entered Dex's slightly after four and scanned the crowd. There were quite a few empty tables; she was ahead of the dinner rush. That made it easy to see Kelly across the room.

Kelly spotted her and stood. "Sally." Kelly insisted on a brief hug. "You look good. Let me guess. New boyfriend."

Sally felt herself blush. "Um, not exactly, no. You look good yourself. The south agrees with you. And engaged? Congratulations."

"Thanks. He's a doctor. The winters in Columbia are nicer, the food is great, but I'll tell you one thing. I'll never be a Southern belle." Kelly sat and smoothed a napkin across her lap. She'd already ordered herself a glass of white wine.

Sally flagged down a passing waiter. "Glass of merlot, please." When the waiter moved off, she looked at her old colleague. "I'm glad you called me."

"Mom said you left a couple messages. I figured it was important, I just didn't think…"

"It had to do with Trafford."

Kelly rearranged her flatware. "You said the news is right."

"Depends on the news."

"Two murders, both shootings. Colin Rafferty from your office, and Alex Costanzo. The ADA with attitude."

Her wine arrived and Sally took a sip before responding. "ADA with attitude?"

Kelly shrugged. "More polite than saying asshole who couldn't keep his hands to himself."

Sally had heard rumors, although she'd never been the object of that kind of attention from him personally. "If that's the case, how come he's never been reported?" That would have been hot courthouse gossip.

"Because the girls on whom his lines worked didn't care, and those who would be offended, like moi, knew enough to stay away."

Made sense. Sort of.

"You said on the phone Trafford was back."

"Yes." Sally filled Kelly in on the latest, including the explosion of the lab. "The police aren't positive it's him."

"But where there's smoke, there's fire." Kelly swirled the contents of her glass. "You think he's involved with these murders?"

"I do. They've arrested someone else in Colin's case, but I think they've got it wrong. The investigating detective doesn't believe me. I need some hard proof and I intend to get it."

"You always were a bit of a spitfire when you wanted to be."

"I have a friend who's a cop. He's the one investigating Alex's death, actually. Jim, my friend, is open to the possibility that Trafford is involved in both shootings, but he has some other angles to investigate." That was nice and vague. Jim wouldn't get in trouble from that. Not that Kelly knew anyone in the PSP she could call and blab to.

Kelly downed the rest of her wine. "And you need a witness who puts both of them together."

"Yes. That's where you come in." Sally studied the other woman's face, a picture of desire to do the right thing versus the desire to stay out of the way. "I understand you've moved away. You're making a good life for yourself. Trafford's not exactly the warm fuzzy type and it's perfectly natural for you to be a little scared of him. Hell, more than a little."

"That's an understatement."

"But Kelly." Sally leaned in. "If you have information that will put him away for double homicide, he's not going to get the opportunity to threaten you. We can talk to the DA. I'm sure Harding will be willing to work with you, especially considering you were once an employee in his office and a damn good one at that."

Kelly was silent. Around them, other diners talked and ate, not a care in the world. She stared at the tablecloth so intently it might have been the most interesting thing in Uniontown.

Sally counted in her head. It was clear to her that Kelly was making a decision. Sally had made her best pitch; it was a waiting game, now.

Kelly exhaled. "I saw Trafford and Mr. Costanzo together. At the DA's office last fall."

Sally pulled a small notebook from her purse. "Mind if I take notes?"

"Go ahead."

"Thanks. Do you remember any details or just that you saw him?"

"It was one of those things that would be hard to forget." Kelly grimaced. "I saw him a couple weeks before I left for Columbia. A lot of folks had gone to lunch. I was on my way out, ready to lock the exterior door. I ran right into him. Trafford. He shoved his way into the office and demanded to see Mr. Costanzo."

"Then what happened?"

"He stormed down the hall, bellowing for Mr. Costanzo. It was terrifying. I had just about worked up the courage to tell him Mr. Costanzo wasn't there when he came out of his office, mad as hell."

Sally scribbled furiously. When she got in her car, she would call Jim. "I know it's been a year, but do you remember what they talked about?"

Kelly had gotten a refill on her wine. She took a gulp before speaking, the memory clearly rattling her. "Mr. Costanzo hustled Trafford into his office pretty quickly, but Trafford was practically shouting. The words were muffled, but I could hear enough."

Sally held her breath.

"He was swearing like a trucker. 'You said you would handle this. I paid money and you said you'd effing handle it.' I remember that."

"What else?"

"Mr. Costanzo replied. He was harder to make out. I think he was trying to get Trafford to calm down. 'Don't worry, he'll be fine.' I remember that. Then I heard the door open and Trafford said 'he looks like a pussy to me, so you better hope that he can keep his mouth shut' or something like that. I didn't want him to see me, so I ducked into one of the conference rooms."

Probably a wise move. "What about Alex? Did he see you?"

Kelly shook her head. "I stayed in the conference room until I heard two doors shut. I checked, saw the empty hallway, and got out as fast as I could."

Sally leaned forward. "Why didn't you say anything before now?"

Kelly's laugh was shaky. "Are you kidding? Have you ever seen or talked to Trafford? I was scared half to death of what would happen if he saw me at that minute. I sure didn't want to say anything afterward. Mr. Costanzo would find out, he'd probably tell his friendly neighborhood criminal…no way. I'd just heard him threaten someone and I had no doubt that threat was physical violence. I wasn't going to let the victim be me."

Sally might have wished her friend had acted otherwise, but she wasn't sure she could blame her for keeping quiet. She closed the notebook. "Thank you for meeting with me. That cop friend of mine. He's in the state police. He's a good guy. If I call him, are you willing to make a statement? To testify?"

"Because if you tell him you heard it from an unnamed source it's hearsay and useless."

"Correct."

Kelly took a deep breath, then nodded. "You're right. I can't let Trafford walk again, for the murder of two attorneys this time. Harding is a good DA, he'll do his best to keep me out of the crossfire. Yeah, I'll talk to your friend."

⁂

As instructed, Duncan and McAllister brought the box of material from Costanzo's office to the barracks. "How long do you think we'll get to keep this?" McAllister asked.

"No idea. That's why the lieutenant gets paid more than we do. To fight those battles." He checked the clock.

"We going to talk to Tyra now?"

"I'm not sure. Let's grab some food and figure out our plan. I think we need to have one this time."

"Are we gonna change into civvies?"

"Wasn't planning on it." Duncan's cell phone buzzed. It was a text from Sally. "Please meet me at home ASAP." What could warrant an urgent visit? Duncan was tempted to respond that he was busy. Then again, if Sally was planning another field trip, maybe he should go over there. He sent a confirmation and turned to McAllister. "We need to make a slight detour."

"Oh?"

"Quick stop at Ms. Castle's apartment." Duncan took in the younger trooper's look and added, "Business, not pleasure."

They could stay in uniform, but not take a patrol car, so they used Duncan's Jeep. It was about five-thirty when they pulled up in front of Sally's building.

"You want I should wait here?" McAllister asked.

"I told you, this is business. Come on." He led her to Sally's apartment and knocked.

There was almost no delay in opening the door. "Jim! I need to—" Sally pulled up when she saw McAllister. "Oh, hi Trooper McAllister."

"Evening." McAllister voice was neutral, but she gave Duncan a look that plainly said "business, huh?"

Sally looked a little wrong-footed as she motioned them in. "Uh, come in. I didn't mean to interrupt a shift."

"You didn't." It was clear to him that Sally had expected him to be alone. McAllister was all professionalism now, but he was sure to hear some ribbing when they got back to their task. Women. "What's so urgent?"

"I was able to connect with a friend at the District Attorney's office today." Sally proceeded to tell Kelly's story, talking so fast the words tumbled over each other. "That's the connection. Trafford, Costanzo…how much you want to bet they were talking about Colin? The threat was made last fall, but it doesn't sound like it came with an expiration date. That proves Trafford's your killer."

"Hold up. You said this woman's name was Kelly Martin?"

Sally nodded.

Duncan looked at McAllister, who was already flipping through her notes. "How'd we miss her? More specifically, how did you miss her?"

McAllister was mumbling to herself as she read. "I didn't, I swear. There is no mention of a Kelly Martin in my notes. Not from the people who were at the office the day of the Costanzo shooting and she wasn't on the list of absentees for follow up."

"Because she doesn't work there," Sally said.

He could feel the headache coming on. "A second ago you said she worked at the DA's office."

"She used to work there." Sally glanced at McAllister, who was still checking her notes. "Didn't I say that?"

"You did not." This was why he didn't like rushing. "My apologies, McAllister."

"No worries." She stuffed her notebook in her pocket. "I knew I didn't miss anyone," she muttered.

Duncan let it go. McAllister had just as much right to be annoyed as he did. "I need her address and phone number."

"Well, she lives in South Carolina; she's in town for a visit. I have her mother's address. This is her cell phone number." Sally held out a piece of paper, took one look at the troopers and added, "She knows she needs to be interviewed. She's a paralegal, she understands the drill. She's good for an interview and testifying, if it comes to that. Understandably nervous, but she'll do it."

He took the paper. "We'll add it to our to-do list."

"But Jim—"

"Don't push me." Duncan took a deep breath and marshaled his professionalism. "Thank you for the information. We will add it to what we know and follow up with Ms. Martin. We'll also inform Detective Killian. Right now, we have something to do. Is there anything else?"

Sally shook her head, shooting a slightly guilty look at McAllister.

"Then we'll be in touch." He opened the door.

"It's nice to meet you again," Sally said to McAllister. "Sorry for interrupting."

McAllister nodded. "Likewise." She headed out and Duncan shut the door. Back in the Jeep, she clicked her seatbelt. "You didn't have to be so sharp with her, Boss. Especially not for my sake. Sounds like she's pretty invested in the outcome of this one."

"She is. I'll apologize later. She'll understand." Sally probably would, too. "I'm sorry for doubting your work."

"No worries. Next up, Tyra?"

"Food first. Then Tyra."

⁂

After Jim and McAllister left, Sally sagged against the door. "Well, that could have gone better." She hadn't figured on Jim turning up with his trainee and she should have made it clear from the start Kelly no longer worked in Fayette County. Jim was reasonable, though. He wouldn't hold anything against McAllister, who did seem like a nice person.

If Sally was honest, she'd hoped for more of a response than "we'll add it to our to-do list." Did he not understand the weight of what she'd said? She finally put Alex and Trafford together in another less-than-friendly discussion. Hell, Trafford had uttered an out-and-out threat and Colin was the only logical target. If that didn't at least deserve to go to the top of Jim's list, she didn't know what did.

Then again, maybe there was something going on he wasn't telling her. That had to be it. Yeah, he was usually pretty generous with information, but Alex had been found in a seedy motel, immediately after sex. Sally had to admit the constant meetings with Tyra, a known prostitute, were legally sketchy at best. Perhaps that was what occupied the rest of Jim's tasks. Although how that trumped a murder investigation, Sally didn't know.

She brewed herself a cup of tea and settled in with her mug, a legal pad, and pen. She made a bullet list of everything she knew. "It doesn't have to be just one thing," she murmured. Alex meets a prostitute. He had some hold over her; that would explain the multiple meetings and the fact that Tyra had clearly not wanted to be near him when Sally found them at that restaurant.

Colin's death she had squared away. He was a threat to Trafford's safety that was eliminated, plain and simple. She still needed to figure out how Trafford had gotten into the courthouse with a gun, but those were details she, or she and Jim, could work out later.

Alex's death, now that was another story. He been at the Twin Oaks, but no way he would be totally anonymous no matter what he'd done to hide. Trafford found out he was there, broke in on them, and shot Alex for whatever reason. Revenge, betrayal, insurance. It didn't matter. "Why didn't he shoot Tyra, too?" After all, the woman would have seen him. Unless she'd been in the bathroom or something. Cleaning up, getting ready to leave. The noise in the bedroom made her stay hidden. When she came out, Trafford was gone and Alex was dead. She didn't call because she was scared or perhaps she was grateful her "customer" had been disposed of.

It was a good theory. Sally liked it. She'd be sure to call Jim and talk it over with him. But he'd looked awfully irritated when he left. She should definitely give him some time to cool off.

CHAPTER 34

Dinner was fast-food drive through. Not Duncan's favorite, but sometimes beggars couldn't be choosers.

"Are we going straight to Tyra's?" McAllister asked around the straw to her milkshake.

It was only six; they might get lucky and Tyra would be at home. Duncan finished off his own shake. "Might as well."

The lights were off at the home and no one answered Duncan's authoritative knock. The trash cans were empty, rolling on the sidewalk with a grating sound.

"You're going to put your fist through the door," McAllister said. "She's not here. Are we going to wait for her?"

"We don't have all night." Duncan got back in the car.

McAllister followed. "Do you know where she'd be on a Wednesday?"

"I'm willing to bet she's working. Yes, on a weeknight. Let's cruise downtown. Keep your eyes open."

It was a mid-October cold snap with the overnight temps dipping to the low 40s. Uniontown didn't quite have the same kind of "red light" district that other cities did. They were on Mt. Vernon Ave, near the Salvation Army, when McAllister pointed. "There. Woman up ahead, under the light. Pretty sure that's her."

Duncan pulled over and squinted. Even if it wasn't Tyra, the woman might know where to find a fellow streetwalker. When she walked away from the pools of light, he could see puffs from her breath. He watched her pace up and down, rubbing her bare arms. A few cars drove by, but no one stopped. Except for the woman, the sidewalk was deserted. With all the surrounding stores closed, it was no surprise business was thin.

"How're we going to play it?" McAllister looked at him. "You want me to come from the back?"

A lot depended on whether Tyra would run. Duncan went with the gut instinct that sympathy, not brute force, was the way to approach. "You talked to her before. You lead."

They split up, Duncan walking down the opposite side of the street, while McAllister made a more direct approach. "Excuse me, Tyra Young? Trooper McAllister. We spoke before. I have some more questions." McAllister's voice cut the night air.

When Duncan crossed the street, he could see Tyra wore a skimpy blue dress with silver threads running through it and shoes with spiked heels so high, it was a shock she could balance on them. She wouldn't run anywhere in those. Still, he positioned himself to cut Tyra off if she proved to be more nimble than anticipated.

She started at the mention of her name, took a few hesitant steps backward, then gasped when she bumped into Duncan. "I don't know anything. I didn't do anything. I was just hanging, I swear." The streetlight gleamed off eyes wide with fear.

"Trooper McAllister has a few questions, that's all." He pointed at McAllister, who had closed the gap, trapping Tyra between them but not crowding her personal space.

"I ain't done nothing." Tyra looked at McAllister and shivered. The cool night breeze made goose pimples stand out on her arms.

McAllister shrugged out of her state-issue jacket. "Put this on. You're going to catch a cold."

Tyra took it, eyes narrow with suspicion. ""I already told you everything I know." Her breath frosted on the night air.

McAllister rested her hands on her hips. "When was the last time you had sex with Alex Costanzo?"

"I don't remember."

"Was it Monday?"

Tyra was silent.

"Ms. Young." McAllister's voice was soft, inviting confidence. "The manager at the Twin Oaks saw a tall woman enter the room where Mr. Costanzo was killed. We found long dark hair at the scene. Hair like yours."

"Okay yeah, I was there."

"Did you go there often?"

"Not really." A car zipped by. "He liked to mix it up, never met me in the same place twice."

"Did he ever take you back to his house?"

Tyra barked a bitter laugh. "You gotta be kidding."

"When did you leave Monday?"

"Two-thirty? Maybe closer to three. Costanzo wasn't much for foreplay, so it never took long. I did what I had to, showered, and left."

Duncan ran over the timeline. She might have seen the shooter after all. "Was he alive when you left?"

Another bitter laugh. "Unfortunately."

"Did you see anyone?"

"Nuh-uh."

"You saw him pretty often according to his calendar," McAllister said. "Did he pay every time or did he have you on retainer?"

Tyra's mouth thinned. "He didn't pay me. He called, I came."

That was an odd arrangement. McAllister must have thought the same because she asked, "Why is that? This is your job. Legalities aside, wouldn't you get paid?"

"I had my reasons." Tyra spit on the sidewalk.

"Ms. Young, where's your brother?" Duncan asked

"I told you, he's in Pittsburgh. Hill District."

"Last time, you said he was in Homewood," McAllister said, voice even. "Which is it, the Hill District or Homewood? Think, because you know we could call the Pittsburgh police and see if he's been picked up."

McAllister had to be feeling the chill without her jacket, but Duncan couldn't see a trace of it on her face. Even though she had to know Tyra was jerking them around, she didn't raise her voice and there was nothing but compassion in her expression.

Tyra's gaze flitted between both troopers, before coming to rest on McAllister. "He ain't done nothing."

"We didn't say he has," McAllister said. "Is he at your house? Somewhere in Uniontown?" She waited, watching Tyra struggle with indecision. "Who hit you? Was it Alex Costanzo?"

Tyra blinked. "Like you care."

"Maybe I can help."

"Don't need it, not now." Tyra sniffled. "That asshole. Using me, never paying me, playing the big man. This one all because I said I wouldn't blow him. I don't do that shit." She touched the bruise on her cheek.

"You could have turned him in. Whatever you've decided to do with your life, you don't deserve to be hit." The steel in McAllister's eyes contrasted with the softness of her voice. Duncan wouldn't have been surprised if the frost in the air was as much the result of the younger trooper's gaze as the temperature.

"Ain't nobody gonna take the word of a hooker over a lawyer." Tyra sniffed again and Duncan handed her his pocket handkerchief.

McAllister glanced at him before continuing. "Elijah is in Uniontown, isn't he."

Tyra used the handkerchief to wipe her nose and nodded.

"Why didn't you tell us?"

"Eli's always in trouble." Tyra jammed her hands into the jacket's pockets. "He ain't got no common sense. Always looking for the big score, fast money. Talking about how he's gonna get us off the streets."

"And you've got to protect your brother."

"Been looking out for him since we was kids, when our mom got sick," Tyra said. "He was smart. Had a scholarship to community college, but he never was patient. He started doing stupid shit. Drugs and stuff."

"How did you wind up in a sexual relationship with Alex Costanzo?"

Tyra's lip curled. "I told you, Eli ain't too bright. He passed on that scholarship, but got himself accepted to some school for mechanics. Then he got arrested with a dime bag. At his bail hearing, I asked if they would go easy on Eli seein' how he was in school. Costanzo said…" She stopped, biting her lip. The planes of her face were harsh in the sodium lighting.

"What?" McAllister's voice was like flint.

"He said he could see his way to helping Eli if I helped him. I thought I'd sleep with him once and that'd be it, but he kept coming back for more, threatening what would happen to Eli if I said no." The tears she'd kept at bay so successfully broke loose. "Guy like Costanzo, he ain't supposed to do that shit."

"How did Elijah feel about Costanzo, the way he treated you?" McAllister said, fists clenched.

"He weren't happy. But again, what's he gonna do?"

McAllister turned to Duncan, her eyes like chips of ice. She licked her lips before returning to Tyra. "Ms. Young, does Elijah own a gun?"

"No, he don't. I swear."

"Is he at your place?"

"Yeah." Tyra sagged again and blew her nose. "I suppose you gonna arrest him now." She looked at the handkerchief, a sodden mess of tears, makeup, and snot. "Looks like I ruined your hanky."

Duncan had no interest in the handkerchief. "We're going to go talk to Elijah. That's all." Sally would argue Trafford had a better motive, but no cop would take Elijah Young off the suspect list after hearing Tyra's story.

"I'd like to give you the jacket," McAllister said, "but I need it back. Here." She fished some cash out of her pocket. "Take the night off and get yourself a hot meal."

Tyra handed the jacket back and took the money. "Thanks."

They returned to the Jeep and Duncan watched Tyra walk down the street. Just when he'd been tempted to give in to Sally's arguments.

He turned his attention to McAllister, her face like carved granite in the street lights. "You've talked to abuse victims before."

"What makes you think that?"

"That was the best interview I've seen you do. Tells me you have experience."

She got in the Jeep. "Costanzo was a piece of shit." She paused. "She'll probably call Elijah. To warn him."

Duncan turned right at a light. "We'll stop and see him anyway." If Elijah knew they'd spoken to his sister, maybe he would open the door.

≽≽≽

They drove in silence until Duncan pulled up outside Tyra's apartment. "You ready to do this?"

"I told you before. I don't like bullies."

He paused. Not the answer he expected, but he stayed quiet, hoping for more.

"Costanzo, Trafford, my uncle...all bullies." McAllister stared out of the window. "It doesn't matter if you're young, short, female, a prostitute, weak, whatever. No one should be allowed to make you feel small. I'm not talking about physical size, either."

Duncan's memory flashed to his one knock-down, drag-out fight in high school. "I sympathize."

"Do you?" She fixed him with a hard-eyed stare. "Were you ever bullied Jim Duncan?" Without waiting for an answer, she got out of the car.

He sat, momentarily taken aback, then he followed her.

She was waiting for him on the sidewalk. As soon as he closed the distance between them, she moved closer to the door and pounded. "Elijah Young, state police." No answer. "Come on, Elijah. We've talked to your sister. Open up."

While she knocked, Duncan scanned their surroundings. Nothing. By now, with the sun well and truly down, the chill was palpable, but not cold enough to freeze his hands.

McAllister raised her hand to knock again when the door opened. A young man stood there, hair cut close and a glittering stud in his left ear. "Tyra sent you here? What'd she do that for?" He hitched up a baggy pair of jeans.

"Are you Elijah Young?"

"What if I am? You gonna arrest me?"

"Depends on what you tell me." McAllister had the bit in her teeth, but she wasn't out of control. "Got a few questions, if you're willing to answer them."

"And if I tell you to get lost?"

"Look, your sister sent us here. I know what Alex Costanzo did to her." McAllister waited.

Duncan watched while Young processed the words. "What do you want?" he finally asked.

McAllister hooked her thumbs on her belt. "How bad did you want to hurt Costanzo for what he did to Tyra?"

Young hawked and spat. "That answer your question?"

"Kind of." Again, McAllister glanced at Duncan. "Monday afternoon. Where were you?"

"You think I killed him?"

Duncan spoke up. "Come on, Elijah. Costanzo was sexually blackmailing and occasionally hitting your sister. I have a sister. I know how I'd feel if it were her. Just answer the question. Where were you?" Duncan watched for any sign of hesitation or evasion in Young's eyes.

He gave a snort of laughter. "I saw on the news how he was shot. Wasn't me, man. Not that I wouldn't have, given half a chance. But I didn't. Not like I expect you to believe me. All you white folks, thinking you're the shit."

McAllister spoke up. "How long has it been since you saw your friend, Marshawn?"

"Last…" Young blinked and looked upward. Then he refocused on McAllister. "Last month. I went up to Pittsburgh. He and I got together for a beer."

"You haven't seen him since then?" Duncan asked.

Another blink. Young stared into the middle distance. "Nope." He blinked again. "You gonna arrest me or not?"

McAllister glanced at Duncan, who gave her a tiny head shake. Hopefully, she'd take the silent suggestion.

"Not," McAllister said. "Thanks for your time. Make sure your sister warms up when she gets home. It's chilly out here."

They turned and went to the Jeep. Behind them, the door slammed and they heard the deadbolt shoot into place.

"Last month my ass." McAllister gave a quick look at the house, jumped into the passenger seat and buckled her seat belt.

Duncan slid into the driver's side. "Agreed, not quite a truthful answer. How come you didn't push him harder?" Duncan wouldn't have done so either, not yet. He wanted to hear McAllister's answer, though.

"Because I got the feeling you didn't want me to," she said, not looking at him. "Are we done for the night? Because I'd really like to go home, change, and have a drink."

"Yeah, we're done." He pulled away. What he really wanted to do was take McAllister out for a beer, see if he could get her to talk some more, especially about her intense dislike of bullies. But there was a rhythm to any good interrogation. "Day off tomorrow. How about we meet for breakfast? My treat."

Her answering look was wary. "Why?"

"It's something I like to do with all my trainees near the end of the assignment. Give you a chance to ask questions not related to the job."

The answer seemed to mollify her. "Okay, sure."

"Meet me at nine, Gray Line Diner on Route 40. It's a greasy spoon, but I find those are the best breakfasts." It was a chance to ask questions. But McAllister wouldn't be the one asking them.

CHAPTER 35

By Thursday morning, Sally was not in such an understanding mood. Jim had not called or sent a text since she saw him last night. Her message that morning—a day she knew he usually had off—had resulted in a brief "I'll be in touch." Yes, he was busy. But she deserved answers, didn't she?

She decided to drive to Confluence and confront him. At his house it would only be the two of them and Rizzo, conditions that were much more conducive to her forcing out some details. She'd call off this morning, talk to him, and be in by lunch.

But before she got on the road, she remembered someone else she had to talk to: Deborah Rafferty. It was just as likely Colin had hidden information for safekeeping as Alex had. Where better than with his mother? There was a whole box of things from Colin's office that needed to be returned to her. The good will Sally earned by doing so might get her an invitation to poke around at anything Colin had sent to Pittsburgh.

Deciding Jim could wait, Sally changed her plans and got on the Turnpike heading east toward Pittsburgh. She called Deborah from the road. Colin's mother would be home all day and would be very grateful for the delivery of her son's possessions.

Sally pulled up in front of the Mt. Lebanon residence under October skies that had returned to a brilliant blue although the temperature was milder after Tuesday's storm. Piles of crisp red, gold, and brown from the shedding oaks and maples skittered across the sidewalk, the air filled with the dusty scent of fall. Deborah's front yard had a thick carpet of color. Sally removed the box from her trunk, walked up to the door, and balanced the load on her hip as she pushed the doorbell.

Deborah answered wearing the same sweatshirt she'd worn on Sally's last visit. "Goodness gracious, come in before you drop that." She held the door open for Sally. "Bring it into the kitchen. Do you want coffee or anything?"

"Coffee would be great, thanks." She deposited the box on the kitchen table. "This is everything from Colin's office. Sorry it took so long to get it to you."

"Don't worry about it. Milk, creamer, sugar?"

"Little bit of creamer, thank you."

Deborah brought the coffee to the table and handed it over. Then she took the top off the box and started unpacking Colin's things. "The Steelers mugs. He was fond of these."

"I know." Sally blew on the coffee, steam still thick. "He told me he was at the games. He never used them, you know. Well, almost never." He'd used them with his killer.

Deborah removed Colin's diplomas, brushing the glass with her fingers. "I was so proud when he graduated law school."

"I'll bet."

It didn't take long to empty the box. "Is this it?"

"Everything from his office, yes. The Uniontown police should be in touch to talk about how you want to dispose of the stuff from his apartment, if they haven't already."

Deborah repacked the box. "Detective Killian called. He said they needed to keep Colin's papers a bit longer, but I could make arrangements for the furniture and clothes. I'll probably give them to a charity in Uniontown. Colin had a few pictures I'd like back and I'll go through his papers to see if I want to save anything."

Sally sipped in silence, letting Deborah spend a few minutes thinking of her son. "Mrs. Rafferty, can I ask you a question?"

"My friend the former English teacher would say that's already a question." Her eyes twinkled. "Call me Deborah, please. Go ahead."

"Did Colin leave anything with you before he died? Papers or books? Maybe a locked box or something?"

Deborah frowned in thought. "He did bring up some boxes last month. He said he didn't have space and instead of renting a storage unit he asked to put them in the basement. I said yes, of course."

"May I look through them?"

"If you think it will help. I haven't touched them since he brought them up. He said they were filled with useless stuff he didn't know how to get rid of." Deborah stood, went to the basement stairs and flicked on a light. "This way."

Sally followed. The basement was unfinished; a concrete floor and block walls, an older washing machine and dryer against the far wall. Across from them were a few packing boxes labeled "stuff." She went over. "Are these the ones?"

Deborah nodded. "Like I said, I haven't touched them."

Sally unfolded the flaps of the first box. It was filled with clothes. She made sure nothing was hidden between the items before moving on to the next box. That one was filled with college text books. She flipped all the pages, but nothing fell out.

The third held old shoes and a metal box with a key taped to the bottom. The key to the box? Why hadn't he kept it on him? So no one would take it, she reasoned. She peeled the key off. "Mind if I open this?"

"Go right ahead. I want to know what's in it as much as you do."

The key fit perfectly. Inside were small tapes, like those from an old-style answering machine. There was also a player and a power cord.

"Bring it upstairs," Deborah said. "I want to hear what's on those tapes, but I think I'd better sit down first."

"Are you sure? I can take them home with me and tell you what's on them, if you'd like."

"No." Deborah's thin form was stiff, her face set. "I want to hear it for myself, even if it's not good."

⚜⚜⚜

Duncan got to the Gray Line early, an unassuming diner northwest of Uniontown on the National Pike beyond the car dealerships, greeted the waitress and snagged a booth in the back. Then he waited. With no sightseeing spots nearby, the Gray Line catered to a very specific local clientele. Hopefully McAllister would show up. He thought maybe he'd sussed out a little of what was going on in mind, but he wanted to hear it in her own words.

A few minutes later, she walked in the door, spotted Duncan, and headed to his booth. She slid in on the opposite bench. "This place looks like a 50s truck stop joint."

"I told you, it serves the best breakfast in the Laurel Highlands." He pushed a menu across the table. "But these aren't truckers. Most of them are off-duty or former cops. Couple of firemen in the back corner." He grinned at her look of confusion. "The owner is a retired PSP trooper. You haven't been on the job long enough. You'll find you start to pick your places to eat and drink carefully."

Duncan ordered coffee and a full meal: eggs, bacon, pancakes, and hash browns. McAllister, after glancing around, went with Mountain Dew and French toast. "What did you want to talk about? You said something about an end of training chat?"

The drinks arrived and Duncan watched her remove the paper from her straw. "You asked me a question yesterday. Figured you deserved an answer."

"What question?"

"Was I ever bullied." The effect of the statement on McAllister was like pouring water on a fire. "The answer, as you may have guessed, is no," Duncan continued. "But there was this kid in high school, David Burkanich. Looked right out of that old movie 'Revenge of the Nerds.' Glasses, pocket protector, the works. One of the football players, Bobby Brennan, never gave David an inch. All the classic stunts: stuffed him in a locker, wedgies, stole his glasses."

"Sounds like real gem," McAllister said, voice flat. "But I don't—"

"One day, I'd had enough. Told Bobby to lay off or he would answer to me. It was the only real fight I ever had in high school."

"Let me guess: you emerged victorious and made a friend for life."

"Not quite." The food arrived. "I got my ass kicked. David, the little weasel, turned Bobby and me in for fighting, and we both got a week of in-school suspension.

McAllister's paused eating, fork in mid-air. "He did what?"

"Bobby and I walked out of the ordeal as best friends. On the last day, he said we should hunt David down and beat him silly." Duncan shook his head at the memory. "I told Bobby if he did that, friend or no I'd have to fight him again and we'd probably end up back in suspension. Since I was still bruised from the first time, I'd appreciate it if he'd give me a couple more days to recover."

"Did you wind up fighting him again?"

"Nope."

McAllister pushed the pieces of her French toast around through the syrup.

"The point is, I do understand. I don't like bullies either. And yeah, sometimes things turn violent. But what beat Bobby was not the fight. It was my willingness to do it all over again." He watched her. Her turn.

She finished her breakfast and moved the plate aside. "My uncle was a jerk. A drunk. I watched him verbally beat up everyone around him, but especially my aunt and cousin. It was worse when he was drinking."

"Did it get physical?"

"Sometimes. Shannon, my cousin, would occasionally have a bruise on her arm she didn't want to talk about. It looked like finger marks to me. But mostly Uncle Jerry was all talk." She took a deep breath. "One night he started in on Shannon because we'd come home a few minutes late. I told him to shut up and leave her alone. He pushed me away pretty easily. Heck, look at me. He was six-foot-two and two hundred pounds. A foot taller and nearly a hundred pounds heavier than me at the time."

Duncan stayed silent, drinking his coffee.

"It didn't really hurt, but I was mad. He pushed me aside again and laughed. He said a little girl like me should learn the world is for the strong. I better get comfortable with the idea, because I'd never be good enough to fight back." The light in her eyes was hard. "I made myself a promise: no one would push me around like that again. After I put on the uniform for the first time, I doubled-down on that promise. It wasn't only for me, it was for others, too."

It was a common story. He'd heard it and at least a dozen variations in his time as an FTO. "Did you ever go back and confront your uncle?"

"I didn't have to. He finally ran into something he couldn't beat down."

"What?"

"An oncoming train. He was drunk and walking the tracks in the dark. The engineer never saw him." Her voice wavered and she went back to looking at the Formica table.

Finally, McAllister steadied herself enough to speak again. "Is this where you tell me I flunked training and I need to find another line of work?"

"Hardly." He leaned on the table. "You are going to be a great trooper. You're smart, you care, you're willing to put yourself out there. But there's something you need to understand. People don't stop trying to push you around just because you wear the uniform. If anything, it'll motivate some people to try and prove they're tougher than you. You're good enough that I think you'll hold your own just fine. But you have to be careful."

"Of what?"

"In your quest to beat the bully, don't become one yourself."

CHAPTER 36

Once again, Deborah's frailty masked her inner strength. "Lead the way," Sally said.

They went back to the kitchen, where Deborah refilled their coffee mugs while Sally plugged in the tape player and sorted through the cassettes. They were dated. She picked one from a few months ago, inserted it, and pressed play. Two voices filled the kitchen, Colin's and a stranger's. After a minute or two, Sally shook her head. "Not what we're looking for." She removed the tape and tried again.

Five tries later, they had plenty of evidence about the extortion, but no threats. Deborah pointed to a cassette. "Try that one."

"Deborah, really. You don't have to listen to this."

"I want to."

Sally picked up the tape. It was dated a few weeks before she and Colin had their Friday Happy Hour where he'd left without a word. She inserted it and pressed play.

"Thanks for coming, Alex." There was a bit of a background hiss, but Colin's voice could clearly be heard.

"What do you want? It's going to look funny, me coming down here when none of my cases have anything to do with you people," Alex said.

"It's the county courthouse. We can always find an excuse."

They were at the Public Defender's, Sally thought. Colin's office? Probably. If Alex had seen the recorder, he'd have said something; he had no idea, which argued for the machine being hidden.

"Whatever. What the hell is so urgent?" Alex asked.

"I heard Aaron Trafford was coming back to the area. Or is back, depending on who you talk to."

"So?"

"I don't want a repeat of last fall. In fact, upon further review, I don't want to continue this at all."

There was a thud, like someone had slapped hands on a surface. Colin's desk? "Oh really?" Alex asked, eerily calm.

"Yeah, really."

Sally tried to picture the scene and had to give Colin credit. Alex had probably been leaning in, getting as close as he could. Colin would have been seated behind the desk. Did he feel he was in danger? Was that the moment he realized he'd not only made a huge mistake with his career, but he'd never get out of the arrangement he agreed to with his life? She shot a sideways glance at Deborah. The older woman's pale face and thin lips said everything about her reaction. Sally reached for the "stop" button.

Deborah grabbed Sally's hand. "Let it play." Her voice was a bit ragged, but firm. Sally withdrew her hand.

"You listen to me." Alex's voice had a harsh edge, the one he often used with hostile witnesses on the stand. "You got into this of your own free will. No one put a gun to your head. Back out now and you might find that to be the case."

"Maybe I don't care."

"You should. Think carefully because your next decision on this matter could dramatically impact your life, whatever's left of it." The conversation ended and hissing filled the room.

Sally shut off the recorder. Nobody could take Alex's statement as anything other than a threat. Considering how Colin died, the words were prophetic and made Sally reconsider her assumptions. Had Alex pulled the trigger or merely made the suggestion to Trafford based on the conversation Sally had just listened to?

"Ms. Castle?"

Sally jerked herself back to the present. "If I'm going to call you Deborah, you have to call me Sally."

Deborah's cheeks were wet, but her face was determined. "Do you know the other man on the tape? The one who threatened Colin."

"Alex Costanzo. He worked in the DA's office in the county. Based on the notebook I found, I'm pretty sure he and Colin were running some kind of extortion racket. These are further proof." Like the notebook, the tapes were Colin's insurance.

"He's dead, right? Mr. Costanzo? I read a story in the paper about an attorney found at a seedy motel down in Fayette County." Seeing Sally's nod of confirmation, Deborah continued. "This recording, is it proof he killed my son?"

"Given the wording of the threat and the fact that Colin was shot in the head, I think it's possible. But no, it's not absolute proof."

"Then I'll never know? Detective Killian, he arrested another man, didn't he?"

"He did, but I think he's going to have to reconsider once he learns of these. I think they'll force the detective to continue investigating until he knows without a doubt who was behind the shooting." Sally stood and put the tapes back in the box. "The only thing that's certain is if the killer was Alex, he won't go to jail. But you'll have the satisfaction of knowing who killed your son." She paused. "I'm sorry you had to hear this, though."

"I'm not." Deborah took a deep breath, then helped Sally finish putting all the recordings away. When they were done, Deborah put the box in Sally's hands. "Take it, all of it. Give it to the detective or whoever you have to. If this Alex Costanzo is responsible, well, I guess I'll have to be satisfied with the fact that someone shot him, too. But if it's someone else…make sure you call me, Sally. I want to be there when they sentence the bastard."

Sally squeezed the woman's thin hand. "Don't worry. I will."

⁂

After returning from breakfast, Duncan devoted himself to autumn chores. He raked leaves and stacked firewood. The mindless work let him ponder the facts in his two major cases. He didn't even mind too much when Rizzo scattered a pile of leaves for the third time. The repetitive motion of the raking freed him to think.

He had finished bagging the last pile and was considering lunch options when Sally's Camry pulled in. "Hey, shouldn't you be at work?"

"Shouldn't you be at a furniture store?"

"I'll get there. Eventually." He leaned on the rake. "What's up?"

"I need to show you something. Or, more accurately, have you listen to something." She removed a box from her trunk and headed to the front door. Like she owned the place. Rizzo, of course, abandoned the stick he'd dragged from the backyard to follow her.

Duncan propped the rake against the porch and went inside. Sally was already in the kitchen, plugging in a small tape player and setting it on the table. "Where did you get that?" he asked.

"Colin's mother. This is what I need you to listen to."

"Hold on." He washed his hands, grabbed a bottle of his favorite Edmund Fitzgerald, and sat. She had queued up a tape and pushed play. He listened to Costanzo and Rafferty, the conversation making him all but forget the bottle in his hand. "Play it again," he said when the recording finished. "This was at Rafferty's?" He listened once more while Sally grabbed a pad from the counter and wrote.

"It was at his mother's house in Pittsburgh," Sally said, finishing whatever she was writing. "It was in a box with a bunch of stuff he brought up to her. He said it was things he wanted to get rid of, but needed her to hang on to until he figured out what to do with them. I went up there to return his office effects, asked if he stashed anything with her, and she let me poke around."

"Any clue as to when that conversation took place?"

"Remember when you saw Colin and me in Lucky 7?"

The night he'd asked her if she wanted him to be jealous. "I do."

"The tape is dated a little more than two weeks before that. Colin was planning his exit strategy."

"Sounds to me like he had planned it and was giving notice to Costanzo. What were you writing?"

She handed him the pad. "A transcript. I know these tapes have to go to Detective Killian. I want a record for myself."

Duncan read Sally's neat handwriting, a word-by-word account of the taped conversation. "Here's what we know. Costanzo and Rafferty had, at some point, agreed on this extortion scam."

"Yes. My guess is maybe twelve to eighteen months ago. That's when Colin's credit cards started showing big payments, at least according to Killian."

"They run with it for a while. The targets include Trafford for his original trial last year."

"We still don't know if that one was bribery or extortion."

"Not relevant right now." He took a drink, focused on his timeline. "Eventually, Rafferty decides he wants out. Crisis of conscience, fear for his safety, the reason doesn't matter. But he knows saying so could be dangerous, so he starts taking precautions."

"Actually, he did that from the beginning. Remember the notebook?"

"That wasn't dated. He could have started at the outset, gone back and filled it in...again. It doesn't matter."

Rizzo laid his head in Sally's lap and she stroked the dog's ears while she spoke. "He knew he was in danger. There was the life insurance with his mother as beneficiary. According to Deborah, the policy was obtained three or so months ago; that must have been when he made his move."

"The last thing he did was record this conversation. At least, that's your thought. He hadn't gone public with the scam yet, had he?"

"I doubt it. Bryan would have said something."

"What did Rafferty plan to do with all the notes and tapes?"

"Turn them in. Or leave it for the cops or for me so that even if he was dead, the scheme would be exposed. Those are the only things I can think of."

A logical conclusion. "The line about a gun to the head. Can't be a coincidence that's how Rafferty was killed."

"No." Her face was pale, but there was no fear in her eyes. "In fact...now it's got me thinking maybe Alex did the shooting. Or he gave Trafford explicit instructions."

"Or he was passing on a statement from Trafford."

"But Trafford's name didn't come up."

"No, it didn't." He set aside the bottle. "You said Costanzo doesn't own a gun."

"I don't think he does. Except he lied about so much, what's to say he didn't lie about that?"

"We can find out." Duncan picked up his cell phone and dialed. "Porter, hey. I need a favor. I need to know if there's a record of Alex Costanzo registering a firearm, specifically anything in the nine millimeter category. Also, did he have a carry permit. Yeah, I know. Yeah. Thanks." He snapped the phone shut.

"What if he doesn't have a permit? Is that a stumbling block?"

"Because he'd only shoot someone if he was licensed to carry?"

Her cheeks turned bright pink. "Okay, okay. Next question: how would he get the gun into the courthouse? We...oh."

"What?"

"I'm so stupid. The employee entrance doesn't have a metal detector."

"It doesn't? You mean anyone can come in?" That was awfully trusting.

"Not anyone. There's a fingerprint scanner for access, so it's not like you can pass off an ID card. There's CCTV coverage, plus there is always loads of people around. It's practically impossible to slip in and out unnoticed, or to meet up with someone who isn't supposed to be there."

"But Costanzo could get a gun in."

Sally bit her lip.

"He could get the gun in without an issue." Duncan shook his head.

"It was Sunday, Jim. How would Trafford get into the courthouse?"

"I don't know. Thomas apparently did."

She must have pulled too hard on Rizzo's ear because he yelped. "Oh, sorry bud." She kissed his head and received a lick in response. "Anyway, we still aren't sure who the shooter is: Alex or Trafford. How do we eliminate one of them?"

"I think it's time I insist on seeing that CCTV footage." And Sally was definitely going with him.

CHAPTER 37

S ally kept her attention on Rizzo, thoughts racing, while Jim called Detective Killian and politely, but firmly, insisted on meeting later that afternoon to review the CCTV video.

"That's settled then." He set down the phone.

"You didn't mention my name."

"Yeah, this kind of falls in the 'better to ask forgiveness' area. I didn't want to spend all day arguing with him. It'll be harder to turn me down if you're standing right there." He checked his watch. "He's going to meet me at four. It's not quite noon. Is that going to work for you?"

"I'll make it work." She stood and Rizzo gave her a mournful look. "I gotta go, bud. You'll have to get your attention from the big guy for a while." She shouldered her purse. "I'll see you later."

It was a good thing she had other things to focus on for the early part of the afternoon. It kept her from obsessing about Colin's recordings and what she might see on the CCTV footage. When she headed to the security office at the courthouse shortly before four, Jim was already there. Dressed in jeans and a sweater, he was talking to Killian and it sounded not quite like an argument, but definitely not friendly cop-to-cop BS, either. Why hadn't Jim put on his uniform? Because he wasn't on duty?

Killian broke off mid-sentence when she walked into the room. "What is she doing here?"

"Oh, you mean Ms. Castle?" Jim waited for Killian's grudging nod before continuing. "She's a courthouse employee who's here every day. She worked with the deceased and she's a witness. I can't think of a better person to help us identify the people on the footage, can you?" His tone was polite, but clearly he wasn't going to take "no" for an answer.

"I told you. There isn't anyone to see. Just Thomas and the maintenance guy. I don't need witness identification," Killian said.

"It always helps." Jim turned to the technician. "Cue it up and hit play, please."

They watched in silence. The maintenance worker came and went, spending approximately the right amount of time off-screen needed to perform his tasks. An hour later, they saw Thomas arrive. Minutes later, he ran across the open space, eyes wide, mouth open.

"There you are," Killian said. "A cleaning guy with no motive. Thomas looking like he's ready to crap his pants. How much you want to bet Rafferty hit him up again? They argued, Thomas shot him, and fled the scene."

"Is there any footage of Rafferty and Thomas?"

"No, why does it matter?"

"Because somebody had to let Thomas into the building, that's why."

Killian had no response.

Sally, who was seeing the video for the first time, sensed something out of sync. "Could you rewind it and replay, please? Just the part with maintenance."

The tech obliged. "Sure thing."

While Killian and Jim held a somewhat strained conversation about the futility of their task, Sally peered at the grainy image. "There. Would you please go back just a few seconds?" The image played a third time. "Pause it please?" She turned to Jim and Killian. "That's not maintenance. At least I don't think it is. The man who worked that night was Roy Pasquale."

"His face is covered by the ball cap, but I can see the name patch on his shirt," Killian snapped. "It says Pasquale."

"Shirts can be stolen or borrowed, Detective," Jim said, staring at Sally. "Ms. Castle, what makes you say that's not Pasquale?"

She glanced at Killian. If she only had to convince Jim this would be easier, but the heavyset, aging detective made her antsy. "I talked to him.

Mr. Pasquale has a large birthmark, just here." She touched the spot on her own neck. "I don't see that on the video."

"His collar is up," Killian said.

As she'd told Jim, she'd learned how to stick to her guns. And his presence and expression gave her extra confidence. "I think it would be visible."

Jim turned to face his counterpart. "Detective, have you interviewed Mr. Pasquale?"

"Yes, I have." Killian lifted his chin. "So what, the guy has a birthmark. He admits he worked and I say the mark could be hidden by the collar."

Jim thanked the tech. "Well, it's a question that's easy to settle." He stood back and motioned Sally toward the door.

"What are you gonna do?" Killian asked.

From behind her, Jim pushed open the door, held it and paused. "We're going to visit Mr. Pasquale. You're welcome to come along if you'd like."

⚜⚜⚜

Duncan drove to Pasquale's house, Sally playing navigator in the passenger seat. Her assertion that the person on the video was not Roy Pasquale was good enough for him, but he understood Killian's position. He didn't support it, but he understood it.

"I don't think Detective Killian is very happy with me. Or you, for that matter," Sally said. "Turn right, here."

Duncan followed her direction. "It's not you as much as me. Cops are used to lawyers exploding their cases. Not their brothers-in-arms."

"Then why isn't he taking it out on you?"

"Because, and this is just my speculation, he sees me as an equal. Plus I get the feeling he's reluctant to light into me because he doesn't know what I'll do in response. Anyway, some of us deal with it, having our conclusions cut down by a fellow officer, better than others. Some of us simply pretend."

"Which are you?"

"I pretend. Don't be fooled; I have an ego, same as anyone else. I hope I've mostly learned how to shelve it when I have to." He slowed. "Is this the place?"

"Yes." The Jeep stopped and she put her hand on the door. "I'm sorry I'm causing you problems."

"Don't be. We all want the right answer. Killian wishes he already had it."

Killian met them on the sidewalk outside the house. "This is a waste of time."

Duncan did his best to stay relaxed and check that ego even though he was increasingly sure Sally was right. "So you've said." Repeatedly. "Let's cross the T's and dot the I's, shall we?" He rapped on the front door.

There was the sound of a latch being undone and a deadbolt sliding back. The door opened to reveal a man with the same dark hair color and similar build as the guy seen on the CCTV, but it was impossible to match the grainy image to this guy's face. A large, wine-colored birthmark stood out on his neck. "Yes?" he asked, holding the door ready to slam shut. Seeing Sally, he added, "Don't I know you? You're the lady from the courthouse."

Duncan held out his badge. "Are you Roy Pasquale?"

"That's me. Am I in trouble?" Pasquale's eyes betrayed a nervousness that he tried to cover with civility.

"Not yet, but we have a few questions. You've told Detective Killian here you worked a week ago last Sunday. To refresh your memory, that's the night before Colin Rafferty from the Public Defender's office was found murdered."

"Yes, that's right. I did."

"Are you sure about that?"

Pasquale's gaze darted from Sally to Killian and then back to Duncan before he answered. "Yes, I'm sure."

Face to face, Duncan could tell Sally was correct. The birthmark on Pasquale's neck should have been visible. "See, there's a problem, Mr. Pasquale. We don't think the man on the CCTV recordings from that night is you." At the sound of Killian's muttering, Duncan added, "Some of us don't at least."

Pasquale licked his upper lip. "You're wrong. It's definitely me."

Sally spoke up. "Mr. Pasquale, do you mind getting your work shirt and bringing it here?"

"What do you want with my shirt?"

"Please? Trooper Duncan and I want to see something."

Pasquale hesitated, then disappeared. When he returned, the shirt was clenched in his fist. He held it out.

"Would you please put it on for me?" Sally asked.

He slipped on the shirt. "Is that all?"

Sally glanced at Duncan. "Would you please button it and flip up the collar?"

Killian muttered again, but Duncan ignored him.

Pasquale looked at each of his visitors in turn, then buttoned the shirt and flipped up the collar. "Like that?"

"Perfect, thank you." Sally faced Killian. "Is that good enough, Detective?"

A good third of the birthmark extended past the upturned collar. The man on the CCTV was not Roy Pasquale. Killian muttered a curse, but said nothing else.

There might not have been a birthmark visible, but there hadn't been any tattoos either. The faux janitor was not Trafford. "Mr. Pasquale, think carefully." Duncan crossed his arms. "Are you absolutely certain you worked that night? Before you answer, I urge you to think hard. Eleven nights ago. Not this past Sunday, the previous week."

"Yes," Pasquale said, more confident now. "I already told that to him, when he said I was on the CCTV." He pointed at Killian.

Killian started to say something but Duncan cut him off. "The thing is, Mr. Pasquale, we've looked at that tape again. There's a little issue." Why was Pasquale so insistent?

"What issue?" Pasquale chin jutted out.

"The man on the video," Killian said. "He doesn't have a birthmark."

Pasquale licked his lips, the nervous light back in his eyes. "You're wrong. It was me. Picture must be bad."

"No picture is that bad," Duncan said. He took in the light sweat on Pasquale's forehead and the muscle twitch in his cheek.

Sally stepped forward. "Mr. Pasquale, why are you lying to us?" Her voice was low and gentle, probably one she used often to get clients and witnesses to trust her. "Whatever you've done, whoever has threatened you, we can't help unless you tell us the truth."

"I didn't have anything to do with that man's death. I only—"

Sally didn't take her eyes off him. "Only what? Mr. Pasquale, please. If you want to change anything about your statement, now is the time to do it."

"I didn't commit a crime," Pasquale said. "At least I don't think so."

Duncan exchanged a sympathetic look with Sally. The man was afraid of something. More likely, someone. "Why don't you let us be the judge of that?"

Pasquale's shoulders slumped. "I didn't work that night."

Killian sputtered, but Duncan held up his hand, then motioned Pasquale to continue.

"Guy came to me on Friday after I got home. He offered me one hundred dollars if I'd loan him my uniform shirt. I said my job was worth more than one hundred so he upped it to five. Christmas is coming, man. My daughter wants one of them American Girl dolls. He said I wouldn't get in trouble. I gave him the shirt. It was outside my door with a bundle of twenties in a plastic grocery bag Monday morning, just like he said they'd be."

Sally had pulled up a picture on her phone. Costanzo. She held it out. "Is this the man?"

"No. I know him, or I've seen him at least. He works in the courthouse."

"He used to. He's dead."

Pasquale flinched. "I had nothing to do with it." Tense panic crept into his voice. "I swear on the Bible."

Duncan's thoughts were running at high speed. If it wasn't Costanzo and it wasn't Trafford, who played the role of janitor that night? They'd go back to the CCTV. See if anything else jumped out.

"Are you going to tell my boss?" Pasquale said, worry apparent in his eyes. "I swear, I just loaned the shirt. I don't know anything about a murder. I needed the money. That's all there was to it, honest."

"I can't say whether you'll lose your job," Duncan said, not without sympathy. "Obviously, your employer is going to find out. If you've violated company policy, that's their business to deal with as they see fit. I'm sure Detective Killian will tell them that you had nothing to do with Mr. Rafferty's murder, should they call. Thank you for your time." They left a dejected Pasquale standing in his doorway.

Duncan made it to the sidewalk, when he heard Sally behind him. "One last question. What about this man? Have you seen him?"

He turned. She held out her phone to Pasquale. Obviously, she'd pulled up another picture to look at.

Killian muttered another curse. "Now what is she doing?"

Duncan thought he knew.

Pasquale turned pale. "That's him. He said. . .he said as long as I did what I was told, it would be okay. I'd get my money and that would be the end of it. But if I talked to anyone, well he made it pretty clear things would not be okay. For me or my family." Pasquale turned a searching look on the two cops. "You gotta understand. I only wanted to protect my wife and kids. Earn a little extra money. I didn't know what was going to happen. And after the news, well, yeah. I was scared. I still am."

Sally grasped his hand. "It's going to be okay, Mr. Pasquale. I promise. No one will know you talked to us unless we absolutely can't avoid it. Thank you very much for your time and honesty."

Pasquale opened his mouth as if to respond, then he swallowed and shut his door.

Sally came down to the sidewalk. "I told you it wasn't him."

Killian ignored the comment. "What did you show him? I mean, it was a picture but of who?"

Sally held out her phone so both Duncan and Killian could see the screen. Aaron Trafford.

CHAPTER 38

S ally wandered back to Jim's Jeep, feeling a bit like a kayak trapped in the rapids at Ohiopyle. Just as she had come to grips with the idea that Alex could have been the killer, events conspired to leave her off balance again.

Killian left them on the sidewalk. He got into his car muttering about needing to go back to the station to complete some paperwork and sped off with a slight screech of tires on pavement. The scent of burnt rubber hung in the air.

Sally watched the receding taillights. "He's not happy."

Jim spun his key ring on his finger. "No, he is not."

"Think he's going to release Thomas?"

"I think Detective Killian is going to go back to his desk and re-evaluate his case, given this new information."

"That's a very diplomatic and vague answer."

"It's appropriate in light of who I'm talking to." He turned to her. "What about you?"

"Actually, I'm feeling the need to re-evaluate the facts myself, preferably with a nice adult beverage in my hand."

"Glass of whiskey?"

She could feel her ears burning and imagined they were a nice shade of red. She let her hair down and shook it forward to cover them.

"No whiskey. A nice red wine will be fine." She swore she heard him murmur "damn" as he held open the Jeep door and let her in.

He rounded the vehicle and climbed in. "Do you want this adult beverage at home or somewhere else?"

Oh God. Not her apartment, especially not if he was going to stick around and his body language gave every indication that was exactly what he intended to do. Normally she'd have jumped at the opportunity to play hostess, but the whiskey comment left her embarrassed enough. Lord only knew what would happen if they went to her place. Of course, he'd probably be the gentleman again and absolutely nothing would happen.

She didn't want Dex's, their usual place. She knew Jim's pickiness over drinking spots and she never challenged him. Sure, she'd seen him at Lucky 7, but that was for a special purpose. "What I really want is a place with a squashy armchair in front of a fire," she said, expecting him to offer an alternative.

He paused, then started the Jeep. "There's that new bar downtown. Bit of a hipster hangout, but they probably have what you're looking for."

"Are you sure?" She knew the one he was talking about; it boasted an extensive list of wine, local brews on tap, and a variety of appetizers.

"Gotta live a little, right? Besides, a couple of the guys at the barracks were raving about their beer selection, so I might as well find out if it lives up to the billing." He pulled away from the curb.

About fifteen minutes later, Sally was relaxing in exactly the kind of chair she wanted in front of a merry fire, although she knew the logs were fake and the flames were gas-fed. Jim had gone to get their drinks. He returned with a glass of his usual dark beer and a wineglass half full of garnet-red liquid.

"Thanks." She accepted the glass. "What is it?"

"No clue." He flopped into the other chair, one that backed close to the wall and where he could survey the room. His favorite kind of seat. "I asked for a red, not too dry, not too sweet, and that's what the bartender gave me. Along with a chocolate stout I've been wanting to try."

She sipped. Whatever it was, the wine was good and exactly what she wanted. "Thanks. So...Pasquale. Not quite what we expected to hear, huh?"

"Not exactly. I mean, the minute you said he wasn't the guy on the video, I knew he'd confirm your observation. But the guy we saw wasn't Trafford, either. If we'd have seen Pasquale's birthmark, we'd have seen Trafford's tattoos."

"Then who was it?"

"The simplest answer is that it was Costanzo."

"Except Pasquale didn't recognize Alex's picture, either. Except from around the courthouse."

"That means he didn't obtain the shirt. Not that he didn't use it."

A young, blonde woman walked up. Of course she was going to hit on Jim. He was relaxed, and a good looking guy; just the sort women would flirt with in a bar. Sally bristled and prepared a retort.

"Boss, what are you doing here? I didn't think this was your kind of place," the woman said.

"McAllister. Have a seat. Unless you're here with someone, of course." He waved at Sally. "You remember Ms. Castle?"

Sally unwound. She hadn't recognized Aislyn McAllister out of uniform. But if Jim was off today, she had to be, too. Hardly a threat. Probably. "Hey."

Aislyn held a tumbler half-filled with a dark, fizzy liquid. She nodded as a greeting. "I don't want to interrupt. Unless this is a business talk?"

Sally pointed at a third chair. "Most of our personal talks wind up revolving around business. Please, sit."

"Just for a minute." Aislyn perched on the edge of the chair. "What are you up to?"

Jim told her about the meeting with Pasquale, while she apparently hung on every word.

Sally sipped her wine silently, studying the younger woman's expression and the way she leaned forward. Sally had heard that sometimes trainees got attached to their supervising officers. Was Aislyn McAllister one of those? She looked to be too young for Jim's tastes. The attraction could be one way, though. "Why do you call him 'boss'?" Sally asked, when Jim had finished.

Aislyn started. "Because he is. The boss, I mean."

"As I've said before, I'm your FTO not your boss." Jim stretched out his legs. "At the end of this month, you'll pass your training period and there will be zero difference in our ranks. Then I'll be even less of a boss."

"You'll always be 'the boss' as far as I'm concerned." Aislyn downed the rest of her drink.

It didn't sound or feel like a flirtatious comment to Sally. Aislyn respected Jim—a lot, that much was obvious. Why wouldn't she? Jim regarded the young woman as a promising new colleague. Satisfied she wasn't dealing with a rival on any level, Sally set down her wineglass. "Does this send us back to square one? Knowing Trafford was the one who borrowed Pasquale's shirt, then threatened him."

Jim scratched his chin. "I don't think so. I never crossed Trafford off the suspect list for the Rafferty killing."

"You didn't?"

"Of course not. You don't cross anyone off until you're certain." He took a drink. "I am interested in who let Thomas into the building that night."

"Because he could identify a third person? Maybe the guy masquerading as Pasquale?" The same question had occurred to Sally. "Did you try asking Thomas?"

Jim grimaced. "I put in a request to interview him. The request was declined by Thomas's court-appointed attorney. He probably doesn't want to open the door to further charges against his client."

Aislyn was staring at the flames. "Where's the gun?"

"The one used to kill Colin?" Sally asked.

"Either of them." Aislyn looked from Sally to Jim, and back again. "You didn't tell her there were two guns?"

"No, he didn't," Sally said.

"Must have slipped my mind," he said. "Ballistics report shows the bullets in the shootings came from two different weapons."

"You don't have either of them?" Sally asked.

"All we know is they are both use nine millimeter ammunition. Since neither gun was recovered, we don't know the type and there are several guns of that caliber out there." He looked at the remaining foam in his glass with a slight frown. Because of the beer or because of the lack of knowledge? His cell phone buzzed and he answered it.

"What we do know," Aislyn added, "is that the ballistics report from the Costanzo shooting matches one from Pittsburgh. But the gun wasn't recovered so it doesn't tell us much except the same weapon fired both shots." She glanced at Jim and turned back to Sally. "Where's the damn gun? One missing I can deal with, but two?"

Jim snapped his phone shut and finished the stout. He brushed the back of his hand across his mouth. "They got the lockbox open, the one we found in Costanzo's office."

"What was in it?" McAllister asked. "Please tell me it was a weapon, at least one of them."

"Unfortunately, no," Jim said. "Almost as interesting, though. Cash, a lot of it. Five thousand dollars in brand-new twenties. Ten stacks of five hundred."

"Doesn't seem like that would fit in the box."

"They were five stacks across and two deep. Just enough room to spare that when we jiggled the box we could hear them." He set down his glass.

"That's a lot of cash," Sally said. "Where'd it come from?"

"Yet another question we don't have an answer to." Jim stared at the flames. "Back to the guns. If Trafford is the shooter in both cases, they're with him. I don't know why a person needs two handguns, but hey, maybe he likes variety. If Costanzo is the actor in the Rafferty killing, I agree we should have found the weapon by now."

"It's not in his office or his home," Sally said. "He doesn't have a rental place for storage, does he?"

"Not that we've found." Jim tapped his thumbs together. "We still don't know if he has a carry license or ever legally purchased a gun. I'll check on that tomorrow. But let's say he got the gun from Trafford."

"Could he have returned it?" Aislyn asked. "Try this. Trafford met him at the Twin Oaks so Costanzo could return the gun, they argued, and Trafford shot him."

It was something Sally hadn't considered. "But not with the borrowed gun used to kill Colin."

"This is why I hate complications," Jim said, scowling. "Another possibility is that Costanzo was shot by a third party, so that gun is with him. Or her."

"Tyra," Sally said. "You think she can handle a gun of that caliber?"

"I use a nine-mil," Aislyn said.

"You're a trained cop," Sally replied. "Tyra Young is a prostitute."

"Who really hated Alex Costanzo."

"That's cold. Have sex with a guy, then shoot him?"

"You know a better way to put a man off his guard?"

The light from the fire flickered across Jim's face, set in a pensive expression. Suddenly he stood. "McAllister. Tomorrow we re-interview Tyra and Elijah Young. We know she was on the scene right before Costanzo was shot. We need to push her on what happened after the sex and see if we can get an alibi for her brother. We'll also re-check to see if Costanzo had a storage unit we missed the first time around. And we need to schedule a meeting with Detective Killian. I'm tired of looking at these cases independently."

Aislyn also stood. "Got it, Boss."

"As far as the money goes, we'll figure out why Costanzo had it and why he hid it. Later."

Sally followed suit as it was quite obvious Jim was ready to leave. "What are you going to do tonight?"

"I'm going to go home and feed my dog," he said. "Right after I take you home."

It was a statement that should have filled Sally with excitement. Except judging by his expression, he wasn't in the mood for a nightcap.

CHAPTER 39

W hen Duncan arrived at the barracks Friday morning, he strode through the desk area. His fellow troopers wisely gave way. He'd called Killian the previous night. The Uniontown detective, still disgruntled over the events of the previous day, had tried to make excuses as to why he couldn't meet. Duncan had politely steamrolled over all of them.

"I'm seeing a new side of you, Boss," McAllister said as they set up in one of the conference rooms.

"Oh yeah? What side?"

"The slightly scary one."

Killian was late, but he did show and was escorted to the conference room. He checked at the door upon seeing McAllister, but he didn't say anything.

"Have you released Thomas?" she asked.

"Not yet." Killian unbuttoned his jacket and sat. "Fine. That lady lawyer proved it wasn't Pasquale working that night. But I still have Thomas on the CCTV and a meeting scheduled in the deceased's planner."

"But no murder weapon," McAllister said, sitting down across from him.

Killian only glared.

"Enough, both of you." Duncan pulled out a chair on Killian's side of the table. No need to make their visitor feel like the state police was

ganging up on him by sitting next to McAllister. "Here's what we know."
He ran over everything: the extortion scandal, Rafferty's apparent desire to
get out, the taped conversation between Rafferty and Costanzo, the
ballistics reports, what they'd learned at the Twin Oaks and from Tyra
Young, and wrapped up with the new information from Pasquale. "Are we
clear on all that?"

"We're still missing two guns and we don't know how Rafferty's
killer bypassed courthouse security," Killian said.

"We're working on finding the guns. Quite frankly, it doesn't
matter how the actor bypassed security. It happened." Duncan turned to
McAllister. "Do you have anything to add?"

"Only that I saw Porter this morning," she said. "He confirmed
that Alex Costanzo does not have a carry permit nor is there any record of
a handgun registered in his name in the state licensing registry."

"But we all know that criminals don't follow gun laws, so that
doesn't exclude the possibility he acquired a gun from someone."

There was a beat of silence, then McAllister spoke again. "Those
crime scene photos. They bother me."

"Oh, they do, huh?" Killian's lip curled.

McAllister colored, but plowed on. "Look at them side by side."
She laid out the pictures they'd brought in with the Costanzo file. After a
second, Killian did the same with his shots. "Look at the differences."

"What's your point? The scenes are different. That happens all the
time." Killian downed a half-empty cup of coffee.

Duncan saw the warning signs. McAllister's ears turned red, her lips
thinned, and her eyes narrowed. "McAllister," he said. "Would you be so
kind as to go find me some ibuprofen? Must be a change in barometric
pressure because I've got the mother of all headaches coming on."

McAllister shot him a look. Then she stalked out of the room,
letting the door bang shut behind her.

"Rookies," Killian said. "They're all the same."

"Detective Killian."

The older man paused and a wary expression settled onto his
features. "Yeah?"

"You've made it pretty clear you're one of those local cops who
doesn't like interference from the PSP. You've been borderline, and often
not so borderline, rude on a number of occasions to me and Trooper
McAllister. You've been dismissive of witnesses. I've put up with it because

we've been on your territory. That and I'm old-fashioned enough to believe you shouldn't rip into another cop in front of a civilian or new officer."

Killian inched his chair away.

"But we're on my turf now. So let me make this simple." Duncan leaned in. "Say something like that again while we're here and I will personally escort you from this barracks. Then I will ask my lieutenant to call your captain, which he will gladly do because he respects me and he stands behind his people. I can guarantee you will not like the results of that conversation. Understood?"

Killian muttered and shuffled the papers.

"I'm waiting for an answer."

"Understood," Killian mumbled.

🌾🌾🌾

On Friday, Sally's workload made her pay for all the off-the-book investigating she'd been doing for the earlier part of the week. Depositions, bail hearings, and meetings on plea agreements occupied the entire morning. But the question of where the gun used in Colin's murder had ended up was never far from her mind.

Trafford was involved in the affair because he'd gotten the shirt from Roy Pasquale. But he wasn't the man on the video. That meant he'd either pressured one of his cronies into killing Colin for him, or he'd obtained the items for Alex. The erstwhile maintenance worker's face had been obscured by a ball cap and he'd been hunched. It might have been Alex or it might not.

Jim would say go with the simplest explanation first. Sally assumed Pasquale's stand-in was Alex. She had no idea if he had a carry license or had purchased a gun, but she was willing to bet the answer to both questions was "no." Either one would draw attention. If Trafford had paid Alex off, he'd also make Alex dispose of any threat Colin might pose. Trafford would gladly provide the weapon. But if that were the case, what did Alex do with the gun after the shooting? He wouldn't keep it. If found in his possession it might be tied back to the crime.

He could have returned it to Trafford, but when? Nothing had passed between them the one time Sally had seen them together. Alex had been shot the next day. Maybe he had refused to return the gun and that had been the reason for the argument, just like Aislyn said. Alex had tried to threaten Trafford by not returning the murder weapon and had gotten

killed for his efforts. It sounded like Trafford's M.O. Don't negotiate with
a threat; eliminate it.

Between meetings, Sally started making a list of every person she
knew Alex was any kind of friendly with. Fellow attorneys, drinking
buddies, ex-girlfriends. It was a pitifully small list and none of them would
have willingly hidden an illegal firearm. But any of them might have been
coerced or tricked into doing so.

Leaving her final engagement of the morning, she glanced at the
clock. Eleven-thirty. She had the next hour and a half to find as many
phone numbers and make the associated calls as she could, and hope that
one of her long shots paid off.

⚜⚜⚜

Duncan was sitting in silence, staring at Killian, when McAllister returned a
few minutes later with a glass of water and packet of Advil. "Am I
interrupting something?"

"Not at all," Duncan said. "Detective Killian and I were merely
clearing up some points of confusion."

Killian didn't reply. He hadn't said anything since Duncan issued
his ultimatum.

"I scared up some ibuprofen and I brought water," she said,
handing them over. "I don't think you want to take those with cold
coffee."

"Thank you." Duncan downed the pills. "Now, what were you
saying about these photos?"

"Never mind. You probably already thought of it."

"I want to hear it from you."

McAllister glanced at Killian, but when he stayed silent she sat and
pushed forward some pictures. "Here's the Rafferty scene. It's clean. Single
shot, few fingerprints, little trace evidence. It's clinical. Professional, for
lack of a better word," she said.

Duncan studied the photos. "Go on."

"Next, consider where he was shot. His office. No signs of a
struggle, no evidence of defensive wounds. He knew who he was meeting
and he felt safe. Or at least he wasn't expecting trouble."

"That would describe a meeting with Thomas," Killian said, voice
considerably more courteous than it had ever been.

"True. But we can't ignore the coffee mugs." She looked between the other two. "Ms. Castle was quite adamant that Rafferty would only use them for an important guest. Not a client."

Duncan could see where she was going. He'd been right; she was smart and observant.

"Now look at Costanzo." She pulled over some more pictures. "It's the exact opposite. The scene was filthy. There was almost too much trace evidence. These shots were angry, emotional. Especially this one." She tapped the area showing Costanzo's mangled genitals. "This is not a killer who is simply eliminating a threat. This is a shooter who was fueled on anger, plain and simple."

Duncan compared the two sets of photos. "I agree."

Killian swore under his breath. "You two are giving me a headache. Are you telling me Rafferty was some kind of contract killing and Costanzo was shot over sex? None of this has anything to do with the extortion scandal?"

McAllister grabbed her bottle of Mountain Dew. "I'm saying Alex Costanzo shot Colin Rafferty. We know it was Trafford who obtained the stuff from the maintenance guy."

Killian didn't look convinced. "Wouldn't Rafferty know something was up the minute his partner entered wearing a janitor's shirt?"

"He probably did."

"So why didn't he react?"

Duncan looked at the photo of the Rafferty shooting again. "He might have. We have no idea. My bet is that Costanzo walked in, shot Rafferty before he had a chance to do anything, spent enough time in the office to set up the video, and left."

McAllister pursed her lips. "The thing that trips me up...why the courthouse on Sunday night? I mean, there have to be loads of better meeting places."

"There may well be, but let's not get hung up on trivialities. The fact is, they did meet there. What was the logic? Who knows. But they did. It's a highly unlikely location, but it's not impossible for them to get in. We may never know the rationale and, in the end, it doesn't matter. They met at the courthouse. End of story."

McAllister pondered that and then continued "I can easily see Trafford bullying Costanzo into taking care of their errant partner, especially since Costanzo had just as much, if not more, to lose if Rafferty spilled the beans. Someone else killed Costanzo. I'm still debating if it was because of sex or not."

Nice job, McAllister. Duncan pushed the photos over to Killian. "Tell me she doesn't have a point."

Killian looked. "Damn it." He shoved the pictures away.

"If you weren't considering releasing De'Shawn Thomas before, you might want to give it serious thought now. Of course if it were me, I wouldn't jump straight to accusing a member of the district attorney's office of murder without knowing for certain. Even if he is dead. But that's your call."

"I need the gun," Killian said, running a hand over his face.

Duncan thought Sally might have reached the same conclusion. But he'd badgered Killian enough for one day. "If we can help in any way, let us know."

McAllister threw her FTO a puzzled look, but let the offer pass without comment. "What about us, Boss?"

Duncan stood. "We're going to talk to the Young siblings again."

"And Trafford?"

"I told you before, one thing at a time."

⍦⍦⍦

As Sally replaced the phone handset, she crossed the last name off her list. Every person she'd talked to had denied taking anything for safekeeping from Alex. It was sad, really. None of them had expressed any real sorrow, either. Regret that a man was dead, sure. But there'd been no heart-rending grief in any of the voices.

Where was the gun? It had to be somewhere, and she was running out of places to look and people to talk to. If Alex really had returned it, the gun was gone. She had as much chance of getting it from Trafford as she had of winning the Power Ball.

But what if he hadn't? Sally couldn't get away from the notion that Alex was too smart to have gotten in bed with a known criminal without taking precautions. That might include keeping the gun he'd used to kill Colin. Heck, she could even envision a scenario where Alex had been very careful not to leave his own prints on the weapon, making sure that if it was ever "found," the only identifying marks, if any could be lifted, were Trafford's.

The PSP had searched Alex's house; his office, twice; his car; his garage; and found nothing. Jim had told her there was no record of Alex renting a storage unit. Come on, Castle, Sally thought. If he could get the gun in, he'd get it out. He'd either keep it or dispose of it. He hadn't given it away. Throwing it away near work would be risky. That meant he'd at least take it home first. She'd start her search at Alex's house and go from there.

Unlike most single men Sally knew, Alex had a small house, not an apartment. She had a vague memory of him deeming the Uniontown offerings as beneath his luxury scale. The house was in a neat neighborhood off Bailey Avenue. The area was quiet in the middle of the day, except for Alex's neighbor. The construction sounds said there was serious renovation going on.

And in the front of the home was a giant, industrial dumpster.

A man in overalls exited the house carrying a load of broken dry wall. He threw it in the dumpster, brushed off his hands, and headed back inside.

Sally hurried to intercept him. "Excuse me." The man paused. "Are you working in this house?"

The man, George from the name badge sewn on his shirt, frowned. "What business is it of yours?"

No business at all. She waved at Alex's house. "My name is Sally Castle. I knew the man who lived over there. I'm...looking for something and he mentioned there was work going on at his neighbor's."

"You looking for home reno?"

What a mess. Sally abandoned any attempt at a ruse. "Not quite. See...I think something might have been thrown away. Evidence in a case. Honestly, I think my colleague might have been involved and I've been looking for places where he might have disposed of this evidence. I came up empty, but when I saw your dumpster I thought maybe he'd used that."

George's eyes narrowed. "No one's supposed to toss random trash in that unit."

"I know, but a man who's already broken the law wouldn't much care about rules, would he?" Sally waited, but there was no answer. "Can you tell me how long the dumpster has been here?"

George eyed her, but must have decided she wasn't a complete lunatic because he answered. "This is a major job. We've been here three weeks."

"Is it always open? I mean, could anybody walk by and toss something in?"

"Yeah. Like I said, they ain't supposed to, but you've got a point. Someone who's broken the law wouldn't give a damn about that."

The dumpster would be there, full of construction debris. And when the job ended, no one would look at the contents, probably. Perfect disposal site. "Would you mind if I looked inside?"

George's stared in frank disbelief. "In a skirt? Lady, are you out of your mind?"

"It's very important I find this evidence."

"There's wall board, nails, all sorts of crap in there. You could get hurt."

Sally gave him what she hoped was a winning smile. "Then could you look for me?"

He stared for a long second, then grabbed the edge of the dumpster, and pulled himself up. "Better than you cutting yourself and suing us, I suppose." Once over the edge, he asked, "What exactly does this evidence look like?"

What was she looking for? "A plastic bag. Could be clear, but it's probably opaque. Green, black, or brown. There will be a heavy-ish object in it that will either look or feel like a gun."

"A gun? Why?"

"Because it is."

George had started pushing aside bags, but he stopped. "I'm outta here."

"Please. It sounds bad...okay it is bad, but I need to find it."

"Why are you looking for a plastic bag with a gun in it in a dumpster full of construction garbage?"

"It's a long story." While George looked, talking under his breath the whole time, Sally looked around the sides of the dumpster, even getting down on her knees to see if the bag had been taped or affixed to the sides. She came up empty. Not surprising. If the idea was to include the bag with the rest of the garbage, it wouldn't be outside the dumpster. It'd be at or near the bottom.

"I might have found something." George dangled a bag of thick, black plastic over the side. It looked like the kind of thing a toner cartridge for a printer would come in. Unlikely to tear, totally opaque.

Sally took it, her fingers touching what definitely felt like the outline of a handgun. It was sealed with heavy tape, wrapped around so it was nearly impossible to peel apart. "Do you have a utility knife or a box cutter?" she asked.

George handed over a knife and Sally used the blade to slit open the end of the bag. She pulled it open as wide as she could and stepped into the sunlight to get a clear look at the contents. The bright autumn sun hit off the dull surface of a black handgun.

CHAPTER 40

It was almost noon on Friday when Duncan and McAllister arrived at Tyra Young's apartment. The trash cans had been knocked over again. This time, some urban scavenger had shredded the cheap bags so that garbage trailed everywhere, the sweet smell of refuse mingling with that of dry leaves and exhaust fumes.

After a minute of knocking, Duncan decided to try the superintendent. He skirted the trash and walked down a few doors to one identical to the others, but marked manager in peeling gold foil, and knocked.

"Just a second," a wheezy voice said. The door was opened a few moments later by an old man with swollen knuckles and chapped hands. "Is there a problem?"

Both troopers held out their badges. "You the manager?" Duncan asked.

"For forty years. Ben Waterhouse." He stuck out his hand. "Not usual for the state police to knock on my door. Nobody's complained, have they?"

"No, sir," McAllister said. "We're looking for Ms. Young, the lady in that unit there. Have you seen her?"

Waterhouse stared at Tyra's door. "Tyra? Nice girl. Little rough around the edges, but nice girl. Let me think." He frowned. "Haven't seen her today, no."

"What about her brother, Elijah?"

Waterhouse blinked his watery eyes. "Check Jimmy-Joe's. They have a pool table. I think Elijah hangs out there a lot. If he's not there, maybe someone's seen him."

They walked back to the patrol car. "Do you think she's working already?" McAllister asked.

"Even for a Friday, it's early." Duncan leaned on the car. "Never mind Tyra. We know she was at the motel. If the shooter was her brother, she's not going to say anything. Let's focus on Elijah."

"Off to Jimmy-Joe's?"

"Yep." Duncan's cell phone buzzed. Caller ID said Sally. "What's up?"

Her voice was strained. "I think I found the gun used to kill Colin."

"Where?"

McAllister shot him a quizzical look, but he mouthed, "just a sec."

"In the dumpster at his neighbor's house, which is being renovated. It's inside a toner cartridge bag. I think Alex, or whoever the killer was, threw it there intending it to be taken away with the construction garbage."

"Did you touch it?"

"No. I know, prints. It looks like it has a rough grip; I'm not sure you'll get anything off it."

"But we might be able to pull something off the magazine and ballistics will definitely tell us if it's the murder weapon."

McAllister walked over. "They found the gun?"

Duncan waved her off. "I don't suppose you can tell me what kind it is?"

"It's black and it's huge," Sally said with a shaky laugh. "Actually, it looks a lot like the one you carry on duty."

It could very well be a Glock or a Sig, then. "Okay, listen. Call Detective Killian and have him meet you, pronto. You give him the entire thing, bag and all."

"Can't you come get it?"

"It's not my case. Call Killian. Trust me, I think you'll find him a little more...amenable to your suggestions."

"What did you say to him?"

"Never mind. I'll call you later." He hung up. "Ms. Castle. She thinks she found the gun used to kill Rafferty."

"So I gather," McAllister said. "Where?"

"Dumpster. Get in and I'll tell you on the way."

⇟⇟⇟

Sally dutifully called Detective Killian as soon as she returned to the courthouse. She knew it was the right way to handle things, but she would have liked to hand over the gun to Jim and let him deal with the grouchy Uniontown detective.

The Killian who walked through her door was not the same man who'd gone with her to see Roy Pasquale, however. His face was grayer and the lines around his eyes were a bit deeper. He took the toner cartridge bag from her and peered inside. "You said you found this in a dumpster?"

"Yes. At the bottom." She told him about going to Alex's house and seeing the ongoing work next door. "It seemed like a good place."

"What made you look there?"

"I asked myself how I'd dispose of a gun without being noticed. Nobody looks twice at a bag of trash."

He dropped the entire thing in an evidence bag and sealed it.

"Coupled with the statement from Roy Pasquale—"

"Yeah, I know." He finished with his chain of custody form and attached it to the bag. "I've already released Thomas and put in a subpoena for Alex Costanzo's financial records. Is there anything else I should know about?"

Sally told him about her conversation with Kelly Martin. "Did Trooper Duncan tell you about the lock-box in Costanzo's office?"

"The one full of cash? Yes. I'll be looking into that." He hefted the bag. "Thank you for your help, Ms. Castle. I'm…I apologize for not listening to you more closely." His words were stiff.

"I understand, Detective. It was not my intention to cause you undue stress. I only wanted to make sure the right thing was done."

He muttered an indistinct goodbye and left.

She might have wished for a more gracious apology, but it was probably as good as she was going to get. She stared at the work in front of her, unable to get the image of the gun and Jim's description of the cash out of her mind. Why did Alex have so much money in his office, and hidden to boot? It didn't make sense.

What if she'd got it backwards? What if Alex hadn't paid Trafford, it was the other way around?

CHAPTER 41

Duncan and McAllister pulled up outside Jimmy-Joe's. The heavy bass beat of hip-hop rattled the cruiser's windows, even though it was barely twelve-thirty. On the sidewalk, the noise poured through the front door every time it opened.

Before they went in, McAllister stepped in front of Duncan. "I want the lead."

He surveyed her. "It might be early, but I can guarantee all of those people have been drinking. At least half of them will want to prove they're tougher than you are. Maybe more. Could get ugly."

"I know."

She'd done some great interviews. But up until now, the good ones had been with sympathetic subjects. When he said "ugly" what he really meant was "disastrous." Duncan ran through possible scenarios. The safe decision would be to tell her "no." But it wasn't the right decision. "I'll be at your six. I'm not going to wait for blood to flow before I step in."

"Understood." She squared her shoulders and they entered the bar.

Duncan scanned the crowd and briefly locked eyes with Elijah Young at the back of the room. Young tried to slink to the fire exit. But he couldn't move fast enough in the mass of bodies.

"Elijah Young, we need to speak with you." Duncan made his voice heard even over the thumping bass.

"Impressive," McAllister muttered.

"Experience." He led her back to Young.

"Mr. Young, we have a few more questions," McAllister said. "Got a minute?"

"Why not? You white officers ain't gonna listen no how. Gonna pin it on the black man no matter what." Young's chin jutted, but the defiance didn't quite cover the wavering of his voice. There was a mutter of agreement from the knot of people around him.

Duncan scanned the building's interior, but he also watched McAllister in the mirror behind the bar. Her posture was relaxed. When she spoke, there was no trace of belligerence, only firm determination.

"We're not here to pin anything on anyone," she said. "We want to know where you were last Monday between one and five. If you don't want to tell us, that's fine."

"Except you'll get a warrant or something," Young replied.

"There's always the possibility we'll come back." McAllister's left hand rested on her hip, the right one on her sidearm. Ready to react, but not overtly threatening. "We told you before. We know what the deal was between Alex Costanzo and Tyra. I'm asking a routine question, that's all. Tell us to leave and we'll leave."

Young snorted. "If you want me to say I'm sorry he's dead and I wouldn't have shot him myself iff'n I'd had the chance, you're gonna be disappointed."

"I want to know where you were last Monday." McAllister didn't break eye contact, her voice even.

"Here."

"What time?"

"Damned if I know. I don't wear no watch."

"Thank you." McAllister started to walk away, then turned back. "Marshawn Watkins. You're sure you haven't seen him recently?"

"I'm sure." Young had been staring at McAllister, but now he looked around at his friends. "Ain't that right?"

The crowd murmured assent, all but one who glanced at the troopers, then back to Young, then shifted his gaze to the floor.

McAllister touched her hat. "We'll see ourselves out."

It was at least twenty degrees cooler outside. Duncan took a deep breath to clear the stuffy air of the bar from his lungs. "Excellent job."

McAllister shrugged. "Except we didn't learn anything. He's lying, I know it. We need to trip him up."

"We will. I have a sneaking suspicion Young's friends aren't all on board with his story," Duncan said. "Did you notice the guy in the corner?"

"The one who wouldn't look anywhere but the floor?"

"Yeah, him. He's the weak link." Duncan was about to suggest ways they could isolate the man in question when he exited the bar.

"Hey. Hey officers. Can I talk to you?" He shot a nervous look behind him. He'd been standing at Young's elbow inside, a thin, reedy black man with a pseudo-afro and scraggly beard. His jeans weren't particularly baggy, but were still threatening to fall off non-existent hips under an oversized T-shirt with some kind of Jamaican-looking logo and a nondescript black hoody.

"Of course. What's up?"

"Uh, I don't wanna—"

"Be seen, right. Let's go over here." Duncan led him a few steps down an alley. The smell of refuse was thick on the air, but they were out of sight. The man had deferred to Young inside and his demeanor told Duncan the guy was anxious not to be seen with the police. "What's your name?"

"Petey Washington. Eli and me go way back."

"What do you want to tell us?" McAllister said.

Washington shuffled his feet. "Like I said, Eli and me go way back. He's got a way of saying things that make him look guilty."

Duncan waited in silence. Someone always wanted to help his buddy. They usually wound up helping the police instead. But now that Washington was outside, he had the appearance of someone who was rethinking his decision. "Is this about Monday afternoon?" Duncan prompted.

"Yeah. He was here like he said, but not until later. Maybe around five. When he came in, he looked wild. But he started drinking, didn't want to talk about it. Said the shit had gone down and he didn't want to think on it no more."

"Have you seen this man before?" McAllister held out the mug shot of Marshawn Watkins.

Washington studied it, tongue between his teeth. "I think he was with Eli Saturday night. The Saturday before the Monday you're asking about."

McAllister put the picture back in her pocket. "Did you speak to him?"

"Nah, he and Eli were in a booth, talking. It was clear to me they didn't want to be bothered. He left early."

"Did he have a gun?" Duncan asked.

"No clue," Washington said. "He was wearing a jacket. I didn't see nothing. You think he shot the guy who was doing Eli's sister?"

Duncan didn't answer, but exchanged a look with McAllister.

"I don't want Eli to get in trouble if there's no trouble to be got." Washington stuffed his hands in his pockets and shot a furtive look at Jimmy-Joe's.

"Understood. Thank you for the information." Duncan nodded and watched as Washington scampered back inside. There was a beat of silence, then the thumping bass started again.

"I knew it. Watkins was here," McAllister said. "Do you think he loaned Elijah the gun? Or what about this. Elijah wants Costanzo hurt, but he's afraid of getting busted himself. He calls his old buddy. Tyra lures Costanzo to the motel, Watkins busts in and winds up getting carried away."

"Costanzo told her to be at the Twin Oaks. It doesn't sound like he was lured there."

"Okay, she told her brother where Costanzo would be, he tells Watkins, and we end up with the same result."

"Let's call Pittsburgh." Duncan headed back to the car. "See if they can locate Mr. Watkins. Let's make it known we want to talk to him."

"I don't suppose there's a way Tyra gets out of this clean."

"She knew what was going to happen and she played along. Conspiracy to commit at the very least."

McAllister slammed her door shut. "I hate it when the victim becomes the bully."

Duncan agreed. It sucked. Unfortunately, the situation was an occupational hazard.

CHAPTER 42

McAllister called the Pittsburgh Bureau of Police from the car. While she was on the phone, Duncan's cell rang. Caller ID: blocked. "Yeah Eddy."

The bookie's girlish voice was strained. "You need to get over to Carrington's house on Wharton Furnace. Now."

"Why?"

"Trafford's clearing the place out. I guess you and your friend made it too hot for him."

Duncan glanced at McAllister, who was still talking to the Pittsburgh police. "You saw this?"

"I've had feelers out for a while. One of my sources brought it to me, so I had Stanley drive me by the place. Yes, I saw it. Trafford and his friend are hauling out boxes. I had Stanley fake engine trouble so we could pull over. I heard just enough to know they aren't moving out books for a library sale."

"Thanks, Eddy." Duncan snapped his phone shut and made the turn that would take them to Carrington's house.

"What's up?" McAllister said.

"Trafford's leaving the house on Wharton Furnace. We need to get there before he ditches the evidence or hauls it away." He nodded toward the glove compartment. "Warrant applications in there. Start one and we'll get a phone approval. Application made based on information from a trusted informant that evidence may be destroyed or removed from the premises."

McAllister pulled out the paper and started writing.

After she turned over the gun, Sally tried to distract herself with the paperwork for a new plea agreement, as well as wrapping up a few other details that had been waiting for her attention. It only half worked. She also called Deborah Rafferty to give her the news. The man who had almost-certainly killed her son was dead. Whether Alex had been paid for a job or done it of his own volition remained to be seen. Sally hated not knowing, but she'd done all she could. It was up to the police now.

Her phone rang around twelve-thirty, jolting her out of her thoughts. "Fayette County Public Defender's office. Sally Castle speaking."

"Uh, you said you were Sally Castle?" The voice was male, high-pitched, and nervous.

A younger man unsure about calling an attorney's office. "Yes, who is this?"

"My uh," the man swallowed, "my name is Devin Carrington. I, uh, need to speak to you."

She pushed aside her paperwork. "We're speaking now, aren't we?" Whoever he was, she needed to put him at ease.

"Yeah, see…I own a house. On Wharton Furnace Road. We…I mean I have information. About Aaron Trafford, Alex Costanzo, and Colin Rafferty."

If the man was calling to rat out Trafford, no wonder he was nervous. "Well, why don't you give me the details and we'll go from there?"

"Not over the phone. It has to be in person."

"I'm in my office. If you have transportation, I can meet you at the courthouse."

"Too public. Can you…can you come to my place?"

His place? No freaking way. Maybe if she played at being cooperative, she could get him to meet elsewhere. "I can't do that. If you won't come to me, I'm afraid I can't help you." Silence from the other end. "I can tell you're nervous and that's understandable. Maybe we can compromise. There's a state police barracks—"

"No! Not there. Trafford…if he finds out…well, you know." Carrington's voice was stressed. He didn't want to make this call, that was crystal clear. Either something had happened to scare him into talking to anyone in the legal system who wasn't a police officer or he was being forced to contact her.

"Then we're at a standstill." More silence. She could hear breathing, so he hadn't hung up. "Mr. Carrington, it's your call."

"Please, I gotta talk to you. It's super important." He paused, breathing heavy. "There's a baseball field on Jumonville Road. How about there?"

A ball field. That could work. There would potentially be people there, but not enough to scare Carrington off. Jim was on duty now. That meant if she arranged to meet Carrington later, she could tell Jim to meet her at the field. "Okay, but I don't leave work until four-thirty. If you won't meet me at the courthouse or the barracks, the best I can do is five o'clock."

"Ball field. Five. Got it. What kind of car do you drive? You know, so I can recognize you."

"A tan Camry." There'd be another car there too, either a state police cruiser there or a dark blue Jeep, but she didn't mention that.

"Tan Camry. Got it. See you then." Carrington hung up.

Sally replaced the receiver and stared at the phone. Then she did a search of county records for Devin Carrington. He did own a house on Wharton Furnace. He had a record; a smattering of misdemeanor drug charges. His mug shot was a reedy guy who didn't look like he weighed a hundred pounds sopping wet. Devin Carrington didn't scare her.

Did she need backup? Was she was overreacting and Carrington was exactly what he sounded like? A guy with information who was scared shitless Trafford would find out. She could be delaying the receipt of key information that would help the police. Considering what Sally knew Trafford might have done, it wasn't an unreasonable fear. But it would be foolish to make assumptions. Carrington looked scrawny in his mug shot, but she heard Jim's voice in her head. "He could decide to shoot you before you ever got close enough to disarm him."

Maybe she should turn this over to the police and not go at all. But what if Carrington truly had information? He had reached out to her, specifically. Perhaps he didn't trust the authorities. If no one pursued this, he might not call again.

She made up her mind, picked up the phone, and dialed Jim's cell. It went to voicemail. "Jim, it's Sally. I just got a call from a Devin Carrington about Trafford. Carrington sounded nervous as hell, asked to meet me at a baseball field on Jumonville Road. From the map, it's by that kids' camp. It might be legit, but I don't want to go alone. I told him I'd be there at five. I really want you with me on this. Call me back."

She hung up. It was irrational to think Jim would answer the first time she called. He was working. He was almost certainly busy. But she hoped he'd get back to her soon.

CHAPTER 43

McAllister ended her call. "Got it. I tried to be as open-ended as I could. The judge was pretty lenient."

"Excellent." Duncan turned onto Wharton Furnace Road. "Do me a favor, check my phone. It's down there, I heard it buzz."

McAllister picked up the tiny handset. "Missed call and voicemail from S Castle. You want me to listen to it?"

"No need." Who knows what Sally had said. It probably wasn't too personal, but he didn't want McAllister listening to his messages. "Send her a text and tell her I'll call her later."

"If I can remember how to use one of these things."

"Very funny."

The clouds had moved out and it was a brilliant day: cool, sunny, and breezy. When they arrived at the house on Wharton Furnace, over half the leaves were gone from the trees in the front yard. Duncan walked up to the front door, pounded, and announced himself while McAllister prowled the roadside and property lines, pushing aside dead grass with gloved hands.

He was about to pound again, when he heard scuffling and the unlocking of the deadbolt. The door opened to reveal Devin Carrington. He was dressed in a dirty T-shirt and grimy jeans. His bloodshot eyes had huge, dark bags, and he sniffled constantly. "What the hell do you want?" he said.

"I'm looking for Aaron Trafford. Is he home?" Pretty convenient for Trafford. One guy, Monahan, to move the drugs. One, Carrington, to store them and provide a home base. How many more flunkies did Trafford have?

"Screw you."

"Then no. You're Devin Carrington, correct?"

The man rubbed his nose. "I said screw you."

"I heard you the first time. We have a search warrant for these premises." Duncan held out the warrant. "You can read it, but I'll summarize. It authorizes us to search the entire property and all buildings for drugs and drug-related paraphernalia."

"Duncan, over here." McAllister's sharp voice came from near the garage.

"Get the hell away from there." Carrington started out of the house. "Ain't none of your business. I'm gonna call the cops."

"We are the cops," Duncan said. He walked over to McAllister, who was standing over a shredded black garbage bag against the garage wall.

She pointed. A large quantity of plastic sandwich bags spilled from the black plastic, along with several empty rolls of duct tape and a pile of cream-colored powder.

Under the powder, Duncan could see a foil disc labeled Enfamil.

"Bet you anything that's formula," McAllister said. "You see any evidence there were babies in this place when we were last here?"

Duncan snapped on a pair of nitrile gloves from his belt and picked up the baggies. "Corners clipped off." He turned. "You're making some mighty small sandwiches and using a lot of duct tape," he said. "Babysitting for someone?"

Carrington had come out as far as the corner of the house. "Get away from that. Ain't none of your business."

"You forget, we have a warrant. It's right there, in your hand." Duncan straightened. In his pocket, his phone buzzed. Probably Sally. She'd have to wait.

⁂

Over the course of the afternoon, Sally alternately called Jim and sent texts. She also tried reaching him at the barracks, but was told he was unavailable and she declined to leave a message. She'd done enough of that.

She looked up the location of the baseball field where Devin Carrington wanted to meet. It was maybe a fifteen or twenty-minute drive. She decided to leave her departure until the last possible minute to give Jim the opportunity to get back to her.

He'd call. Or text. He would. At this point, they knew what had happened to Colin. Jim, however, had more to deal with. He still had to figure out who killed Alex and deal with the drugs, although now they'd proven Trafford was at least peripherally involved in one murder, it increased the odds he was connected to both of them. Jim had to be positive, though. He was probably hip-deep in investigation right now. He'd get back to her as soon as he could.

But the time rolled by and there was no call. What was he doing? Perhaps he was arresting Trafford at that very minute. But maybe not. What if he didn't have the information he needed for an arrest warrant? This meeting with Carrington could provide the last bit of evidence Jim needed for his case.

⇟ ⇟ ⇟

Carrington's house turned out to be a bonanza. A new marijuana grow in the attic. Drying racks and packaging in the basement. In the garage was a heavy, padlocked deck container. "McAllister, get the bolt cutters from the trunk," Duncan said.

Carrington, who had stood by while the troopers raided his house, turned red. "You don't need to open that."

"Right, because what we've found already isn't enough."

"None of this is my shit. It's all Trafford's."

"Stored in your house with your knowledge. That's possession with the intent to distribute. In fact, let's make it official." Duncan cuffed him, eliciting twisting, swearing, and protests.

"I'm telling you that isn't my stuff. I didn't do nothing, you stupid shit! Lemme go!"

Duncan ignored all of it and led Carrington to the patrol car. After he shut the door, he took a moment to check his phone, which had been buzzing for the last couple of hours. He knew it couldn't be anyone from the barracks; they would have radioed as a follow-up to the phone. He checked the screen: Sally. He'd said he would call her later. Well, okay. It was later and he hadn't been in touch. She must be going crazy waiting for information. He'd send her a quick text, find out what she wanted.

McAllister jogged up with the bolt cutters, interrupting him. "Shall I do the honors?"

He snapped his phone shut. It was four-thirty. He'd wrap this up, then get back to Sally. "Be my guest."

It didn't take long to get rid of the lock. McAllister popped off the lid and whistled. Stacked inside were cans originally from coffee and formula, both filled with baggies containing crystal rocks that were visible through the translucent lids. "Jackpot."

"All right, let's get it boxed up and get the hell out of here. I want to get this into evidence, ASAP."

McAllister looked up from the chain of custody form. "What about Trafford?"

"Not to worry. I'm betting once Mr. Carrington gets to a comfy cell down at the county jail, he'll be only too happy to help us find his buddy."

❧❧❧

Minutes ticked by while Sally sat and willed her phone to ring. It was four forty-five. If she left now, she'd only be five or ten minutes later than when she'd promised to be at the baseball field. Not even that. Maybe Jim would call her while she was en route and meet her there.

She'd try one more time. Again, she got his voicemail. "Jim, it's Sally. I have to leave. I can't risk Devin Carrington running out when he has information that might help. But seriously, I don't want to do this alone. Hopefully you've gotten these messages. If you can't respond, well, I'll see you at the field on Jumonville, yeah? Thanks."

She picked up her purse. Devin Carrington's mug shot and arrest records indicated he was a scrawny guy. On the phone he'd sounded weak, indecisive. She could hold him off easily. All she had to do was stall him until Jim arrived.

CHAPTER 44

Duncan parked the patrol car at the barracks and shut the door. "I told you he'd cooperate."

Carrington had started talking before they'd even gotten to Uniontown. By the time they put him into a cell, the troopers had four possible locations for Trafford.

"Now we have to round up Trafford," McAllister said as they entered the building.

Duncan pulled out his phone. It was a little after five. He'd call Sally, ask her out for a celebratory drink, and fill her in on all the details. All he really needed to make the afternoon perfect was to make a collar in the Costanzo homicide. Before he could dial, his phone buzzed. It was a Pittsburgh number. "Duncan."

"Trooper Jim Duncan? This is Detective David Bonetti, Pittsburgh Bureau of Police."

"How can I help you?"

"It is my understanding you are interested in a man named Marshawn Watkins."

McAllister grabbed the bottle of Mountain Dew she'd purchased from the vending machine and unscrewed the top. "Who is it?"

"Detective Bonetti, just a second. I'm going to put you on speaker." Duncan laid the phone on a desk so he and McAllister could hear. "Yes, I want to question Watkins about a homicide down here in Fayette County."

"Today's your lucky day," Bonetti said. "We picked him up late last night. Or early this morning, take your pick. Possession with intent. If you're looking at him for a murder, he had a couple items that might interest you."

"Like what?"

"A Glock nine-millimeter, unregistered, and a receipt from a Uniontown McDonald's dated a week ago."

McAllister pumped her fist.

"Did Mr. Watkins have any explanation for those items or has he already asked for a lawyer?" Duncan asked.

Bonetti chuckled. "Funny you should ask. We questioned him about the gun. First he said it wasn't his, then he said it was a recent purchase. He tried to play dumb when we pointed out it wasn't registered, so it couldn't have been a legal purchase, but we weren't buying his act."

"What about the receipt?"

"He denied being in Fayette County. We said he had a receipt that showed otherwise. He said he might have visited a friend. When we asked who this friend was, he reversed course and said he hadn't been near Uniontown."

Duncan glanced at McAllister, who was shaking her head. "He never asked for a lawyer?" Duncan asked.

"We Mirandized him, but he didn't bother to ask for an attorney until after he'd bungled his story."

It was true. More crimes were solved by stupid criminals than brilliant law enforcement. "I'd really like to see the ballistics report on that gun. Do you think you could put a rush on it?"

"Already did. I faxed you the results." Bonetti paused for effect. "It's a match."

McAllister whooped.

"Detective Bonetti, you have no idea how happy you've made me," Duncan said. "First round's on me."

"I'll put it on my calendar. We'll work out the jurisdiction, but I suspect your murder charge is going to trump my narcotics bust." Bonetti hung up.

McAllister toasted Duncan with her bottle. "Not bad for a day's work. A revenge killing. Young got fed up with his sister being mistreated and called his friend Watkins. You think Watkins did the shooting or just provided the gun?"

"I don't know, but it doesn't matter. It's murder and conspiracy to commit any way you slice it."

"I can't believe Trafford wasn't involved in either homicide. What are the odds?"

"As weird as it sounds to say it, Trafford is just a drug dealer. Nothing more than what he said he was. But yes, this is what you call 'a good day.' Now I can call Sally back, let her know I just need to wrap up the paperwork—"

"Make plans for the evening?" McAllister's blue eyes twinkled.

"Be quiet." But he grinned. First, he should see what all these texts and messages said, just in case Sally had already made plans. He scrolled through them and the temperature in the room felt like it plunged.

McAllister set down her pop, all traces of mirth gone from her face. "What's wrong?"

He tried to keep his hand from shaking and punched the code for his voicemail. As he listened, his breathing and heartbeat sped up.

"Jim, it's Sally. Still haven't heard from you. I'm about five minutes out from the meet. I'm hoping I see you there. If not, I'll try to stall Carrington until you arrive. See you soon."

The profanity hissed out, his voice barely a whisper.

"If a Boy Scout like you is saying that, I know it's serious. What's up?

He shook his head as he dialed Sally's number. Voicemail. He hung up, then slid the phone into his pocket. "McAllister, can you handle things on this end? Start with the stuff from the drugs. Then we need arrest warrants. Meth production and distribution for Trafford, murder and conspiracy to commit for Watkins, and Tyra and Elijah Young. I've gotta go."

"You want company?"

"No. I've got this, you focus on the paper. We don't want all our hard work to go to waste. I'll call for back-up from the road."

"Where are you going?" McAllister asked.

"I've gotta get to a baseball field." He rushed out of the room, snatched keys from his desk, and ran for a cruiser.

☙☙☙

Sally parked in the lot at the field, expecting to see at least a few other cars. But it was deserted except for an old, beat-up Buick; a sign indicated the field was closed temporarily because of a ground bee infestation in the infield. The wind stirred dry brown leaves on the ground making an eerie rustle. Most significantly, Jim was not there. She couldn't have missed a marked state car or his Jeep.

She got out of her Camry and locked it, an automatic response. He'd be there any minute. She could handle Devin Carrington until he did.

One problem. The person who came out of the Buick was not Devin Carrington.

She stopped, grasping her keys. The man was stocky, slightly taller than she was, and at least fifty pounds heavier. His hair was shaved close and the tattoos on his arms and neck were obvious under the plain white T-shirt, the hem of which bunched around a large, black handgun at his waist.

It was Aaron Trafford. She hadn't bargained for this. Where the hell was Jim?

"I was beginning to think you'd skipped out on me, legal eagle," the man said. His voice was rough and low.

Legal eagle. Trafford had used the same phrase to describe Colin. Even if she hadn't recognized Trafford from his mug shot, the words would have confirmed the identification. "I'm looking for Devin Carrington." She paused by the front of her car. Would she have time to back up, unlock the door, get into the car, start the engine, and drive off before he closed the distance between them? Maybe, but the presence of the gun made that irrelevant. She stayed perfectly still, hoping the lack of movement would keep any action on his part at bay.

He laughed, a low growl that wasn't a pleasant sound. "Yeah, Devin isn't here. Seems he got himself in a bit of a jam with the cops. They kept him busy with all the searching and stuff at his place. They carted him off at the end, him and all the drugs they found."

"If he was so busy with the police, how did he call me?" Keep him talking until Jim arrived.

Another evil chuckle. "That's the great thing about being me. I got all kinds of friends who will do favors. Getting arrested for drug possession. Making phone calls and pretending to be someone else."

It hadn't been Carrington on the phone. Trafford had coerced one of his "friends" into calling and giving a false name in case she looked up arrest records and property ownership. Which she had. No wonder the man on the phone had been nervous. He'd probably made the call while Trafford pointed that gun at him. "Well, then. This seems to be a mistake. I'll just go." She took a step backward, leaves crunching underfoot.

"Don't move." He pulled the weapon from his waistband and pointed it at her. "I'm disappointed. You didn't bring your cop friend."

"I was told not to." The gun was big. The same one used to kill Alex? "You're Aaron Trafford, I presume." Jim, any time now would be good, she thought.

"That's me." He jerked his head. "I was sure telling you not to call the cops would guarantee that was exactly what you'd do."

Sally said nothing, but listened for the reassuring sounds of a siren. All she heard was birds chirping, wind in the grass, and the dead leaves brushing the ground. Had Jim not gotten her messages?

"First, your boyfriend shuts down my lab. Then he harasses Gran. Then he takes my product. All this after I had to pay off your lawyer-buddy and his pet DA last year. Although I think that's the other way around. Your DA friend and his pet defense lawyer. You people sure do make it hard to earn a living."

Sally found her voice. "What does that have to do with me? Why lure me out here?"

"Leverage. I've seen you with that state cop. I have you, he'll come here. Trashing his house didn't quite have the effect I was hoping for. Maybe if I'd been able to kill his pooch he'd have gotten the message. Dropped his investigation and this whole situation could have been avoided." The hand holding the gun never moved and Trafford took another step forward. "Now he's screwed everything. I can't let that slide. It's bad for my reputation. You understand."

How had he seen them? Where? It didn't matter. She wasn't the only one who could do illicit surveillance. She and Jim had been together plenty of times. She took another step back.

"I said don't move." His grip on the gun tightened.

He might not want to kill her. Yet. Wounding was another matter. "He wouldn't have stopped. You're breaking the law. Killing his dog would have pissed him off that much more."

"Screw the law." His eyes glinted. "I don't force people to buy drugs. I'm sure you've heard of supply and demand. I'm using the money to take care of Gran, not leaving her to the state. Family first and all that. I've been taken care of by the state, you know. They suck at it." He took another step.

"Mr. Trafford. I can't hurt you. You said the cops have already seized all your…product. You can't get anything of value from me. I'll get back in my car, drive off, and leave you to do whatever it is you're planning to do. There's no need for this." No need to mention what Trafford was doing right now constituted a fresh wave of law-breaking and would summon the police again. Hopefully on her way back to Uniontown she'd see Jim and he could deal with the situation. If she didn't, she'd definitely make the call to 911.

"I've got a better idea. You and I sit tight, and wait for your boyfriend to show."

"I told you. I didn't call him." She lifted her chin, trying to sell the bluff. Now she didn't know whether to hope Jim arrived or not. Maybe Trafford intended to shoot her either way. Even if she used the remote to unlock her car, it wouldn't help. Trafford would fire as soon as he heard the beep. Her palms were slick as she grasped the keys and fought to control her breathing, suddenly hot even thought it was cool in the twilight.

"Well, I guess you'll have to call him now."

She might as well try to get a confession. "You hired Alex Costanzo to kill Colin Rafferty, and then you killed Alex to shut him up."

The gun didn't move, targeted square on her chest. "Wrong. I wanted to be left alone. Killing people would defeat the purpose. I've made plenty of threats, but I've never killed anyone."

"Then you can still walk away."

"Like I said, that would be bad for my reputation. Sure, I can set up business somewhere else, but if word gets out I let the cops run me out of Fayette County, no one will take any of my threats seriously. So I'll go, but the cop has to go first."

"And me?"

"You're…what do they call it? Oh yeah. Collateral damage."

He had to be lying. But looking in his eyes, Sally could tell he wasn't. Aaron Trafford was many things, but he wasn't a liar. Or a murderer. Yet.

If there hadn't been a gun pointed at her, the realization would have hurt more than it did. Now what? She knew gun defenses, but he was too far away for those. What a friggin' mess. She'd called Jim, trusted him. He said he'd be there for her. Where the hell was he?

The sound of a siren cut the air.

"Thought you said you didn't call the cops," Trafford said, a sly grin on his lips.

She tried for a last-ditch lie. "I didn't. Something else must have tipped them off." It had to be Jim. At least, she hoped it was. The gun was enormous, at least to her eyes.

"Either way gets me what I want." Trafford lunged.

Sally tried to sidestep, but her heel caught in the gravel and she nearly fell. Trafford grabbed her wrist and spun her. He pulled her close, arm wrapped around her shoulders, and pressed the gun to her side.

The marked state car skidded to a halt behind hers and Jim emerged from the driver's side, his own gun in his hand.

"Well, lookee here," Trafford said. His breath tickled Sally's ear. "We got ourselves a real party now, don't we?"

CHAPTER 45

Duncan brought the state Ford to halt in the middle of the parking lot. The baseball field should have been full of people, but it wasn't. A bright yellow sign fluttered from the fence and yellow tape marked off the infield. The ball field was closed. No wonder Trafford picked it for the meet.

Duncan got out and muttered curses under his breath as he crouched behind the engine block as a barrier. He keyed the mic. "Trooper Jim Duncan again requesting backup." He rattled off the location. "I've got one shooter with a handgun. This is a hostage situation." Hopefully that would make people drive faster.

"Copy that. Additional cars are en route." The response crackled through the radio.

Backup would come, but would it be in time? Trafford had Sally in front of him, his arm clasped around her, using her as a very effective human shield. Brown leaves drifted past on the gentle breeze. Only part of his face was visible behind her head. A black semi-automatic handgun was pressed to her right side.

"State police. Down on the ground."

"Make me," Trafford said, lip curled.

The gun trained on Sally was larger than a 9mm. A .45? A .357? Either way, the cover provided by the car was flimsy. The engine block might stop a round, but the bullet would pierce the metal body easily. The massive oak at the edge of the lot would be better at shielding Duncan's body. But his line of sight would be crap. That and the tree was at least thirty feet away. How good was Trafford's aim? Hitting a moving target was harder, but did Duncan want to risk injury with Sally's well-being on the line? He was better off staying put.

Why had she come out here? Because she didn't know who she'd meet. She thought she was meeting a scared witness in a case she didn't know was closed. The news of the drug raid had not yet hit the news. She didn't know about the collaboration between the Youngs and Watkins.

How many times had he started to call? All he needed to have done was send a quick text. Something to let her know what was going on. He hadn't because he'd been "too busy." Damn it.

"Let her go," he said, holding his Sig steady. "Put down your gun and get on the ground."

"That would give up my advantage," Trafford said. "You've been giving me a lot of trouble. I knew putting her in the line of fire would get you here."

"Down on the ground."

"Nah, I don't think so. See, I gotta get rid of both of you now. You, because you screwed me good and I can't let that go. Her, because I don't need witnesses, especially ones I know will continue to cause problems."

Duncan didn't have a clean shot. All he could do was hope backup was close. "You're going to be outmatched and outgunned here pretty soon. Nobody wants this to get messy. Let her go and put down the gun."

"Screw you. Unless you want to see her die right now, come out from behind that car and take what's coming like a man." Trafford jammed the gun into Sally's side.

🌲🌲🌲

Trafford's arm tightened around Sally. "What's it going to be?"

She could feel his hot breath on her neck, rancid with the scent of onions and beer, and the barrel of the gun at her midsection. She fought to control her breathing. Trafford's body hummed with tension.

"I told you. Let her go. Down on the ground, arms out." Ahead of her in the late-afternoon light, she saw Jim stand firm, covered by the car, steady hands holding his own gun. He could have been carved from rock. Irresistible force meet immovable object.

For her own part, she stood stock still, palms sweaty. Her mouth was dry and her heart pounded as it tried to escape her chest. Okay. Something had happened and he didn't get her message on time. He was here now. What could she do to help him? He didn't move, but he wouldn't do anything with her in the way. They couldn't stand like this forever. He wouldn't have come without calling for backup, but that might cause a shoot-out, at which point anything could happen. She needed to help him bring this to a close now.

Aaron Trafford hadn't killed anybody.

She pushed the thought from her mind. There would be time later to go over where she'd messed up. Right now she needed to focus on the situation at hand. Her thoughts skittered through her head, frightened mice looking for an escape hole. All those self-defense courses and she couldn't think of a single technique. Through the turmoil, her instructor's words came to her: target the squishy parts.

Trafford shifted to keep her in front of him and she wobbled on her heels. Her heels. Three and a half inches ending in a spike. Trafford was wearing canvas sneakers. Taking deep breaths, as deep as she could, she formulated a plan.

Trafford's voice growled in her ear. "Last chance. Come out from behind that car or I swear I'll shoot her right now."

She tried to catch Jim's eye, give him some hint of what she was going to do. But he crouched behind the car's engine area, a solid figure in gray, betraying no clue he'd seen her do anything. It was now or never.

Holding her breath, she made her move and scraped her instep down Trafford's shin bone, finishing by slamming her heel into his foot. He howled and loosened his grip enough that she twisted and slammed her elbow into his solar plexus. She was rewarded by hearing his breath whoosh, rippling her hair.

"Bitch!"

She pulled free as she felt him strike her between the shoulder blades. She stumbled and tried to catch herself, but she hit the gravel hard and her head struck the bumper of the Buick. Pain exploded in her head and her knees.

The last thing she heard before the darkness consumed her was the roar of gunfire.

CHAPTER 46

H er head hurt. Her knees hurt. Even her hair hurt.

I can't be dead. It wouldn't hurt this much.

She heard a rustling noise and tried to open her eyes. It was like her eyelids were glued shut. Eventually, she forced them up. Wherever she was, it was dim, soft, and chilly. She could make out a blurry shape next to her. Gasping, she sat up. A wave of nausea hit her and she choked.

"Take it easy." A hand grasped her shoulder and gently pushed her back. She blinked and a nurse swam into focus.

"What the hell happened?" Her voice was raspy. "Where am I?"

"Uniontown General Hospital." The nurse handed her a glass, holding the straw in it to her lips. "Here. Small sips."

That's why Sally was so cold. She was in a thin hospital gown. The cool water was a balm to her scratchy throat. "What happened?"

"I only know they brought you here unconscious. There's a trooper waiting. I think he wants to talk to you, if you're up to it."

She didn't want to talk to anyone, but she wanted to see Jim. "I'll see him." The nurse left.

The trooper who walked through the door was not Jim, nor was it Aislyn McAllister. This was a lean man, runner's build, shorter than Jim. He had coffee-colored skin and dark brown eyes filled with a solemn sadness. He pushed the door shut behind him.

Tension knotted in her chest. "Who are you? Where's Jim?"

The trooper touched his hat. "Trooper Alan Porter, ma'am. I'm afraid Trooper Duncan isn't available."

The oxygen left the room and she struggled to breathe. "He's not, did he, was he…" She couldn't bring herself to say the words.

Porter said nothing, the picture of professional efficiency.

"Oh God. I know you're not supposed to tell me, but please. He's a friend. I have to know." Her voice cracked and she clutched the blanket so tightly she could feel her fingernails in her palms through the flimsy fabric.

Porter must have decided to take pity on her. He glanced at the closed door and his voice became soft. "He's fine. He's completing paperwork after the incident and he's on administrative leave pending an investigation."

The tension relaxed a smidge. "Someone was shot. I heard the gunfire." Too much for one gun. "What about Aaron Trafford? Is he alive?" It was easier to ask about Trafford. After all, he'd have shot her and Jim without a second thought.

Porter's professional mask came back. "I'm sorry. I can't disclose any details."

Looking in his eyes, Sally knew. Aaron Trafford was dead and Jim had shot him. The vise around her chest tightened again. She should have been patient, waited for Jim to call. He never ignored her. Ever. She should have known, not rushed off, so sure she was right.

"I'm here to take your statement," Porter said. "The nurse said you were willing, but we can do this tomorrow."

"I want to get it over with." Except it wouldn't be over with, not really. This one moment would be over, but she'd feel the repercussions for a long time. She could postpone it by speaking to Porter, but all that did was delay the inevitable. What had Jim said to her when he'd come to her apartment after the explosion?

She grasped the blanket and talked. About the phone call she'd gotten, allegedly from Devin Carrington. How she'd called Jim for backup, but never reached him. Arriving at the baseball field, the confrontation with Trafford, Jim's eventual arrival, and the conclusion as she knew it.

"Is that all?" When she nodded, Porter closed his notebook. "Thank you, Ms. Castle. I hope you feel better soon. Representatives from the investigative board will be in touch if they need to ask you any questions."

The what? Of course. This was a police-involved shooting. "He did his job. Trooper Duncan. He didn't do anything wrong. I was at risk, Trafford had a gun. He would have killed me."

Porter said nothing.

The tension knot was back, making it difficult to breathe. "Can I talk to him? Trooper Duncan?"

"I'm afraid that won't be possible. At least not tonight." Porter gave her a sympathetic smile. "I'll leave my card in case you need to add anything to your statement." He touched his hat, then glanced at the closed door. "I shouldn't say this but...Duncan will come out of this okay. Well, as 'okay' as you can be under the circumstances." He nodded at her and left.

Under the circumstances. Porter had been too diplomatic to say "after killing someone." A situation Jim wouldn't have been in if she hadn't been so cocky. As soon as she hadn't seen a state car or the Jeep, she should have driven off.

"If you're wrong, it'll crush you," he'd said. She should have listened. At that moment, all she wanted was the reassurance of his presence. Except he might not forgive her for what she'd done that afternoon.

She wasn't sure she could ever forgive herself.

‌   ⸙⸙⸙

The paperwork had taken forever. Hours to cover thirty seconds. Duncan knew the routine. There'd be a hearing, but he wasn't worried. It was a clean shooting. When Sally pulled free, Trafford had fired his gun; he'd presented a clear threat before that. After the specified three days, Duncan would give his statement. They'd recover the bullet from his patrol car. Ballistics would match it to Trafford's gun. The video and audio recordings from the in-dash recorder would show what happened. Sally would corroborate, if asked.

That all was the easy part.

His body ached with exhaustion. Begged him to go home and drink a bottle or six of the weizenbock beer he'd picked up at the last barracks beer swap and try to forget the afternoon ever happened, although there was little chance of that.

His brain had other ideas. The last time he'd seen Sally, she'd been unconscious and loaded on a gurney in the back of an ambulance. He needed to make sure she was okay. She'd called, asked for his help. He'd failed her. Yeah, she was a witness and that meant contact was off limits. At least according to protocol.

The hell with protocol.

He did take the time to stop home and change, reasoning that he'd be far less conspicuous in street clothes. Rizzo seemed to sense his owner was on a mission, because the dog refrained from the jubilant barking and antics that usually marked a homecoming.

At the hospital, Duncan professed himself a friend of a patient and obtained Sally's room number from the information desk. Just as he headed to the elevator bank, he spotted a figure in a gray uniform coming his way. It was Porter. At least they'd sent a competent, sensitive trooper to follow up with Sally. Porter wouldn't bust Duncan for trying to check on a friend. Still, Duncan ducked over to the gift shop where he could stay out of sight and watch Porter exit the hospital. He wouldn't blow the whistle, but he would try to dissuade Duncan from going up.

Wasn't going to happen.

Once upstairs, Duncan made his way to Sally's room. He checked at the door. Sally was asleep, head resting on a pillow that was way too thin to be comfortable. But she was almost certainly as worn out as he was. Maybe more. Her brown hair, loosed from its typical twist, was in a soft pile, partially obscuring her face.

He couldn't wake her, no matter how much he wanted to talk to her. That would be cruel. At the same time, he couldn't leave without letting her know he'd been there. He asked at the nurses' station for a pen and sheet of paper, thought a moment, and wrote.

Sally, I stopped to check on you, but you were asleep. After today, I sure as hell wasn't going to wake you up. I hope you're okay. Well, as okay as you can be. I'll be out of touch for a while. I hate it, but that's how it's gotta be until the investigation is complete. But I promise. Once it's over, I'll take you out to Dex's for dinner and a glass of wine. Or a glass of whiskey, your choice. Jim

Thanking the nurse on duty, he returned the pen and went back to Sally's room. Should he leave the note on her bedside table or somewhere else? It had to be a place she'd see it.

As she lay in the bed her arm was beside her, hand partially open. He folded the note and put it in on her palm. She'd notice it when she woke. Then he bent down to drop a kiss on the top of her head and crept out.

He didn't know if dinner and drinks would make it up to her. But he was damn sure going to try.

The End

ABOUT THE AUTHOR

Erin McClain Studio

Liz Milliron has been making up stories, and creating her own endings for other people's stories, for as long as she can remember. She is the author of The Laurel Highlands Mysteries. Her short fiction has been published in multiple anthologies, including Malice Domestic 12: Mystery Most Historical and the Anthony-award-winning Bouchercon 2016 Anthology Blood on the Bayou. Visit her at http://lizmilliron.com.

Made in the USA
Middletown, DE
15 November 2018